MY SECRET LIFE
BOOK ONE

MY
SECRET LIFE

BOOK ONE

'WALTER'

WORDSWORTH CLASSICS

The paper in this book is produced from pure wood
pulp, without the use of chlorine or any other substance
harmful to the environment. The energy used in its
production consists almost entirely of hydroelectricity
and heat generated from waste material, thereby
conserving fossil fuels and contributing little to the
greenhouse effect.

This edition published 1995 by
Wordsworth Editions Limited
Cumberland House, Crib Street
Ware, Hertfordshire SG12 9ET

ISBN 1 85326 602 7

Printed and bound in Denmark by Nørhaven

CONTENTS

3

INTRODUCTION

In 18 — my oldest friend died. We had been at school and college together, and our intimacy had never been broken. I was trustee for his wife and executor at his death. He died of a lingering illness, during which his hopes of living were alternately raised, and depressed. Two years before he died, he gave me a huge parcel carefully tied up and sealed. "Take care of but don't open this," he said; "if I get better, return it to me, if I die, let no mortal eye but yours see it, and burn it."

His widow died a year after him. I had well nigh forgotten this packet, which I had had full three years, when, looking for some title deeds, I came across it, and opened it, as it was my duty to do. Its contents astonished me. The more I read it, the more marvellous it seemed. I pondered long on the meaning of his instructions when he gave it to me, and kept the manuscript some years, hesitating what to do with it.

At length I came to the conclusion, knowing his idiosyncrasy well, that his fear was only lest any one should know who the writer was; and feeling that it would be sinful to destroy such a history, I copied the manuscript and destroyed the original. He died relationless. No one now can trace the author; no names are mentioned in the book, though they were given freely in the margin of his manuscript, and I alone know to whom the initials refer. If I have done harm in printing it, I have done none to him, have indeed only carried out his evident intention, and given to a few a secret history, which bears the impress of truth on every page, a contribution to psychology.

PREFACE

I began these memoirs when about twenty-five years old, having from youth kept a diary of some sort, which perhaps from habit made me think of recording my inner and secret life.

When I began it, had scarcely read a baudy book, none of which, excepting *Fanny Hill*, appeared to me to be truthful: that did, and it does so still; the others telling of récherché eroticisms or of inordinate copulative powers, of the strange twists, tricks, and fancies of matured voluptuousness and philosophical lewedness, seemed to my comparative ignorance as baudy imaginings or lying inventions, not worthy of belief; although I now know, by experience, that they may be true enough, however eccentric and improbable, they may appear to the uninitiated.

Fanny Hill's was a woman's experience. Written perhaps by a woman, where was a man's written with equal truth? That book has no baudy word in it; but baudy acts need the baudy ejaculations; the erotic, full-flavored expressions, which even the chastest indulge in when lust, or love, is in its full tide of performance. So I determined to write my private life freely as to fact, and in the spirit of the lustful acts done by me, or witnessed; it is written therefore with absolute truth and without any regard whatever for what the world calls decency. Decency and voluptuousness in its fullest acceptance cannot exist together, one would kill the other; the poetry of copulation I have only experienced with a few women, which however neither prevented them nor me from calling a spade a spade.

I began it for my amusement; when many years had been chronicled I tired of it and ceased. Some ten years afterwards I met a woman, with whom, or with those she helped me to, I did, said, saw, and heard well nigh everything a man and woman could do with their genitals, and began to narrate those events, when quite fresh in my memory, a great variety of incidents extending over four years or more. Then I lost sight of her, and my amorous amusements for a while were simpler, but that part of my history was complete.

7

After a little while, I set to work to describe the events of the intervening years of my youth and early middle age, which included most of my gallant intrigues and adventures of a frisky order; but not the more lascivious ones of later years. Then an illness caused me to think seriously of burning the whole. But not liking to destroy my labor, I laid it aside again for a couple of years. Then another illness gave me long uninterrupted leisure; I read my manuscript and filled in some occurrences which I had forgotten but which my diary enabled me to place in their proper order. This will account for the difference in style in places, which I now observe; and a very needless repetition of voluptuous descriptions, which I had forgotten and had been before described; that however is inevitable, for human copulation, vary the incidents leading up to it as you may, is, and must be, at all times much the same affair.

Then, for the first time, I thought I would print my work that had been commenced more than twenty years before, but hesitated. I then had entered my maturity, and on to the most lascivious portion of my life, the events were disjointed, and fragmentary and my amusement was to describe them just after they occurred. Most frequently the next day I wrote all down with much prolixity; since, I have much abbreviated it.

I had from youth an excellent memory, but about sexual matters a wonderful one. Women were the pleasure of my life. I loved cunt, but also who had it; I like the woman I fucked and not simply the cunt I fucked, and therein is a great difference. I recollect even now in a degree which astonishes me, the face, colour, stature, thighs, backside, and cunt, of well nigh every woman I have had, who was not a mere casual, and even of some who were. The clothes they wore, the houses and rooms in which I had them, were before me mentally as I wrote, the way the bed and furniture were placed, the side of the room the windows were on, I remembered perfectly; and all the important events I can fix as to time, sufficiently nearly by reference to my diary, in which the contemporaneous circumstances of my life are recorded.

I recollect also largely what we said and did, and generally our baudy amusements. Where I fail to have done so, I have left description blank, rather than attempt to make a story coherent by inserting what was merely probable. I could not now account for my course of action, or why I did this, or said that, my conduct seems strange, foolish, absurd, very frequently, that of some women equally so, but I can but state what did occur.

In a few cases, I have, for what even seems to me very strange, suggested reasons or causes, but only where the facts seem by themselves to be very improbable, but have not exaggerated anything willingly. When I have named the number of times I have fucked a woman in my youth, I may occasionally be in error, it is difficult to be quite accurate on such points after a lapse of time. But as before said, in many cases the incidents were written down a few weeks and often within a few days after they occurred. I do not attempt to pose as a Hercules in copulation, there are quite sufficient braggarts on that head, much intercourse with gay women, and doctors, makes me doubt the wonderful feats in coition some men tell of.

I have one fear about publicity, it is that of having done a few things by curiosity and impulse (temporary aberrations) which even professed libertines may cry fie on. There are plenty who will cry fie who have done all and worse than I have and habitually, but crying out at the sins of others was always a way of hiding one's own iniquity. Yet from that cause perhaps no mortal eye but mine will see this history.

The Christian name of the servants mentioned are generally the true ones, the other names mostly false, tho phonetically resembling the true ones. Initials nearly always the true ones. In most cases the women they represent are dead or lost to me. Streets and baudy houses named are nearly always correct. Most of the houses named are now closed or pulled down; but any middle-aged man about town would recognize them. Where a road, house, room, or garden is described, the description is exactly true, even to the situation of a tree, chair, bed, sofa, pisspot. The district is sometimes given wrongly; but it matters little whether Brompton be substituted for Hackney, or Camden Town for Walworth. Where however, owing to the incidents, it is needful, the places of amusement are given correctly. The Tower, and Argyle rooms, for example. All this is done to prevent giving pain to some, perhaps still living, for I have no malice to gratify.

I have mystified family affairs, but if I say I had ten cousins when I had but six, or that one aunt's house was in Surrey instead of Kent, or in Lancashire, it breaks the clue and cannot matter to the reader. But my doings with man and woman are as true as gospel. If I say that I saw, or did, that with a cousin, male or female, it was with a cousin and no mere acquaintance; if with a servant, it was with a servant; if with a casual acquaintance, it is equally true. Nor if I say I had that woman, and did this or that with her, or felt or did aught else with a man, is there a word of untruth, excepting as to the place at which the incidents occurred. But even those are mostly correctly given; this is intended to be a true history, and not a lie.

SECOND PREFACE

Some years have passed away since I penned the foregoing, and it is not printed. I have since gone through abnormal phases of amatory life, have done and seen things, had tastes and letches which years ago I thought were the dreams of erotic mad-men; these are all described, the manuscript has grown into unmanageable bulk; shall it, can it, be printed? What will be said or thought of me, what became of the manuscript if found when I am dead? Better to destroy the whole, it has fulfilled its purpose in amusing me, now let it go to the flames!

———————————

I have read my manuscript through; what reminiscences! I had actually forgotten some of the early ones; how true the detail strikes me as I read of my early experiences; had it not been written then it never could have been written now; has anybody but myself faithfully made such a record? It would be a sin to burn all this, whatever society may say, it is but a narrative of human life, perhaps the every day life of thousands, if the confession could be had.

What strikes me as curious in reading it is the monotony of the course I have pursued towards women who were not of the gay class; it has been as similar and repetitive as fucking itself; do all men act so, does every man kiss, coax, hint smuttily, then talk baudily, snatch a feel, smell his fingers, assault, and win, exactly as I have done? Is every woman offended, say "no," then "oh!" blush, be angry, refuse, close her thighs, after a struggle open them, and yield to her lust as mine have done? A conclave of whores telling the truth, and of Romish Priests, could alone settle the point. Have all men had the strange letches which late in life have enraptured me, though in early days the idea of them revolted me? I can never know this; my experience, if printed, may enable others to compare as I cannot.

Shall it be burnt or printed? How many years have passed in this indecision? why fear? it is for others' good and not my own if preserved.

11

CHAPTER I

Earliest recollections. — An erotic nursemaid. — Ladies abed. — My cock. — A frisky governess. — Cousin Fred. — Thoughts on pudenda. — A female pedlar. — Baudy pictures. — A naked baby.

My earliest recollections of things sexual are of what I think must have occurred some time between my age of five and eight years. I tell of them just as I recollect them, without attempt to fill in what seems probable.

She was I suppose my nursemaid. I recollect that she sometimes held my little prick when I piddled, was it needful to do so? I don't know. She attempted to pull my prepuce back, when, and how often, I know not. But I am clear about seeing the prick tip show, of feeling pain, of yelling out, of her soothing me, and of this occurring more than once. She comes to my memory as a shortish, fattish, young female, and that she often felt my prick.

One day, it must have been late in the afternoon for the sun was low but shining — how strange I should recollect that so clearly — but I have always recollected sunshine, — I had been walking out with her, toys had been bought me, we were both carrying them, she stopped and talked to some men, one caught hold of her and kissed her, I felt frightened, it was near a coach stand, for hackney coaches were there, cabs were not then known, she put what toys she had on to my hands and went into a house with a man. What house? I don't know. Probably a public-house, for there was one not far from a coach stand, and not far from our house. She came out and we went home.

Then I was in our house in a carpeted room with her; it could not have been the nursery I know, sitting on the floor with my toys; so was she; she played with me and the toys, we rolled over each

13

other on the floor in fun, I have a recollection of having done that with others, and of my father and mother being in that room at times with me playing.

She kissed me, got out my cock, and played with it, took one of my hands and put it underneath her clothes. It felt rough there, that's all, she moved my little hand violently there, then she felt my cock and again hurt me, I recollect seeing the red tip appear as she pulled down the prepuce, and my crying out, and her quieting me.

Then of her being on her back, of my striding across or between her legs, and her heaving me up and down, and my riding cockhorse and that it was not the first time I had done so; then I fell flat on her, she heaved me up and down and squeezed me till I cried. I scrambled off of her, and in doing so my hand, or foot, went through a drum I had been drumming on, at which I cried.

As I sat crying on the floor beside her, I recollect her naked legs, and one of her hands shaking violently beneath her petticoats, and of my having some vague notion that the woman was ill; I felt timid. All was for a moment quiet, her hand ceased, still she lay on her back, and I saw her thighs, then turning round she drew me to her, kissed me and tranquillised me. As she turned round I saw one side of her backside, I leant over it and laid my face on it crying about my broken drum, the evening sunbeams made it all bright, it had at some time been raining, I recollect.

I expect I must have seen her cunt, as I sat beside her naked thigh. Looking towards her and crying about my broken drum, and when I saw her hand moving no doubt she was frigging. Yet I have not the slightest recollection of her cunt, nor of anything more than I have told. But of having seen her naked thighs I am certain, I seem often to have seen them, but cannot feel certain of that.

The oddest thing is that whilst I early recollected more or less clearly what took place two or three years later on, and ever afterwards, on sexual matters, and what I said, heard, and did, nearly consecutively, this, my first recollection of cock and cunt, escaped my memory for full twenty years.

Then one day, talking with the husband of one of my cousins, about infantine incidents, he told me some thing which had occurred to him in his childhood; and suddenly, almost as quickly as a magic lantern throws a picture on to a wall, this which had occurred to me came into my mind. I have since thought over it a hundred times, but cannot recollect one circumstance relating to the adventure more than I have told.

My mother had been giving advice to my cousin about nurse-maids. They were not to be trusted. "When Walter was a little fel-low, she had dismissed a filthy creature, whom she had detected in abominable practices with one of her children"; what they were my mother never disclosed. She hated indelicacies of any sort, and us-ually cut short allusion to them by saying, "It's not a subject to talk about, let's talk of some thing else." My cousin told her husband, and when we were together he told me, and his own experiences, and then all the circumstances, came into my mind, just as I have told here.

I could not, as the reader will hear, thoroughly uncover my prick tip without pain till I was sixteen years old, nor well then when quite stiff unless it went up a cunt. My nursemaid I expect thought this curious, and tried to remedy the error in my make, and hurt me. My mother, by her extremely delicate feeling, shut herself off from much knowledge of the world, which was the reason why she had such implicit belief in my virtue, until I had seen twenty-two years, and kept, or nearly so, a French harlot.

I imagine I must have slept with this nursemaid, and certainly I did with some female, in a room called the Chinese room, on ac-count of the color of the wall papers. I recollect a female being there in bed with me, that I awoke one morning feeling very hot and stifled, and that my head was against flesh; that flesh was all about me, my mouth and nose being embedded in hair, or some thing scrubby, which had a hot peculiar odour. I have a recollection of a pair of hands suddenly clutching and dragging me up on to the pillow, and of daylight then. I have no recollection of a word being uttered. This incident I could not long have forgotten, having told my cousin Fred of it before my father did. He used to say it was the governess. I suppose I must have slipped down in my sleep, till my head laid against her belly and cunt.

Some years afterwards, when I got the smell of another wom-an's cunt on my fingers, it at once reminded me of the smell I had under my nose in the bed; and I knew at a flash that I had smelt cunt before, and recollected where, but no more.

How long after I have no idea, but it seems like two or three years, there was a dance in our house, several relations were to stop the night with us, the house was full, there was bustle, the shifting of beds, the governess going into a servant's room to sleep, and so on. Some female cousins were amongst those stopping with us; going into the drawing-room suddenly, I heard my mother saying to one of my aunts, "Walter is after all but a child, and it's only for one night." "Hish-hish," both said as they saw me, then my mother sent me out of the room, wondering why they were talking about me, and feeling curious and annoyed at being sent away.

I had been in the habit then of sleeping in a room either with another bed in it or close to a room leading out of it, with another bed, I cannot recollect which; I used to call out to whoever might have been there when I was in bed: for being timid, the door was kept open for me. It could not have been a man who slept there, for the men-servants slept on the ground-floor, I have seen their beds there.

The night I speak of, my bed was taken out, and put into the Chinese-paper room, one of the maids who helped to move it sat on the pot and piddled; I heard the rattle, and as far as I can recollect it was the first time I noticed anything of the sort, tho I recollect well seeing women putting on their stockings and feeling the thigh of one of them just above her knee. I was kneeling on the floor at the time and had a trumpet, which she took angrily out of my hand soon afterwards, because I made a noise.

I recollect the dance, that I danced with a tall lady, that my mother, contrary to custom as it seems to me, put me to bed herself, and that it was before the dance was over, for I felt angry and tearful at being put to bed so early. My mother closed the curtains quite tightly all round a small four post bed, and told me I was to lie quietly and not get up till she came to me in the morning; not to speak, nor undo my curtains, nor to get out of bed, or I should disturb Mr. and Mrs. *** who were to sleep in the big bed; that it would make them angry if I did. I am almost certain she named a lady and her husband who were going to stay with us; but can't be sure. A man then frightened me more than a woman, my mother I dare say knew that.

I dare say, for it was the same the greater part of my early life that I went to sleep directly I laid down, usually never awaking till the morning. Certainly I must have gone fast asleep that night; perhaps I had had a little wine given me, who knows; I have a sudden consciousness of a light, and hear someone say, "He is fast asleep, don't make a noise"; it seemed like my mother's voice. I rouse myself and listen, the circumstances are strange, the room strange, it excites me, and I rise on my knees, I don't know whether naturally, or cautiously, or how; perhaps cautiously, because I fear angering my mother, and the gentleman; perhaps a sexual instinct makes me curious, though that is not probable. I have not in fact the slightest conception of the actuating motive, but I sat up and listened. There were two females talking, laughing quietly and moving about, I heard a rattling in the pot, then a rest, then again a rattle and knew the sound of piddling. How long I listened I don't know, I might have dozed and awakened again, I saw lights moved about; then I crawled on my knees, with fear that I was doing wrong, and pushed a little aside the curtains where they met at the bottom of the bed. I recollect their being quite tight by the tucking in, and that I could not easily make an opening to peep through.

There was a girl, or young woman, with her back to me, brushing her hair, another was standing by her, one took a night gown off the chair, shook it out, and dropped it over her head, after drawing off her chemise. As this was done I saw some black at the bottom of her belly, a fear came over me that I was doing wrong and should be punished if found looking, and I laid down wondering at it all; I fancy I again slept.

Then there was a shuffling about, and again it seems as if I heard a noise like piddling, the light was put out, I felt agitated, I heard the women kiss, one say "Hish! you will wake that brat," then one said, "Listen" then I heard kisses and breathing like some one sighing, I thought some one must be ill and felt alarmed and must then have fallen asleep. I do not know who the women were, they must have been my cousins, or young ladies who had come to the dance. That was the first time I recollect seeing the hair of a cunt, though I must have seen it before, for I recollect at times a female (most likely a nursemaid) stand naked, but don't recollect noticing anything black between her thighs, nor did I think about it at all afterwards.

In the morning my mother came and took me up to her room, where she dressed me; as she left the room, she said to the females in bed they were not to hurry up, she had only fetched Wattie.

But all this only came vividly to my mind when, a few years

after, I began to talk about women with my cousin, and we told each other all we had seen, and heard, about females.

Until I was about twelve years old I never went to school, there was a governess in the house who instructed me and the other children, my father was nearly always at home. I was carefully kept from the grooms and other men servants; once I recollect getting to the stable yard and seeing a stallion mount a mare, his prick go right out of sight in what appeared to me to be the mare's bottom, of father appearing and calling out, "What does that boy do there?" and my being hustled away. I had scarcely a boy acquaintance, excepting among my cousins, and therefore did not learn as much about sexual matters as boys early do at schools. I did not know what the stallion was doing, I could have had no notion of it then, nor did I think about it.

The next thing I clearly recollect, was one of my male cousins stopping with us, we walked out, and when piddling together against a hedge, his saying, "Shew me your cock, Walter, and I will shew you mine." We stood and examined each other's cocks, and for the first time I became conscious that I could not get my foreskin easily back like other boys. I pulled his backwards and forwards. He hurt me, laughed and sneered at me, another boy came and I think another, we all compared cocks, and mine was the only one which would not unskin, they jeered me, I burst into tears, and went away thinking there was some thing wrong with me, and was ashamed to shew my cock again, tho I set to work earnestly to try to pull the foreskin back, but always desisted, fearing the pain, for I was very sensitive.

My cousin then told me that girls had no cock, but only a hole they piddled out of, we were always talking about them, but I don't recollect the word cunt, nor that I attached any lewed idea to a girl's pidding hole, or to their cocks being flat, an expression heard I think at the same period. It remained only in my mind that my cock and the girl's hole were to piddle out of, and nothing more, I cannot be certain about my age at this time.

Afterwards I went to that uncle's house often, my cousin Fred was to be put to school, and we talked a great deal more about girls' cocks, which began to interest me much. He had never seen one, he said, but he knew that they had two holes, one for bogging and the other to piddle from. They sit down to piddle said he, they don't piddle against a wall as we do, but that I must have known already, afterwards I felt very curious about the matter.

One day, one of his sisters left the room where we were sitting. "She is going to piddle," he said to me. We sneaked into a bedroom of one of them one day and gravely looked into the pot to see what piddle was in it. Whether we expected to find any thing different from what there was in our own chamber pot I do not know. When talking about these things my cousin would twiddle his cock. We wondered how the piddle came out, if they wetted their legs and if the hole was near the bum hole, or where; one day Fred and I pissed against each other's cocks, and thought it excellent fun.

I recollect being very curious indeed about the way girls piddled after this, and seeing them piddle became a taste I have kept all my life. I would listen at the bed room doors, if I could get near them unobserved, when my mother, sister, the governess, or a servant went in, hoping to hear the rattle and often succeeded. It was accompanied by no sexual desire or idea, as far as I can recollect; I had no cock-stand, and am sure that I then did not know that the woman had a hole called a cunt and used it for fucking. I can recall no idea of the sort, it was simple curiosity to know something about those whom I instinctively felt were made different from myself. What sort of a hole could it be, I wondered? Was it large? Was it round? Why did they squat instead of stand up like men? My curiosity became intense.

How long after this the following took place I can't say, but my cock was bigger. I have that impression very distinctly.

One day, there were people in one of the sitting rooms; where my mother and father were I don't know; they were not in the room, and were most likely out. There were one or two of my cousins, some youths, my big sister and one brother, besides others, our governess, and her sister, who was stopping with us, and sleeping in the same room with her. I recollect both going into the bed room together, it was next to mine. It was evening, we had sweet wine, cake, and snap-dragon, and played at something at which all sat in a circle on the floor. I was very ticklish, it nearly sent me into fits, we tickled each other on the floor. There was much fun, and noise, the governess tickled me, and I tickled her. She said as I was taken to bed, or rather went, as I then did by myself, "I'll go and tickle you." Now at that time, when I was in bed, a servant, or my mother, or the governess took away the light and closed the door; for I was still frightened to get into bed in the dark, and used to call out, "Mamma. I'm going to get into bed." Then they fetched the light, they wished to stop this timidity, often scolded me about it, and made me undress myself, by myself, to cure me of it.

I expect the other children had been put to bed. My mother keeping all the younger ones in the room near her. The nursery was also upstairs; my room, as said, was next to the governess.

When in bed, I called out for some one to put out the light, up came the governess and her sister. She began to tickle me, so did her sister, I laughed, screeched, and tried to tickle them. One of them closed the door and then came back to tickle me. I kicked all the clothes off and was nearly naked, I begged them to desist, felt their hands on my naked flesh, and am quite sure that one of them touched my prick more than once, though it might have been done accidentally. At last I wriggled off bed, my night-gown up to my armpits, and dropped with my naked bum on to the floor, whilst they tickled me still, and laughed at my wriggling about and yelling.

Then what induced me heaven alone knows; it may have been what I had heard about the piddling-hole of a woman, or curiosity, or instinct, I don't know; but I caught hold of the governess' leg as she was trying to get me up on to the bed again, saying, "That will do, my dear boy, get into bed, and let me take away the light." I would not; the other lady helped to lift me, I pushed my hands up the petticoats of the governess, felt the hair of her cunt, and that there was something warm, and moist, between her thighs. She let me drop on to the floor, and jumped away from me. I must have been clinging to her thigh, with both hands up her petticoats, and one between her thighs, she cried out loudly — "Oh!"

Then slap-slap-slap, in quick succession, came her hand against my head. "You . . . rude . . . bad . . . boy," said she, slapping me at each word. "I've a good mind to tell your mamma, get into bed this instant," and into bed I got without a word. She blew out the light and left the room with her sister, leaving me in a dreadful funk. I scarcely knew that I had done wrong, yet had some vague notion that feeling about her thighs was punishable. The soft hairy place my hand had touched, impressed me with wonder, I kept thinking there was no cock there, and felt a sort of delight at what I had done.

I heard them then talking and laughing loudly thro the partition. "They are talking about me; oh, if they tell mamma, oh! what did I do it for?" Trembling with fear, I jumped out of bed, opened my door, and went to theirs, listening; theirs was ajar; I heard: "Right up between my thighs. I felt it! He must have felt it; ah! ah! ha! would you ever have thought the little beast would have done such a thing!" They both laughed heartily. "Did you see his little thing?" said one. "Shut the door, it's not shut"; — breathless I got back to my room and into bed, and laying there heard them through the partition roaring with laughter again.

That is the first time in my life I recollect passing an all but sleepless night. The dread of being told about, and dread at what I had done, kept me awake. I heard the two women talking for a long time. Mixed with my dread was a wonder at the hair, and the soft, moist feel I had had for an instant on some part of my hand. I knew I had felt the hidden part of a female, where the piddle came from, and that is all I did think about it, that I know of, I have no recollection of a lewed sensation, but of a curious sort of delight only.

It must have been from this time, that my curiosity about the female form strengthened, but there was nothing sensual in it. I was fond of kissing, for my mother remarked it; when a female cousin, or any female, kissed me, I would throw my arms round her and keep on kissing. My aunts used to laugh, my mother corrected me and told me it was rude. I used to say to the servants, "Kiss me." One day I heard my godfather say: "Walter knows a pretty girl from an ugly one doesn't he?"

I had a dread of meeting the governess at breakfast, watched her and saw her laugh at her sister, I watched my mother for some days after, and at length said to the governess, who had punished me for something, "Don't tell mamma." "I have nothing to tell about, Walter," she replied, "and don't know what you mean." I began to tell her what was on my mind. "What's the child talking about? You are dreaming, some stupid boy has been putting things into your head, your papa will thrash you, if you talk like that." "Why, you came and tickled me," said I. "I tickled you a little when

I put your light out," said she, "be quiet." I felt stupefied, and suppose the affair must have passed away from my mind for a time, but I told my cousin Fred about it afterwards. He thought I must have been dreaming, and I began to wonder if it really had occurred, I never thought much about it until I began to recall my childhood for this history.

I must have been twelve years old when I went to an uncle's in Surrey and became a close friend of my cousin Fred, a very devil from his cradle, and of whom much more will be told: before then I had only seen him at intervals. We were then allowed, and it seems to me not before that time, to go out by ourselves. We talked boyish baudiness. "Ain't you green," said he, "a girl's hole isn't called a cock, it's a cunt, they fuck with it," and then he told me all he knew. I don't think I had heard that before, but can't be sure.

From that time a new train of ideas came into my head. I had a vague idea, though not a belief, that a cock and cunt were not made for pissing only. Fred treated me as a simpleton in these matters and was always calling me an ass; I have quite a painful recollection of my inferiority to him in such things, and of begging him to instruct me. "They make children that way," said Fred. "You come up and we will ask the old nurse where children come from, and she'll say 'out of the parsley-bed,' but it's all a lie." We went and asked her in a casual sort of way. She replied, "The parsley-bed," and laughed. The nurse at my house told me the same when I asked her afterwards about my mother's last baby. "Ain't they liars?" Fred remarked to me. "It comes out of their cunts, and it's made by fucking."

We both desired to see women piddling, though both must have before seen them at it often enough. Walking near the market-town with him, just at the outskirts, and looking up a side-road, we saw a pedlar woman squat down and piss. We stopped short and looked at her: she was a short-petticoated, thick-legged, middle-aged woman; the piss ran off in a copious stream, and there we stood, grinning. "Be off, be off, what are you standing grinning at, yer damned young fools," cried the woman. "Be off, or I'll heave a stone at yer," and she pissed on. We moved a few steps back, but, keeping our faces toward her, Fred stooped and put his head down. "I can see it coming," said he jeeringly. He was rude from his infancy, bold in baudiness to the utmost, had the impudence of the Devil. The stream ceased, the woman rose up swearing, took up a big flint and threw it at us. "I'll tell on yer," she cried. "I knows yer, wait till I see yer again." She had a large basket of crockery for sale, it was put down in the main-road at the angle; she had just turned round into the side lane to piss. We ran off, and, when well away, turned round and shouted at her. "I saw your cunt," Fred bawled out; — she flung another stone. Fred took up one, threw it, and it crashed into the crockery, the woman began to chase us, off we bolted across the fields home. She could not follow us that way; it was an eventful day for us. I recollect feeling full of envy at Fred's having seen her cunt. Though writing now, and having in my mind's eye exactly how the woman squatted, and the way her petticoats hung, I am sure he never did see it; it was brag when he said he had, but we were always talking about girls' cunts, the desire to see one was great, and I then believed that he had seen the pedlar woman's.

Then one of Fred's companions shewed us a baudy picture, it was coloured. I wondered at the cunt being a long sort of gash. I had an idea that it was round, like an arse-hole. Fred told his friend I was an ass, but I could not get the idea of a cunt not being a round hole quite out of my head, until I had fucked a woman. We were all anxious to get the picture, and tossed up for it, but neither I nor Fred got it, some other boy did.

Soon after that, Fred came to stop with us and our talk was always about women's privates, our curiosity became intense. I had a little sister about nine months old, who was in the nursery. Fred incited me to look at her cunt, if I could manage it. The two nurses came down in turns, to the servants' dinner, I was often in the nursery, and, soon after Fred's suggestion, was there one day when the oldest nurse said: "Stop here, master Walter, while I go downstairs for a couple of minutes. Mary (the other nurse) will be up directly, and don't make a noise." My little sister was lying on the bed asleep. "Yes, I'll wait." Down went nurse, leaving the door open; quick as lightning, I threw up the infant's clothes, saw her little slit, and put my finger quite gently on it, she was laying on her back most conveniently. I pulled one leg away to see better, the child awakened and began crying, I heard footsteps and had barely time to pull down her clothes, when the under nursemaid came in. I only had had a momentary glimpse of the outside of the little quim, for I was not a minute in the room with the child by myself altogether and was fearful of being caught all the time I was looking.

There must have been something in my face, for the nursemaid said, "What is the matter, what have you been doing to the baby?" "Nothing." "Yes, you are colouring up, now tell me." "Nothing, I have done nothing." "You wakened your sister." "No, I have not." The girl laid hold of me and gave me a little shake. "I'll tell your mamma if you don't tell me, what is it now?" "No, I have done nothing, I was looking out of the window when she began to cry." "You're telling a story, I see you are," said the nursemaid; and off I went, after being impudent to her.

I told Fred, and he tried the same dodge, but don't recollect whether he succeeded or not. His sisters were some of them older, and we began to scheme how to see their cunts, when I was on a visit to his mother's (my aunt), which was to come off in the holidays. The look of the little child's cunt, as I described it, convinced him that the picture was correct, and that a cunt was a long slit and not a round hole. That cast doubt on males putting their pricks into them, and we clung somehow to the idea of the round hole, and we quarrelled about it.

It must have been about this time that I was walking with my father and read something that was written in chalk on the walls. I asked him what it meant. He said he did not know, that none but low people, and blackguards wrote on walls; and it was not worth while noticing such things. I was conscious that I had done wrong somehow, but did not know exactly what. When I went out, which I was now allowed to do for short distances by myself, I copied what was on the walls, to tell Fred, it was foul, baudy language of some sort, but the only thing we understood at all, was the word cunt.

Just then being out with some boys, we saw two dogs fucking. I have no recollection of seeing dogs doing that before. We closed round them, yelling with delight as they stuck rump to rump, then one boy said that was what men and women did, and I asked, did they stick together so, a boy replied that they did; others denied it, and, all the remainder of the day, some of us discussed this; the impression left on my mind is that it appeared to me very nasty; but it seemed at the same time to confirm me in the belief that men put their pricks up into women's holes, about which I seem at that time to have had grave doubts.

After this time my recollection of events is clearer, and I can tell not only what took place, but better what I heard, said, and thought.

CHAPTER II

My godfather. — At Hampton-Court. — My aunt's backside. — Public baths. — My cousins' cunts. — Haymaking frolics. — Family difficulties. — School amusements. — A masturbating relative. — Romance and sentiment.

My godfather (whose fortune I afterwards inherited) was very fond of me; somewhere about this time he used perpetually to be saying, "When you get to school, don't you follow any of the tricks yourself that other boys do, or you will die in a mad-house; lots of boys do." And he told me some horrible tales; it was done in a mysterious way. I felt there was a hidden meaning and, not having knowledge of what it was, asked him. I should know fast enough, said he, but mark his words. He repeated this so often that it sunk deeply into my mind, and made me uneasy, something was to happen to me, if I did something — I did not know what — it was intended as a caution against frigging, and it had good effect on me I am sure in various ways in the after time.

One day talking with Fred, I recollected what I had done to the governess. I had kept it to myself all along for fear. "What a lie," said he. "I did really." "Oh! ain't you a liar," he reiterated, "I'll ask Miss Granger." The same governess was with us then.

At this remark of his, an absolute terror came over me, the dread was something so terrible that the recollection of it is now painful. "Oh don't, pray, don't, Fred," I said, "oh, if Papa should hear!" He kept on saying he would. I was too young to see the improbability of his doing anything of the sort. "If you do, I'll tell him what we did when the pedlar woman piddled." He did not care. "Now, it's a lie, isn't it, you did not feel her cunt?" In fear, I confessed it was a lie. "I knew it was," said Fred. He had kept me in a state of terror about the affair for days, till I told a lie to get quit of the subject.

I was evidently always secret, even then, about anything amorous, excepting with Fred (as will be seen), and have continued so all my life. I rarely bragged or told anyone of my doings; perhaps this little affair with the governess was a lesson to me, and confirmed me in a habit natural to me from my infancy. I have kept to myself everything I did with the opposite sex.

We now frequently examined our pricks, and Fred jeered me so about my prepuce being tight that I resolved no other boy should see it; and though I did not keep strictly to that intention, it left a deep-seated mortification on me. I used to look at my prick with a sense of shame and pull the prepuce up and down, as far as I could, constantly, to loosen it, and would treat other boys' cocks in the same way, if they would let me, without expecting me to make a return; but the time was approaching when I was to learn much more.

One of my uncles, who lived in London, took a house in the country for the summer near Hampton-Court Palace. Fred and I went to stay there with him. There were several daughters and sons, the sons quite young. People then came down from London in vans, carts, and carriages of all sorts, to see the Palace and grounds (there was no railway), they were principally of the small middle classes, and used to picnic, or else dine, at the taverns when they arrived; then full, and frisky, after their early meal, go into the parks and gardens. They do so still, but times were different then, so few people went there comparatively, fewer park-keepers to look after them, and less of what is called delicacy amongst visitors of the class named.

Our family party used to go into the grounds daily, and all day long nearly, if we were not on the river banks. Fred winked at me one day, "Let's lose Bob," said he, "and we'll have such a lark." Bob was one of our little cousins, generally given into our charge. We lost Bob purposely. Said Fred, "If you dodge the gardeners, creep up there, and lay on your belly quietly, some girls will be sure to come and piss, you'll see them pull their clothes up as they turn round, I saw some before you came to stay with us." So we went, pushing our way among shrubs and evergreens, till a gardener, who had seen us, called out, "You there, come back, if I catch you going off the walks, you'll be put outside." We were in such a funk, Fred cut off one way, I another, but it only stopped us for that day. Fred so excited me about the girls' arses, as he called them, that we never lost an opportunity of trying for a sight, but were generally baulked. Once or twice only we saw a female squat down, but nothing more, till my mother and Fred's came to stop with us.

Fred's mother, mine, the girls, Fred and I went into the park gardens, one day after luncheon. A very hot day, for we kept on the shady walks, one of which led to the place where women hid themselves to piss. My aunt said, "Why don't you boys go and play, you don't mind the sun," so off we went, but when about to leave the walk, turned round and saw the women had turned back. Said Fred, "I'm sure they are going to piss, that's why they want to get rid of us." We evaded the gardeners, scrambled through shrubs, on our knees, and at last on our bellies, up a little bank, on the other side of which was the vacant place on which dead leaves and sweepings were shot down. As we got there, pushing aside the leaves, we saw the big backside of a woman, who was half standing, half squatting, a stream of piss falling in front of her, and a big hairy gash, as it seemed, under her arse; but only for a second, she had just finished as we got the peep, let her clothes fall, tucked them between her legs, and half turning round. We saw it was Fred's mother, my aunt. Off aunt went. "Isn't it a wopper," said Fred, "lay still, more of them will come."

Two or three did; one said, "You watch if anyone is coming," squatted and piddled, we could not see her cunt, but only part of her legs, and the piddle splashing in front of her. Then came the second, she had her arse towards us, sat so low that we could not even see the tips of her buttocks. Fred thought it a pity they did not stand half up like his mother. On other occasions, we went to the same place, but though I recollect seeing some females' legs, don't recollect seeing any more. Nevertheless the sights were very delightful to us, and we used to discuss his mother's "wopper" and the hair, and the look of the gash, but I thought there must be some mistake, for it was not the idea I had formed of a cunt.

Fred soon after stopped with us in town, we had been forbidden to go out together without permission, but we did, and met a boy bigger than either of us, who was going to bathe. "Come and see them bathing," he said. My father had refused to take me to the public baths. Disregarding this, Fred and I paid our six pence each, and in we went with our friend; we did not bathe, but amused ourselves with seeing others, and the pricks of the men. None, as far as I can recollect, wore drawers in those days, they used to walk about hiding their pricks generally with their hands, but not always. I was astonished at the size of some of them, and at the dark hair about them and on other parts of their bodies. I wondered also at seeing one or two, with the red tip shewing fully, so different from mine. All this was much talked over by us afterwards, it was to me an insight into the male make and form. Fred told me he had often seen men's pricks in their fields, and in those days, living in the country as he did, I dare say it was true, but I don't recollect ever having seen the pricks of full grown men, or a naked man, before in my life.

It must have been in the summer of that same year that I went after this to spend some days at my aunt's at H°°°dfs°°°l°°°, Fred's mother. We slept in the same room and sometimes got up quite at daybreak to go fishing. One morning Fred had left something in one of his sisters' rooms, and went to fetch it, though forbidden to go into the girls' bed-rooms. The room in question was opposite to ours. He was only partly dressed, and came back in a second, his face grinning. "Oh! come Wat, come softly, Lucy and Mary are quite naked, you can see their cunts, Lucy has some black hair on hers." I was only half dressed, and much excited by the idea of seeing my cousins' nudity. We both took off our slippers and crept along through the door half open, then went on our knees! but why we did so, to this day I don't understand, and so crept to the foot of the bed, then raising ourselves, we both looked over the foot-board.

Lucy, fifteen years old, was laying half on her side, naked from her knees to her waist, the bed-clothes kicked off (I suppose through heat), were dragging across her feet and partly laying on the floor; we saw her split, till lost in the closed thighs, she had a little dark short hair over the top of her cunt, and that is all I can recollect about it.

Mary-Ann by the side of her, a year younger only, laid on her back, naked up to her navel, just above which was her night-gown in a heap and ruck; she had scarcely a sign of hair on her cunt, but a vermillion line lay right through her crack. Projecting more to-

wards the top, where her cunt began, she had what I now know
was a strongly developed clitoris; she was a lovely girl and had long
chestnut hair.

Whilst we looked she moved one leg up in a restless manner,
and we bobbed down, thinking she was awaking; when we looked
again, her limbs were more open, and we saw the cunt till it was
pinched up, by the closing of her buttocks. In fear of being caught,
we soon crept out, closed the door ajar, and regained our bed-room,
so delighted that we danced with joy as we talked about the look of
the two cunts; of which after all we had only had a most partial,
rapid glimpse.

Lucy was a very plain girl, and was so as a woman. She had,
I recollect, a very red bloated looking face as she lay (it was so hot);
she it was, who in after-life my mother cautioned about leaving her
infant son to a nursemaid.

Mary-Ann was lovely. I used afterwards to look and talk with
her, thinking to myself: "Ah! you have but little idea, that I have
seen your cunt." She was unfortunate; married a cavalry officer,
went to India with him, was left at a station unavoidably by her
husband, who was sent on a campaign, for a whole year; could not
bear being deprived of cock, and was caught in the act of fucking
with a drummer boy, a mere lad. She was separated from him, came
back to England, and drank herself to death. She was a salacious
young woman, I think, from what I recollect of her, and am told
was afterwards fucked by a lot of men; but it was a sore point with
the family, and all about her was kept quiet.

One of Lucy's sons, in after years, I saw fucking a maid in a
summer-house: both standing up against a big table; I was on the
roof. Many years before that I fucked a nursemaid, she laying on
that table in the very same summer-house, as I shall presently tell.

Fred and I used to discuss the look of his sisters' and mother's
cunts, as if they had belonged to strangers. The redness of the line
in Mary-Ann's quim astonished us. I do not recollect having even
then formed any definite notion of what a girl's cunt was, though
we had seen the splits, but had still, and till much further on, the
notion that the hole was round, and close to where the clitoris is,
having no idea then of what a clitoris was, though we had got an
Aristotle and used to read it greedily; the glimpses of the two cunts

were but momentary, and our excitement confused our recollections.

Fred and I then formed a plot to look at another girl's cunt; who the girl was I don't know, it may have been another of Fred's sisters, or a cousin by another of my aunts, but I think not; at all events, she was stopping in aunt's house, and from her height, which was less than that of Fred and myself, I should think a girl of about eleven or twelve years of age. I scrupulously avoid stating anything positively unless quite certain. Some years afterwards when we were very young men, we did the same thing with a female cousin (but not his sister), as I shall tell.

There was haymaking. We romped with the girl, buried each other in hay, pulled each other out, and so on. I was buried in the hay and dragged out by my legs by Fred and the girl. Then Fred was; then we buried the girl, and as Fred pulled her out he threw up her clothes, I lay over her head, which was covered with hay. Fred saw, winked, and nodded. It came to my turn again to be buried, and then hers; I laid hold of her legs and pulling them from under the hay, saw her thighs, I pushed her knees up, and had a glimpse of the slit, which was quite hairless. My aunt and others were in the very field, but had no idea of the game we were playing, the girl romping with us had no idea that we were looking at her cunt, and an instantaneous peep only it was.

What effect sensuously these glimpses of cunt had on me, I don't know; but have no recollection of sexual desire, nor of mine nor Fred's cock being stiff. I expect that what with games and our studies, that, after all, the time we devoted to thinking about women was not long, and curiosity our sole motive in doing what we did. I clearly recollect our talking at that time about fucking, and wondering if it were true or a lie. We could repeat what we had read and heard, but it still seemed improbable to me that a cock should go up a cunt, and the result be a child.

Then a passionate liking for females came over me; I fell in a sort of love with a lady who must have been forty, and had a sad feeling about her, that is all I recollect. Then I began to follow servants about, in the hope of seeing their legs or seeing them piddle, or for some undefined object: but that I was always looking after them I know very well.

Then (I know now) my father got into difficulties, we moved into a smaller house, the governess went away, I was sent to another school, one of my brothers and sisters died; my father went abroad to look after some plantations, and after a year's absence came back and died, leaving my mother in what, compared with our former condition, were poor circumstances, but this in due course will be more fully told.

I think I went to school, though not long before what I am going to tell of happened, but am not certain; if so, I must have seen boys frigging; yet as far as I can arrange in my mind the order of events, I first saw a boy doing that, in my own bed-room at home.

I was somewhere, I suppose, about thirteen years of age when a distant relative came from the country to stay with us, until he was put to some great school. He was the son of a clergyman, and must have been fifteen, or perhaps sixteen, years old, and was strongly pitted with the small-pox. I had never seen him before and took a strong dislike to him; the family were poor, this boy was intended for a clergyman. I was excessively annoyed, that he was to sleep with me, but in our small house there was just then no other place for him.

How many nights he slept in my bed I don't recollect, it can have been but few. One evening in bed he felt my prick; repulsing him at first, I nevertheless afterwards felt his, and recollect our hands crossing each other and our thighs being close together. Awakening one morning, I felt his belly up against my rump, and his feeling or pushing his prick against my arse, putting my hand back, I pushed him away; then I found it pushing quickly backwards and forwards between my thighs, and his hand, passed over my hips, was grasping my cock. Turning round, I faced him; he asked me to turn round again, and said I might do it to him afterwards, but nothing more was done. An unpleasant feeling about sleeping with him is in my memory, but as said, I disliked him.

The next night, undressing, he showed me his prick stiff, as he sat naked on a chair; it was an exceedingly long but thin article; he told me about frigging, and said he would frig me, if I would frig him. He commenced moving his hand quickly up and down on his prick, which got stiffer and stiffer, he jerked up one leg, then the other, shut his eyes, and altogether looked so strange that I thought he was going to have a fit, then out spurted little pasty lumps, whilst he snorted, as some people do in their sleep, and fell back in the chair with his eyes closed; then I saw stuff running thinner over his knuckles. I was strangely fascinated as I looked at him, and at what was on the carpet, but half thought he was ill; he then told me it was great pleasure, and was eloquent about it. Even now, as it did then, the evening seemed to me a nasty, unpleasant one, yet I let him get hold of my prick and frig it, but had no sensation of pleasure, He said, "Your skin won't come off, what a funny prick"; that annoyed me, and I would not let him do more, we talked till our candle burnt out; he stamped out the sperm on the carpet, saying the servants would think we had been spitting. Then we got into bed.

Afterwards he frigged himself several times before me, and at his request I frigged him, wondering at the result, and amused, yet at the same time much disgusted. When frigging him one day, he said it was lovely to do it in an arse-hole, that he and his brother took it in turns that way: it was lovely, heavenly! would I let him do it to me. In my innocence I told him it was impossible, and that I thought him a liar. He soon left us and went to college. I saw him once or twice after this, in later years, but at a very early age he drowned himself. I told my cousin Fred about this when I saw him; Fred believed in the frigging, but thought him a liar about the arse-hole business, just as I did. This was the first time I ever saw frigging and male semen, and it opened my eyes.

Though now at a public school, I was shy and reserved, but greedily listened to all the lewed talk, of which I did not believe a great deal. I became one of a group of boys of the same tastes as myself. One day some of them coaxed me into a privy, and there, in spite of me, pulled out my cock, threw me down, held me, and each one spat upon it, and that initiated me into their society. They had what they called cocks-all-round: anyone admitted to the set was entitled to feel the others' cocks. I felt theirs, but again, to my mortification, the tightness of my prepuce caused jeering at me; I was glad to hear that there was another boy at the school in the same predicament, though I never saw his. This confirmed me in avoiding my companions, when they were playing at cocks-all-round; being a day scholar only, I was not forced at all times into their intimacy, as I should have been had I been a boarder.

We had a very large playground; beyond it were fields, or-
chards, and walks of large extent reserved for the use of the two
head-masters' families, many of whom were girls. On Saturday half-
holidays only, if the fruit was not ripe, we were allowed to range
certain fields, and the long bough-covered paths which surrounded
them. Two or three boys of my set told me mysteriously one afternoon that when the others had gone ahead we were to meet in the
playground privy, in which were seats for three boys of a row,
and I was to be initiated into a secret without my asking. I was
surprised at what took place, there was usually an usher in the
playground in play-hours, and if boys were too long at the privy,
he went there, and made them come out. On the Saturdays, he
went out with the boys into the fields: there was no door to the
privy; I should add, it was a largish building.

One by one, from different directions, some dodging among
trees which bordered one side of the playground, appeared boys.
I think there were five or six together in the privy, then it was cocks-
all-round, and every boy frigged himself. I would not, at first. Why?
I don't know. At length incited, I tried, my cock would not stand,
and vexed and mortified, I withdrew, after swearing not to split on
them, on pain of being kicked and cut. I don't think I was one of
the party again, though I saw each of the same boys frig himself in
the privy when alone with me, at some time or another.

After this a boy asked me to come to a privy with him in school
time, and he would show me how to do it. Only two boys were allowed to go to those closets at the same time, during school time.
There were two wooden logs with keys hung up on the wall by
string: A boy, if he wanted to ease himself, looked to see if a log
and key was hanging up, and if there was, stood out in the centre
of the room; by that the master understood what he wanted. If he
nodded, the boy took the key and went to the bog-house (no water-
closets then), and when he returned, he hung up the log in its
place. Those privies were close together, and separate, there were
but two of them.

You wait till there are two logs hanging up, and directly I get
one, you get up and come after me. Soon we were both in one privy
together. "Let's frig," said he; we were only allowed to be away
five minutes. Out he pulled his prick, then out I pulled mine; he
tried to pull my skin back, and could only half do it, he frigged

himself successfully, but I could not. He had a very small prick compared with mine. How I envied him the ease with which he covered and uncovered the red tip. I frigged that boy one day, but finding my cock was becoming a talk among our set, I shrunk from going to their frigging parties, which I have seen even take place in a field, boys sitting at the edge of a ditch whilst one stood up to watch if anyone approached. When they were frigging in the privy, a boy always stood in the open door on the watch, and his time for frigging came afterwards. With this set I began to look through the Bible and study all the carnal passages; no book ever gave us perhaps such prolonged, studious, baudy amusement; we could not understand much, but guessed a good deal.

Before I had seen anyone frig, I had been permitted to read novels, not a moment of my time when not at studies was I without one. My father used to select them for me at first, but soon left me to myself, and, now he was dead, I devoured what books I liked, hunting for the love passages, thinking of the beauty of the women, reading over and over again the description of their charms, and envying their lovers' meetings. I used to stop at print-shop windows and gaze with delight at the portraits of pretty women, and bought some at six pence each, and stuck them into a scrapbook. Although a big fellow for my age, I would sit on the lap of any woman who would let me, and kiss her. My mother in her innocence called me a great girl, but she nevertheless forbade it. I was passionately fond of dancing and annoyed when they indicated a girl of my own age, or younger, to dance with.

These feelings got intensified when I thought of my aunt's backside, and the cunts of my cousins, but when I thought of the heroines, it seemed strange that such beautiful creatures should have any. The cunt which seemed to have affected my imagination was that of my aunt, which appeared more like a great parting, or division of her body, than a cunt as I then understood it; as if her buttock parting was continued round towards her belly, and as unlike the young cunts I had seen as possible. Those seemed to me but little indents. That the delicate ladies of the novels should have such divisions seemed curious, ugly, and unromantic. My sensuous temperament was developing, I saw females in all their poetry and beauty, but suppose that my physical forces had not kept pace with my brain, for I have no recollection of a cock-stand when think-

ing about ladies; and fucking never entered into my mind, either
when I read novels or kissed women, though the pleasure I had
when my lips met theirs, or touched their smooth, soft cheeks, was
great. I recollect the delight it gave me perfectly.

After having seen frigging, it set me reflecting, but it still
seemed to me impossible, that delicate, handsome ladies, should allow pricks to be thrust up them, and nasty stuff ejected into them. I
read Aristotle, tried to understand it, and thought I did, with the
help of much talk with my schoolfellows; yet I only half believed it.
Dogs fucking were pointed out to me; then cocks treading hens, and
at last a fuller belief came.

I began then, I recollect, to think of their cunts when I kissed
women, and then of my aunt's; I could not keep my eyes off of her,
for thinking of her large backside and the gap between her thighs;
it was the same with my cousins. Then I began to have cock-stands
and suppose a pleasurable feeling about the machine, though I do
not recollect that. I then found out that servants were fair game,
and soon there was not one in the house whom I had not kissed. I
had a soft voice and have heard an insinuating way, was timorous,
feared repulse, and above all being found out; yet I succeeded.
Some of the servants must have liked it, who called me a foolish
boy at first; for they would stop with me on a landing, or in a room,
when we were alone, and let me kiss them for a minute together.
There was one, I recollect, who rubbed her lips into mine, till I felt
them on my teeth, but of what she was like I have no recollection,
and I did not like her doing that to me.

My curiosity became stronger, I got bolder, told servants I
meant to see them wash themselves, and used to wait inside my
bed-room till I heard one of them come up to dress. I knew the time
each usually went to her bed-room for that purpose, the person
most in my way was the nurse: she after a time left, and mother
nursed her own children. "Let's see your neck; do, there is a dear,"
I would say. "Nonsense, what next?" "Do, dear, there is no harm;
I only want to see as much as ladies show at balls." I wheedled one
to stand at the door in her petticoats and show her neck across the
bed-room lobby. The stays were high and queerly made in those
days, the chemises pulled over the top of them like flaps. One or
two let me kiss their necks, a girl one day said to my entreaties,

"Well, only for a minute"; and easing up one breast, she showed me the nipple, I threw my arms round her, buried my face in her neck and kissed it. "I like the smell of your breast and flesh," said I. She was a biggish woman, and I dare say I smelt breasts and armpits together; but whatever the compound, it was delicious to me, it seemed to enervate me. The same woman, when I kissed her on the sly afterwards, let me put my nose down her neck to smell her. We were interrupted, "Here is some one coming," said she, moving away.

"What makes ladies smell so nice?" said I to my mother one day. My mother put down her work and laughed to herself. "I don't know that they smell nice." "Yes, they do, and particularly when they have low dresses on." "Ladies," said mother, "use patchouli and other perfumes." I supposed so, but felt convinced from mother's manner that I had asked a question which embarrassed her.

I used to lean over the backs of the chairs of ladies, get my face as near to their necks as I could, quietly inhale their odours, and talk all the time. Not every woman smelt nice to me, and when they did, it was not patchouli, for I got patchouli, which I liked, and perfumed myself with it. This delicate sense of the smell of a woman I have had throughout life, it was ravishing to me afterwards when I embraced the naked body of a fresh, healthy young woman.

From about this time of my life I recollect striking events much more clearly, yet the circumstances which led up to them or succeeded them I often cannot. One day Miss Granger, our former governess, came to see us. I kissed her. Mother said: "Wattie, you must not kiss ladies in that way, you are too big." I sat Miss Granger on my lap in fun (my mother then in the room), and romped with her. Mother left us in the room, and then, seating Miss Granger on my lap again, I pulled her closely to me. "Kiss me, she's gone," I said. "Oh! what a boy," and she kissed me, saying, "Let me — go — now — your mamma is coming." It came into my mind that I had had my hand up her clothes, and had felt hair between her legs. My prick stiffened; it is the first distinct recollection of its stiffening in thinking of a woman. I clutched her hard, put one hand on to her and did something, I know not what. She said: "You are rude, Wattie." Then I pinched her and said: "Oh! what a big bosom you have." "Hish! hish!" said she. She was a tallish woman with brown hair; I have heard my mother say she was about thirty years of age.

A memorable episode then occurred. There were two sisters, with other female servants, in our house. My father was abroad at that time; I was growing so rapidly that every month they could see a difference in my height, but was very weak. My godfather used to look at me and severely ask if I was up to tricks with the boys. I guessed then what he meant, but always said I did not know what he meant. "Yes, you do; yes, you do," he would say, staring hard at me, "you take care, or you'll die in a mad-house, if you do, and I shall know by your face, not a farthing more will I give you." He had been a surgeon-major in the Army, and gave me much pocket-money. I could not bear his looking at me so; he would ask me why I turned down my eyes.

About this time, I had had a fever, had not been to school for a long time, and used to lie on the sofa reading novels all day. Miss Granger had come to stop with my mother. One day I put my hand up her clothes, nearly to her knees; that offended her, and she left off kissing me. One of my little sisters slept with her, in a room adjoining my mother's room; I slept now on the servants' floor, at the top of the house. Again I recollect my cock standing when near Miss Granger, but recollect nothing else.

I was then ordered by my mother to cease speaking to the servants, excepting when I wanted anything, though I am sure my mother never suspected my kissing one. I obeyed her hypocritically, and was even at times reprimanded for speaking to them in too imperious a tone. She told me to speak to servants respectfully. For all that, I was after them, my curiosity was unsatiable, I knew the time each went up to dress, or for other purposes, and if at home, would get into the lobby, or near the staircase, to see their legs, as they went upstairs. I would listen at their door, trying to hear them piss, and began for the first time to peep through keyholes at them.

CHAPTER III

A big servant. — Two sisters. — Armpits. — A quiet feel. — Baudy reveries. — Felt by a woman. — Erections. — My prepuce. — Seeing and feeling. — Aunt and cousin. — A servant's thighs. — Not man enough.

A big servant, of whom I shall say much, had most of my attention; she went to her room usually when my mother was taking a nap in the afternoon; or when out with my sisters and brother. When I was ill in bed, this big woman usually brought me beef-tea; I used to make her kiss me, and felt so fond of her, would throw my arms round her, and hold her to me, keeping my lips to hers and saying how I should like to see her breasts; to all which she replied in the softest voice, as if I were a baby. I wonder now if my homage gave the big woman pleasure, or my amatory pressures made her ever feel randy. She was engaged to be married, but I only heard that at a later day, when my mother talked about her; her sister was also with us, as already said.

The sister was handsome, according to my notions then (I now begin to remember faces clearly); both had bright, clear complexions. I kissed both, each used to say, "Don't tell my sister," and ask, "Have you kissed my sister?" I was naturally cunning about women, and always said I had done nothing of the sort. The two were always quarrelling, and my mother said she must get rid of one of them.

The youngest was often dancing my little sister round in the room, then swinging herself round, and making cheeses with her petticoats. As I got better, I would lay on the rug with a pillow, and my back to the light reading, and say it rested me better to be on the floor, but in hope of seeing her legs as she made cheeses. I often did, and have no doubt now that she meant me to do so, for she would swing round, quite close to my head so that I could see to her knees, and make her petticoat's edge, as she squatted, just cover my head, immediately snatching her petticoats back and saying: "Oh! you'll see more than is good for you."

It used to excite me. One day as she did it, and squatted, I put out my hand and pulled her clothes, she rolled on to her back, threw up her legs quite high, and for a second I saw her thighs; she recovered herself, laughing. "I saw your thighs," said I. "That you didn't." One day she let me put my hand into her bosom; I sniffed. "What's there to smell?" said she. I have some idea that she used to watch me closely when I was with her sister, as she was always looking after her, and before she kissed me would open the door suddenly or go out of the room and then return. I've seen the other sister just outside the door of the room, when suddenly opened.

The big sister must have been five feet nine high, and large in proportion; the impression on my mind is that she was two and twenty: that age dwells in my recollection, and that my mother remarked it. She had brown hair and eyes, I recollect well the features of the woman. Her lower lip was like a cherry, having a distinct cut down the middle, caused she said by the bite of a parrot, which nearly severed her lip when a girl. This feature I recollect more clearly than anything else. My mother remarked that, though so big, she was lighter in tread than anyone in the house, her voice was so soft; it was like a whisper or a flute, her name was I think Betsy.

I had none of the dash, and determination towards females, which I had in after life; was hesitating, fearful of being repulsed or found out, but was coaxing and wheedling. Betsy used to take charge of my two little sisters (there was no regular nursery then), and used to sit with them in a room adjoining our dining room; it had a settee and a large sofa in it, we usually breakfasted there. She waited also at table, and did miscellaneous work. I am pretty certain that we had then no man in the house. I used to lie down on the sofa in this room. One day I talked with her about her lip, put my head up and said: "Do let me kiss it." She put her lips to mine, and soon after, if I was not kissing her sister, I was kissing her regularly, when my mother was out of the way.

One day when she went up to her bed-room, I went softly after her, as I often did, hoping to hear her piddling. Her door was ajar, one of my little sisters was in the room with her, I expect I must have had incipient randiness on me. She taught the child to walk up stairs in front of her, holding her up, and in stooping to do so, I had glimpses of her fat calves. At the door, I could not see her wash, that was done at the other side of the room, but I heard the splash of water and, to my delight, the pot moved, and her piddle rattle. The looking-glass was near the window. Then she moved to the glass and brushed her hair, her gown off, and now I saw her legs, and most of her breast, which looked to me enormous.

Then I noticed hair in her armpits; it must have been the first time I noticed any thing of the sort, for I told a boy afterwards, that brown women had hair under their armpits; he said every fool knew that. When she had done brushing, she turned round, and passing the door, shut it: she had not seen me.

I fell in love with this woman, an undefined want took possession of me, I was always kissing her, and she returned it without hesitation. "Hush! your mamma's coming"; then she would work, or do something with the children if there, as demurely as possible. I declare positively as I write this that I believe I gave that woman a lewed pleasure in kissing me, her kisses were so much like those I have had from women I have fucked in after years, so long, and soft, and squeezing.

One day I was in the sitting-room laying on the sofa reading, she sitting and working; where the children were, where my mother was, I can't say: they must have been out; why this servant was in the room with me alone, I don't know. On a table was something the doctor had ordered me to sip from time to time. "Come and sit near me, I like to touch you, dear" (I used to say "dear" to her). She drew her chair to the sofa, so that her thighs were near my head, she handed me my medicine, I turned on one side, put my head on her lap, and then my hand on her knee. "Kiss me." "I can't." I moved my head up and she bent forward and kissed. "Keep your face to mine, I want to tell you something." Then I told her I had seen her brushing her hair, her breasts, her armpits. "Oh! you sly boy! you naughty boy! you must not do it again, will you?" "Won't I, if I get the chance; put your head down, I've something more to tell you." "What?" "I can't if you look at me; put your ear to my mouth." I was longing to tell her, and could not do it whilst she looked at me. I recollect my bashfulness perfectly, and more than that, my fear of saying what I wanted to say.

She bent her ear to my mouth. "I heard you piddle." "Oh! you naughty!" and she burst into a quiet laugh. "I'll take care to shut the door in future." I let my hand drop by the side of the sofa, laid hold of her ankle, then the calf of her leg (without resistance); then up I slid it gently, and gradually above her garter, and felt the flesh; she was threading a needle. As I touched the thigh, she pressed both hands down on to her thighs, barring further investigation. "Now, Wattie, you're taking too much liberty, because I've let you feel my ankles." I whined, I moaned. "Oh, do, dear, do, kiss me dear; only for a minute." I tried very gently to push my hand (it was my left hand) further. "What do you want?" "I want to feel it, oh! kiss me — let me, — do, — Betsy, do," and I raised my head.

Sitting bent forward towards me as I lay, until she was nearly double, she put her lips to mine and, kissing me, said: "What a rude boy you are, what do you expect to find?" "I know what it's called, and it's hairy, isn't it, dear?" Her hands relaxed, she laughed, my left hand slid up, until I felt the bottom of her belly. I could only twiddle my fingers in the hair, could feel no split, or hole, was too excited to think, too ignorant of the nature of the female article; but of the intense delight I felt at the touch of the warm thighs, and the hair, which now I knew was outside the cunt, somewhere, I recollect my delight perfectly.

She kept on kissing me, saying in a whisper, "What a rude boy you are." Then I whispered modestly, all I had read, told of the Aristotle I had hidden in my cupboard, and she asked me to lend her the book. I touched nothing but hair, her thighs must have been quite closed, and a big stay-bone dug into my hand and hurt it, as I moved it about. I have felt that obstacle to my enterprise in years later on, with other women.

Then came over me a voluptuous sensation, as if I was fainting with pleasure, I seem to have a dream of her lips meeting mine, of her saying oh! for shame! of the tips of my fingers entangling in hair, of the warmth of the flesh of her thighs upon my hand, of a sense of moisture on it, but I recollect nothing more distinctly.

Afterwards she seems to have absorbed me. I ceased speaking to her sister, and could think of nothing but her neck, legs and the

hair at the bottom of her belly. I was several times in the same room
with her, and was permitted the same liberties, but no others. I lent
her Aristotle, which I had borrowed, and one day recollect my
prick stiffening, and a strange overwhelming, utterly indescribable
feeling coming over me, of my desire to say to her "cunt," and to
make her feel me, and at the same time a fear and a dread overtook
me, that my cock was not like other cocks, and that she might laugh
at me. After that, I used to pull the skin down violently every day,
I bled, but succeeded; it became slightly easier to do so, yet I have
no recollection of having a desire to fuck that woman, all that I
recollect of my sensations I have here described.

I was still ill, for there was brought me to my bed at nights a
cup of arrowroot. My mother usually did this, but sometimes the
big woman did; I was so glad when my mother did not. Then I
would kiss her as if I never wanted to part with her, but my hand out
of bed, scramble it up her clothes, till I could feel the hair. Then she
would jut her bum back, so that I could not touch more. One night
my prick stood, "Take the light outside," I said, "I've something to
say to you." The door was half open when she had complied; the
gleam of the light struck across the room, my bed was in the shade,
"Do let me feel you further, dear and kiss me." "You naughty boy!"
but we kissed. Again I felt her thighs, belly, and hair. "What good
does it do you, doing that," she said. I took hold of her hand, and
put it under the bed-clothes on to my prick. She bent over me,
kissing and saying, "Naughty boy," but feeling the cock, and all
around it, how long, I can't say, "Oh! I'd like to feel your hole," I
said. "Hish!" said she, going out of the room, and closing the door.

She felt me several times afterwards. When my mother brought
me the arrowroot, she having an idea that I liked her to do so, I
would not take it, saying it was too hot. She said, "I can't wait,
Wattie, while it cools." "Don't care, mamma, I don't want it." "But
you must take it." "Put it down then." "Well, don't go to sleep, and
I'll send Betsy up with it in a few minutes." Up Betsy would come,
and quickly and voluptuously kissing, keeping her lips on mine for
two or three minutes at a time, she would glide her hand down and
feel my cock, whilst my fingers were on her motte, her thighs closed,
then she would glide out of the room. I never got my hand between
her thighs, I am sure.

I used to long to talk to her about all I had heard, but don't think I ever did more than I have told, for I had a fear about using baudy words to a woman, though I already used them freely enough among boys. I used to talk only of her hole, my thing, of doing it, and so forth; but what made her laugh was my calling it pudendum, a word I had got out of Aristotle and my Latin dictionary. In spite of all this, and of the voluptuous sensations which used to creep over me, I have no clear, defined, recollection of wishing to fuck her, nor did I ever say anything smutty, if I could see her face.

I got better. Then she refused either to feel me, or let me feel her, on account of my boldness. One day, just at dusk, she was closing the dining-room shutters, I went behind her, and after pulling her head back to kiss me, stooped and pulled up her clothes to her waist; it exposed her entire backside. Oh how white and huge it seemed to me. She moved quickly round not holloring out but saying quietly: "What are you doing? Don't, now!" As she turned round, so did I, gloating over her bum, then laid both hands on it, slid them round her thighs, and rapidly kneeling down, put my lips on to the flesh, her petticoats fell over my head. She dislodged me, saying she would never speak with me again. She never either felt me or permitted me any liberties afterwards, and soon left. One or two years after that, she came to see my mother with her baby. She smiled at me. I don't recollect what became of her sister, but think she soon left us also.

My physique could not then have been strong, nor my sexual organs in finished condition, because I am sure that up to that time, I had not had a spend; perhaps my growing fast and the fever may have had something to do with it. My father came home brokenhearted I have heard, and ill. Soon after we only kept two female servants, a man outside the house, and a gardener. Father was ordered to the sea-side, my mother went with him, taking the children and one servant (all went by coach then). One of father's sisters, my aunt, a widow, came to take charge of our new house, and brought her daughter, a fair, slim girl, about sixteen years old.

I remained at home, so as to go to school; the servant left in the house was a pleasant, plump young woman, dark haired, and was always laughing; she was to do all the work. My godfather, who lived a mile or two away from us and whose maiden sister kept house for him, was to see me frequently, and did so till I was sick of him. Every half-holiday, he made me spend with him in walking, and riding; he insisted on my boating, cricketting, and keeping at athletic games when not at my studies. The old doctor I expect guessed my temperament, and thought, by thoroughly occupying and fatiguing me, to prevent erotic thoughts. He wanted me to stay at his house, but I refused, and it being a longer way from school, it was not persisted in.

My aunt slept in my parents' bed-room, my cousin in the next room. I was taken down, during my parents' absence, from the upper floor to sleep on the same floor as my aunt. They had not been in the house a week before I had heard my cousin piddle, and stood listening outside her bed-room door, night after night, in my bed-gown, trying to get a glimpse of her charms through the key-hole, but was not successful.

I made up to the servant, beginning when she was kneeling, by putting myself astride on her back. It made her laugh, she gave her back a buck up, and threw me over; then I kissed her, and she kissed me. She and my aunt quarrelled, my aunt was very poor and proud, and wanted a hot dinner at seven o'clock, I my dinner in the middle of the day. The servant said she could not do it all. The girl said quietly to me, "I'll cook for you, don't you go without, let her do without anything hot at night." She did not like her. My aunt said she was saucy and would write to my mother and complain that she wasted her time with the gardener. Godfather then renewed his offer for me to stay with him, but I would not, for I was getting on very comfortably with the servant in kissing, and things settled themselves somehow. I learnt the ways of my aunt, and tried to get home when she was out, so as to be alone with the servant; but to escape both aunt and godfather was difficult. I did so at times by saying I was going out with the boys somewhere, on my half-holidays, or something of the sort, but was rarely successful.

The servant went to her bed-room, one afternoon; with palpitating heart I followed her, and pushed her on to the bed. She was a cheeky, chaffing, woman, and I guess knew better than I did, what I was about. I recollect her falling back on to the bed, and showing to her knees. "Oh! what legs!" said I, "Nothing to be ashamed of," said she. Whatever my wishes or intentions might have been, I went no further. My relations were of course out.

Another day we romped, and pelted each other with the pillows from her bed, she stood on the landing, I half way down the

stairs, and kept when I could, my head just level with the top of
the landing on which she was, so that as she whisked backwards
and forwards, picking up the pillows to heave at me, I saw up to
her knees. She knew what she was about, though I thought myself
very cunning to manage to get such glimpses. On the landing I
grappled with her for a pillow, and we rolled on the floor. I got my
hand up her clothes, to her thighs, and felt the hair. "That's your
thing," said I with a burst of courage. "Oh! oh!" she laughed,
"what did you say?" "Your thing!" "My thing! what's that?" "The
hole at the bottom of your belly," said I, ashamed at what uttered.
"What do you mean? who told you that? I've no hole." It is strange,
but a fact, that I had no courage to say more, but left off playing,
and went down stairs.

On occasions afterwards, I played more roughly with her and
felt her thighs; but fear prevented me from going further up. She
gave me lots of opportunities, which my timidity prevented me
from availing myself of. One day she said, "You are not game for
much, although you are so big," and then kissed me long and furiously, but I never saw her wants, nor my chances that I know of,
though I see now plainly enough that, boy as I was, she wanted me
to mount her.

About that time, — how I got it, I know not, — I had a book
describing the diseases caused by sacrificing to Venus. The illustra-
tions in the book, of faces covered with scabs, blotches, and erup-
tions, took such hold of my mind, that for twenty years afterwards,
the fear was not quite eradicated. I showed them to some friends,
and we all got scared. I had no definite idea of what syphilis, and
gonorrhea were, but that both were something awful we all made
up our minds. My godfather also used to hint now to me about ailments men got, by acquaintance with loose, bad, women; perhaps
he put the book in my way. Frigging also was treated of, and the
terrible accounts of people dying through it, and being put into
straight waistcoats, etc., I have no doubt were useful to me. Several
of us boys were days in finding out what the book meant by masturbation, onanism, or whatever the language may have been. We
used dictionaries and other books to help us, and at last one of the
biggest boys explained the meaning to us.

One evening, my aunt being out (it was not I think any plan on
my part), I had something to eat and then went into the kitchen,

where the servant was sitting at needle-work by candle-light. I talked, kissed, coaxed her, began to pull up her clothes, and it ended in her running round the kitchen, and my chasing her; both laughing, stopping at intervals, to hear if my aunt knocked. "I'll go and lock the outer gate," said she, "then your aunt must ring, if she comes up to the door, she will hear us, for you make such a noise." She locked it and came back again.

The kitchen was on the ground-floor, separated from the body of the house by a short passage. I got her on to my knees, I was now a big fellow, and though but a boy, my voice was changing, she chaffed me about that; then my hand went up her petticoats, and she gave me such a violent pinch on my cock (outside the clothes), that I hollowed. Whenever I was getting the better of her in our amatory struggles, she said, "Oh! hush! there is your aunt knocking," and frightened me away, but at last she was sitting on my knees, my hand touching her thighs, she feeling my prick, she felt all round it and under. "You have no hair," she said. That annoyed me, for I had just a little growing. Then how it came about I don't recollect, but she consented to go into the parlor with me, after we had sat together feeling each other for a time, if mine could be called feeling, when my fingers only touched the top of the notch. I took up the candle. "I won't go if you bring a light," said she, so I put down the candle, and, holding her by the arm, we walked through the passage across the little hall to the front parlour; she closed the door, and we were in the dark. And now I only recollect generally what took place, it seems as if it all could but have occupied a minute, or two, though experience tells me it must have been longer.

We sat on a settee or sofa, she had hold of my prick, and I her cunt, for she now sat with thighs quite wide open. It was my first real feel of a woman, and she meant me to feel well. How large and hairy and wet it seemed; its size overwhelmed me with astonishment, I did not find the hole, don't recollect feeling for that, am sure I never put my finger in it, all seemed cunt below her belly, wet, and warm, and slippery. "Make haste, your aunt will be in soon," said she softly, but I was engrossed with the cunt, in twiddling it and feeling it in delighted wonder at its size and other qualities. "Your aunt will be in," and leaving off feeling my cock, she laid half on, half off the settee. "No, no, not so," I recollect the words, but what I was doing, know not; then I was standing by her side, my cock stiff, and still feeling her cunt in bewilderment. "I can't . . . stop . . . get on to the sofa." I laid half over her, my prick touched something — her cunt of course. Whether it went in or not, God knows, I pushed, it felt smooth to my prick, then suddenly came over me, a fear of some horrible disease, and I ceased whatever I was doing. "Go on, go on," said she, moving her belly up. I could not, said nothing, but sat down by her side, she rose up, "You're not man enough," said she, laying hold of my prick. It was not stiff, I put my hand down, and again the great size — as it seemed to me — of her cunt, made me wonder.

What then she did with me, I know not, she may have frigged it, I think she did, but can't say, a sense of disgrace had come over me as she said I was not man enough, disgrace mixed with fear of disease. "Let me try," said I; again she laid back, I have a faint recollection of my finger going in somewhere deep, again of my prick touching her thighs and rubbing in something smooth, but nothing more. "You're not man enough," said she again. A ring . . . "Hark! it's your aunt, go!" and it was.

I went into the adjoining room, where my books were and a lamp, she went to the street-door. My aunt and cousin came in and went up to their bed-rooms, I sat smelling my fingers; the full smell of cunt that I had for the first time. I smelt and smelt almost out of my senses, sat poring over a book, seeming to read, but with my fingers to my nose and thinking of cunt, its wonderful size and smell. Aunt came down. "Have you got a cold, Wattie?" "No, aunt." "Your eyes look quite inflamed, child." Soon after again, she said: "You have a cold?" "No, aunt." "Why are you sniffing so, and holding your hand to your mouth?" Suddenly the fear of the pox came over me, I went up to the bed-room, soaped and washed my prick, and had a terrible fear on me.

I was overwhelmed with a mixed feeling of pride, at having had my prick either touch or go up a cunt, fear that I had caught disease, and shame at not being man enough. Instinct told me I had lost, in the eyes of the woman, and my pride was hurt in a woeful manner. I tried to avoid seeing her, instead of as before getting excitedly into a room where she was likely to be alone for a minute. I did that for three days, then fear of disease vanished, and my hopes of feeling her cunt again, or of poking — I don't know which — impelled me towards her.

During those three days I washed my prick at every possible opportunity, and thought of nothing else but the incident; all seemed to me hurry, confusion, impossible; I wondered, and wonder still, whether my prick went into her or not; but above all, the largeness of the cunt filled me with wonder; for though I had had rapid glimpses of cunts as told, and had now seen a few pictures of the long slit, I never could realise that that was only the outside of the cunt, until I had had a woman. My fingers had no doubt slipped over the surface of hers, from clitoris to arse-hole; the space my hand covered filled me with astonishment, as well as the smell it left on my fingers, I thought of that more than anything else. This seems to me now laughable, but it was a marvel to me then.

When I sneaked into the kitchen again, I was ashamed to look at her, and left almost directly, but one day I felt her again. Laughing she put her hand outside my trowsers, gave my doodle a gentle pinch and kissed me. "Let's do it!" I said. "Lor! you ain't man enough," and again I slunk away ashamed.

CHAPTER IV

My first frig. — My godfather. — Meditations on copulation. — Male and female aromas. — Maid and gardener. — My father dies. — A wet dream. — Bilked by a whore.

The frequency of my cock-stands up to this time I don't know. Voluptuous sensation I have no clear recollection of; but no doubt during that half swooning delight, which I had when big Betsy allowed me to lay my head on her lap and feel her limbs, that impulse towards the woman was accompanied by sensuous pleasure, though I don't recollect the fact, but soon my manhood was to declare itself.

Some time after I had felt this servant's quim, I noticed a strong smelling, whitish stuff, inside my foreskin, making the underside of the tip of the prick sore. At first I thought it disease, then pulling the foreskin up, I made it into a short of cup, dropped warm water into it, and working it about, washed all round the nut, and let the randy smelling infusion escape. This marked my need for a woman, I did not know what the exudation was, it made me in a funk at first. One day I had been toying with the girl, had a cock-stand, and felt again my prick sore, and was washing it with warm water, when it swelled up. I rubbed it through my hand, which gave me unusual pleasure, then a voluptuous sensation came over me quickly so thrilling and all pervading that I shall never forget it. I sunk on to a chair, feeling my cock gently, the next instant spunk jetted out in large drops, a full yard in front of me, and a thinner liquid rolled over my knuckles. I had frigged myself, without intending it.

Then came astonishment, mingled with disgust, I examined the viscid, gruelly fluid with the greatest curiosity, smelt it, and I think tasted it. Then came fear of my godfather, and of being found out; for all that, after wiping up my sperm from the floor, I went up to my bed-room and, locking the door, frigged myself until I could do it no more from exhaustion.

I wanted a confidant and told two schoolfellows who were brothers, I could not keep it to myself, and was indeed proud though ashamed to speak of the pleasure. They both had bigger pricks than mine, and never had jeered at me because I could not retract my prepuce easily. Soon after they came to see me, we all went into the garden, each pulled my prepuce back, I theirs, and then we all frigged ourselves in an out-house.

Then I wrote to Fred, who was at a large public school, about my frigging. He replied that some fellows at his school had been caught at it and flogged; that a big boy just going to Oxford had had a woman and got the pox badly. He begged me to burn his letter, or throw it down the shit-house directly I had read it, adding that he was in such a funk for he had lost mine; and that I was never to write to him such things at the school, because the master opened every day indiscriminately one or two letters of the boys. He knew my mother was away and so did not mind writing to me. When I heard that he had lost my letter, I also was in a funk; the letter never was found. Whether the master got it, or sent it to my god-father or not, I can't say, but it is certain that just after I had one night exhausted myself by masturbation, my godfather came to see me.

He stared hard at me. "You look ill." "No, I am not." "Yes, you are, look me full in the face, you've been frigging yourself," said he just in so many words. He had never used an improper word to me before. I denied it. He raved out "No denial, sir, no lies, you have, sir; don't add lying to your bestiality, you've been at that filthy trick, I can see it in your face, you'll die in a mad-house, or of consumption, you shall never have a farthing more pocket-money from me, and I won't buy your commission, nor leave you any money at my death." I kept denying it, brazening it out. "Hold your tongue, you young beast, or I'll write to your mother." That reduced me to a sullen state, only at times jerking out: "I haven't!" He put on his hat angrily, and left me in a very uncomfortable state of mind.

I knew that my father was not so well off as he had been, my mother always impressed upon me not to offend my godfather, and now I had done it. I wrote Fred all about it, he said the old beggar

was a doctor, and it was very unfortunate; he wondered if he really
did see any signs in my face, or whether it was bounce; that I was
not to be a fool and give in, and still say I hadn't, but had better
leave off frigging.

From that time my godfather was always at my heels, he waited for me at the school-door, spent my half-holidays with me, sat
with me and my aunt of an evening till bed-time, made me ride and
drive out with him, stopped giving me pocket-money altogether,
and no one else did; so that I was not very happy.

The pleasure of frigging, now I had tasted it (and not before),
opened my eyes more fully to the mystery of the sexes, I seemed
at once to understand why women and men got together, and yet
was full of wonder about it. Spunking seemed a nasty business, the
smell of cunt an extraordinary thing in a woman, whose odour generally to me was so sweet and intoxicating. I read novels harder
than ever, liked being near females and to look at them more than
ever, and whether young or old, common or gentle, was always
looking at them and thinking that they had cunts which had a
strong odour, and wondering if they had been fucked; I used to
stare at aunt and cousins, and wonder the same. It seemed to me
scarcely possible, that the sweet, well dressed, smooth-spoken ladies who came to our house, could let men put the spunk up their
cunts. Then came the wonder if, and how, women spent; what
pleasure they had in fucking, and so on; in all ways was I wondering
about copulation, the oddity of the gruelly, close-smelling sperm
being ejected into the hole between a woman's thighs so astonished
me. I often thought the whole business must be a dream of mine;
then that there could be no doubt about it. Among other doubts,
was whether the servant's quim, which had made my fingers smell,
was diseased, or not.

Fear of detection perhaps kept me from frigging, but I was
weak and growing fast, and have no recollection of much desire,
though mad to better understand a cunt. It does not dwell in my
mind now that I had a desire to fuck one, but to see it, and above
all, to smell it; the recollection of its aroma seems to have had a
strange effect on me. I did not like it much, yet yearned to smell it
again. Watching my opportunity one day, I managed to feel the
servant; it was dusk, she stood with her back up against the wall,
and felt my prick whilst I felt her; it was an affair of a second or

two, and again we were scared. I went to the sitting-room, and passed the evening in smelling my fingers and looking at my cousin. This occurred once again, and I think now, that the servant must just have been on the point of letting me fuck her, for she had been feeling my prick and in a jeering way saying, "You are not man enough if I let you," I emboldened, blurted out that I had spent, I recollect her saying, "Oh! your story," and then something put us to flight, I don't now know what. I certainly was not up to my opportunities, that I see now plainly.

I had a taste for chemistry, which served my purpose, as will be seen further on, and used to experimentalise in what was called a wash-house, just outside the kitchen, with my acids and alkalis; that enabled me to slip into the kitchen on the sly, but the plan of the house rendered it easy for my aunt to come suddenly into the kitchen.

My bed-room window overlooked the kitchen yard, in which was this wash-house, a knife-house, and a servant's privy, etc., etc., the whole surrounded by a wall, with a door in it, leading into the garden. Just outside on the garden side, was a gardener's shed; the servant in the morning used to let the gardener in at the kitchen entrance; and he passed through this kitchen yard into the garden. I was pissing in the pot in my bed-room early one morning, and peeping through the blind, when I saw the servant's head just coming out of the gardener's shed, she passed through the kitchen yard into the kitchen in great haste, looking up at the house, as if to see if anyone was at the windows. Then it occurred to me, that if I got quite early to the kitchen, I could play my little baudy tricks without fear, for my relatives never went down till half-past eight to breakfast, whilst the servant went down at six.

The next morning, I went down early to the kitchen, did not see the wench, and thinking she might be in the privy in the kitchen yard, waited. The shutters were not down, after some minutes delay, in she came; she started. "Hulloh! what are you up for?" I don't think I spoke, but making a dash, got my hand up her clothes and on to her cunt. She pushed me away, then caught hold of the hand with which I had touched her cunt, and squeezed it hard with a rubbing motion, looking at me as I recollected (but long afterwards), in a funny way. "Hish! hish! here is the old woman," said she. "It is not." "I'm sure I heard the wires of her bell," and sure enough there came a ring. Up I went without shoes, like a shot to my bed-room, began to smell my fingers, found they were sticky, and the smell not the same. I recollect thinking it strange that her cunt should be so sticky, I had heard of dirty cunts, — it was a joke among us boys — and thought hers must have been so, which was the cause that the smell and feel were different.

Two or three days afterwards my mother came to town by herself, there was a row with the servant, I was told to leave the room; the servant and gardener were both turned off that day and hour, a char-woman was had in, a temporary gardener got, and my mother went back to my sick father. Years passed away, and when I had greater experience and thought of all this, concluded that my aunt had found the gardener and the servant amusing themselves too freely, had had them dismissed, and that the morning I found my fingers sticky the girl had just come in from fucking in the gardener's shed.

With all the opportunities I had, both with big Betsy and with this woman, I was still virgin.

When I saw Fred next, he told me he had felt the cunt of one of their servants. I told him partly what I had done, but kept to myself how I had failed to poke when I had the opportunity, fearing his jeers; and as I was obliged to name some woman, mentioned one of my godfather's servants. He went there to try his chances of groping her as well, but got his head slapped. We talked much about the smell of cunt, and he told me that one day after he had felt their servant, he went into the room where his sisters were, and said, "Oh, what a funny smell there is on my fingers, what can it be? Smell them." Two of his sisters smelt, said they could not tell what it was, but it was not nice. Fred used to say that he thought they knew it was like the smell of cunt, because they colored up so.

I had noticed a strong smell on my prick, whenever the curdy exudation had to be washed out. Fred's talk made me imitative, so I saturated my fingers with the masculine essence one evening, and, going to my female cousin, "Oh, what a queer smell there is on my fingers," said I, "smell them." The girl did. "It's nasty, you've got it from your chemicals," said she. "I don't think I have, smell them again, I can't think what it can be, what's it like?" "I don't think it's like anything I ever smelt, but it is not so nasty, if you smell it close, it's like southern wood," she replied. I wonder if that young lady when she married, ever smelt it afterwards, and recognized it. I did this more than once, it gave me great delight to think my slim cousin had smelt my prick, through smelling my fingers; what innate lubricity comes out early in the male.

Misfortunes of all sort came upon us, the family came back to town, another brother died, then my father, who had been long ill, died, and was found to be nearly bankrupt; then my godfather died, and left me a fortune, all was trouble and change, but I only mention these family matters briefly.

My physique still could not have been strong, for though more than ever intensely romantic, and passionately fond of female society, I don't recollect being much troubled with cock-standings, and think I should, had I been so. My two intimate school-friends left off frigging, the elder brother, who had a very long red nose, having come to the conclusion with me that frigging made people mad, and worse, prevented them afterwards from fucking and having a family. Fred, my favorite cousin, arrived at the same conclusion — by what mental process we all arrived at it I don't know.

When I was approaching my sixteenth year, I awakened one night with a voluptuous dream, and found my night-shirt saturated with semen, it was my first wet dream; that set me frigging again for a time, but I either restrained myself or did not naturally require much spending at that time, for I certainly did not often do so.

But our talk was always about cunt and women, I was always trying to smell their flesh, look up their petticoats, watch to see them going to piddle; and the wonder to me now is that I did not frig myself incessantly; and can only account for it on the grounds, that though my imagination was very ripe, my body was not. The fact of hair under the arms of women had a secret charm for me about that time. I don't recollect thinking much about it before, though it had astonished me when I first saw it; and why it came to my imagination so much now I do not know, but it did. I have told of the woman under whose arms I first saw hair.

One afternoon after my father's death, and that of my godfather, Fred was with me, we went to the house of a friend, and were to return home about nine o'clock. It was dark, we saw a woman standing by a wall. "She is a whore," said Fred, "and will let us feel her if we pay her." "You go and ask her." "No, you." "I don't like." "How much money have you got?" We ascertained what we had, and after a little hesitation, walked on, passed her, then turned round and stopped. "What are you staring at, kiddy," said the woman. I was timid and walked away; Fred stopped with her. "Wattie, come here," said he in a half whisper. I walked back. "How much have you got?" the woman said. We both gave her money. "You'll let us both feel?" said Fred. "Why of course, have you felt a woman before?" Both of us said we had, feeling bolder. "Was it a woman about here?" "No." "Did you both feel the same woman?" "No." "Give me another shilling then, you shall both feel my cunt well, I've such a lot of hair on it." We gave what we had, and then she walked off without letting us. "I'll tell your mothers, if you come after me," she cried out. We were sold; I was once sold again in a similar manner afterwards, when by myself.

These are the principal baudy incidents of my early youth, which I recollect, and have not told to friends; many other amusing incidents told them are omitted here, for the authorship would be disclosed if I did. One or two were peculiar and most amusing, yet I dare not narrate them; but all show how soon sexual desires developed in me, and what pleasure early in life even these gave me and others.

I now had arrived at the age of puberty, when male nature asserts itself in the most timid and finds means of getting its legitimate pleasure with women. I did, and then my recollection of things became more perfect, not only as to the consummations, but of what led to them; yet nothing seems to me so remarkable as the way I recollect matters which occurred when I was almost an infant.

CHAPTER V

*Our house. — Charlotte and brother Tom. — Kissing and groping.
— Both in rut. — My first fuck. — A virginity taken. — At a baudy
house. — In a privy. — Tribulations. — Charlotte leaves. — My despair.*

After father's death, our circumstances were further reduced.
At the time I am going to speak of, we had come to a small house
nearer London; one sister went to boarding-school, an aunt (I had
many) took another, I went to a neighboring great school or college,
as it was termed, my little brother Tom was at home; but reference
henceforth to members of my family will be but slight, for they had
but little to do with the incidents of this private life, and unless they
were part actors in it, none will be mentioned.

Our house had on the ground-floor a dining-room, a drawing-
room, and a small room called the garden parlour, with steps leading into a large garden. On the first floor, my mother's bed-room and
two others; above were the servants' room, mine, and another much
used as a lumber-room; the kitchens were in the basement, outside
them a long covered way led to a servants' privy, and close to it a
flight of stairs leading up into the garden; at the top of the stairs
was a garden-door leading into the fore-court, on to which opened
the street-door of the house. This description of plan is needful to
understand what follows.

I was about sixteen years old, tall, with slight whiskers and
moustache, altogether manly and looking seventeen or eighteen, yet
my mother thought me a mere child, and most innocent; she told
our friends so. I had developed, without her having noticed it, love
of women, and the intensest desire to understand the secrets of
their nature had taken possession of me; the incessant talk of fuck-

57

ing with which the youths I knew beguiled their leisure, the stories they told of having seen their servants or other girls half, or quite, naked, the tricks by which they managed this, the dodges they were up to, inflamed me, sharpened my instinctive acuteness in such matters, and set me seeking every opportunity to know women naked, and sexually. Frigging was now hateful to me; I had never done so more than the times related, that is as far as I now can recollect, frightened, as said, by my godfather telling me that it sent men mad and made them hateful to women. So although boiling with sensuality, I was still all but a virgin, and actually so in fucking.

A housemaid arrived just as I came home from college; the cook stood at the door, she was a lovely woman about twenty-five or -six years old, fresh as a daisy, her name was Mary. The housemaid was in a cart, driven by her father, a small market gardener living a few miles from us. I saw a fresh, comely girl about seventeen years old in the cart as I passed, and when I got inside our fore-court, turned round to look, she was getting down, the horse moved, she hesitated. "Get down," said her father angrily. Down she stepped, her clothes caught on the edge of the cart, or step, or somehow; and I saw rapidly appear white stockings, garters, thighs, and a patch of dark hair between them by her belly; it was instantaneous, and down the clothes came, hiding all. I stood fascinated, knowing I had seen her cunt hair. She, without any idea of having been exposed, helped down with her box, I went into the parlour ashamed of having, as I thought, been seen looking.

I could think of nothing else, and when she brought in tea, could not take my eyes off her, it was the same at supper (we led a simple life, dining early and having supper). In the evening my mother remarked, "That girl will do," I recollect feeling glad at that.

I went to bed, thinking of what I had seen, and stared whenever I saw her the next day, until, by a sort of fascination, she used to stare at me; in a day or two I fancied myself desperately in love with her, and indeed was. I recollect now her features, as if I had only seen her yesterday, and, after the scores and scores of women I have fucked since, recollect every circumstance attending my having her, as distinctly as if it only occurred last week; yet very many years have passed away.

She was a little over seventeen years, had ruddy lips, beautiful teeth, darkish hair, hazel eyes, and a slightly turn-up nose, large shoulders and breasts, was plump, generally of fair height, and looked eighteen or nineteen; her name was Charlotte.

I soon spoke to her kindly, by degrees became free in manner, at length chucked her under her chin, pinched her arm, and used the familiarities which nature teaches a man to use towards a woman. It was her business to open the door, and help me off with my coat and boots if needful; one day as she did so, her bum projecting upset me so that as she rose from stooping I caught and pinched her. All this was done with risk, for my mother then was nearly always at home, and the house being small, a noise was easily heard.

I was soon kissing her constantly. In a few days got a kiss in return, that drove me wild, her cunt came constantly into my mind, all sorts of wants, notions, and vague possibilities came across me; girls do let fellows feel them, I said to myself, I had already succeeded in that. What if I tell that I have seen it outside? will she tell my mother? will she let me feel her? what madness! yet girls do let men, girls like it, so all my friends say. Wild with hopes and anticipations, coming indoors one day, I caught her tightly in my arms, pulled her belly close to mine, rubbed up against hers saying, "Charlotte, what would I give, if you would . . ." it was all I dared say. Then I heard my mother's bed-room door open, and I stopped.

Hugging and kissing a woman never stopped there, I told her I loved her, which she said was nonsense. We now used regularly to kiss each other when we got the chance; little by little I grasped her closer to me, put my hands round her waist, then cunningly round to her bum, then my prick used to stand and I was mad to say more to her, but had not the courage. I knew not how to set to work, indeed scarce knew what my desires led me to hope, and think at that time, putting my hand on to her cunt, and seeing it, was perhaps the utmost; fucking her seemed a hopelessly mad idea, if I had the expectation of doing so at all very clearly.

I told a friend one or two years older than myself how matters stood, carefully avoiding telling him who the girl was. His advice was short. Tell her you have seen her cunt, and make a snatch up her petticoats when no one is near; keep at it, and you will be sure to get a feel, and some day, pull out your prick, say straight you want to fuck her, girls like to see a prick, she will look, even if she turns her head away. This advice he dinned into my ears continually, but for a long time I was not bold enough to put his advice into practice.

One day, my mother was out, the cook upstairs dressing, we had kissed in the garden parlour, I put my hand round her bum, and sliding my face over her shoulder half ashamed, said, "I wish my prick was against your naked belly, instead of outside your clothes." She with an effort disengaged herself, stood amazed, and said, "I never will speak to you again."

I had committed myself, but went on, though in fear, prompted by love or lust. My friend's advice was in my ears. "I saw your cunt as you got down from your father's cart," said I, "look at my prick (pulling it out), how stiff it is, it's longing to go into you, 'cock and cunt will come together.'" It was part of a smutty chorus the fellows sang at my college; she stared, turned round, went out of the room, through the garden, and down to the kitchen by the garden stairs, without uttering a word.

The cook was at the top of the house, I went into the kitchen reckless, and repeated all I had said. She threatened to call the cook. "She must have seen your cunt, as well as me," said I; then she began to cry. Just as I was begging pardon, my friend's advice again rang in my ears, I stooped and swiftly ran both hands up her clothes, got one full on to her bum, the other on her motte; she gave a loud scream, and I rushed off upstairs in a fright.

The cook did not hear her, being up three pairs of stairs; down I went again, and found Charlotte crying, told her again all I had seen in the court yard, which made her cry more. She would ask the cook, and would tell my mother — then hearing the cook coming downstairs, I cut off through the passage up into the garden.

The ice was quite broken now, she could not avoid me, I promised not to repeat what I had said and done, was forgiven, we kissed, and the same day I broke my promise; this went on day after day, making promises and breaking them, talking smuttily as well as I knew how, getting a slap on my head, but no further, my chances were few. My friend, whom I made a half confidant of, was always taunting me with my want of success and boasting of what he would have done had he had my opportunities.

My mother just at that time began to resume her former habits, leaving the house frequently for walks and visits. One afternoon she being out for the remainder of the day, I went home unexpectedly; the cook was going out, I was to fetch my mother home in the evening; Charlotte laid the dinner for me; we had the usual kissing, I was unusually bold and smutty. Charlotte finding me not to be going out, seemed anxious. All the dinner things had been taken away, when out went the cook, and there were Charlotte, my little brother and I alone. It was her business to sit with him in the garden parlour when mother was out, so as to be able to open the street-door readily, as well as go into the garden if the weather was fine. It was a fine day of autumn, she went into the parlour and was sitting on the huge old sofa, Tom playing on the floor, when I sat myself down by her side; we kissed and toyed, and then with heart beating, I began my talk and waited my opportunity.

The cook would be back in a few minutes, said she. I knew better, having heard mother tell cook she need not be home until eight o'clock. Although I knew this, I was fearful, but at length mustered courage to sing my cock and cunt song. She was angry, but it was made up. She went to give something to Tom, and stepping back put her foot on the lace of one boot which was loose, sat down on the sofa and put up one leg over the other, to relace it. I undertook to do it for her, saw her neat ankle, and a bit of a white stocking. "Snatch at her cunt," rang in my ears, I had never attempted it since the afternoon in the kitchen.

Lacing the boot, I managed to push the clothes up so as to see more of the leg, but resting as the foot did on one knee, the clothes tightly between, a snatch was useless: lust made me cunning, I praised the foot (though I knew not at that time how vain some women are of their feet). "What a nice ankle," I said, putting my hand further on. She was off her guard; with my left arm, I pushed her violently back on to the large sofa, her foot came off her knee, at the same moment, my right hand went up between her thighs, on to her cunt; I felt the slit, the hair, and moisture.

She got up to a sitting posture, crying, "You wretch, you beast, you blackguard," but still I kept my fingers on the cunt; she closed her legs, so as to shut my hand between her thighs and keep it motionless, and tried to push me off; but I clung round her. "Take your hand away," said she, "or I will scream." "I shan't!" Then followed two or three loud, very loud screams. "No one can hear," said I, which brought her to supplication. My friend's advice came again to me: pushing my right hand still between her thighs, with my left I pulled out my prick, as stiff as a poker. She could not do otherwise than see it; and then I drew my left hand round her neck, pulled her head to me, and covered it with kisses.

She tried to get up and nearly dislodged my right hand, but I pushed her back, and got my hand still further on to the cunt. I never thought of pressing under towards the bum, was in fact too ignorant of female anatomy to do it, but managed to get one of the lips with the hair between my fingers and pinch it; then dropped on to my knees in front of her and remained kneeling, preventing her getting back further on the sofa, as well as I could by holding her waist, or her clothes.

There was a pause from our struggles, then more entreaties, then more attempts to get my right hand away; suddenly she put out one hand, seized me by the hair of my head, and pushed me backwards by it. I thought my skull was coming off, but kept my hold and pinched or pulled the cunt lip till she hollowed and called me a brute. I told her I would hurt her as much as I could, if she hurt me; so that game she gave up; the pain of pulling my hair made me savage, and more determined and brutal, than before.

We went on struggling at intervals, I kneeling with prick out, she crying, begging me to desist; I entreating her to let me see and feel her cunt, using all the persuasion and all the baudy talk I could, little Tom sitting on the floor playing contentedly. I must have been half an hour on my knees, which became so painful that I could scarcely bear it; we were both panting, I was sweating; an experienced man would perhaps have had her then; I was a boy inexperienced, and without her consent almost in words would not have thought of attempting it; the novelty, the voluptuousness of my game was perhaps sufficient delight to me; at last I became conscious that my fingers on her cunt were getting wet; telling her so, she became furious and burst into such a flood of tears that it alarmed me. It was impossible to remain on my knees longer; in rising, I knew I should be obliged to take my hand from her cunt, so withdrawing my left hand from her waist, I put it also suddenly up her clothes, and round her bum, and lifted them up, showing both her thighs, whilst I attempted to rise. She got up at the same instant, pushing down her clothes, I fell over on one side, — my knees were so stiff and painful — and she rushed out of the room upstairs.

It was getting dusk, I sat on the sofa in a state of pleasure, smelling my fingers. Tom began to howl, she came down and took him up to pacify him, I followed her down to the kitchen, she called me an insolent boy (an awful taunt to me then), threatened to tell my mother, to give notice and leave, and left the kitchen, followed by me about the house; talking baudily, telling her how I liked the smell of my fingers, attempting to put my hand up her clothes, sometimes succeeding, pulling out my ballocks, and never ceasing until the cook came home, having been at this game for hours. In a sudden funk, I begged Charlotte to tell my mother that I had only come home just before the cook, and had gone to bed unwell; she replying she would tell my mother the truth, and nothing else. I was in my bed-room before cook was let in.

Mother came home later, I was in a fright, having laid in bed cooling down and thinking of possible consequences; heard the street-door knocker, got out of bed, and in my night-shirt went half way downstairs listening. To my relief, I heard Charlotte, in answer to my mother's enquiry, say I had come home about an hour before and had gone to bed unwell. My mother came to my room, saying how sorry she was.

For a few days I was in fear, but it gradually wore off, as I found she had not told; our kissing recommenced, my boldness increased, my talk ran now freely on her legs, her bum, and her cunt, she ceased to notice it, beyond saying she hated such talk, and at length she smiled spite of herself. Our kissing grew more fervid, she resisted improper action of my hand, but we used to stand with our lips close together for minutes at a time when we got the chance, I holding her to me as close as wax. One day cook was upstairs, mother in her bed-room, I pushed Charlotte up against the wall in the kitchen, and pulled up her clothes, scarcely with resistance; just then my mother rang, I skipped up into the garden and got into the parlour that way, soon heard my mother calling to me to fetch water, Charlotte was in hysterics at the foot of the stairs — after that, she frequently had hysterics, till a certain event occurred.

My chances were chiefly on Saturdays, a day I did not go to college; soon I was to cease going there and was to prepare for the army.

I came home one day, when I knew Charlotte would be alone — the cook was upstairs — I got her on to the sofa in the garden parlour, knelt and put my hands between her thighs, with less resistance than before, she struggled slightly but made no noise. She kissed me as she asked me to take away my hand; I could move it more easily on her quim, which I did not fail to do; she was wonderfully quiet. Suddenly I became conscious that she was looking me full in the face, with a peculiar expression, her eyes very wide open, then shutting them "Oho — oho," she said with a prolonged sigh, "do — oh, take away — oh — your hand, Walter dear, — oh I shall be ill, — oho, — oho," then her head dropped down over my shoulder as I knelt in front of her; at the same moment, her thighs seemed to open slightly, then shut, then open with a quivering, shuddering motion, as it then seemed to me, and then she was quite quiet.

I pushed my hand further in, or rather on, for although I thought I had it up the cunt, I really was only between the lips — I know that now. With a sudden start she rose up, pushed me off, snatched up Tom from the floor, and rushed upstairs. My fingers were quite wet. For two or three days afterwards, she avoided my eyes and looked bashful, I could not make it out, and it was only months afterwards, that I knew, that the movement of my fingers on her clitoris had made her spend. Without knowing indeed then that such a thing was possible, I had frigged her.

Although for about three months I had been thus deliciously amusing myself, anxious to feel and see her cunt, and though I had at last asked her to let me fuck her, I really don't think I had any definite expectation of doing it to her. I guessed now at its mutual pleasures, and so forth, yet my doing it to her appeared beyond me; but urged on by my love for the girl — for I did love her — as well as by sexual instinct, I determined to try. I also was quickened by my college friend, who had seen Charlotte at our house and not knowing it was the girl I had spoken to him about, said to me, "What a nice girl that maid of yours is, I mean to get over her, I shall wait for her after church next Sunday, she sits in your pew, I know." I asked him some questions, — his opinion was that most

girls would let a young fellow fuck them, if pressed, and that she
would (this youth was but about eighteen years old), and I left
him fearing what he said was true, hating and jealous of him to
excess. He set me thinking, why should not I do it if he could, and
if what he said about girls was true? — so I determined to try it on,
and by luck did so earlier than I expected.

About one hour's walk from us was the town house of an aunt,
the richest of our family and one of my mother's sisters. She alone
now supplied me with what money I had, my mother gave me next
to nothing. I went to see aunt, who asked me to tell my mother to
go and spend a day with her, the next week, and named the day.
I forgot this until three days afterwards, when hearing my mother
tell the cook, she could go out for a whole holiday; I said, that my
aunt particularly wished to see mother on that day. My mother
scolded me for not having told her sooner, but wrote and arranged
to go, forgetting the cook's holiday. To my intense joy, on that day
she took brother Tom with her, saying to Charlotte, "You will have
nothing to think of, but the house, shut it up early, and do not be
frightened." I was as usual to fetch my mother home.

In what an agitated state I passed that morning at school, and
in the afternoon went home, trembling at my own intentions.
Charlotte's eyes opened with astonishment at seeing me. Was I not
going to fetch my mother? I was not going till night. There was no
food in the house, and I had better go to my aunt's for dinner. I
knew there was cold meat, and made her lay the cloth in the kitch-
en. To make sure, I asked if the cook was out, — yes, she was, but
would be home soon. I knew that she stopped out till ten o'clock on
her holidays. The girl was agitated with some undefined idea of
what might take place, we kissed and hugged, but she did not like
even that, I saw.

I restrained myself whilst eating, she sat quietly besides me;
when I had finished she began to remove the things, the food gave
me courage, her moving about stimulated me, I began to feel her
breasts, then got my hands on to her thighs, we had the usual
struggles, but it seems to me as I now think of it that her resistance
was less and that she prayed me to desist more lovingly than was
usual. We had toyed for an hour, she had let a dish fall and smashed
it, the baker rang, she took in the bread, and declared she would not
shut the door unless I promised to leave off. I promised, and so

soon as she had closed it, pulled her into the garden parlour, having been thinking when in the kitchen how I could get her upstairs. Down tumbled the bread on the floor, on to the sofa, I pushed her, and after a struggle she was sitting down, I kissing her, one arm round her waist, one hand between her thighs, close up to her cunt. Then I told her I wanted to fuck her, said all in favour of it I knew, half ashamed, half frightened, as I said it. She said she did not know what I meant, resisted less and less as I tried to pull her back on the sofa, when another ring came: it was the milkman.

I was obliged to let her go, and she ran down stairs with the milk. I followed, she went out, and slammed the door, which led to the garden, in my face; for the instant, I thought she was going to the privy, but opened and followed on; she ran up the steps, into the garden, through the garden parlour, and upstairs to her bed-room just opposite to mine, closed and locked the door in my face, I begged her to let me in.

She said she would not come out till she heard the knocker or bell ring; there was no one called usually after the milkman, so my game was up, but nothing makes man or woman so crafty as lust. In half an hour or so, in anger, I said I should go to my aunt's, went downstairs, moved noisily about, opened and slammed the street-door violently, as if I had gone out, then pulled off my boots, and crept quietly up to my bed-room.

There I sat expectantly a long time, had almost given up hope, began to think about consequences if she told my mother, when I heard the door softly open and she came to the edge of the stairs. "Wattie!" she said loudly, "Wattie!" much louder, "he has," said she in a subdued tone to herself, as much as to say that worry is over. I opened my door, she gave a loud shriek and retreated to her room, I close to her; in a few minutes more, hugging, kissing, begging, threatening, I know not how; she was partly on the bed, her clothes up in a heap, I on her with my prick in my hand, I saw the hair, I felt the slit, and not knowing then where the hole was or much about it, excepting that it was between her legs, shoved my prick there with all my might. "Oh! you hurt, I shall be ill," said she, "pray don't." Had she said she was dying I should not have stopped. The next instant a delirium of my senses came, my prick throbbing and as if hot lead was jetting from it, at each throb; pleasure mingled with light pain in it, and my whole frame quivering with emotion; my sperm left me for a virgin cunt, but fell outside it, though on to it.

How long I was quiet I don't know; probably but a short time; for a first pleasure does not tranquillise at that age; I became conscious that she was pushing me off of her, and rose up, she with me, to a half-sitting posture; she began to laugh, then to cry, and fell back in hysterics, as I had seen her before.

I had seen my mother attend to her in those fits, but little did I then know that sexual excitement causes them in women and that probably in her I had been the cause. I got brandy and water and made her drink a lot, helping myself at the same time, for I was frightened, and made her lay on the bed. Then, ill as she was, frightened as I was, I yet took the opportunity her partial insensibility gave me, lifted her clothes quietly, and saw her cunt and my spunk on it. Roused by that, she pushed her clothes half down feebly and got to the side of the bed. I loving, begging pardon, kissing her, told her of my pleasure, and asked about hers, all in snatches, for I thought I had done her. Not a word could I get, but she looked me in the face beseechingly, begging me to go. I had no such intention, my prick was again stiffening, I pulled it out, the sight of her cunt had stimulated me, she looked with languid eyes at me, her cap was off, her hair hanging about her head, her dress torn near her breast. More so than she had ever looked was she beautiful to me, success made me bold, on I went insisting, she seemed too weak to withstand me. "Don't, oh pray, don't," was all she said as, pushing her well on the bed, I threw myself on her and again put my doodle on to the slit now wet with my sperm. I was, though cooler, stiff as a poker, but my sperm was not so ready to flow, as it was in after days, at a second poke, for I was very young; but nature did all for me; my prick went to the proper channel, there stopped by something it battered furiously. "Oh, you hurt, oh!" she cried aloud. The next instant something seemed to tighten round its knob, another furious thrust, — another, — a sharp cry of pain (resistance was gone), and my prick was buried up her, I felt that it was done, and that before I had spent outside her. I looked at her, she was quiet, her cunt seemed to close on my prick, I put my hand down, and felt round. What rapture to find my machine buried! nothing but the balls to be touched, and her cunt hair wetted with my sperm, mingling and clinging to mine; in another minute nature urged a crisis, and I spent in a virgin cunt, my prick virgin also. Thus ended my first fuck.

My prick was still up her, when we heard a loud knock; both started up in terror, I was speechless. "My God, it is your mamma!" Another loud knock. What a relief, it was the postman. To rush downstairs, and open the door was the work of a minute. "I thought you were all out," said he angrily, "I have knocked three times." "We were in the garden," said I. He looked queerly at me and said, "With your boots off!" and grinning went away. I went up again, found her sitting on the side of the bed, and there we sat together. I told her what the postman had said, she was sure he would tell her mistress. For a short time, there never was a couple who had just fucked, in more of a foolish funk then we were; I have often thought of our not hearing the thundering knocks of a postman, whilst we were fucking, though the bed-room door was wide open; what engrossing work it is so to deafen people. Then after unsuccessfully struggling to see her cunt, and kissing, and feeling each other's genitals, and talking of our doings and our sensations for an hour, we fucked again.

It was getting dark, which brought us to reason; we both helped remake the bed, went downstairs, shut the shutters, lighted the fire which was out, and got lights. I then, having nothing to do, began thinking of my doodle, which was sticking to my shirt, and pulling it out to see its condition, found my shirt covered with sperm smears, and spots of blood; my prick was dreadfully sore. I said to her that she had been bleeding, she begged me to go out of the kitchen for a minute, I did, and almost directly she came out and passed me, saying she must change her things before the cook came home. She would not let me stay in the room whilst she did it, nor did I see her chemise, though I had followed her upstairs; then the idea flashed across me that I had taken a virginity; that had never occurred to me before. She got hot water to wash herself. I did not know what to do with my shirt; we arranged I should wash it before I went to bed. We thought it best to say I had not been home at all, and that I should go and fetch my mother. After much kissing, hugging, and tears on her part, off I went, hatching an excuse for having fetched mother earlier, and we came home with Tom in my aunt's carriage, I recollect.

Before going to bed, I ordered hot water for a footbath. How we looked at each other as I ordered it. I washed my shirt as well as I could, and looked sadly at my sore prick, I could not pull the skin back so much as usual, it was torn, raw, and slightly bleeding.

Awake nearly all night, thinking of my pleasure and proud of my success, I rose early and, looking at my shirt, found stains still visible, and that I had so mucked it in washing that an infant could have guessed what I had been doing. I knew that my mother, who now did household duties herself, selected the things for the laundress; and in despair hit on a plan: I filled the chamber-pot with piss and soap-suds, making it as dirty as I could, put it near a chair and my shirt hanging over it carelessly, so as to look as if it had dropped into the pot by accident; left it there, and put on a clean shirt. After breakfast my mother, who usually helped to make my bed and her own as well, called out to me; up I went with my heart in my mouth, to hear her say she hoped I would be a little more careful and remember that we had no longer my poor father's purse. "Look," said she, "a disgraceful state you left your shirt in, I am ashamed to have it sent to the laundress, have been obliged to tell the housemaid to partly wash it first, you are getting very careless." Charlotte afterwards told me that, when mother gave her the shirt to rough wash, she felt as if she should faint.

I need not repeat about my prepuce, which as said I could now pull down with a little less difficulty. Lacerated and painful over night, it was much more swollen and sore the next morning, when I pissed it smarted, the thinking and smarting made me randy: risking all, whilst my mother was actually in the adjoining room, the poor girl in horrid fear and looking shockingly ill, I thrust my hand up her clothes and on to her split. She whispered, "What a wretch you are!" I went to college, came back at three o'clock, thinking always on the same subject; my prick got worse, I took it into my head, that Charlotte had given me some disease, and was in a dreadful state of mind. I washed it with warm water and greased it, having eased it thus a little, got the skin down, then could not get it back again; it got stiff; as it did so, sexual pleasures came into my mind, and worse got the pain. I greased it more, my pain grew less, I touched the tip with my greasy finger, it gave a throb of pleasure, I went on without meaning, almost without knowing, the pleasure came, and spunk shot out. I had frigged myself unintentionally again.

I watched my penis shrink, its tension lessen, its high colour go, then came the feeling of disgust at myself that I have always felt after frigging, a disgust not quite absent even when done by the little hands of fair friends, to whose quims I was paying similar delicate attentions. I was able to pull up the skin again, but the soreness got worse, I told the poor girl that my prick was very sore, and that I thought it strange. It did not wound her feelings, for she did not know my suspicions. The next morning being no better, I with much hesitation told a college friend, he looked at my prick, and thought it either clap or pox. Frightened to go to our own doctor, I at his advice went to a chemist, who did a little business in such matters; we dealt there, but my friend assured me that the man never opened his mouth to any one, if youths consulted him, and many he knew had.

With quaking I said to the chemist, that I had something the matter with my thing. "What?" said he. "I don't know." "Let me see it." I began to beg him not to mention it to my mother, or any-one. "Don't waste my time," said he, "show it to me, if you want my advice." Out I pulled it as small as could be, but still with the skin over it. "Have you been with a woman?" said he. "Yes." He looked at my shirt, there was no discharge, then he laid hold of my prick with both hands, and with force pulled the skin right down, I howled. He told me there was nothing the matter with me, that the skin was too tight, that a snip would set me to rights, and ad-vised me soon to have it done, saying, "It will save you trouble and money if you do, and add to your pleasure." I declined. "Another day, then." "No." He laughed and said, "Well, time will cure you, if you go on as you have begun," gave me a lotion, and in three days I was pretty right: warm water I expect would have had the same effect. I had simply torn the skin in taking the virginity.

Of course I wanted Charlotte again, she seemed in no way to help me, and used to cry, still there was a wonderful difference be-tween then and before the happy consummation: she tried to pre-vent my hands going up her petticoats, but, once up, objection ceased, and my hands would rove about on the outside and inside of all, we stood and kissed at every opportunity. "When shall we do it again?" She replied, "Never!" for she was sure it would bring punishment on us both.

I neglected my studies absolutely; all I thought about was her, and how to get at her, it must have been a week or more before I did. Ready for any risk, that day my mother was out, I came home, had the early dinner; the cook after that always went up to dress, or, as she said, clean herself, and there she always was an hour. Waiting till I heard her go up, I went into the garden parlour, where as usual Charlotte was with my little brother. Going at her directly, I was refused, but now how different, once she would not rest until my hand was altogether away from her. Now I begged and besought her, with my hand up her clothes, my fingers on her quim. No — if we had not been found out, we were fortunate, but never, never, would she do it again; was I mad, did I wish to ruin her, was not the cook upstairs, might she not come down, whilst we did it? How light the room was, the sun was coming in. I dropped the blinds, her resistance grew less, as her cunt felt my twiddling. "No — now no — oh, what a plague you are; hush! it is the cook." I open the door, listen, there is no one stirring. "What will she think if she finds you here?" "What does it matter? Now do — let me, — I'll bolt the door, if she comes I will get under the sofa, you say you don't know how it got bolted." Such was my innocent device, but it sufficed, for both were hot in lust. I bolted it. My prick is out, I pull her reluctant hand on to it, my hands are groping now, but too impatient for dallying, I push her down on the sofa — that dear cunt. "Don't hurt me so much again, oh, don't push so hard." Oh! what delight! in a minute we are spending, together this time.

I unlock the door, go back to the dining-room, she strolls out into the garden, cook speaks to her out of the window. "Where is master Wattie?" "In the dining-room, I suppose." Soon out I stroll into the garden, play with Tommy of course, she can scarcely look me in the face, she is blushing like a rose. "Was it not lovely, Charlotte, is not your thing wet?" In she rushes with Tom, soon I follow, cook is still upstairs. "Come, be quick." Again the bolt, again we fuck, she walks off into the garden with Tommy, her cunt full, and cook and she chat from the window. How we laughed about it afterwards.

Modesty retired after this, we gave way to our inclinations, she refusing but always letting me if we got a chance! We were still green and timid, at the end of three weeks we only had done it a dozen times or so, always with the cook in the house, always with fear. I was longing for complete enjoyment of all my senses, had never yet seen her cunt, except for a minute at a time, was mad for "the naked limb entwined with limb," and all I had read of in amatory poetry. I had gained years in boldness and manhood, and, although nervous, began to practice what I had heard.

I heard of accommodation houses, where people could have bed-rooms and no questions were asked; and found one not far from my aunt's, although she lived in the best quarter of London. Just before Charlotte's day out, I went to my aunt, complained of my mother's meanness, and she gave me a sovereign. On my way home, I loitered a full hour in the street with the baudy house, marked it so as to know it in the day, and saw couples go in, as my knowing friend who had told said I should. The next day, instead of going to college and risking discovery, I waited till Charlotte joined me, took a hackney coach to the street, and, telling Charlotte it was a tavern, walked to the door with her; to my astonishment it was closed. Disconcerted, I nearly turned back, but rang the bell. Charlotte said she would not go in. The door opened, a woman said, "Why did you not push the door?" Oh! the shame I felt as I went into that baudy house with Charlotte; the woman seemed to hesitate, or so I fancied, before she gave us a room.

It was a gentleman's house, although the room cost but five shillings: red curtains, looking-glasses, wax lights, clean linen, a huge chair, a large bed, and a cheval-glass, large enough for the biggest couple to be reflected in, were all there. I examined all with the greatest curiosity, but my curiosity was greater for other things; of all the delicious, voluptuous recollections, that day stands among the brightest; for the first time in my life I saw all a woman's charms, and exposed my own manhood to one; both of us knew but little of the opposite sex. With difficulty I got her to undress to her chemise, then with but my shirt on, how I revelled in her nakedness, feeling from her neck to her ankles, lingering with my fingers in every crack and cranny of her body; from armpits to cunt, all was new to me. With what fierce eyes, after modest struggles, and objections to prevent, and I had forced open her reluctant thighs, did I gloat on her cunt; wondering at its hairy outer covering and lips, its red inner flaps, at the hole so closed up, and so much lower down and hidden than I thought it to be; soon, at its look and feel, impatience got the better of me; hurriedly I covered it with my body and shed my sperm in it. Then with what curiosity I paddled my fingers in it afterwards, again to stiffen, thrust, wriggle, and spend. All this I recollect as if it occurred but yesterday, I shall recollect it to the last day of my life, for it was a honey-moon of novelty; years afterwards I often thought of it when fucking other women.

We fell asleep, and must have been in the room some hours, when we awakened about three o'clock. We had eaten nothing that day, and both were hungry, she objected to wash before me, or to piddle; how charming it was to overcome that needless modesty, what a treat to me to see that simple operation. We dressed and left, went to a quietish public-house, and had some simple food and beer, which set me up, I was ready to do all over again, and so was she. We went back to the house and again to bed; the woman smiled when she saw us; the feeling, looking, titillating, baudy inciting, and kissing recommenced. With what pleasure she felt and handled my prick, nor did she make objection to my investigations into her privates, though saying she would not let me. Her thighs opened, showing the red-lipped, hairy slit; I kissed it, she kissed my cock, nature taught us both what to do. Again we fucked, I found it a longish operation, and when I tried later again, was surprised to find that it would not stiffen for more than a minute, and an insertion failed. I found out that day that there were limits to my powers. Both tired out, our day's pleasure over, we rose and took a hackney coach towards home. I went in first, she a quarter of an hour afterwards, and everything passed off as I could have wished.

From that day, lust seized us both; we laid our plans to have each other frequently, but it was difficult: my mother was mostly at home, the cook nearly always at home if mother was out; but quite twice a week we managed to copulate, and sometimes oftener. We arranged signals. If, when she opened the door, she gave a shake of the head, I knew mother was in; if she smiled and pointed down with her finger, mother was out, but cook downstairs; if it pointed up, cook was upstairs; in the latter case, to go into the garden parlour and fuck was done off hand. If cook was known to be going out, Charlotte told me beforehand, and if mother was to be out, I got home, letting college and tutors go to the devil. Then there was lip kissing, cunt kissing, feeling and looking, tickling and rubbing each other's articles, all the preliminary delights of copulation, and but one danger in the way: my little brother could talk in a broken way; we used to give him some favorite toy and put him on the floor, whilst we indulged voluptuously. On the sofa one day, I had just spent in her when I felt a little hand tickling between our bellies, and Tommy, who had tottered up to us, said, "Don't hurt Lotty, der's a good Wattie." We settled that Tom was too young to notice or recollect what he saw, but I now think differently.

Winter was coming on, she used to be sent to a circulating library to fetch books, the shop was some distance off; a few houses, long garden-walls, and hedges were on the road. I used to keep out, or go out just before she went, and we fucked up against the walls. I took to going to church in the evening also, to the intense delight of my mother, but it was to fuck on the road home. One day, hot in lust, we fucked standing on the lobby near my bed-room, my mother being in the room below, the cook in the kitchen. We got bold, reckless, and whenever we met alone, if only for an instant, we felt each other's genitals.

At last we found the servant's privy one of the best places. I have described its situation near to a flight of steps, at the end of a covered passage which could be seen from one point only in the garden; down there, anyone standing was out of sight. If all was clear, I used to ring the parlour bell, ask for something, and make a sign; when she thought it safe, there she would go, I into the garden, to where I could see into the passage by the side of the garden stairs. If I saw her, or heard "ahem," down I went into the privy and was up her cunt in a second, standing against the wall and shoving to get our spend over, as if my life depended on it; this was uncomfortable, but it had its charm. We left off doing it in the privy, being nearly caught one day there.

We thought cook was upstairs, mother was out, I was fucking her, when the cook knocked saying, "Make haste, Charlotte, I want to come." We had just spent, she was so frightened I thought she was fainting, but she managed to say "I cannot." "Do," said cook, "I am ill." "So am I," said Charlotte. Said cook, "I can sit on the little seat." "Go to misses' closet, she's out." Off cook went, out we came, and never fucked in that place again; one day I did her on the kitchen table, and several times on the dining-room table.

We in fact did it everywhere else, and often enough for my health, for I was young, weak, and growing, and it was the same with her. The risks we ran were awful, but we loved each other with all our souls. Both young, both new at the work, both liking it, it was rarely we got more than just time to get our fucking over and clothes arranged before we had to separate, for her to get to her duties. Many times I have seen her about the house, cunt full and with the heightened colour and brilliant eyes of a woman who had just been satisfied. I used to feel pleasure in knowing she was bringing in the dinner, or tea, with my spunk in her cunt; not having had the opportunity to wash or piddle it out.

When she had another holiday, we went to the baudy house, and stayed so long in it that we had a scare; just asleep, we heard a knocking at the door. My first idea was that my mother had found me out, and, although I ruled her in one way, I was in great subjection to her, from not having any money. She thought her father was after her. What a relief it was to hear a voice say: "Shall you be long, sir, we want the room?" I was having too much accommodation for my money. That night we walked home, for I had no money for a coach, and barely enough to get us a glass of beer and a biscuit; we were famished and fucked out; my mother had refused to give me money, and another aunt whom I had asked said I was asking too often, and refused also.

Although we went to this baudy house, I always felt as if I was going to be hanged when I did, and it was with difficulty I could make her go: she called it a bad house, and it cost money. Something then occurred which helped me, penniless as I was.

At the extreme end of our village were a few little houses; one stood with its side entrance up a road only partially formed, and without thoroughfare; its owner was a pew-opener, her daughter a dressmaker, who worked for servants and such like; they cut out things for servants, who in those days largely made their own dresses. Charlotte had things made there. At a fair held every year near us, of which I shall have to tell more, my fast friend, who had put me up to so much and who, I forgot to say, tried to get hold of Charlotte, I saw with the dressmaker's daughter. Said he, talking to me next day, "She is jolly ugly, but she's good enough for a feel. I felt her cunt last night and think she has been fucked (he thought that of every girl); her mother's a rum old gal too, she will let you meet a girl at her cottage, not whores, you know, but if they are respectable." "Is it a baudy house?" I asked. "Oh, no, it's quite respectable, but if you walk in with a lady, she leaves you in the room together, and, when you come out, if you just give her half a crown, she drops a curtsy, just as she does when she opens the pew-doors and anyone gives her six pence, but she is quite respectable — the clergyman goes to see her sometimes."

Charlotte asked to go out to a dressmaker, I met her as if by chance at the door, the old pew-opener asked if I would like to walk in and wait. I did. Charlotte came in after she had arranged about her dress. There was a sofa in the room, and she was soon on it; we left together, I gave two or three shillings (money went much further then), and the pew-opener said, "You can always wait here when your young lady comes to see my daughter."

When we went a second time, she asked me if I went to St. Mary's Chapel (her chapel). We went to her house in the day that time. When we were going away, she said, "Perhaps you won't mind always going out first, for neighbours are so ill-natured." The old woman was really a pew-opener, her daughter really a dress-maker, but she was glad to earn a few shillings by letting her house be used for assignations of a quiet sort; she would not have let gay women in, from what I heard. She had lived for years in the parish and was thought respectable. She had not much use of her house in that way, wealthy people going to town for their frolics, — town only being an hour's journey — and no gay women being in the village that I knew of.

At this house, I spent Charlotte's third holiday with her, in a comfortable bed-room. We stopped from eleven in the morning, till nine at night, having mutton chops and ale, and being as jolly as we could be. We did nothing the whole day long but look at each other's privates, kiss, fuck, and sleep outside the bed. It was there she expressed curiosity about male emissions. I told her how the sperm spurted out, then discussing women's, she told me of the pleasure I had given her when fingering her in the manner de-scribed already; we completed our explanations by my frigging my-self to show her, and then my doing the same to her with my finger. I bungled at that, and think I hear her now saying, "No, just where you were is nicest." "Does it give you pleasure?" "Oh, yes, but I don't like it that way, oh! — oh! — I am doing it — oh!" I had no money that day, Charlotte had her wages, and paid for everything, giving me her money to do so.

One day we laughed at having nearly been caught fucking in the privy. "She must have a big bum, must Mary," said I, "to sit on that little seat at the privy." Said Charlotte, "She is a big woman, twice as big as me, her bottom would cover the whole seat." This set us talking about the cook, and as what I then heard affected me much at a future day, I will tell all Charlotte said, as nearly as I can recollect.

"Of course I have seen her naked bit by bit — when two women are together they can't help it, why should they mind — if you sit down to pee, you show your legs, and if you put on your stockings you show your thighs, then we both wash down to our waists, and if you slip off your chemise or night-gown you show yourself all over. Mary's beautiful from head to foot; one morning in the summer, we sleeping in the same bed, were very hot. I got out to pee, we had kicked all the clothes off, Mary was laying on her back with night-clothes above her waist fast asleep, I could not help looking at her thighs, which were so large and white — white as snow." "Had she much hair on her cunt?" said I. "What's that to you?" said she, laughing, but went on: "Oh! twice as much as I have, and of a light brown." "I suppose her cunt is bigger than yours?" said I reflectively. "Well, perhaps it is," said Charlotte, "she is a much bigger woman than me, what do you think?" I inclined to the opinion it must be, but had no experience to guide me; on the whole we agreed that it was likely to be bigger.

"Then," said she, "I suppose some men have smaller things than yours?" I told her that as far as I knew they varied slightly, but only had knowledge of youthful pricks, and could not be certain whether they varied much when full grown or not. We went on about Mary. "I know I should like to be such a big, fine woman." "But," said I, "I don't like light hair, I like dark hair on a cunt, light hair can't look well, I should think." "I like her," said Charlotte, "she is a nice woman, but often dull, she has no relatives in London, never says anything about them or herself, she used to have letters, and then often cried; she has none now; the other night she took me in her arms, gave me a squeeze and said, 'Oh! if you were a nice young man now,' then laughed and said, 'perhaps we would put our things together and make babies.' I was frightened to say anything, for fear she should find out I knew too much; I think she has been crossed in love."

I was twiddling Charlotte's quim, as I was never tired of doing, something in the sensation I suppose reminded her, for, laughing, she went on: "You know what you did to me the other night?" "What?" said I, not recollecting. "You know, with your finger." "Oh! frig." "Yes, well, Mary does that; I was awake one night, and was quite quiet, when I heard Mary breathing hard, and felt her elbow go jog, jog, just touching my side, then she gave a sigh, and all was quiet. I went to sleep, and have only just thought of it." She had heard or felt this jog from the cook before, so we both concluded that she frigged herself; Charlotte knew what frigging was.

"Do you recollect your mamma's birthday?" said Charlotte. "She sent us down a bottle of sherry, the gardener was to have some, but did not; so we were both a little fuddled when we went to bed. When Mary was undressed she pulled up her clothes to her hips, and looking at herself said, 'My legs are twice as big as yours.' Then we made a bet on it and measured; she lost, but her thigh was half as big again round as mine; then she threw herself on her back and cocked up her legs, opening them for a minute. I said 'Lord, Mary, what ever are you doing?' 'Ah!' said she, 'women's legs were made to open,' and there it ended. I never heard her before say or do anything improper, she is most particular." If Charlotte had been older or wiser, she would not have extolled the naked beauties of a fellow servant to her lover, for the description of the big bum, white thighs, and hairy belly bottom, the jog, jog of the elbow, and all the other particulars, sank deep into my mind.

We fucked more than ever, recklessly — it is a wonder we were not found out, for one evening, it being dark, I fucked her in the forecourt, outside our street-door; but troubles were coming.

Her father wrote to know why she had not been home at her holidays, she got an extra holiday to go and pacify him; then we had a fright because her courses stopped, but they came on all right again. One of my sisters came home and diminished our opportunities; still we managed to fuck somehow, most of the time they were uprighters. The next holiday she went home by coach (the only way), I met her on the return, and we fucked up against the garden wall of our house. A month slipped away, again we spent her holiday at the pew-opener's; no man and woman could have liked each other more, or more enjoyed each other's bodies, without thinking of the rest of the world. I disguised nothing from her, she told me all she knew of herself, the liking she took for me, her pleasure yet fear and shame when first I felt her cunt, the shock of delight and confusion when, on my twiddling it, she had spent; how she made up her mind to run out of the house when the milkman came, the hysterical faint when I first laid my prick between her slit and spent, the sensation of relief when I had not done, as instinct told her I should, in spending outside, the sort of feeling of "poor fellow, he wants me, he may do as he likes," which she had; I told my sensations. All these we told each other, over and over again, and never tired of the conversation; we were an innocent, reckless, randy couple.

We had satisfied our lusts in simple variety, but I never put my tongue in her mouth, nor do I know that I had heard of that form of lovemaking — but more of that hereafter. I did her on her belly, and something incited me to do it to her dog fashion, but it was never repeated; we examined as said each other's appendages, but once satisfied, having seen mine get from flaccid to stiff, the piddle issue, the spunk squirt, she never wanted to see it again, and could not understand my insatiable curiosity about hers. She knew, I think, less than most girls of her age about the males, having never, I recollect, nursed male children, and I don't think she had brothers.

How is it that scarcely any woman will let you willingly look at her cunt after fucking, till it is washed? Most say it is beastly, gay or quiet; it is the same. Is it more beastly to have it spurted up, to turn and go to sleep with the spunk oozing on to a thigh, or an hour afterwards to let a man paddle in what has not dried? They don't mind that, but won't let you look at it after your operations, willingly — why?

A modest girl lays quietly after fucking, and does not wash till you are away. A young girl who has let you see her cunt and take her virginity, won't wash it at all until you point out the necessity. A gay woman often tries to shove back her bum just as you spend, gets the discharge near the outlet, uncunts you quickly, and at once washes and pisses at the same time. A quiet young girl wipes her cunt on the outside only. A working man's wife does the same. I have fucked several, and not one washed before me. I incline to the opinion that poor women rarely wash their cunts inside, their piddle does all the washing. "What's the good of washing it?" said

a poor but not a gay girl to me, "it's always clean and feels just the
same an hour afterwards, whether washed or not." Is the unwashed
cunt less healthy than one often soaped and syringed? I doubt it.
An old roué said to me he would not give a damn to fuck a cunt
at night which has been washed since the morning.

About sexual matters each of us knew about as much as the
other, and we had much to learn. A girl, however, in the sphere of
life of Charlotte, usually knows more about a man's sex than a youth
of the same age does of a woman's; they have nursed children and
know what a cock is; a girl is never thought too young to nurse a
male child, no one would trust a boy after ten years of age to nurse
a female child; but she had never nursed. From Charlotte I had my
first knowledge of menstruation and of other mysteries of her sex
Ah! that menstruation was a wonder to me, it was marvellous, but
all was really a wonder to me then.

After Christmas, my sister went back to school, our chances
seemed improving, we spent another holiday at the pew-opener's.
I had got money, and we were indiscreet enough to go to see some
wax-works. Next day her father came to see her; he ordered her
to tell where she had been. She refused, he got angry, and made
such a noise that mother rang to know what it was. He asked to see
her, apologized, and said his daughter had been out several holidays without his knowing where she had been. My mother said it
was very improper, and that he ought. A friend was with us in the
room, and I sat there reading and trembling. My mother remarked
to the lady, "I hope that girl is not going wrong, she is very good
looking." Mother asked me to go out of the room, then had Charlotte up, and lectured her; afterwards Charlotte told me, for the
first time, that her father was annoyed because she would not
marry a young man.

A young man had called at our house several times to see her;
she saw him once and evaded doing so afterwards. He was the son
of a well-to-do baker a few miles from Charlotte's home, and wished
to marry her; his father was not expected to live, and the young
man said he would marry her directly the father died. Her mother
was mad at her refusing such a chance. Charlotte showed me his
letters, which then came, and we arranged together the replies.

She went home, and came back with eyes swollen with crying;
some one had written anonymously to say she had been seen at the

wax-works with a young man, evidently of position above her, and had been seen walking with a young man. The mother threatened to have a doctor examine her to see if she had been doing anything wrong; no one seemed to have suspected me; her father would have her home, her mother had had suspicion of her for some time, "The sooner you marry young Brown the better, he will have a good business and keeps a horse and chaise, you will never have such a chance again, and it will prevent you going wrong, even if you have not already gone wrong," said her mother.

It was a rainy night, I had met her on her return, and we both stood an hour under an umbrella, talking and crying, she saying, "I knew I should be ruined; if I marry he will find me out, if I don't they will lead me such a life; oh! what shall I do!" We fucked twice in the rain against a wall, putting down the umbrella to do it. Afterwards we met at the dressmaker's, talked over our misery, and cried, and fucked, and cried again. Then it was nothing but worry, she crying at her future, I wondering if I should be found out; still, with all our misery, we never failed to fuck if there was a clear five minutes before us. Then her mother wrote to say that old Brown was dead, and her father meant to take her away directly; she refused, the father came, saw my mother, and settled the affair by taking back Charlotte's box of clothes. I had not a farthing; at her age a father had absolute control, and nothing short of running away would have been of use. We talked of drowning ourselves, or of her taking work in the fields. I projected things equally absurd for myself. I tended in her agreeing to go home, — she could not help that, — but refusing to marry.

Charlotte wrote me almost directly after her return. My mother had reserved the right of opening my letters, although she had ceased to do so. That morning seeing she had one addressed to me, in fear I snatched it out of her hand. She insisted on having it back, I refused, and we had a row. "How dare you, sir, give it me." "I won't, you shan't open my letter." "I will, a boy like you!" "I am not a boy, I am a man, if you ever open a letter of mine, I will go for a common soldier, instead of being an officer." "I will tell your guardian." "I mean to tell him how shamefully short of money I am; Uncle *** says it's a shame, so does aunt." My mother sank down in tears; it was my first rebellion; she spoke to my guardian, never touched my letters again, and gave me five times the money

I used to have; but, to make sure, I had letters enclosed to a friend, and fetched them.

Charlotte was not allowed to go out alone and was harassed in every way; for all that, I managed to meet her at a local school, one Saturday afternoon when it was empty; some friendly teacher let her in, and she let me in. We fucked on a hard form, in a nearly dark room, about the most difficult poke I ever had, it was a ridiculous posture. But our meeting was full of tears, despondency, and dread of being with child. She told me I had ruined her, even fucking did not cheer her. A week or so afterwards, having no money, I walked all the way to try to see her, and failed. Afterwards, in her letters, she begged me never to tell anyone about what had passed between us. Her father sent her away to his brother's, where she was to help as a servant; for somehow he had got wind that she had met some one at the school-house. There she fell ill and was sent home again. Then she wrote that she should marry, or have no peace, wished I was older, and then she could marry me; she did not write much common sense, although it did not strike me so then. She was coming to London to buy things, would say she would call on my mother on the road, but would meet me instead. How she humbugged the young woman who came to town with her, I don't know, but we met at the baudy house, cried nearly the whole time, but fucked for all that till my cock would stand no longer; then, vowing to see each other after she was married, we parted.

She married soon, my mother told me of it; she lived twelve miles from us, and did not write to me. I went there one day, but, although I lingered long near their shop, I never saw her. I did that a second time, she saw me looking in, and staggered into a back room. I dared not go in for fear of injuring her. Afterwards came a letter not signed, breathing love, but praying me not to injure her, as might be if I was seen near her house. Money, distance, time was all against me; I felt all was over, took to frigging, which, added to my vexation, made me ill. What the doctor thought I don't know; he said I was suffering from nervous exhaustion, asked my mother if I was steady and kept good hours. My mother said I was the quietest and best of sons, as innocent as a child, and that I was suffering from severe study — she had long thought I should; the fact being that for four months I had scarcely looked at a book, excepting when she was near me, and had, when not thinking of Charlotte, spent my time in writing baudy words and sketching cunts and pricks with pen and ink.

Thus I lost my virginity, and took one; thus ended my first love or lust; which will you call it? I call it love, for I was fond of the girl, and she of me. Some might call it a seduction, but thinking of it after this lapse of years, I do not. It was only the natural result of two people being thrown together, both young, full of hot blood, and eager to gratify their sexual curiosity; there was no blame to either, we were made to do it, and did but illustrate the truth of the old song, "Cock and cunt will come together, check them as you may," and point to the wisdom of never leaving a young male and female alone together, if they were not wanted to copulate.

In all respects we were as much like man and wife as circumstances would let us be. We poked and poked, whenever we got a chance; we divided our money, if I had none, she spent her wages; when I had it, I paid for her boots and clothes — a present in the usual sense of the term I never gave her; our sexual pleasures were of the simplest, the old fashioned way was what we followed, and altogether it was a natural, virtuous, wholesome, connexion, but the world will not agree with me on that point.

One thing strikes me as remarkable now: the audacity with which I went to a baudy house; all the rest seems to have begun and followed as naturally as possible. What a lovely recollection it is! nothing in my career since is so lovely as our life then was; scarce a trace of what may be called lasciviousness was in it; had the priest blest it by the bands of matrimony, it would have been called the chaste pleasure of love and affection — as the priest had nothing to do with it, it will be called, I suppose, beastly immorality. I have often wondered if her husband found out that she was not a virgin, and, if not, whether it was owing to some skill of hers, or to his ignorance? I heard afterwards that they lived happily.

CHAPTER VI

Mary the cook. — A bloody nose and broken piss pot. — An involuntary spend. — A feel and a poke. — A new sensation. — At a baudy house. — Mary's history. — She leaves.

As the certainty that all was finished between us came to me, I got better, my grief moderated, my prick expected occupation, I was horrified at having frigged myself, and ceased doing it. Then, naturally, I looked at the servants. The new housemaid was ugly as sin, so I turned to Mary the cook. I was then about seventeen years old.

She was now I think twenty-six or -eight years old; big, stout, but, as it seemed to me then, symmetrical; she had exquisite teeth, blue eyes, and a fine complexion — so fine that my mother remarked it. She was quiet in a remarkable degree and treated me as a boy. Nine months before this I should as soon have dared to think of fucking my aunt, but experience had altered me. I thought of the light hair on her cunt, and of all I could not see, which Charlotte had innocently described to me; and the conclusions we had arrived at, that she frigged herself. Then I thought that, after all, old as she was, and young as I was, she might, like Charlotte, let me do her. I had once kissed her when Charlotte was with us, and she had taken it as if she was letting a child kiss her; I now tried it again, and got a quiet kiss in return; it was done with the air and manner of "There, there, you troublesome boy," which mortified me much.

I had now special tutors at home and was at home when I liked, yet my chances with the cook were fewer than they had been with Charlotte, owing to her occupations. I was studying elementary chemistry, and, when making some experiments in the garden parlour, burnt a table cover. My mother, angry, said I had better experiment in the back kitchen again, so, under that pretence, I managed to be downstairs frequently.

I used to watch Mary slipping out into the outside passage leading to the servants' privy, and take pleasure in the idea of her piddling there. One day I watched her coming back; she gave her clothes a tuck between her legs, and I knew it was to dry her cunt; opened the door just as she did it, she knew that I saw the action by my grin, and her face turned scarlet. I kissed her that day, asked her timidly if she had dried it properly that morning. "Dried what?" said she innocently. "What I saw you drying when you came from the closet." She turned away without saying a word.

A day or two after, as she went upstairs to the parlour, I stooped, saw her legs, and told her she had jolly fat legs. She wished I would go upstairs, for I was in the way with my chemicals, and after that ceased talking to me. But it was difficult to avoid me, I got rude, would tuck my coat between my legs, laugh and make believe to stoop down to see her ankles, but she took no notice. Begging her to kiss me one day, she gave me two or three at once, saying, "There now, go on with your chemicals," in such a motherly way that it mortified me excessively, making me feel the difference in our ages, as a barrier to my hopes.

But if discouraged one day, I got courage the next; impelled by a cock-stand, and my mother being out, I said, "Should I not like to see your legs." For a wonder she answered, "Look at your own." "Oh!" I replied, they are not the same, you have got a slit between them, I have got something hanging, and ready to put into the slit." "I wish you would go upstairs," said she, "you are always down here now." Then she told mother I was in her way, — I promised only to go to the back kitchen when it suited the cook, but did not keep my word.

She was alone one evening, I went home and downstairs, kissed and fondled, and would not be repulsed. At some time every woman is more yielding than at others, they always are if randy. Getting my courage up, I said I wished she would let me feel her thing, then said, "Let me do you," in a whisper. It was quite dusk down there when I said it. She was speechless for a full minute, whilst I kept repeating my demand. At length she replied, "How dare a boy like you speak like that to a woman like me." "I am not a boy," said I in anger; "I have had many women, I know all about a woman's pleasure, I know where your thing is, I know why you tuck your hand outside your clothes after you have piddled." Then she pushed me out of the kitchen, but I thought she smiled.

Our family habits were much as they had been, but, the weather getting finer, mother often took both Tom and the housemaid with her out for a walk; but not until the cook had dressed herself after our early dinner. Unless she took the housemaid out, I was worse off than ever. Yet my chance came.

Cook one day was alone in the kitchen darning a stocking; it was cold — the beginning of March — her feet were on the old fashioned iron fender, I sat myself down on the fender, and we talked, I laid my hand on her lap, and tried quietly, without letting her know it, to feel where she gartered. I felt the knot distinctly above her knee, thought how near it was to the cunt I was burning to feel, then put my hand up her clothes, and felt her naked leg under the knee.

She told me to leave off, my prick was standing, "Have you not jolly big white thighs, I have heard of them," said I. "Heard?" said she. "Yes, and a good lot of hair between them." "Who, to look at you, would believe you were such a liar, such a young monkey? Get out of the kitchen." She arose, drew some water, took it in one hand, some clean clothes in the other, and went upstairs, taking no further notice of me. I followed her a few steps up, then pushed my hands up her clothes on to her thighs, just beneath her backside; round she swung facing me, and sat down on the stairs; in swinging round my hand came just into contact with the hair of her cunt; then with a push she sent me downstairs tumbling. As I got up she said quite quietly, "It's your fault if you are hurt; if you follow me, I will push you down again, I am stronger than you." I sang out, "I don't care, so long as I can feel you." "If I was not so comfortable here in many ways, I would leave to-morrow," said she, continuing to go upstairs, and thinking she had settled me; but I followed, tried again, and she threw the whole jug of water over me. "Now tell your mamma," said she, "and I'll surprise her, she don't know her son," and again she pushed me down. That did not stop my tongue, for I now got angry and reckless, sang out my wants, bawling out about her cunt, and said, "Did you ever sit on a little privy seat, Mary, tell me?" She went up and locked herself in her bed-room, till I was tired of waiting.

I had been a month at this fun, and, as in Charlotte's case, seemed not getting on at all, my experience was confined to one woman, and naturally I used to compare everything taking place with what had taken place with her. To my inexperienced mind there was a difference between the two women which I could not understand: when I first got my hand up Charlotte's clothes, she was as quick as me, struggled, screeched, and got my hand away, seemed in dread and astonished. When I got my hand on Mary's flesh, which I did repeatedly afterwards, she would turn round quite quietly, remove my hand with force, look at me if she were collecting her thoughts, did not seem at all alarmed, but gave me a lecture. When she kissed me afterwards, it seemed to be upon reflection, but she did it with force, looked me full in the face, then turned away. One day she said, "I would not leave a sister of mine here, if she were young, for five times my wages, but I am old enough to keep you in your place."

Soon after, mother was one day out, I at home, housemaid and Tom in the garden; it was a clear, bright day, there was a fire in the garden parlour, the garden window-door was shut, and I bolted it; it was about half-past three o'clock, the cook was dressing, I burning with lust, went to my bed-room, opposite then to her door, and listened. I heard the rattle of piddle, excitement got the better of my fears, I knocked. "It's not locked," she called out, thinking it was the housemaid; I opened the door, went in, and closed it.

She was standing before the glass brushing her hair, with but stays on; over her chemise, I saw at a glance big white breasts and big white legs up to her knees. She turned round and, seeing me, put her hands up to cover her breasts, stepped backwards till the bedstead stopped her, and said, "Go out, Master Walter," but I threw my arms round her, clasping her tightly and kissing her on her breasts before she could repeat her request, and said, "Oh! do Mary, do let me."

She did not answer, but disengaged herself from my arms. Crafty with lust and doubtless thinking of former experience, I dropped on my knees, in an instant had her chemise up, both hands round her great bum, and my mouth buried in the hair, kissing the outside of her cunt; she sat down nearly crushing my hands, between her bum and the bedstead, I withdrew them with a cry of pain.

She pushed me away; being on my knees, back I tumbled; as I did so, caught her chemise and lifted it; she put her hands down to prevent it; I kept my hold tightly, and it tore up, with a noise, to where her stays stopped it from going further; but the rent disclosed thighs, belly and motte simultaneously. She rose, tried to hide her nakedness and stop the chemise going further, her legs got somehow entangled with mine, I fell back, and she fell clean over me. As I fell, my head struck the pot and overturned it, I felt the warm piddle round my neck and head, and at the same instant a heavy sort of blow on my nose, and hair on my lips — it was her naked belly and motte which struck me as she fell on me. We rolled over and struggled for a second, I saw white thighs, a huge bum, and then we were both up. She opened the window and shouted out, "Eliza, Eliza, I want you."

Then she turned to me with her eyes wide open, her bosom palpitating, and said, "Get out, you are a nice young blackguard, I would not have believed it, had I not found you out." And in the same breath hurriedly, "Oh! my God, Wattie, what is the matter?" I felt a funny trickling sensation on my upper lip, and putting my hand up to feel, removed it covered with blood, the result of the blow of her motte on my nose, which was pouring down blood copiously, and dropping on to my shirt. The sight of blood always made me furious. "It's a blow from your belly," said I, "you did it purposely." She saw by that time it was not serious and said, "It serves you right, and directly your mamma comes in I will tell her." "Do," said I. She repeated, "You are a young blackguard."

In the excitement of opening the window, calling out, and seeing my nose bleeding, she had forgotten her torn chemise; and I had thought about nothing but my bleeding nose. Standing by the table to open the window, her form had been hidden, but she moved, disclosed the torn chemise, partly one of her hips, thigh, leg, and partially the hair of her cunt. "I can see your cunt," said I staunching my nose. She snatched up the torn chemise, hiding herself with it. "Oh! go, go," said she, "oh! that mess, what shall I do!" and she stooped to set up the piss-pot which was laying on one side; I rushed forward, nose still bleeding, and tried to feel the half-naked thigh. "For God's sake go," said she, "here is Eliza coming." I heard Tom lumping up, step by step, slowly, assisted by the housemaid, and bolted into my room.

I held the door ajar and listened. "Where is Master Walter?" said the housemaid as she got to the top landing. "I don't know," said Mary, "is he not in the drawing-room?" "I don't know," replied Eliza, "what do you want?" The door closed, I heard no more, but I felt sure that Mary did not mean to tell. My nose left off bleeding, I washed it, and crept quietly downstairs.

Eliza and Tommy went down again into the garden; shortly afterwards, down went cook into the kitchen, five minutes after, down I went. It was always dullish in the afternoon there. I had thought what I might risk, and, as I passed the door from the kitchen leading into the garden, shot the bolt so that, had the housemaid come down that way, she could not get in also.

Mary was sitting close to the fire. "No more nonsense, I hope," said she. There was a kiss and forgiveness soon given me, in her tranquil way.

Again I sat down on the huge kitchen fender, and the next instant was thinking what I had best do. I had seen those wonderfully large, white thighs, seen the thicket of lightish hair between them, had felt no cunt fully for weeks, and was dying with lust. She was as serene as if nothing had happened and kissed me, but in the usual motherly sort of way. She rose up saying, "I must begin to shut up; what is Eliza staying out so late in the garden with that child for?" That instant I thrust my hand up her clothes, got it on to the motte, and clutched the hair between my fingers; it was easy enough, for it was about the longest and thicket motte thatch I have yet felt. Down she sat, and tried to push me away, but I had firm hold of the hair, and as I did on a similar occasion with Charlotte, pulled and hurt her; she ceased to push me off, and there I stopped, my prick throbbing, and every fibre in me palpitating with the lust of long continence. Then I pulled and hurt her again, threatening to hurt her more still unless she let me feel her; knowing the housemaid must knock before she could get in suddenly, I was bold.

She bore my tugs with a little flinching and never answered my entreaties. I had found my courage and used the words cunt and fuck; it was getting dark; looking at me steadily she said, "So young and yet so cruel, five minutes ago you were saying you were so fond of me, and now you are trying to hurt me; you promised you would not touch me again, now you are doing it; you are all alike, young and old, cruel and liars." I felt ashamed, but was mad with lust. "A youth like you, and so quiet as you look." "Youth! I am a man, have had women, feel me, let me feel you, oh! do feel me." I had my prick out. To get better at her, got from the fender on to my knees, and was pushing my hand between her thighs with energy. Putting her bum back, she stooped, and her face came near mine. "Kiss me, feel me, and I will indeed leave off, I have seen your belly, let me feel it, and I will leave off." "You will break your word again," said she. "I swear not." She put her face to mine and kissed me, her right hand dropped, and gently laid hold of my prick, her thighs just so little opened that my fingers passed the hair and felt the smooth inner face of the lips; it was too much for me, for some hours my prick had been standing off and on, I had been pulling it about, longing and hoping to use it, and for a long time no emission had left it.

I felt my sperm coming and could not stop it, my arse jogged and pushed my prick involuntarily between her fingers, pleasure suddenly overwhelmed me, and, kissing her, I spent in her hand — all the work of half a minute. Then burning shame came over me, I could kiss her no longer, dared not look her in the face, nor keep my hand between her thighs, but rose quickly and, without a word, ushed upstairs to my bed-room.

I have done for myself, I thought, what a beast she will think me, I shall never dare to speak to her again, and was ready to cry; little knowing then that every step in baudiness is a step towards the end, and that my spunk on her hand, would help me to shed some in her elsewhere.

Feeling so uncomfortable, I went out; calling out to the housemaid that I should be home about eight o'clock, went to a friend's, had dinner, but could not talk or scarcely eat. My friend joked and asked if I was in love. My prick was standing again after I had eaten, I went home, making up my mind to go to bed early, preferring solitude and my own thoughts; it was about seven p.m., to my astonishment Mary opened the door. I felt my face hot, and could scarcely look at her; she was as tranquil as ever, nothing ever seemed to disturb that woman. This tranquillity reassured me, the more so when I found mother was still out. The housemaid had gone out to make a few purchases, leaving Mary alone with Tommy, whom she was just going to put to bed, and upstairs she went with him for that purpose, without speaking to me.

What a chance! oh! if I had not been such a beast. My prick rose stiff, the afternoon's spend was the first I had had for a long time, a stiff prick gives courage, and darkness helps. We are alone, she said nothing as I spent in her hand, indeed went on kissing me when spending; what if I ask her again? What an age she seemed putting Tommy to bed; at last I heard her say, "Go to sleep, mamma will be home soon," and she went up to her bed-room. She is going, thought I, to sit there till Eliza knocks, and did not dare go up, but stood listening in the hall, feeling my prick and longing; at last I heard her coming down with slow, measured steps. In the hall, I flung my arms round her, kissing and begging her to forgive me. "I could not help it," said I in a whisper, "you do not know how I longed for you." "Let me go downstairs," said she.

The garden parlour door was open. "Come in here and talk." I pulled her in with but little difficulty, pushed her down on the sofa, and put both arms round her. The door closed, leaving a small opening; there was no light but the gleam which shot from the hall-lamp through the door ajar; I could barely see her face and sat by her begging forgiveness and kissing, but got no reply. My prick was more than stiff, I put my hand down on her lap, on to her knees, then down to her feet, waiting a second at each advance — no movement. My hand slipped up bit by bit, it passed her ankle, her garter, and was on the flesh above — still no movement. I hesitated and begged — no reply. Up further went my hand, the thighs were not closed, but let my hand slip between them, a long drawn sigh came from her as my fingers buried themselves in a fat, warm, quim. I pushed her back gently and put her hand on to my prick; she held it tight and, in a whisper said, "Will you never tell any-one?" By my body and soul I swore it; the thighs opened wider, her body fell back and disposed itself on the sofa, my hands roved over a large expanse of flesh, I could see the white mass only, the rest seemed dark. I kissed the hair on her cunt which I could not see, felt the smooth velvety haunches, and threw myself on one of the finest, whitest, and broadest bellies I ever yet have had close to mine. The thighs opened to receive me, and the next moment my prick was gliding up her cunt — she was not a virgin.

What a heavenly sense of satisfaction at being up a cunt again. I could scarcely realize my success; my hands felt between the fat lips, to ensure my being in all right. I was conscious of a difference between her and Charlotte, the way she lay, the size of the thighs, the quantity of hair, and a quiescent manner made her as different as possible from my former sweetheart. Novelty made me think this one more delicious, but nature would not postpone and was impelling her as well as me; was tightening her cunt round my prick, her body was thrilling for a spend. I pushed; as her cunt, tightening, roused me, tighter was my prick grasped within her; her arms folded across me, drew me towards her like a vice; her belly moved up quite slowly to mine, as if to throw me off, then moved twice or thrice as if in a spasm — a sigh, and her belly sank down as slowly as it had risen up, drawing my sperm into her, as she spent.

We lay without stirring or uttering a word for a long time, supremely happy; my prick lingered, as if it intended to stop permanently in its trap; she made no effort to dislodge it; at last it began to shrink, then curiosity began, down went my hand between our bellies, wet as if from a bath of gruel was my doodle and her quim. Then she spoke — the first words uttered — "No — no." The feel had such an effect on me, that my prick began again to stiffen. I had with Charlotte failed ignominiously two or three times, in a third fuck on the same day, and feared a failure now. I kissed and felt her, as far as my hands and our clothes would let me, she moved her bum up gently to let my hand under it, but not a word could I get from her. "Can I do it again?" thought I, and began pushing — yes it was stiffening, again was that cunt tightening. I push harder, — with a gentle heave the belly comes up, I am off on the ride without having withdrawn; was this the first time I had ever been man enough to do it twice without uncunting? I think so.

The passage of privates was longer, I felt more movement in her buttocks, her sighs were stronger, her hand moved more restlessly over my back, our mouths got glued together. Her lips are wet, or is it mine which are getting wet? There is a new, voluptuous sensation I never experienced before, it delights me; I glue my lips tighter to hers, our heaves are quicker, our sighs shorter, I feel the least bit of her tongue touching my lips. I had never heard of that voluptuous accompaniment of fucking, and it was to me an inspiration; shooting out my tongue into her mouth, — hers comes out to meet it; they are exchanging liquids, — the delight spreads electrically through our bodies, — up comes her belly, — shorter are my shoves, — a quivering wriggle to get deeper up her — and we both spend together, as it seems with more pleasure than I ever did before. How strange I should recollect this all so clearly.

The delights of the wet kisses are new to me; although not able to see them, I thought of her exquisite teeth and rolled my tongue over them. She kisses me, still holds me, again my hand goes down to feel the parts now separating, slobbered and sticky with past joy; out comes my prick, and then she speaks. "No — no," she sits up, I by her side, my hand on her naked thighs for a minute. She gets up, gives me a long kiss, goes to her room, and soon after comes down, her eyes wet with crying. "Don't come near me, don't be unkind, let me alone," she says. Her manner was so commanding that I let her go to the kitchen without following her. Shortly Eliza, and then my mother, came home.

Mad for her again, I took to my chemistry in the back kitchen constantly, you may be sure. When I got the chance, spoke of our pleasures and my hopes. "We ought," said she, "both to be ashamed of ourselves, but I especially, who am so many years older than you, ought to have known better; if I am punished it will serve me right. Oh! if you don't hold your tongue! my risk is more than you have any idea of." All was said in a way as if she were preaching, and looking me full in the face.

She refused what I wanted and avoided me, but it was impossible for her altogether to escape me. Risking everything, emboldened by impunity with Charlotte, I used to clutch her knees, and put my head up her clothes, kissing and smelling her motte, I began to love the smell of it. She used to dislodge me, and neither made a noise nor uttered a word in doing so — indeed she rarely spoke at any time. But it is difficult for a woman who has been fucked by a man to refuse him again; I watched my opportunities; my conversation, broken as it was, and rarely but for a minute at a time, was one repetition of lustful wants and prayers; I used to pull my prick out, beg her to see and feel it. At length she did, saying, "May God forgive me for my weakness." That day I fucked her again standing in the kitchen, and a second time a few hours afterwards in the dusk, which experience began to show me was the time she was most accessible; the other servant was somewhere in the house at the time, I recollect.

After that her manner changed, she ceased to resist; but when I asked her to go to a house with me, she said, "No, no, I am not coming to that." Now, though tranquil, she was more capricious, sometimes letting me feel her or do it to her with impatience; at other times with evident desire to please; but I was so often baulked, and I plagued her so incessantly to meet me somewhere that at length she did, saying, "Well, it little matters, as I have made my bed, so I must lie on it." I did not know then what she meant by that.

She got a holiday, we had food at a tavern, went to the house to which I first took Charlotte, and into the same room; what a reminiscence! As I got to the door, she looked nervously round and said, "I may as well be hung for a sheep as a lamb." It was a joyous day for me. Once in the house she became gay and amatory, threw off all restraint, and abandoned herself to sexual enjoyment in a way she never did but twice again.

She was simply dressed as was customary with servants in those days. Soon I had her standing naked before me with but boots and stockings on. And what a sight she was. Quite five feet eight high, stout, yet, as it seemed to me then, without a single part of her body either flabby or shapeless; her skin was of such dazzling whiteness that her white stockings looked dull by contrast, very light brown hair, which, when pulled out, nearly hung to her waist, the hair of her cunt and arm-pits in quantity of a lighter golden brown; all looked much darker than their true colour, against the dazzling whiteness of the skin. Ample calves and thighs, breasts firm as ivory, her arms to match in plumpness and whiteness, her hands alone, discoloured by work, looked dark against the rest of her glorious person. I recollect this all well, and that at that time I disliked light-haired women; but in her, suddenly, the light hair appeared to me lovely.

She changed in manner that day from a condescending matron to a lover of my own age; had the complacency of a gay woman, tempered with modesty. I had no notion of baudily posturing women which I learned in after life, but had an innate love and perception of all that was beautiful and began placing her in attitudes favourable to the contemplation of her charms. She complied with all; from belly to side, from side to back, I turned her; she smiled as if pleased, curious, and astonished; and when I turned to quench my passion in her, she met me with an ardour less demonstrative, but more stifling and satisfying, than Charlotte; it was a worry to think that I had twice fucked her, and seemed to have finished each time before I had begun fucking.

The firmness of her flesh impressed me, whether I put my finger between the cheeks of her arse or between her thighs, I could with difficulty get it away; she could have cracked a nut between either. The next wonder was the hair of her cunt, which was long but curly; I now see that she could not have pissed without wetting it, which accounted for her always what we youths used to call mopping it, after she had piddled. The cunt looked twice as big as Charlotte's, but the prick-hole seemed to me smaller; and whether my finger, or my prick was in it, seemed to grasp it tightly. My prepuce used to give me then at times pain just before or when I spent in Charlotte; in Mary I scarcely seemed to feel it, and afterwards a quiet sort of grinding of her cunt prolonged my pleasure until my penis left it. I was so new to the work that all these differences impressed me, I compared and thought of them constantly.

She gave no violent writhes or twists, nor jerked her arse, nor wriggled as she spent, but just as my short thrusts came on, her belly used gradually to heave up and grow into mine; her cunt almost seemed to be sucking my prick, whilst it throbbed and jetted its sperm into her; my hardest thrusts never hurt; Charlotte used to complain if my prick was too vigorous in her. Then when her pleasure was over, lolling her tongue against mine, and sucking my very breath from me, she quietly subsided; leaving me to lay in her, until, with a kiss, she would gently doze off with me in her arms.

A taste had developed as said, which I have retained to the present time. I loved to see a woman piddle, used to make Charlotte do it as often as I could, to place my hand under the stream, and feel its splash on my fingers; and if chance let me hear the rattle in a pot, or see a woman rising up from the attitude, my prick used to stand. I did this with her, greatly to her astonishment, she resented it so much that I never repeated it: singular that a woman who would let me lay and kiss her cunt, or put finger and prick up it, should refuse to let me see the water come from it — but so it was.

Charlotte I loved, and used to feel as if she were part and parcel of me for life when I was up her; with Mary I thought of thighs, backside, cunt, and her other parts, without much liking her beyond the desire of spending in her. My impression is that I must have fucked that day as much as I ever did in my life on one day; my mother remarked that I looked ill and worn out when I got home and again fell on her favorite belief that I was overstudying. How she could have permitted a young man to be so often in the kitchen, and near to female servants, seems to me a marvel of stupidity, — but she did.

Nothing opens a man's and woman's heart to each other like fucking. A woman laying satisfied by your side, her cunt bedewed with your spunk, with fingers touching your prick, and mouth fresh from contact with yours, will tell you more than she will at any other time. She did that day. She had thought me a mere boy, getting baudy with coming manhood, and had liked me. My quiet, demure manner made her imagine that such an attack from me was among the most improbable things; when I began she made up her mind to leave, but then came the mystery, — there were circumstances which rendered it needful for her to stay where she was, if possible — what they were she would not say. My assault on her in the bed-room and all that followed upset all her ideas, filled her mind with images of lust and pleasure, and left that undefined sensation and unsatisfied longing which is known as randiness. I suddenly seemed a man to her. My spending in her hand upset her still more. I asked if that had made her let me have her. She replied, "I gave up the self denial of years, abandoned my intentions, and let you do it; when you pushed me into the garden parlour I intended to let you as I went in, I had not quite intended before."

There was the greatest difficulty after that day in getting her, for my mother seemed always in my way, and objected to my being in the kitchen. Mary never helped me as Charlotte used; as cook indeed she could not. She ran no risks, and was never in a hurry, so where I had Charlotte half a dozen times, I could scarcely get Mary once.

She met me out again, and in a fortnight asked for another holiday. It astonished my mother, for for more than a year she scarcely had gone out and never had taken a whole holiday. What another day of ballocking it was, in that old, snug, baudy house — but we had a quarrel there.

Even with my inexperience, I knew she was different from Charlotte at the first poke. I used in my mind to compare the differences. Charlotte's curiosity, the manifest novelty of fucking to her, even for a couple of months after her splitting and bleeding, was so different from the steady, quiet, well-satisfied way with which Mary copulated. Pondering over this, I wondered if she had been done before, how often, and by how many, or had I been the first? The idea of asking her was always floating through my brain. That day I said to her as her face was towards mine on the pillow, and I was toying with her bubbies, "I wonder who had you before me." She sat up, looked me steadily in the face, and replied, "You have no right to ask me, you are not my husband." "But tell me." "I shall not, it is an impertinence; how can a youth like you know anything about first or second." I blurted out, "Because when first I did it to Char — " the name was almost out of my mouth, but I stopped in time, "when I first had a young woman (correcting myself), I could not easily get into her, it tore my prick, and she bled." "Who was it?" said she. "Oh! a young woman." "But who was it?" I did not reply. "Was it Charlotte?" and she looked me hard and full in the face. "No," said I. "Now was it? Tell me," said she bending over, kissing and coaxing me. "No, it was not." "I believe it was, you once said she was young, and had dark brown hair — it was she." In vain I denied it. "I feel sure it was, and a youth like you! Is it possible you can have harmed that nice girl! What a wretched, wicked lot you all are, you will be as bad as the others." Then she suddenly said, "Mind, you have sworn solemnly never to mention to any living soul about me; ah! once forget yourself, and it's all up with a woman." Then she laid down, again her manner became quiet and voluptuous — another fuck followed. I again tried the question. She settled me by saying, "If ever you ask me that question again, I will not let you have me afterwards," and I never did ask her that I can recollect, until just before she left us.

But she for some time after asked me questions about my first woman: Was she tall? were her teeth so good as hers? and so on. How far she satisfied herself that it was Charlotte, she never said; for I don't recollect that she mentioned her name again, and I gave wrong descriptions; but she may have got more information than I meant her to have, as she asked me at odd times when I was off my guard.

A third time, to the still greater surprise of my mother, she took a holiday. We spent it at the house, and she exhausted me and herself. For a day or two afterwards she gave me every chance at home, and we fucked furiously. She took to calling me a dear fellow, when her tongue was not against mine, but which was always the case when our mouths got together, and I imagine now must have been a greater luxury to her than it was then to me. Soon after she received several letters which I said were from her lover. "I wish they were," said she. Then she took ill, and when better, refused me altogether. I had opportunities, but she would not. I said I wished I had never seen her; she said she wished so too, for she was fond of me, although it was ridiculous at her age and mine. Afterwards, when mother was one evening at the bottom of the garden, Eliza gone out to the library, I seized Mary as she closed the shutters, kissing and begging her. She opened her thighs, my fingers were on her clitoris; she, kissing me at intervals, said, "Oh! no, oh! I can't, dear — I dare not — Walter, Walter, you must not; I am a married woman, and am going home to my husband most likely."

Soon afterwards she told me her history. Married seven years previously, her husband became dissipated and unfaithful, and from being a well-to-do tradesman brought himself to the condition of a labourer. She forgave him until he gave her a disease, then she left him as she had threatened to do. Nothing he could say would induce her to have anything more to do with him. "Is there anything about me that a man could not be satisfied with for a year?" she asked, as if I were a judge.

She went home to her mother. He appears to have been fond of her. Love of women was his great fault; but the disease so set her against him, that all his entreaties were useless. Nevertheless she was his wife, and getting into the mother's house one day, when she was alone (Mary), he fucked her with violence — and violent it must have been, for she was as strong as a horse. Directly afterwards she left and went to service in London, confiding only her address to her mother, taking a false name, and writing him that if ever he found her out and annoyed her, she would go abroad. Her husband made the mother a sort of promise to keep steady for three months, but failed in doing so, went to America, had never ceased to write affectionate letters which came to her through her mother, and had recently written to say he had made a large sum of money and was coming home. He had sent money home to the mother with instructions to settle it on Mary how she liked, provided she would come back to him. Afterwards she showed me his letters; they were well written, and in a style above a man of his position in life.

She had lived in service ever since; with us she had then been a year and a half, and had had but two other places. One she left because a grown up son began to pay her too much attention. At the other the master — a married man — made love to her, and one day tried to force her. I knew the last place, it was about three miles from us.

This news came like a cold bath on me. It suited my taste to have a woman in the house. The idea of losing her was terrible. She refused me my pleasures. I doubted her truth at times, but whenever I did, she would fetch a letter as proof saying, "Now will you believe me?" She refused to say where her home had been and what her real name was. I used to try to make out the postmark on her letters, but could not. They were negligent in those days in such matters, and postage was dear.

And now I again asked if she had had any other but her husband and me; by all that was holy she declared she had not. "How came you to let me?" "God in heaven knows!" said she, "months ago if anyone had said such a thing was possible I should have said it was ridiculous; I only thought of you as a tall boy, but that day I felt that my life was passing away without the pleasures of a woman; what you did kneeling down in the kitchen upset me, then I let you; though I thought I should ruin myself by doing so."

She cared but little for her husband, for he had caused her to lead the life of a widow for years. "Suppose I had done anything wrong," said she, "and he had found it out, he would have cast me away; but you men can do what you like, and we poor women have to submit." "But why go back?" "Four months ago I would not have done so, but you have made me find out I am a woman after all; you will understand that better as you grow older. Not many would have kept chaste as I have done until that night. Now I mistrust myself. I am getting fond of you, but what could come of it? And if anything came to the ears of my mother and friends, who are respectable, I should drown myself. I have got plenty of will of my own, although I am quiet."

"You don't care much about poking?" "I have had my wants but suppressed them," she replied. "What did you do?" "Oh!" said she in an off hand way, "what other unmarried women do, I suppose." "Frigged yourself?" She gave a nod and said, "And not often that." I thought of what Charlotte had told me, but held my tongue.

I tried to get at her at intervals, but it was no use. "It's caprice," said I with my prick out, "you let me when I wanted it three weeks ago, why not now?" "I can't, — I dare not, — it might be certain ruin now." What does a fellow care about ruin when his hand is outside a cunt and his prick is like an iron rod? Twice as strong as me, she could at all times have escaped me, unless sexual desire was strong on her; desire gives a man force, but it takes away a woman's force. She rose up, nor would she continue talking until I had buttoned up my prick and promised not to touch her; that done, she said, "Would you wish to ruin me? you might if I let you, I have been very ill as you know, was in the family way, my monthlies stopped, and I have brought them on. When I was in trouble that way, I let you do what you like, now I am going home, what would become of me if I were in the family way then?" This explained all.

I had never given her a present, I never gave Charlotte one, having then so little money. I never thought about it. I had now more and offered to give her some if she wanted any. She showed me a saving-bank's book. She had got nearly fifty pounds. I bought a pair of gold earrings for her, it was the first present I had ever given a woman, and she was much pleased. I had, I think, some vague notion that it would induce her to let me have her; but if so, I was deceived.

Mother seemed to be keeping at home to baulk me. My chemicals had been taken back into the garden parlour. I knew she wanted to go to my aunt's; but one morning it was too hot, then it rained, and so on. How I restrained myself from frigging I don't know, for I used to walk up and down my bed-room with my prick out stiff, and looking at it; at length a chance came — my last.

Mother went to aunt's, the ugly housemaid said, "As Master Tom won't be at home, do you mind my going out for a couple of hours?" "No," said my mother, "when the cook is ready." "Please will you tell cook Mamm'," said she, "or she won't let me go." I ha then a tutor in mathematics who came on that day, but promised to fetch mother home. I had many times broken my promises to do so, to enable me to get at Mary. Mother said, "I hope you mea· what you say, you are getting a man, and should never break your word." Anxious to know when the housemaid would go, I asked her. "I am not going till five o'clock, sir," said she, "unless you particularly want the books." "That will be too late, for I am to fetch mamma home, — never mind."

I finished with my tutor, and out I went. But at about five o'clock came home near to the house, wondering if the housemaid had gone (Mary I had not spoken a word to), waited in sight of the house, and at last saw a form I guessed to be the housemaid going off fast towards the village; five minutes afterwards I knocked, and Mary opened the door. Said she, "What brings you home?" I said I was unwell, had a bad cold, could not go for my mother, would go to bed, would she fetch me a foot-bath, and went to my bed-room. I had been two days planning the thing, an old dodge it was, though.

It was hot and quite light, but I drew down the blinds, undressed and put on my nightgown; she brought the bath, we talked. She had not heard from her mother again, it was strange, — was she being played with? It took weeks then to get to America. I kissed and got closer to her, we were on the edge of the bed; I spoke of our meetings and our pleasures, she avoided the subject, said I should take cold, prayed me to have the foot-bath and go to bed. Gradually I got my hand on her thighs, how could she help it? — a woman who had been fucked by me lots of times. But she was firm in refusing me. I lifted my night-shirt, my prick stood up, the shirt hanging at the back of it like clothes on the hook of a prop. Finding that useless, I threatened to frig myself and began the operation. She said I ought to be ashamed of myself, that she would leave if I did not desist and turned to go, when I pulled her on to the bed. Soon my fingers were on her slit, her fingers on my

prick. "I dare not let you, — oh! pray!" she said, but she was vanquished, silent, and tranquilly laid down on the bed; nature was too
strong for her.

I lifted her chemise, had a glimpse of the lovely plump calves
and large, fleshy thighs as I threw myself impetuously upon her.
My belly closed with hers, and pushing my knuckles through the
hairs, I guided my prick towards her cunt, but alas! too late. The
long abstinence and the excitement were too much for me: just as
my fingers opened the cunt-lips, and my prick touched her cunt,
throb — throb — gush — gush, and over my fingers, over her thighs,
into the thicket of hair, on to the clitoris, on to the smooth, round
bum-cheeks below — anywhere — everywhere excepting the right
place, my sperm spurted out; and only the last drop remained just
as I buried my prick in her. Then, instead of meeting her humid
tongue with mine, I sank on her breast, kissing, yet damning and
cursing like a dragoon at my spoiled pleasure, — I had spend out of
sheer copiousness of spunk, and excitement.

Said she, "It is as well as it is, get off." I made no reply, hoping
my sexual force would return, for my prick was in her sheath. She
moved to release herself. Stronger far than me, she could in any
other attitude have easily done so; but the most difficult position
for a woman to disengage herself from a man is when he is on the
top of her, well between her thighs, and clasping her backside
tightly. As she moved there was no strong will in it; how could it
be otherwise? she in the prime of life had been without it for weeks,
nature was pleading for me, my prick was in her, my spunk all about
her. To gain time I promised to get off in a minute. "Kiss me." Our
mouths and tongues met. It was like magic. A voluptuous throb
passed through both of us, my prick stiffened to the full, a sympathetic grind of her cunt responded; again we were in the full tide
of pleasure, fucking and spending together, the future was forgotten as we sank quietly down. I had spent twice without uncunting;
scarcely was it over than she pushed me off and washed out her
cunt in my foot-bath.

We sat on the side of the bed, kissing and feeling each other,
it was like the old time, the door wide open to hear the street door
knocks. When the housemaid knocked, into bed I got; an hour afterwards home came my mother and into my bed-room. She approved
of the hot foot-bath, but insisted on my taking a febrifuge. To keep

up the sham, I took it. Mary brought it and stood by whilst my mother gave it to me; my prick was again standing like a prop at the sight of Mary, and as my mother pulled the bed-clothes over me, she might, if she had had eyes, seen my prick pushing them almost up.

Next morning she gave notice to leave. I never had her again. On one or two occasions I felt her, and if there had been more time might perhaps have had her. At the end of a fortnight she told me that her monthlies were all right. From that day she resolutely refused to even let me feel her. "I don't much care about going back," said she; "I don't think I shall be happy, but I do it for the best; at all events I shall have a home." The day before she went she said, "Goodbye, God bless you, you are a good fellow, but you will play mischief with many a poor girl here before you have done. I like you very much, and shall always think of you." I never heard of her after, and with her passed from me the woman who is still in my recollection as one of the most beautiful and perfect in form, as one who gave me the greatest sexual pleasure, — but I was of course very young and inexperienced.

My mother remarked that she was the most trustworthy servant she ever had; but that there was a mystery about her. Her boxes were labelled for a place that the coach would not take her to, and her boxes were not like a servant's. "I think she has been crossed in love and ran away," said mother. Said I, "Perhaps she has gone off with a bobby," it was a current joke then, policemen not having been long invented. My mother said in her severe way, "She is a virtuous woman, a youth like you should not utter ignorant jokes about women, especially about the humbler classes, to whom good reputation is everything." I began to see plainer than ever that I could humbug mother after that.

Many of our conversations are told here in her very words, others as nearly as I can recollect them. I have often wondered at the way this woman behaved to me, talked to me, and all about her. The circumstances, as they occurred, even at the time seemed peculiar; I felt as if I was wicked in getting into her, almost as if I was going to poke my mother, but I cannot attempt to analyse motives or sensations, I simply narrate facts. Certain it is that I never have had a woman who in behaviour resembled Mary, in manner, conversation, and general behaviour, — I always felt as if she were a superior person to me, as if she were obliging me and not herself, and was putting me under an obligation by letting me fuck her.

Again lonely, I not only wanted cunt but also the society of a woman, it was so sweet to see and talk to some one I fucked; to do so secretly, was an additional charm, and I used to feel quite sad. I was then about in my eighteenth year.

CHAPTER VII

At the Manor house. — Fred's amours. — Sarah and Mary. — What drink and money does. — My second virgin. — My first whore. — Double fucking. — Gamahuching. — Minette. — A Belly up and down.

One aunt as said lived in H°°°shire, a widow; her son, my cousin Fred, was preparing for the Army. I wanted a change and went by advice to stay there. Fred was a year older than me, wild and baudy to the day of his death, he talked from boyhood incessantly about women. I had not seen him for some time, and he told me of his amours, asking me about mine. I let him know all, without disclosing names; he told me in nearly the words that it was "a lie," for he had heard my mother say that I was the steadiest young fellow possible, and she could trust me anywhere. This, coupled with my quiet look and the care I took not to divulge names, made him disbelieve me; but I disclosed so many facts about women's nature that he was somewhat astonished. He told me what he had done, about having had the clap, and what to do if I got it; then he had seduced a cottager's daughter on the estate; but his description of the taking did not accord with my limited experience. One day he pointed the girl out to me at the cottage door, and said he now had her whenever he wanted.

She was a great coarse wench, whom he had seen in my aunt's fields. He had caught her piddling on one side of a hedge; she saw him looking at the operation from a ditch, and abused him roundly for it; it ended in an acquaintance, and his taking her virginity one evening on a hay-cock, — that was his account of it.

Her father was a labourer on my aunt's estate, the girl lived with him and a younger sister, her name was Sarah; he expatiated

105

on her charms from backside to bubbies, but it was soon evident
to me that with this woman it was no money, no cunt; for he borrowed money of me to give her. I had squeezed money out of my
aunt, my guardian, and mother, and had about ten pounds, — a
very large sum for me then, — so I lent him a few shillings.

He had his shove, as he called it, and triumphantly gave me
again such account of his operations and the charms of the lady
that I, who had been some time without poking, wondered if the
girl would let me; arguing to myself, he gives her money — my girls
never wanted money, — why should his? He had been dinning into
my ears that all women would let men for money, or presents, or
else from lust. "Kiss and grope, and if they don't cry out, show
them your prick and go at them." These maxims much impressed
me.

"Fred," said my aunt at breakfast, "ride over to Brown about
his rent, you will be sure to find him at the corn market," and she
gave him other commissions at the market town. I promised to ride
with him, but had been tortured with randiness about this great
wench of his; so made some excuse and, as soon as he was well off,
sauntered towards the cottage, which was about half a mile from the
Hall.

It was one of a pair in a lane. Scarcely anyone passed them,
excepting people on my aunt's lands. One was empty. The girl was
sweeping in front of the cottage, the door was wide open. I gave
her a nod, she dropped a respectful curtsey. Looking round and
seeing no one, I said, "May I come in and rest, for it is hot and I
am tired?" "Yes, sir," said she, and in I went, she giving me a chair;
then she finished her sweeping. Meanwhile I had determined to
try it on. "Father at home?" "No, sir, he be working in the seven-
acre field." "Where is your sister?" "At mill, sir," — meaning a paper
mill. I thought of Fred. It was my first offer, and I scarcely knew
how to make it, but, chucking her under the chin, said, "I wish you
would let me — " "What, sir?" "Do it to you," said I boldly, "and I
will give you five shillings," producing the money; I knew it was
what Fred gave her usually.

She looked at me and the five shillings, which was then more
than her wages for a week's work in the fields, burst into laughter
and said, "Why, who would ha' thought a gentleman from the Hall
would say that to a poor girl like me." "Let me do it," said I hurried-

ly, "if you won't I must go — I will give you seven and six pence." "You won't tell the young squire?" said she — meaning Fred. "Of course not." She went to the door, looked both ways, then at the clock, shut the door, and bolted it without another word.

The house consisted of a kitchen, a bed-room leading out of it, and a wash-house. She opened the bed-room door, there were two beds which almost filled the room; at the foot of one was a window, by its side a wash-stand. She got on to the largest bed saying, "Make haste." I pulled up her clothes to her navel and looked. "Oh! make haste," said she. But I could not, it was the third cunt I had seen, and I paused to contemplate her. Before me lay a pair of thick, round thighs, a large belly, and a cunt covered with thick brown hair, a dirty chemise round her waist, coarse woollen blue stockings darned with black, and, tied below the knees with list, thick hob-nailed boots. The bed beneath was white and clean, which made her things look dirtier; it was different to what I had been accustomed to. I looked too long, "Better make haste, for father will be home to dinner," said she.

I put my hand to her cunt, she opened her thighs, and I saw the cleft, with a pair of lips on each side like sausages, a dark vermillion strong clitoris sloped down and hid itself between the lips, in the recesses of the cock-trap; the strong light from the window enabled me to see it as plainly as if under a microscope. I pushed my finger up, then my cock knocked against my belly, asking to take the place of my finger, and so up I let it go. No sooner was I lodged in her, than arse, cunt, thighs and belly, all worked energetically, and in a minute I spent. Just as I pulled out, her cunt closed round my prick with a strong muscular action, as if it did not wish the warm pipe withdrawn, a movement of the muscles of the cunt alone, and it drew the last drop of lingering sperm out of me.

I got on my knees, contemplating the sausage lips half open, from which my sperm was oozing, and then got off sorry it had been so quick a business. She laid without moving and looking kindly at me said, "Ye may ha me agin an yer loike." "But your father will be home?" "In half an hour," said she. "I don't think I can," said I. Such coolness in a woman was new to me, I scarcely knew what to make of it. She got hold of my tool, I had not had a woman for some time, soon felt lust entering my rod again, and sought her cunt with my hands. She opened her legs wider in a most condescending manner, and I began feeling it. I was soon fit, which she very well knew, for immediately with a broad grin on her face she pulled me on to her and put my prick in her cunt herself, lodging it with a clever jerk of her bum, a squeeze, and a wriggle.

I fucked quietly, but it was now her turn; she heaved and wriggled so that once she threw my prick out of her, but soon had it in again. "Shove, shove," said she suddenly, and I shoved with all my might, she clipped my arse so tightly that she must have left the marks of her fingers on it, then, with a close wriggle and a deep sigh, she lay still, her face as red as fire, and left me to finish by my own exertions.

I felt the same squeeze of the cunt as I withdrew, one of those delicious contractions which women of strong muscular power in their privates can give; not all can do it. Those who cannot never can understand it. Those who can will make a finger sensible of its clip, if put up their cunts.

She got up and tucked her chemise between her legs to dry her split, she did not wash it. "I am always alone," said she, "between eight and twelve just now," and as any woman just then answered my wants, I made opportunities, and I had her again two or three times, till a rare bit of luck occurred to me.

We were in the bed-room one hot day; to make it cooler I took off trowsers and drawers, laid them on a chair, carefully rolled my shirt up round my waist, so as to prevent spunk falling upon it, and thus naked from my boots to waist, laid myself on the top of my rollicking, belly-heaving, rump-wriggling country lass.

I always gave her five shillings before I began; she had taken a letch for me, or else, being hot cunted and not getting it done to her often, dearly liked my poking her; and, seeming to want it that day unusually, began her heaving and wriggling energetically. We were well on towards our spend, when with a loud cry of "Oh! my God!" she pushed me off and wriggled to the bed-side. I got off and saw a sturdy country girl of about fifteen or sixteen years standing in the bed-room door, looking at us with a broad grin, mixed with astonishment, upon her face.

For an instant nobody spoke. Then the girl said with a malicious grin, "Pretty goings on Sarah, if fearther knowed un — " "How dare you stand looking at me?" said Sarah. "It's my room as well as yourn," said Martha, for that was her name; and nothing further was said then. But Martha's eyes fixed on me as I sat naked up to my waist with my prick wet, rigid, red, throbbing, and all but involuntarily jerking out its sperm. I was in that state of lust, that I could have fucked anything in the shape of a cunt, and scarcely knew, in the confusion of the moment, where I was, and what it was all about. Sarah saw my state, and began pulling down my shirt. "Go out of the room," said she to her sister. "Damn it I will finish, I will fuck you," said I making a snatch at her cunt again. "Oh! for God's sake, don't, sir," said she. With a grin out went young sister Martha into the kitchen, and then Sarah began to blubber, "If she tells fearther, he will turn me out into the streets."

"Don't be a fool," said I, "why should she tell?" "Because we are bad friends." "Has she not done it?" "No, she is not sixteen." "How do you know she has not?" "Why we sleep together, and I know." "Who sleeps in the other bed?" "Fearther." "In the same room?" "Yes." "Don't you know anything against her?" "No, last haymaking I seed a young man trying to put his hands up her clothes, that's all; she has only been a woman a few months." If she tells of her, she will tell of me, I thought. It might come to my aunt's ears, Fred would know, and I should get into a scrape.

"It is a pity she has not done it," said I, "for then she would not tell." "I wish she had," she replied. One thing suggested another. "She knows all about what we were doing?" Sarah nodded. "Get her to promise not to tell, and get her to let me do it to her, and I will give you two pounds," said I, taking the money out of my purse.

It was more money than she had ever had in her life at one time, her eyes glistened; she was silent a minute as if reflecting, then said, "She has always been unkind to me, and she shan't get me turned out if I can help it." Then, after further talk, some hesitation, and asking me if I was sure I would give her the money, she said, "I'll try, let's have a jolly good drink, then I'll leave you together," and we went into the kitchen. I saw her dodge.

Martha was leaning, looking out of the window, her bum sticking out, her short petticoats showing a sturdy pair of legs; she turned round to us, it was about eleven o'clock in the day, the old man was at work far off and had taken his dinner with him that day, Sarah had told me.

"You won't tell fearther," said Sarah in a smooth tone. No reply but a grin. "If you do, I will tell him I saw young Smith's hand up your clothes." "It's a lie." "Yes, he did, and you know you have seen all he has got to show." "You are a liar," said Martha. Sarah turned to me and said, "Yes, she did, we both saw him leaking, and a dozen more chaps." "She saw their cocks?" said I. "Yes." "You took me to see them, you bitch," said Martha, bursting out in a rage. "You did not want much taking; what did you say, and what did you do in bed that night, when we talked about it?" "You are a wicked wretch, to talk like that before a strange young man," said Martha and bounced out of the cottage.

In a short time she came in again; the eldest told me scandals she knew about her sister and made her so wild that they nearly fought. I stopped them, they made it up, and I sent off the eldest to fetch shrub, gin and peppermint; it was a good mile to the tavern in the village.

When she had gone, I told Martha I hoped she would do no mischief. She was nothing loath to let me kiss her, so there was soon acquaintance between us. She had seen me half naked, how long she had been watching I knew not, but it was certain she had seen me shoving as hard as I could between the naked thighs of her sister, and that was well calculated to make her randy and ready for the advances of a man. "Here is five shillings, don't say anything, my dear." "I won't say nothing," said she, taking the money. Then I kissed her again, and we talked on.

"How did you like him feeling you?" I asked, "was he stiff?" No reply. "Was it not nice when he got his hand on your thigh?" Still no reply. "You thought it nice when in bed, Sarah says." "Sarah tells a wicked story," she burst out. "What does she tell?" "I don't know." "I will tell you my dear; you talked about Smith's doodle and the other men's you saw pissing." "You are the gentleman from London stopping at the Hall," she replied, "so you had better go back and leave us poor girls alone," and she looked out of the window again.

"I am at the Hall," said I, putting my hand round her waist, "and like pretty girls," and I kissed her until she seemed mollified and said, "What can you want in troubling poor girls like us?" "You are as handsome as a duchess, and I want you to do the same as they do." "What is that?" said she innocently. "Fuck," said I boldly. She turned away looking very confused. "You saw me on your sister, between her thighs, that was fucking; and you saw this," at the same time pulling out my prick, "and now I am going to feel your cunt."

I put my hand up her clothes and tried to feel, but she turned round, and after a struggle half squatted on the floor to prevent me. The position was favorable, I pushed her sharply half on to her back on the floor, got my fingers on to her slit, and in a moment we were struggling on the floor, she screaming loudly as we rolled about.

She was nimble, got up, and escaped me, but by the time her sister came back I had felt her bum, pulled her clothes up, and talked enough baudiness; she had hollowed, cried, laughed, abused, and forgiven me, for I had promised her a new bonnet, and had given her more silver.

Sarah brought back the liquors; there was but one tumbler and a mug, we did with those; the weather was hot, the liquor nice, the girls drank freely. In a short time they were both frisky, it got slightly into my head; then the girls began quarrelling again and let out all about each other, the elder's object being to upset the younger one's virtue and make her lewed. I began to get awfully randy, and told Sarah I had felt her sister's cunt whilst she had been out. She laughed and said, "All right, she will have it well felt some day, she's a fool if she don't." We joked about my disappointment in the morning, I asked Sarah to give me my pleasure then. "Aye," said she, "and it is pleasure; when Martha has once tasted it, she will like it again." Martha, very much fuddled, laughed aloud, saying, "How you two do go on." Then I put my hands up Sarah's clothes. "Lord how stiff my prick is, look," and I pulled it out, Martha saying, "I won't stand this," rushed from the room. I thought she had gone, and wanted to have Sarah; but she thought of the two pounds, and, shutting Martha's mouth, "Try her," said she, "she must have it some day, she'll come in soon." When the girl did, we went on drinking. What with mixing gin, peppermint, and rum shrub, both got groggy, and Martha the worst. Then out went Sarah saying she must go to the village to buy something, and she winked at me.

She had whilst the girl was outside told me to bolt the front door, and if by any chance her father came home, which was not likely, to get out of the bedroom window, and through a hedge, which would put me out of sight in a minute. Directly she was gone I bolted the door and commenced the assault. Martha was so fuddled, that she could not much resist my feeling her bum and thighs, yet I could not get her to go and lie down; she finished the liquor, staggered, and then I felt her clitoris.

I was not too steady, but sober enough to try craft where force failed. I wanted to piss, and did, holding the pot so that she could see my cock at the door, but she would not come into the bed-room. Then I dropped a sovereign, and pretending I could not find it, asked her to help me; she staggered into the bed-room laughing a drunken laugh. The bed was near, I embraced her, said I would give her two sovereigns if she would get on the bed with me. "Two shiners?" said she. "There they are," said I laying them down. "No — no," but she kept looking at them. I put them into her hand, she clutched them saying, "No — no," and biting one of her fingers, whilst I began again titillating her clitoris, she letting me. From that moment I knew what money would do with a woman. Then I lifted her up on to the bed and lay down besides her. All her resistance was over, she was drunk.

I pulled up her clothes; she lay with eyes shut, breathing heavily, holding the gold in her hand. I pulled open her legs, with scarcely resistance, and saw a mere trifle of a hair on the cunt; the novelty so pleased me that I kissed it; then for the first time in my life I licked a cunt, the spittle from my mouth ran on to it, I pulled open the lips, it looked different from the cunts I had seen, the hole was smaller. "Surely," thought I, "she is a virgin." She seemed fast asleep, and let me do all I wanted.

In after life, I should have revelled in the enjoyment of anticipation before I had destroyed the hymen; but youth, want, liquor, drove me on, and I don't remember thinking much about the virginity, only that the cunt looked different from the three others I had known. The next instant I laid my belly on hers. "Oh! you are heavy, you smother me," said she rousing herself, "you're going to hurt me, — don't, sir, it hurts," all in a groggy tone and in one breath. I inserted a finger between the lips of her quim and tried gently to put it up, but felt an impediment. She had never been opened by man. I then put my prick carefully in the nick, and gave the gentlest possible movement (as far as I can recollect) to it.

Her cunt was wet with spittle, I well wetted my prick, grasped her round her bum, whilst I finally settled the knob of my tool against it, then, putting my other hand round her bum, grasped her as if in a vise, nestled my belly to hers, and trembling with lust, gave a lunge, — another, — and another. I was entering. In another minute it would be all over with me, my sperm was moving. She gave a sharp "oh!" A few more merciless shoves, a loud cry from her, my prick was up her, and her cunt was for the first time wetted with a man's sperm; with short, quiet thrusts I fell into the dreamy pleasure, laying on the top of her.

Soon I rolled over to her side; to my astonishment she lay quite still with mouth open, snoring and holding the two sovereigns in her hand. I gently moved to look at her; her legs were wide open, her gown and chemise (all the clothing she had on) up to her navel, her cunt showed a red streak, my spunk was slowly oozing out, streaked with blood, a little was on her chemise; but I looked in vain for that sanguinary effusion which I saw on Charlotte's chemise and on my shirt when I first had her; and, from later experience, think that young girls do not bleed as much as full grown women, when they lose their virginity.

Her cunt, as I found from ample inspection afterwards, was lipped like her sister's; the hair, about half an inch long, scarcely covered the mons, and only slightly came down the outer lips, her thighs were plump and round, her calves big for her age; she was clean in her flesh, but alas! hick blue stockings with holes and darns, bit boots with holes at the sides, a dirty ragged chemise, dark garters below the knees, made an ugly spectacle compared with the clean whiteness of Charlotte's and Mary's linen.

But the sight took effect, my prick had her blood on it, quietly I slid my finger up her cunt, it made her restless, she moved her legs together, shutting my hand in them; she turned on her side, and showed a plump white bum, over one side of which a long streak of bloody sperm had run. I pulled her on to her back and got on to her, then she awakened struggling and called out loudly, but I was heavy on her, my prick at her cunt's mouth, and I pushed it up until it could no further, whilst she kept calling out, I was hurting her.

"Be quiet, I can't hurt you, my prick is right up you," said I, beginning the exercise. She made no reply, her cunt seemed deliciously small, whenever I pushed deep, she winced as if in pain, I tried to thrust my tongue into her mouth, but she resisted it. Suddenly she said, "Oh! go away, Sarah will be home and find us." I had my second emission, and went to sleep with my prick up her, — I was groggy. She slept also.

I awakened, got up tired with heat, excitement, drink and fucking. She got up, and sat on the side of the bed, half sobered but stupid, dropped a sovereign, and did not attempt to pick it up. I did, and put it back into her hands; she took it without saying a word. When buttoned up, I asked her what she was going to do, but all the reply I could get was, "You go now." I went into the kitchen, banged the door, but held the latch, the door remained ajar, and I peeped through.

She sat perfectly still so long, that I thought she was never going to move; then sat down on the chair and laid her head against the bed, looking at the sovereigns at intervals; then put them down, put her hand up her petticoats carefully feeling her cunt, looked at her fingers, burst into tears, sat crying for a minute or two, then put a basin with water on to the floor, and, unsteady, partially up-set it, but managed to wash, and got back on to the chair, leaving the basin where it was. Then she pulled up the front of her che-mise and looked at it, again put her fingers to her cunt, looked at them, again began crying, and leaned her head against the bed, all in a drowsy, tipsy manner. Whilst so engaged, her sister knocked and I let her in; she looked at me in a funny way; I nodded; she went into the bed-room and closed the door, but I heard most of what was said.

"What are you sitting there for?" No reply. "What's that basin there for?" No reply. "You have been washing your grummit?" No reply. "What have you been washing it for?" "I was hot." "Why, you have been on the bed!" "No, I ain't." "You have, with he." "No, I ain't." "I know he have, and been atop a you, just as he were atop on me this morning." "No, he ain't." Then was a long crying fit. Sarah said, "What's the good of crying, you fool, no one ain't going to tell, I shan't, and the old man won't know." Then their voices dropped, they stood together, but I guessed she was asking what I had given her.

Then I went in. "You have done it to my sister," said Sarah. "No," said I. "Yes, you have," and to Martha crying, "Never mind, it's better to be done by a gent than by one of them mill-hands, I can't abear 'em; leave off, don't be a fool." I went out of the room,

Sarah followed me, and I gave her the two sovereigns. "You know," she said, "some one would ha done it to her; one of them mill-hands, or Smith would, he's allus after her, and I knows he got his hands upon her."

Fred went up to London next day, and I was at the cottage soon after; the girls were there, the elder grinned, the younger looked queer, and would not go to the bed-room. "Don't be a fool," said the elder, and soon we were alone together there. Half force, half entreaty got her on to the bed, I pulled up her clothes, forced open her legs, and lay for a minute with my belly to hers in all the pleasure of anticipation, then rose on my knees for a close look. My yesterday's letch seized me, I put my mouth to her cunt and licked it, than put my prick up the tight little slit and finished my enjoyment.

Afterwards when I had her she was neat and clean underneath, although with her every day's clothes on. She was frightened to put on her Sunday clothes. She was a nice plump round girl, with a large bum for her size, with pretty young breasts and a fat-lipped little slit; the lining of it, instead of being a full red like Charlotte's, Mary's, and Sarah's cunts, was of a delicate pink. I suppose it was that which attracted me. Certain it is that I had never licked a cunt before, never had heard of such a thing, though "lick my arse" was a frequent and insulting invitation for boys to each other.

I saw her nearly every day for a week, and her modesty was soon broken. Sleeping in the same room with her father, accustomed to be in the fields or at a mill, such girls soon lose it; but she seemed indifferent to my embraces, and all the enjoyment was on my side. "I've not much pleasure in that," said she, "But more when you put your tongue there." I could not believe that was so in a young and healthy lass, but being always in a hurry to get my poking done lest her father came home, used to lick, put up her, spend quickly, and leave; but she soon got to rights. I licked so hard and long the next time I had her, at the side of the bed, that all at once I felt her cunt moving, her thighs closed, then relaxed, and she did not answer me. I looked up, she was laying with eyes closed and said, that what I had done was nicer than anything. I had gamahuched her till she spent.

After that she spent like other women, when I had her. I tell this exactly as I recollect it, and can't attempt to explain. She worked at a paper mill; slack work was the reason of her being at home, now she was going back to work; I feared a mill hand would get her and offered to pay her what she earned; but if she did not go to the mill her father would make her work in the fields, and she dare not let him see she had money.

Indeed the two sisters did not dare to buy the finery they wanted, because they could not say how they got the money. So back to the mill she went, it being arranged that she should stay away now and then, for me to have her. "Oh! won't she," said Sarah, "she takes to ruddling natoral, I can tell you." Sarah said she told her everything I had done to her, including the licking, and I felt quite ashamed of Sarah knowing that I was so green, as I shall tell presently.

Fred returned, and I had difficulty in getting her often. My cousins walked out in the cool of the evening, I with them; often we passed the cottage, and I made signs if I saw the girls. I sometimes then had her upright in a small shed or by a hay-stack in the dark, where the hay pricked my knuckles.

Fred was soon to join his regiment, was always borrowing money of me "for a shove," and never repaid me; but he was a liberal, good-hearted fellow; and when in after life I was without money and he kept a woman, he said, "You get a shove out of ° ° °," meaning his woman, "she likes you, and I shan't mind, but don't tell me." I actually did fuck her, nor did he ever ask me, — but that tale will be told hereafter. Nothing till his death pleased him more than referring to our having looked at the backside of his mother and at his sisters' quims, he would roar with laughter at it. He was an extraordinary man.

One day we rode to the market-town, and, putting up our horses, strolled about. Fred said, "Let's both go and have a shove." "Where are the girls?" said I. "Oh! I know, lend me some money." "I only have ten shillings." "That is more than we shall want." We went down a lane past the Town-Hall, by white-washed little cottages, at which girls were sitting or standing at the doors making a sort of lace. "Do you see a girl you like?" said he. "Why, they are lacemakers." "Yes, but some of them fuck for all that; there is the one I had with the last half-a-crown you lent me." Two girls were standing, together; they nodded. "Let's try them," said Fred. We went into the cottage; it was a new experience to me. He took one girl, leaving me the other; I felt so nervous; she laughed as Fred (who had never in his life a spark of modesty) put his hands up her companion's clothes. That girl asked what he was going to give her, and it was settled at half-a-crown each. Fred then went into the back-room with his woman.

I never had had a gay woman. A fear of disease came over me. She made no advances, and at length, feeling my quietness was ridiculous, I got my hands up her clothes, pulling them up and looking at her legs. "Lord! I am quite clean, sir," said she in a huff, lifting her clothes well up. That gave me courage, I got her on to an old couch and looked at her cunt, but my prick refused to stand; her being gay upset me. She laid hold of my prick, but it was of no use. "What 'is the matter with you?" said she, "don't you like me?" "Yes, I do." "Have you ever had a girl?" I said I had. Fred who had finished, bawled out, "Can't we come in?" This upset me still more, and I gave it up. In Fred and his girl came, and he said, "There is water in the other room." I went in and feigned to wash myself, and hearing them all laughing, felt ashamed to come out, thinking they were laughing about me; though such was not the case, it was because Fred was beginning to pull about my woman.

I had more money than I had told Fred, and when he said he was thirsty, offered to send for drink, thinking my liberality would make amends for my impotence. Gin and ale was got; then I began to feel as if I could do it. "She's got a coal-black cunt," said Fred, and I seemed to fancy his woman; then he said to mine, "What colour is yours?" and began to lift her clothes; "let's change and have them together," and we went at once into the back room, whither the two girls had gone. One was piddling, Fred pulled her up from the pot, shoved her against the side of the bed, bawling out, "You get the other," and pulled out his prick stiff and ready. An electric thrill seemed to go through me at this sight, I pulled the other into the same position by the side of Fred's; then the girls objected, but Fred hoisted up his girl and plunged his prick into her. Mine got on to the bed, leaving me to pull up her clothes. The same fear came over me, and I hesitated; Fred looked and laughed, I pulled up her clothes, saw her cunt; fear vanished, the next moment I was into her, and Fred and I, side by side, were fucking.

All four were fucking away like a mill, then we paused and looked at our pricks, as they alternately were hidden and came into sight from the cunts. Fred put out his hand to my prick, I felt his, but I was coming; my girl said, "Don't hurry." It was too late, I spent, laid my head upon her bosom, and opening my eyes, saw Fred in the short shoves. The next instant he lay his head down.

I believe now that really all four felt ashamed, for directly after we were all so quiet, one of the girls remarked, "Blest if I ever heard of such a thing afore, you Lunnon chaps are a bad lot." A long time afterwards, I again had the girl for two and sixpence; Fred was then in Canada; she recollected me well, and asked me whether gals and chaps usually did such things together in London.

Fred and I used to examine our pricks for a few days after, to see if there were any pimples on them. Fred soon forgot his fear and shame and offered to bet me the fee of the gals that he would finish first, if we went and repeated the affair, but we did not.

Martha became very curious about me and my doings with Sarah. New to fucking as she was, she got jealous at the idea of anyone sharing my cock with her. She was curious too to know about her sister's pleasures; the elder had, I think, got all she wanted to know from the younger, and had made but little return for it in information.

Then my amatory knowledge was increased by an event unlooked for, unthought of, unpremeditated; I am quite sure I had neither heard nor read of such a thing before, and should, at that period of my life, have scouted the idea as beastly and abominable, though I had done it. How I came to lick Martha's cunt even then astonished me, I thought that it was the small size, the slight hair, and youthfulness of the article; but I used to lick it very daintily, wiping my mouth, spitting frequently, and never venturing beyond the clitoris. It occurred to me one day instead of kneeling, to lay down and lick; so I laid on the bed, my head between her thighs, my cock not far from her mouth, and indulging her in the luxury; for it was much the idea of pleasing her which made me do it. She played with my cock and wriggled as my tongue played over her clitoris, then grasped my prick hard, which gave me a premonitory throb of pleasure. "Do to me what I am doing to you," said I, "put it in your mouth," scarcely knowing what I said and without any ulterior intention. She with her pleasure getting intense, impelled by curiosity, or by the fascination of the cock, or by impulse, the result of my tongue on her cunt, took it in her mouth instantly. How far my prick went in, whether she sucked, licked, or simply let it enter, I know not, and I expect she did not either; but as she spent I felt a sensation resembling the soft friction of a cunt, and instantly shot my sperm into her mouth and over her face. Up she got, calling me a beast. I was surprised and ashamed of this unlooked for termination, and said so to her.

I had as said arranged signs, as I passed the cottage, about our meetings, yet had difficulty now in getting at her without being found out, and never should, excepting for the elder sister, to whom I gave every now and then money. She took care of the house, rarely went out, but worked at a coarse sort of lace and earned money that way. She used to sit outside the cottage door if fine, working, and curtseying when we, who were called the Hall folks, passed. My aunt said one day, "What a strapping wench that is, don't you think so, Walt? you always look at her as you pass." I might have replied, "Yes, she is, and her arse is remarkably like yours," but I did not and was after that more on my guard. Fred had not had the girl for a long time, that freed me a little. Then Martha shammed ill two days to stay from the mill and let me have her, and I spent a good many hours with her. As I turned my head quickly one day, I thought I saw the bed-room door close, and it occurred to me, that the elder had been watching; she looked lecherously at me as I came out.

I went one day soon after and found Sarah alone. She made some excuse about her sister being obliged to go to work. I was going away angry, when she asked me to look at her new boots and stockings. Amused at her vanity I looked, and she put them on. "Them fits fine," said she, showing her legs amply. I was not excited about it, and was going. "Ain't you never going to ha me agin?" said she. "I've no money." "We are old friends, never mind money, if I hadn't got you Martha we moight ha been good friends still, — ar wish a had'nt." "You did it to save us," said I. "Ah, but yer shouldn't leave old friends, and I ha watched and made yer both comfortable." Well, thought I, this is an invitation to fucking, — she had a wonderful clip in her cunt, and I began to rise. "You have lots of friends," said I. "I take my oath, that no friend has seen me since the day you got my sister; ain't I been allus on watch for yer? did yer ever pass without seeing me?"

A woman who wants fucking is not easy to resist, even if she

is ugly and middle-aged. There she sat, the picture of health, her
petticoats nearly up to her knees; I had never before seen them excepting in coarse blue woollen stockings. I rolled her clothes up,
saw the big thighs, the next instant had my fingers in the slit; up
knocked my doodle. She shut the shutter, locked the door, and with
a pleased look got on to the bed. Her cunt struck me as quite a
novelty, and I got ready for insertion.

"You like her better than me," said she. It was a poser, but a
man always likes the woman he is going to poke better than any
other, and so I denied it. "Why don't you do to me what you do to
she then?" "What is that?" "You knows." "No." "Yes you do." "I
feel it like this." "More than that." "What?" "You know." "I don't,
tell me." There was a pause. It came into my head that she knew I
had licked Martha's quim, and it had such an effect on me, that
down went my doodle, and I was almost ashamed to look at her;
for, as said, until I licked Martha I had never done such an act, and
did it with a sort of belief that I was a great beast, and should have
said so of any man who did anything of the sort. Indeed after
spending in her mouth, I had felt so very much disgusted with myself that I left off the licking altogether and had made the girl
promise she would never tell her sister, nor refer to the matter
again. So I was silent, standing with one hand on her belly just
above her split, and in an uncomfortable state of mind.

She broke the silence. "Do it as you do it to she." "I don't know
what you mean," I again stammered. "Yes yer do now." "What has
Martha told you?" "Nothing, but I knows." And finding I was about
to get on the bed, "Naw, naw, kiss it." So I put my mouth down on
to the hair and gave a loud kiss. "Naw," said she, "do it as you do it
to she, I am a finer woman than she by long chalks; what is't yer
sees to take to her so? you knows you tickles hers with yer tongue."
The murder was out. I wanted to mount her, she baulked me, and
kept repeating in a jocular, playful manner her request. So I got her
to the side of the bed, her large thighs wide open, and legs hanging
down in a favorable position, intending to please her; she gave her
cunt a dry rub with her chemise.

I began with dislike, but there was something in the novelty
which warmed me. What a difference between her and her sister.
I could lick the younger one's all but hairless orifice with comfort,

and she always laid quiet; but I had to pull open this one's sausage lips and hold back the dark thick fringe, which got into my eyes and tickled my nose. No sooner had my tongue touched her clitoris, than the lips closed round my mouth, and, as my saliva worked up on to the cunt-hair by her movement, it wetted my nose and face, she heaved and bounced her arse so much. Then her thighs closed round my head tightly enough to squeeze it off, she buried her hands in the hair of my head, and up went cunt again, bringing my nose into the hole, then with a jerk she got her cunt away from me. I was not at all sorry to desist.

"Oh! do it natural, — do it natural," said she, and her thighs opened and hung down, showing a slobbered cunt. I went into her, just as she lay at the side of the bed, and in a minute her cunt was wetter than ever.

I have no doubt that the wench spent almost directly I licked, but I did not know it. When I asked her if she liked it, she said, "The old fashioned way be the best, but I have done the same as she." I questioned her, but never knew whether her sister had told her or not, or whether she had peeped and seen us together at it.

I made her promise she would never tell her sister what I had done. She hoped I would see her again, but having promised Martha that I would not have Sarah again, told her so. She said she was tired of watching for us. The sisters were often quarrelling, and I believe out of jealousy about me, yet I fucked her again.

I may mention the risks I ran, that I was once with Martha on the bed when I heard my cousin's voice asking Sarah, who was at the door, if she had seen me pass.

I could not get the younger readily enough, had been long from home, and was about returning. I had spent all my money, and told Sarah one day after I had poked her that I was going away. Her sister was then at the mill. Said she, "What will Martha do?" I supposed she would get another sweetheart. She shook her head, "Martha be poisoned." "What?" "Don't be afraid," said she, "she be in the family way, we call it poisoned in these parts, when a girl ben't married." It was true. The girl had only menstruated once or twice before I first had her, and now her courses had stopped. There was no attempt at making a market of me, all needed was to get her right again. The elder took Martha to a fortune-teller, and she got better of her difficulty. I borrowed money of my aunt and, giving Martha all I could, went back to London. She left the neighbourhood.

I saw Martha two years afterwards, when visiting again my aunt; she was in household service, and was out for the day. I waylaid her, hoping to have her again; we kissed and fondled, and with difficulty I felt her quim but could not accomplish my wishes; she was going to be married, and soon after I heard that she was.

Sarah also was going to be married to a farm labourer, and when I joked her about his finding her out, she laughed and said, "Lord, he war my first sweetheart," from which I inferred that cousin Fred was mistaken about taking her virginity.

My first cunt-licking, and cock-sucking took place with Martha; I had never before played such amatory pranks, and all came about by instinct. For a long time I was ashamed of myself and never breathed a word on such subjects to anyone; I don't think I should have done so even to Fred, but he was then away. Gradually I was learning by instinct the whole art of love. What made me offer money to get Martha I can't say, I don't think that I had ever heard of tempting women's virtue by money, but I never forgot the lesson, and much improved on it as time went on.

I now had had four women. The difficulties in the way of getting at them were very useful in preventing excesses, and kept me in health. It seems surprising to me now how little I seemed to have thought of baudy attitudes, and lascivious varieties; for belly-to-belly poking on the bed was nearly all I did. I had still the modest, demure demeanour which deceived my mother (coupled with her ignorance of life generally) and relations, and, though very proud of my achievements, kept them much to myself, never disclosing the names of my women, and only telling one or two intimate friends of what I had done; who reciprocated by telling me their achievements. Fucking had eased my prepuce. I made a practice of pulling it backward and forward several times a day; in fact, whenever I piddled. My prick had grown bigger in the two years, which pleased me much, but about the size of it I had a curious doubt, which will be told of further on.

I was, though demure, quite a man in manner and look, and with women behaved in a way which one or two of my relatives remarked. I used to think to myself when talking to them, "Ah! I know what sort of opening you have at the bottom of your belly." The cousins, whose cunts I had had a partial glimpse of, I used to like to dance with, wondering how much the hair had grown on them. I used also to think about my sister's cunt that I had seen when in the cradle, but just then she died. My experiences indeed much increased the charm of female society to me.

Chance had given me two virgins out of four women; that was a luxury unthought of, uncared for, and in no way appreciated; the virgins were no more liked by me than the others.

Cousin Fred will appear at less frequent intervals; he was away sometimes for months, then for years, but he is named whenever he played an important part in my adventures, — he was participator in others which will never be written about here.

CHAPTER VIII

Fanny Hill. — Masturbation. — Friend Henry. — Under street-gratings at the gunmaker's. — A frigging match. — Sights from below. — In a back street. — A prick in petticoats. — Evacuations. — Ladies scared.

I went back to London and resumed my preparations. Penniless, I tried to get money from my mother, but could not. I tried to feel our ugly housemaid, who threatened to tell. Just then a friend lent me *Fanny Hill,* how well I recollect that day, it was a sunshiny afternoon, I devoured the book and its luscious pictures, and although I never contemplated masturbation, lost all command of myself, frigged, and spent over a picture as it lay before me. I did not know how to clean the book and the table-cover.

Fascinated although annoyed with myself, I repeated the act till not a drop of sperm would come; and the skin of my prick was sore. The next day I had a splitting headache, but read at intervals, and again frigged; and did this for a week, till my eyes were all but dropping into my head. In a fever and worn out; the doctor said I was growing too fast and ordered strong nourishment; but I used to take the infernal book with me to bed, and lay reading it, twiddling my prick, and fearing to consummate, knowing the state I was in. It was indeed almost impossible to do it, and when emission came it was accompanied by a fearful aching in my testicles.

My friend had his book back; my erotic excitement ceased, I grew stronger, felt ashamed of myself, and soon found a new excitement.

I had a friend who, like me, was intended for the Army, his father was a gun manufacturer. The eldest son died, and the old man saying that five thousand a year should not be lost to the family, made

124

his other son — my friend — go into the business. He resisted, but had no alternative but to consent. Their dwelling-house was just by ours, but the old man now insisted on his son residing largely at the manufactory, where he invited me to stay at times with him; which I did.

Several houses adjoining belonged to the old man, at the East-End of London, where the manufactory was. Some faced an important thoroughfare, the rest faced two other streets, and at the back, a place without a thoroughfare, on one side of which was the manufactory and workmen's entrance; on the other side, stables. The whole property formed a large block.

The house faced the better street; the family had for forty years lived in it before they became rich, and it was replete with comfort. The old man had since lived there principally, for his love was in his business, and he had made all arrangements for his convenience. He had a private staircase leading from a sitting-room into the manufactory, and could go into the warehouse, or the back street, or out of the front door of the house unnoticed. The people employed never knew when to expect him. He was a regular Tartar, but for all that a kind-hearted man.

There now lived in the house an old servant with her sister, who had been many years in the family. One was married to a foreman, in whom his master had much confidence; these three were in fact in charge of the premises, although nominally the keys were given up to my friend, whom we will call Henry. The old man wished his son to be happy, allowed friends to visit him, there was good wine, put out by the old man in small quantities from time to time, good food, good attendance, and all to make things comfortable; but the old man resolutely forbade his son to be out later than eleven o'clock, and kept him, as my mother kept me, almost without money. I expect that the old servants were told to keep an eye on the doings of Henry.

The basement was used as store-room for muskets, put into wooden boxes which stood in long rows upon each other like coffins. It was a large place and originally only went under the factory, but the old gentleman gradually, as he acquired the adjacent houses, let them, but retained most of the basements, so that his stores ran not only under the premises he occupied, but largely under half a dozen other houses of which he only let the shops and upper portions. On four sides this large basement had glimpses of light let into it, by gratings in the footways of the streets.

At one end and on the principal street was a row of windows, beneath what was then a first-class linen draper's shop — first-class I mean for the East-End — a large place for those days, and always full. Women used to stand by dozens at a time, looking into the shop windows, which were of large plate-glass — a great novelty in those days — people waiting for omnibusses used also to stand up against the shop.

Henry and I were old school friends; I had seen and felt his cock, he mine; I had not been with him an hour before he said, "When the workmen go to dinner, I will show you more legs than you ever saw in your life." "Girls?" said I. "Yes, I saw up above the garters of a couple of dozen yesterday in an hour." "Could you see their cunts?" "I did not quite, but nearly of one," said he. I thought he was bragging, and was glad when twelve o'clock came.

At that hour, down we went, through the basement stored with muskets; it seemed dark as we entered, but soon we saw streams of light coming through the windows at the end; they had not been cleaned for years. We rubbed the glass and looked up. Above us was a flock of women's legs of all sizes and shapes flashing before us, thick and thin, in wonderful variety. We could see them by looking up, it being bright above; but, dark and dusty below, they could not, by looking down, see us through the half cleaned windows, or notice round clean spots on the glass, through which two pairs of young eyes almost devoured the limbs of those who stood over them.

As our only way lay through the work-shop and we did not wish it known that we were there (there was no business done there, unless arms were being stored or taken out), we went back before the workmen returned from their meals; but for several days did we go into the place, gloating over such of the women's charms as we could discern; legs we saw by the hundreds, garters and parts of the thighs we saw by scores: quite enough to make young blood randy to madness, but the shadowy mass between the thighs we could not get a glimpse of.

"There are vaults," said I, "if there, we could see right up, and be at the back of the women." We tried unused keys to find one to open the door, and at length, to our intense delight, it unclosed.

We stepped across the little open space under the gratings into the empty vaults, and, there arranging to take our turns of looking up at the most likely spots, we put out our heads and took our fill at gazing. We were right under the women, who, as they looked into the shop windows, jutting out their bums in stooping, tilted their petticoats exactly over our heads. If there was no carriage passing, we could at times hear what they said, but that was rarely the case.

In those days even ladies wore no drawers. Their dresses rarely came below their ankles, they wore bustles, and, standing over a grating, anyone below them, saw much more, and more easily, than they can in these days of draggling dresses and cunt-swabbing breeches, which the commonest girl wears round her rump. For all that, so close to the thighs do chemise and petticoats cling, that it was difficult to see the hairy slits, which it was our great desire to look at. Garters and thighs well above the knees we saw by scores. Every now and then, either by reason of scanty clothing or short dresses, or by a woman's stooping and opening her legs to look more easily low down at the window, we had a glimpse of the cunt; and great was our randiness and delight when we did. On the whole we were well rewarded. Many as the legs and thighs are that I have since seen, I doubt whether I have seen so many pairs of legs half-way up the thighs, and all but to the split, as I saw in the times we stood under that big linen-draper's shop window. Old and young, thin and fat, dirty and clean, ragged and neat; there was every possible variety and number of legs and their coverings.

There were two states of the weather which favoured us: if muddy, women lifted their clothes up high. Having no modern squeamishness, all they cared about was to prevent them getting muddy; and then, with the common classes, we got many a glimpse of the split. But a brilliant day was the best. Then the reflected light being strong, we could see higher up if the lady was in a favourable position. We could see if they had clouts round their cunts, and had some strange sights of which I will only tell one or two.

One day, quite at the end of the gratings, two women, neat, clean, plump, and of the poorer classes (for we could soon tell the poorer classes from their legs and underclothing), stood close together. It was my five minutes. Henry was at my back. They had been standing talking, close together, not seeming to be looking at the shop, in fact they were at the spot where the shop window finished. One put her leg up against a ledge, keeping the other on the grating; it was a bright day, and I saw the dark hair of her cunt as plainly as if she were standing to show it to me. The next minute she gathered up her clothes a little high, and squatted down on her heels as if to piddle, her bum came down within four or five inches of the grating, and I saw through the bars, her cunt open just as a woman does when she pisses. I thought she was going to do so, when a plaintive cry explained it all; she had a baby, and all the movements were to enable her to do something to it conveniently. At the same time her companion dropped on one knee, pulling her clothes a little up, and arranging them so as to prevent soiling them, she put the other leg out in front, and sat back on the heel of the kneeling leg. Then was another split, younger and lighter-haired, partly visible from below, but not so plainly as the dark-haired one; and they did something in that position for five minutes to the squalling child.

I lost all prudence, whispered to Henry; and together we stood looking, till they moved away. "My prick will burst," said I. "So will mine," said he. The next instant both our pricks were out, and, looking up at the legs, stood we two young men, frigging till two jets of spunk spurted across the area. It would have been a fine sight for the women had they looked down, but women rarely did. They stood over the gratings usually with the greatest unconcern, looking at the shop windows, or only glanced below for an instant, at the dark, uninhabitated-looking area.

This was the beginning of a new state of things. We got reckless; Henry had business to attend to, I none, — I ceased to think about what might be said of our being so much in the store-house; and used to go by myself and stay there two or three hours at a time. Then I gave way to erotic excesses. My prick would stand as I went down the stairs. I used to wait prick in hand, playing with it, looking up and longing for a poke until I saw a pair of thighs plainly, then able to stand it no longer, frigged, hating myself even whilst I did it, and longing to put my spunk in the right place. I used to catch it in one hand, whilst I frigged with the other, then fling the spunk up towards the girls' legs. It was madness; for although the feet of the women were not three feet above my head, yet the smallness of the quantity thrown (after what stuck to my fingers), and the iron bars above, seemed to make it impossible that any of it should reach its intended destination; but I think it did one day. A youngish female was stooping, and showing part of her thighs. I flung up what I had just discharged; suddenly her legs closed, she stepped quickly aside, looked down and went away. I am still under the impression that a drop of my sperm must have hit her naked legs.

We both also grew more lascivious, having frigged before each other, we took to frigging each other. I went to my home; on going back, I found he had taken other young men to see the legs. One night five of us had dinner, we smoked and drank, our talk grew baudier and baudier; we had mostly been schoolfellows, and dare say we had all seen each other's doodles, but I cannot assert that positively. We finished by showing them to each other now, betting on their length and size, and finished up by a frigging sweepstakes for him who spent first.

At a signal, five young men (none I am sure nineteen years old) seated on chairs in the middle of the room began frigging themselves, amidst noise and laughter. The noise soon subsided, the voices grew quiet, then ceased, and were succeeded by convulsive breathing, sighs and long-drawn breaths, the legs of some writhed and stretched out, their backsides wriggled on the chairs, one suddenly stood up. Five hands were frigging as fast as they could, the prick-knobs standing out of a bright vermillion tint looking as if they must burst away from the hands which held them. Suddenly one cried "f — fi — fir — first," as some drops of gruelly fluid flew across the room, and the frigger sank back in the chair. At the same instant almost the other jets spurted, and all five men were directly sitting down, some with eyes closed, others with eyes wide open, all quiet and palpitating, gently frigging, squeezing, and titillating their pricks until pleasure had ceased.

Afterwards we were quiet, then came more grog, more allusion to the legs of women, their cunts and pleasures, more baudiness, more showing of pricks and ballocks, another sweepstakes, another frigging match, and then we separated.

I do not think that, excepting to Henry, that baudy evening ever was referred to by me.

I got up I recollect next day ashamed of myself, and felt worse, when he remarked, "What beasts we made ourselves last night." What changes since then. Two of the five found graves in the

Crimea, the third is dead also; Henry and I alone alive. He with a big family, with sons nearly as old as he was at the time of the frigging matches. I wonder if he ever thinks of them, wonder if he ever has told his wife.

I spent much time now in this leg inspection and frigging myself, till I could scarcely get semen out of me. I hated myself for it, yet went on doing it, when luckily I lost the exciting sights. Some women happened to look down and saw us. A man without a hat came several times and looked down the gratings. Henry's father came to the manufactory, as he often did, went into the stores, asked who had opened the area-door, locked it up, had a new lock put on, and forbade anyone to go into the stores, excepting to get out the guns, and so we lost our game. We never asked a question, nor made a remark on the matter, and came to the conclusion that some one had complained to the linen-draper that persons were looking up the women's legs, and that he had written to Henry's father on the matter.

I went home used up and in a state of indescribable disgust with myself, entirely ceased masturbation, and in a month went again to visit my friend, — he had found out another grating.

The back of the manufactory as said was in a cul-de-sac. There were but the manufactory and stables in it. The workmen entered that side. There were gratings, and coal-vaults beneath the street similar to those beneath the linen-draper's shop. Workmen's wives, bringing their husbands' dinners, used to stand and sometimes sit down over the gratings, but their legs when seen were rarely worth the seeing; it was usually but a sight of dingy petticoats and dirty stockings. We were, however, content to look up at them, for they belonged to women, but soon tired of doing so.

One night (we had never been there at night before), for some reason or the other which I don't recollect, we went down and found two women pissing down the grating, then a man and woman together, and discovered it to be the pissing-place of the gay women, in the main thoroughfare; and where if the nights were dark, couples used to come for a grope, a frig, or even for a fuck at times. The pissing often took place over a grating, we could hear, and feel, but not see.

Then we got a common dark lantern, had the top shade taken off, and a funnel, or short chimney put with a slide, so that when we pushed the slide off, the light shot up through the chimney, and threw a strong light on a circle about one foot across. With this we went down waiting till we heard some one above, then opened the light and saw what was to be seen. Sometimes we waited for hours without seeing anything, but it is astonishing what cunt-loving, baudy young men will go through for the sake of seeing a woman's privates. At other times we saw a good deal. If it were a light night, we saw nothing. No one knew we went down at those hours, the workmen had gone, and the private staircase from the dwelling-house at any time let us into the factory; from the factory we could go anywhere on the premises.

When we heard feet, or a rustle of petticoats over the grating, then taking up the light we sometimes saw a white bum, a split gaping like a dog with its throat cut, and a stream of water splashing from it. We never used to move, but sooner than not see it all and as well as possible, let the stream come over us. Sometimes two women came together; sometimes we could hear to our mortification that they were pissing on the pavement close by, without coming over the grating. We could often hear their conversation. Now and then a woman shit down the grating, we used to watch the turds squeeze out with a fart or two, with great amusement. Once a man did the same, we saw prick, balls, and turd, all hanging down together, we could not help laughing, and off he shuffled as if he had been shot. He must have heard us.

There was one woman whose face we never saw, but who came and pissed over a grating so regularly every evening, and sometimes twice, that we knew her arse perfectly. We lost sight of her and used to wonder if she had found us out, for she finished one night with such a loud fart, that we laughed out, — and she must have heard us.

One night half a dozen ladies came, we knew they were ladies by their manner and conversation, which we could hear perfectly, there being no carriage traffic in the street. "Can anyone see?" said one. "No," said another, "make haste." We heard the usual leafy rustle, and immediately a tremendous stream was heard; then two more sat down close together. I turned on the light at all risks. there were two pretty white little bums above us, with the gaping cunts, they were of quite young girls, without a hair on them; the women then were scared, I suppose, for they moved. One said,

"Make haste, don't be foolish, nobody is coming." A rustle again, off went the slide, up went the light; what a big round bum, what a great, black-haired, open cunt did we see, and a stream of water as if from a fire-engine. "Oh! there is a light down there," said one. Up went the bum, piss still straining down, down went the clothes, and all were off like lightning.

Another night we heard two pairs of feet above us, one was the heavy footstep of a man. "Don't be foolish, he won't know," said a man in a very low tone. "Oh! no, — no, I dare not," said a female voice, and the feet with a little rustling moved to another grating. Henry and I moved on also. "You shall, no one comes here, no one can see us," said the man in a still lower tone. "Oh! I am so frightened," said the female. A little gentle scuffling now took place, and then all seemed quiet but a slight movement of the feet. "Are they there?" whispered Henry from the vault. I nudged him to be quiet, and putting the light as high up as I could, pushed aside the slide a little only.

We were well rewarded. Just above our heads were two pair of feet, one pair wide apart; and hanging only partly down at her back the garments of a female; in front the trousers of a man, with the knees projecting slightly forward between the female's legs, and higher up a bag of balls were hanging down hiding nearly the belly and channel, which the prick was taking. The distended legs between which the balls moved, enabled us however to get a glimpse of the arse-hole end of a cunt. The movement of the ballocks showed the vigor with which the man was fucking, but there must have been some inequality in height; and either he was very tall, or she very short; for his knees and feet moved out at times into different positions. He then ceased for an instant his shoving, as if to arrange himself in a fresh and more convenient posture, and then the lunges recommenced. He must have had his hands on her naked rump, from the way her clothes hung, showing her legs up to her belly, or to where his breeches hid it, or where the clothes fell down which were over his arm.

Once, I imagine, the lady's clothes were in his way, for there was a pause, his prick came quite out, her feet moved, her legs opened wider. He did not need his fingers to find his mark again, his long, stiff, red-tipped article had slidden in the direction of her bum-hole; but no sooner had they readjusted their legs than it moved backwards, and again it was hidden from sight in her cunt. The balls wagged more vigorously than ever, quicker, quicker; the lady's legs seemed to shake, we heard a sort of mixed cry, like a short groan and cry together, and a female voice say, "Oh! don't make such a noise," then a quiver and a shiver of the legs, and all seemed quiet.

When I first had removed the slide, I did so in a small degree, fearing they might look below and see it; but if the sun had shone from below, I believe now they must have been in that state of excitement that they would not have noticed it. To see better I opened the slide more, and gradually held the lantern higher and higher, until the chimney through which the light issued was near to the grating. I was holding it by the bottom at arms length; and naturally, so as to best see myself. Henry could not see as well, although standing close to me, and our heads nearly touching. "Hold it more this way," said he in an excited whisper. I did not. Just then the lady said "Oh! make haste now, I am so frightened." Out slipped the prick, — I saw it. At the very instant, Henry pulled my hand, to get the lantern placed so as to enable him to see better. I was holding it between the very tips of my fingers, just below the feet of the copulating couple. His jerk pulled it over, and down it went with a smash, just as the lady said, "Make haste, I am so frightened." A huge prick as it seemed to me drew out, and flopped down, a hand grasped it, the petticoats were falling round the legs, when the crash of the lantern came. With a loud shriek from the lady, off the couple moved, and I dare say it was many a day before she had her privates moistened up against a wall again, and over a grating.

Henry and I, laughing, picked up the lantern and got back to the house; I went to my bedroom in a state of indescribable randiness. I had for some time broken myself of frigging, and now resisted the desire, tried to read but could not, undressed, and went to bed. My prick would stand. If it went down for a minute and my thoughts were diverted, the very instant my mind recurred to those balls wagging above my head, up it went again. I tried to piss, the piss would not run. At that time, when my prick was stiff, I used to pull the prepuce back, so as to loosen it. I laid down on the bed, prick stiff. If it could have spoken, it would have said, "Frig or fuck you shall, before I give you rest." So I pulled the prepuce slowly back, — only once, — and as the knob came handsomely into view, out shot my spunk all over the bed-clothes.

Getting up to wipe and make things clean, I saw something on the brim of my cap which I had worn; the cap was on the table. I took it up and found a large spot of sperm which had come from the happy couple, it must have followed the withdrawal of the prick; and had my head been a little more turned up, it must have tumbled on my face. I did not mind wiping up my own sperm, but doing so to theirs seemed beastly. Yet what was the difference?

We heard one night someone squat down, and turned up the light; there were petticoats, legs, and an arse, but instead of the usual slit, we saw to our astonishment a prick and balls hanging down between the legs, it was a man in woman's clothes, and he was shitting. The sight alarmed us, we talked it over for many a day afterwards, for we did not then know that some men are fond of amusing themselves with other men.

I never saw but that one couple fucking, but we could hear groping and frigging going on close by. We heard women say, "Oh! don't!" Gay women we heard say, "Here is a good place," but they did not often select the gratings, why I cannot tell, for they were partly in recesses in the wall which enabled people to get more hidden. The bars were wide apart, and I suppose the regulars did not like that, yet they often used the gratings for pissing down.

These sights did not occur all at once, I went home, stopped, returned, and so on; in the meanwhile not having women, I then frigged, left off, then took to it again, and so time went on. Fewer women came at last up the street, we imagined that, with all our care, they had found out that people were beneath the gratings, and avoided them. The favourite place was the recess at the workmen's door to the factory, at which were two steps; we could hear but not see when a couple was there, we used then to go up into the factory and listen at the door. Generally, feeling and frigging was only going on, bargaining for money first. "Give me another shilling. Oh! your nails hurt. What a lot of hair you have. What a big one! Oh! I am coming! Don't spend over my clothes," and so on, we heard at times.

Meanwhile, there was either no servant at my home worthy of a stiff one, or those who would not take one; and I had no alterna-

tive but to frig. Money my mother again kept from me. What I got
I sent to the poor girl Martha, who then had not got rid of her big
belly; gay women I had fear of; devoured by desire to get into a
woman again, I even looked longingly at the wife of the foreman
who took charge of the house in which Henry lived, although she
was fifty. I recollect seeing her making my bed one morning, and
getting a cock-stand at the sight of the woman so near a place to
lay down on.

CHAPTER IX

Mrs. Smith. — A brutal husband. — My second adultery. — A chaste servant. — Road harlots. — A poke in the open. — Use for a silk handkerchief. — A shilling a tail. — Clapped.

Henry had now much business to attend to, I none. I used to wander into the back street just as the men's wives brought them their dinners, so as to look at them. They were not allowed inside, but if the men chose to eat inside they could do so, their wives waiting outside. Six or eight men had their dinners brought, the rest went away. The women most frequently sat on a door-step, or loitered over the gratings up which we used to look at night, or squatted down against the wall. I had once or twice looked up their clothes, but found little inviting, with the exception of a plump little pair of legs which belonged to a Mrs. Smith. She looked about twenty-six years of age, her husband twenty years older, a good workman but a brutal fellow. He bore a bad character among his fellows and was thought a brute to his wife. Some said his wife drank; there was often a row in the street between them at dinnertime, he used to sit on the door-step and eat his dinner outside, she standing near him, and her legs came at times over a grating. I used to dodge downstairs at times at the workmen's dinner-hour and have a look up, and that is how I saw and began to think of the legs of Mrs. Smith.

I took a sort of fancy to her, or rather her legs, so plump and clean. I saw she had a nice clean face with bright brown eyes, and then had a desire to fuck her. I again had desisted from frigging, had sworn to myself not to do so again, and now, getting strength, wanted a woman badly. Our eyes had often met, I had even got out of her way when passing her, a courtesy not often then shown by gentlemen to work-people. I used to stare at her so that she began to look confused when I did. The husband never seemed to notice anything but his dinner, at which he usually swore. Sometimes I spoke to him about gun-making. I wanted to poke Mrs. Smith, but there did not seem to be the remotest chance, nor had I any intention of attempting it, but used to look at her with my cock standing, and wondering what sort of cunt she had. I had been brought up religiously, and the idea of having a married woman seemed shocking. I was shocked when I found that Mary was married. At length I nodded, smiled, and established a sort of intimacy in that way without speaking, managing to meet her as it were quite casually when going to or leaving the work-shop.

One day the man dined on the step, his wife standing by his side; down I went to peep up her clothes and heard him rowing. Why the hell had she not got him beef instead of mutton; God damn her, why were there no potatoes! That was his style. Angry words passed, the voices grew louder, I heard a loud smack and a strong oath, he had hit his wife and gone back into the work-shop.

There was a great gabbling of female voices over the grating round Mrs. Smith. "I would not stand it," said one. "It is a shame," said another. "He ought to be proud of such a wife, an old beast," said another. The husband came out again. "I have done my best," said she, "you are not a man anyhow, or anywhere, for two pins I would run away from you." A loud oath and another smack followed.

I heard Mrs. Smith sobbing. "I have had a little drink," said she, "I told him so. He makes me so unhappy, I must; but I spend scarce a trifle and it's what I earns myself. Ain't I clean? don't I bring him good meals?" "You do, you do," said they. "It's a shame," she went on, "he is not a man, not in bed, not anywhere, not anyhow, I don't aggravate him, I put up with everything, it's full six months since he's been a husband to me, although we sleeps in the same bed," she added in a significant way, "yes, six months full." "Lor," said half a dozen voices together, then said one, "Don't he do anything to you then?" Things quieted, off went Mrs. Smith with some of the women, two remained waiting for their husbands' platters, they squatted down on the step.

"They're a miserable couple," said one. "Yes, and likely, he is never at home, no wonder she do take a drop of comfort." "No, it ain't." "She is a nice little woman, and no man gets his meals nicer." "No, that they don't." "He's too old for her, but he ain't jealous." "No, of course not." "Why he ain't done it to her for six months," said one. They both chuckled then. "Why, my old man don't forget me like that, and he is ten years older than Smith," said the other. "Ah!" said the first, "he's a bad'un altogether, men be a bad lot, the best on 'em." The time-bell rang, their husbands brought out their dinner-cans, and off the women went.

I can scarcely tell what followed exactly, or how it came about, for even now to me it seems astonishing. I was but between eighteen and nineteen and had not had the remotest idea of getting Mrs. Smith, though I longed for her lewedly when my cock stood. I was timid with women until I knew them well, I could never begin with our own servants until they had been in the house a few days; yet, directly I heard this conversation, a chance seemed in my way, and without meaning it I followed it up.

With but little idea of married life or habits, I saw that not only were they a wretched couple but that for months Smith had never touched his wife. I imagined then that married people were always doing it, that women were randier than men, — a common belief of young people. I thought: how she must want a poke! how she would enjoy it! Out I went to see if Mrs. Smith was about, and saw her walking off with a group of sympathizers, who dropped off gradually, until she was left with one, with whom she went into a public-house. In a few minutes they came out and parted. On she went alone, met another woman, had a long talk, and went into another public-house, and then, wiping her eyes as she came out, went her way alone; I after her, lewed and thinking to myself, "She has not had it for six months," and so on. She went into a public-house now by herself. I waited till she came out, and saw she had been taking too many drops of comfort.

Without any definite intention as far as I can remember, but simply for lewed gratification, I went up to and addressed her. She recognized me and stood stock still. She had a small bottle of what I found afterwards to be gin in her hand, which she put into her husband's dinner can. I told her I was sorry for her, having heard the row and all she had said. The reference to her wrongs roused her, and she said vehemently, "He is not a man anyhow or anywhere," and then was silent. I did not know what to say more, and walked on by her side. After a time she said, "Why are you walking with me, sir?" The only reply I made was that I liked it, and was sorry she had such a bad husband. She said she would rather be alone, but I walked on with her, she carrying the little tin can with a cover. I, not knowing what to do, offered to carry it for her, but she would not let me.

Then, she remarked, "You are very good, but don't come any further, it won't look well for a poor woman to be walking with a gentleman; neighbours make mischief, and God knows I have enough to bear already." My boldness having quite left me, I shook hands with her, which seemed to astonish her, and off she went. I followed her at a distance to her house, which was one of a row of small cottages fronting a ditch, and a field on which carpets were beaten and boys played, a scrubby poor place, as you may be sure.

I turned back, hesitating, one moment wondering at my boldness and wickedness in thinking of a married woman, the next thinking I was a fool for not having asked her to let me, when I saw, in the path, the top of the tin can she had been carrying. Here was a chance. I walked about for half an hour before I mustered up courage to go to the house. She opened her eyes wide when she saw me. "What do you want?" "Here is the top of the dinner-can," said I innocently. "Oh!" said she, "I am so glad, he would have hit me if I had lost it." As she took it I entered and closed the door.

She had finished the gin, for the empty bottle was on the table. She may have been more than fuddled, I cannot say; for I was so excited that I recollect only the most prominent circumstances. I was in a funk, but my cock was stiff, and that overcame all scruples. The house had but two rooms: a kitchen I was standing in, the street-door opened on to it. An open door showed a neat bed in a clean, white-washed bed-room. How I began I know not, but recollect telling what I had heard, and that for months he had not been a husband to her. That set her off talking wildly, and she said it all over again. She was sure he was spending his money on some dolly, hoped she might catch her, than cried, wiped her eyes, and said, "Well, that is no business of yours, I am a fool for talking to a young gentleman like you, I don't know what you are doing here."

"Let me do it to you," said I, "I have seen up your clothes, let me, — you are so nice, and I want you so badly; why should you not, he is no husband to you, and you such a nice woman." That was my artless beginning, or something like it. Fright at my impudence was struggling against my cock-stand. For a second she seemed speechless, then replied, "Well sir, you ought to be ashamed, — a married woman like me." "He is no husband to you, he never does it to you, you know, — I heard you tell the women so; they laughed and said he had some hussy whom he did it to." "That's no business of yours, but he is a bad one," and she began crying again. "Now go, sir, go, — if he came home he would murder me if he found you here."

I don't know how the next came off, but I know I was kissing her, that I got my hand up her clothes on to her cunt, that I pulled out my prick, that the struggling ceased, that I edged her to the bed-room, and that up against the bed she made a stand. "Oh! my God, sir, I am a married woman, pray don't." Paying no heed, I got her clothes up and, as she stood, was bending and trying to get my cock up her; but she was little, and I could not; it shoved up against her navel and motte. That I suppose, stirring her lust, overcame her, for she got on the bed, I got on her, and up her in a second.

I was in a bursting state of randiness, and she must have been the same. I was ready to spend, she readier; for I had no sooner entered her than her breath shortened, she clasped me tight, quivered and wriggled, and we both spent. I lay up her, cock ready for further work. Up to that time I had not properly felt her, nor seen her body. I began fumbling about, put my hand down, feeling cautiously round the stem of my cock and my ballocks. All was wet, I slid my finger below her cunt (feeling even near to an arsehole was then beyond me), there it felt wetter; that stimulated me, and on I went grinding. She lay with her eyes closed, without speaking. Soon we both spent again, I had fucked her twice without uncunting.

The quiet dreamy enjoyment had barely begun, when she pushed me off and sat up, saying, "What have I done? what have I done? I am a married woman!" Then came tears, then a kiss from me, then talk, then tears, and at intervals she told me a story of a bad, brutal, morose husband, who had not fucked her for months. Half frightened, half hysterical, it seemed as much pleasure to her to tell me her misery as it had been to have me doing her husband's work. We moved off the bed. "Oh! my God," said she, "look at the bed." I saw one wet patch as large as a tea-cup, and another as large as a crown at the spot where her bum had laid on the counterpane. "What shall I do?" "Wash it." "But I have no other." It was a bore, no doubt. I left without being able to get permission to see her again, but only tears, and an expression of her conviction that she was a wicked woman.

Although she had not asked me not to tell anyone, which women so often do who commit these little slips, I did not mention it to Henry. For three or four days afterwards she did not come to the factory. I went to her cottage. She was out. At length at the dinner-hour I met her face to face by the factory. She looked ready to drop. An hour afterwards seeing her surly husband at work, off to her house I went, and gave a single knock. She opened the door, nearly fell back with surprise, and before she could recover herself I was indoors. I had an altercation, a refusal, almost a fight, but I conquered. Again she was fucked on the bed, and now for the first time I had a look at her charms, her cunt unwashed.

She was a plump little woman, dark-haired on head and tail, her quim was neither large nor small, her thighs round and white, she was an ordinary person, neither handsome nor plain, and my curiosity was soon satisfied. She kept exclaiming, "Oh! if he should come home!" I fell to work again with vigor, and soon again spent. As I got off I observed under her bum again a large wet place, but now on her chemise. "What a lot of spending you have done," said I. "I can't help it," said she. My experience was small, but I knew that from no other woman whom I had stroked had such an effusion taken place. Before I had spent I had felt her wetness on my fingers. I had her on another occasion, and the same thing occurred. I notice this because I only recollect meeting one other such case since; Mrs. Smith, like the other to whom I refer, used after a few pushes up her, to squeeze her cunt, shiver, and discharge quite copiously, to be followed with a second pleasure and discharge when I spent. I only reflected on Mrs. Smith's peculiarity some years afterwards.

In about a week I had her again at her cottage. Then she said if I came any more she would have trouble, for neighbours had already remarked a gentleman at the house. I disregarded this, went and knocked. She opened the door cautiously with the chain up, and seeing me, shut it in my face. I was then about going to my own home, and feared I should not have her again, but found out that the husband spent his evening at a tavern (I had a strange pleasure in looking at him after I had had his wife), that he was to be at some workman's carousel, watched him to the public-house, then ran to his cottage, gave a single loud knock at the door, which was this time opened unsuspiciously, and in I pushed before she could scarcely see who it was.

I had difficulty in persuading her to let me, she was more timid than ever, but promised that I would never come again.

Then she got on to the bed. The crisis was just over when we heard a knock. With a shriek she pushed me off and got up. "He will murder me, he will murder me," said she. I stood blank with bewilderment, relieved by another knock and a voice crying "beer." She fell on the floor fainting, and so alarmed me, that I nearly called in the neighbours. I put a pillow under her head. I don't know what induced me, for not three minutes before I was frightened out of my life, but as she laid there close by the fire (at the knock we had rushed into the kitchen), I pulled up her clothes. The flickering of the fire showed her thighs and cunt in a strange light to me. As I pulled her legs asunder, I felt ashamed, but lust was strong. I looked at the cunt, the novelty of an insensible woman on the floor excited me, the next instant spite of her, for she recovered just as I laid on her, my prick was up her, and my knuckles on the hard bit of dingy carpet, and as I grasped her bum, it seemed that my poke was most delicious. So much for novelty and imagination. I left immediately afterwards.

Then I went home to my mother. In about three weeks, went to see Henry again as I said, but really to get to Mrs. Smith, and found her husband had been discharged. I went off to the cottage, it was empty. They had gone no one knew where, and he had half murdered his wife. I wondered if it had been about me. Then my conscience upbraided me with having committed adultery. I took to going to church more regularly, and repeated the commandments emphatically.

I was now approaching nineteen years, was at home doing nothing but study, and with scarcely a farthing of money. I tried to get into one of our servants unsuccessfully, she was a plain lass, but had a cunt, which was all I wanted. I began to kiss and fondle her, which she submitted to demurely. Then by surprise one day got my hand up her clothes, and between her cunt-lips. She loudly screamed, which luckily was unheard, for my mother was out. Her cunt felt wet, and I found from my fingers afterwards that she was poorly. She rushed downstairs crying violently, the next day gave warning and left, much to my relief. She never I am sure told my mother, but I was in a fright until she had left.

I restrained myself from frigging, although sorely tempted to do so, and luckily found cheaper and better relief. Having had but one gay woman, and having a dread of them, nevertheless my mind involuntarily turned to them, especially as I now defied my mother, stopped out of nights latish, and consequently saw more of them. But I had no money.

Between London and our suburb, there were some lengths of road bounded by fields and only lighted feebly by oil-lamps. At places small houses were being built in side-roads, which were altogether without light. Gay women of a poor class were then of an evening about the darkest parts, or they used to walk there with those who met them where the roads were lighter. They were of that class who go with labouring men, and were not attractive, although cleaner and better-looking than the same class now is.

One evening I worried an aunt out of two pounds, which I had with a solitary shilling besides, and was returning when a woman accosted me. She walked by my side and talked, but I could not afford a sovereign, which was a much larger sum then than it now is, and a shilling seemed to me a ridiculous sum, so I determined to run, for fear I should be fool enough to let her have a sovereign. "I can't," said I, "good night, I only have a shilling." "Make it two," said she. "I have not got more." "Give it me then." I stopped in astonishment at the idea of her taking such a trifle. "She is going to take it and go off," thought I, for I had known such a thing, but I gave her the shilling and then stood still. "Well, are you not going to have it?" said she, "make haste." It was a dark night, but I saw from a white gleam that her clothes were up, felt where the nick was, and in much agitation thrust my tool up it.

Having a woman in the open up against a field fence, and without seeing her cunt, or even her face, was a novelty to me. For a long time I had been bottling up my sperm. All fear left me, and it seemed the most delicious fuck I ever had had. In a few pushes I spent, and kept my belly up against hers in silent delight, till I felt sperm trickling down over my balls. Telling me to take care of my shirt she drew her bum back. Scarcely recovered from my pleasure and still wondering how I had such pleasure with so poor a woman, I suppose I must have said something of the sort, for she remarked, "Why not? we are all made the same way, and if some of us had more cheek, we might have as good clothes as the best, but there are plenty of real gents glad enough to have us," and so we talked for a minute. I had not felt her and now longed to do so, but was too timid to ask her. She turned away. I had been wiping my cock with a silk pocket-handkerchief, to prevent any sperm getting on to my shirt. A happy idea came. "Let me feel you, and do it again, and I will give you this silk handkerchief, for I have no more money." Laughing and saying, "I suppose it is silk," she accepted it. I think now of the exquisite delight with which I felt the thighs and bum of that poor woman, who might, for all I could see, have had the great or the small pox, or have been as ugly as the devil; but I stroked her belly, twiddled her wet cunt-hair (she had pissed), plunged my fingers into her wet cunt, and at length spent again in it, with more delight than I have had with some of the most dashing women since that time.

After funking about pox and clap for a few days, out I sped one evening to try to get her again, delighted at the economical rate at which I found it now possible to have women. But I always was liberal, and gave her three or four shillings. Several times I had had her afterwards and never saw her face. At length I insisted on going where I could see her. She refused until tempted by an offer, then agreed to meet me at a place which she named, saying, "And I will put on a clean chemise and stockings." I met her, and found her to be about thirty-five years old, and one of the ugliest women I ever saw.

She was so plain that all desire left me. I looked her all over, to which she made no objection, remarking as she pulled up her clothes, "Ah! you may look, I am clean as any woman, although I am what I am." I went on looking at, and fiddling her about, but no erection came. She gave an uneasy motion with her bum and said, "Oh! you are tickling me so, why don't you get on?" I said I did not want it yet, which so astonished her that she sat upright and looked at me and at my tool. Then she made me lay down on the poor bed, and mutual feeling soon brought me to a proper state. "Don't you be quick or you will spoil me," said she. Her manner was quite different from what it had been on the high road, it was amorous. I forgot her ugliness, and fucking with all my heart, spent when her hard breathing, tightening cunt, and clasping arms told me she enjoyed it also.

Then the miserable room, and her ugliness revolted me. I moved to get off, but she retained me, asking me to talk. Somewhat against my inclination I did. She laid hold of my prick, pinching it. The gentle pleasure returned, and it ended in my doing her again, as much to her delight as mine. She said so. Instead of feeling pleased, it made her seem to me more ugly. I went away, and although I argued with myself, especially when I only had a shilling or two, yet I never could bring myself to have her again. When I saw her on the road, I went the other side of the way, and soon after lost sight of her.

Finding that I had not suffered by my indiscretion, I got bolder, took the run of the road, and must have had a dozen girls at a shilling a tail. One night as I fumbled a girl, she frigged me vigorously. "I will do it this way," said she, "you will like it so." But I refused. "I will give you such pleasure," said she again, "all the gents say I do it better than any girl." But again I refused. "I am afraid my monthlies are just coming on," said she. But up I put it, and went home satisfied. Two or three mornings afterwards I felt a slight itching at the tip of my prick, but took no notice of it; the next morning, piddling, to my horror I saw a little yellowish fluid oozing, and sat down in consternation. I had got a clap.

This laid me up for weeks; I went to a strange doctor and managed to keep it from my mother, but was in anxiety as to how I was to pay the doctor. Fortune and misfortune often follow each other. My long promised appointment came from the W***-Office just as I was getting well. With overwhelming joy I saw some chance of a little money, beyond what I got by begging from relatives; and then also my mother, at the advice of an uncle, who pointed out that in a year and a half I could not be kept out of my property, allowed me a fair monthly stipend.

I now found out that women of a superior class were to be had much cheaper, than my great friends used to talk of; but at the time I write of a sovereign would get any woman and ten shillings as nice a one as you needed. Two good furnished rooms near the Clubs could be had by women for from fifteen to twenty shillings per week, a handsome silk dress for five or ten pounds, and other things in proportion. So cunt was a more reasonable article than it now is, and I got quite nice girls at from five to ten shillings a poke, and had several in their own rooms, but sometimes paying half-a-crown extra for a room elsewhere.

When with but little money, I used to take out my best silk handkerchiefs, and give them with money, and once or twice I gave nothing else. One night to a nice-looking girl I said I could give her nothing but a handkerchief. "All right," said she without a murmur. When I had fucked her, she laid still on the bed and before she washed her cunt examined the handkerchief very carefully. "It's a rare good new one, it will pop for half-a-crown where I am known, where did you prig it?" looking at me as she spoke, and then added, "Yet you look like a gentleman too." I recollect it as well as if it were yesterday. I at that time used to take pleasure in laying as long as I could after I had spent, then getting up and kneeling between the girl's legs opening her cunt and watching the spunk at the mouth, or the big drops rolling down between the cheeks of her bum. I was kneeling so then, and was not a little shocked at her remark. That girl was young, handsome, well made, and in the Haymarket would now get anything from one to five pounds, yet I had her several times for three and four shillings a time.

CHAPTER X

A big cunted one. — Sister Mary. — A wet dream. — Charlotte re-appears. — Consequences. — My first child. — Cook Brown, and housemaid Harriet. — Masturbation and foolscap. — A deaf relative. — An uncomfortable pudendum. — A lacerated penis. — Sudden dismissals.

Just at this time the following incident occurred. Going one Saturday night up Granby Street, Waterloo Road, then full of women who used to sit at the windows half naked; two or three together at times in the same room on the ground-floor, with the bed visible from the street, and which street I often walked in for the pleasure of looking at the women. A woman standing at a door seized my hand, asking me in, and at the same time pulling me quite violently into the little passage. I had barely seen her, and upon her saying, "Come and have me," replied that I had scarcely any money. "Never mind," said she, "we will have a fuck for all that." She shut the door, closed rapidly the other wooden shutters, which all the ground-floor windows had in that street, and began to kiss me and feel for my prick. I then saw she was half drunk. Quickly she pulled me towards the bed, threw herself on it, pulled up her clothes to her navel, and cried aloud, "Fuck me, — fuck me, — fuck me, — oh! how I want a fuck, make haste." She was a tall woman with dark hair on her cunt, neither very long nor thick. As I looked at it, I saw the inner lips hanging out a full inch, I put my finger, two, then three fingers up her cunt easily. It was enormous. It shocked me, having never seen such a cunt before I am quite sure. She meanwhile did nothing but jerk, and wriggle her arse about, shouting out, "Fuck me, — put your prick in, — fuck me, — fuck me."

The look of her thing, its size, and her manner so shocked me

147

that my prick refused its work, and I told her so. She jumped off of
the bed, fell on her knees, and began sucking my prick violently,
made it stiff spite of me, got on to the bed again, and recommenced
crying out for me to do it to her. With a feeling of disgust I got
on her, slipped my prick up and began, but it felt nowhere. I could
not make out that it was up a cunt at all, so loose was it. If it had
been in a wet bladder, it could not have felt looser, and it shrunk
up again to nothing. "I can't do it," said I in fright, for her manner
was so lewed, and became so ferocious, that it quite upset me.
"What! a fine young man like you can't do it," said she. "No" (and
as an apology), "I often can't do it." Again she got it stiff by sucking it. That quite disgusted me, but on to the bed and into her
again I got. My doodle in a minute began to shrink, but whilst in
her, she wriggled and jerked away so hard, that I think she must
have got a pleasure, for she laid quiet for a time. I was very glad to
get off; but was not to be let off so easy. "I *will* give you a pleasure,"
said she, "I can if anyone can," and although it disgusted me, for
such a thing had never been done to me before and I tried to stop
her, she dropped upon her knees saying, "You will come to see me
again I know, for a man can always do it one way or another," put
my prick in her mouth and sucked and palated it. I was too young
and too full not to feel it. Spite of myself I spent, and just as I did,
grasping my balls with one hand and frigging the stem with the
other, she drew back her mouth about two inches, kept it wide
open, went on frigging, and the sperm squirted out into her mouth
and on to her face; then she resumed sucking it until every drop
was out of me.

That over, she rose and said, "You will come to me again,
won't you? I will always do that to you, and anything else you
like." I gave her a shilling and promised, but never felt so sick and
disgusted with a woman before. Everything about the woman was
repulsive. I have since met four or five women with very large cunt-
holes, but hers was the largest. I am perfectly certain I could have
put my fist up it. I avoided the street for some months, which was
a great loss to me, for I often used to go through it to gloat on the
charms of the women as they lolled out of the windows. When I
thought of my prick being sucked, it used to disgust me awfully,
and it was many years before I knew what pleasure it was to a

man, at times; but it never has been done to me again, in the manner that woman did it.

Then I saw the woman in taking whose virginity I lost my own, — Charlotte.

Our cook married. A new cook and housemaid came, the latter a pretty dark-eyed girl of about eighteen years of age, named Mary. Directly I set eyes upon her I liked her, and thought I would try to get her. My clap and cheap pokes had not made me much in love with gay women, whose free-and-easy ways somewhat shocked my timidity. Some time had elapsed since I had had any others, and my mind naturally reverted to the nice pokes I had had with servants. My chances were fewer than ever. One of my sisters was now frequently at home, Tom no longer needed a servant to be with him, and the housemaid was less frequently away from the kitchen. But I felt myself more a man, my good fortunes made me feel more sure of success, more prompt and determined in attack.

At first I watched her closely and thought I must have seen her before. A resemblance struck me, and I remarked to my mother, "How like that girl is to Charlotte, who lived with us." "She is her sister," said she. I was startled, for a feeling came over me that I ought not to try her.

But it brought my liaison with Charlotte vividly to my recollection. The first meeting, the glimpse of her cunt as she got down from the cart, my first grope, our first poke, were now constantly before me; and I longed with all my heart to have her again, though I knew it was hopeless.

Gradually my mind centered itself on Mary, and as I saw the resemblance to her sister I used to wonder how far the resemblance extended. Whether her haunches were as large, her thighs as round, her cunt so made, fringed, and dark, and so on; until I desired to have her, as much for her resemblance to Charlotte, as for herself. Yet I had fear and reluctance to make advances, because she was Charlotte's sister.

Meanwhile I was chaste, was in good health, and wanted a woman awfully. Then I had a wet dream; dreamed I had Charlotte in my arms, that she ran away and left me with Mary, who pulled up her clothes, and invited me to fuck her. Before I could get in to her, I awakened, found that I was on my back and was spending on my night-gown.

I had heard much of these dreams, had had one partially, and now had experienced a complete one. It threw me into a state of irritation, but seemed to fix the hidden charms of Mary strongly in my imagination. Desire so carried me away that, from gently rubbing and titillating myself, I passed to frigging a discharge, whilst thinking of Mary's cunt.

In the morning I had the enervation I have always since felt after these dreams, and my usual disgust at having frigged myself; a feeling which was not allayed when I looked at my night-shirt. I had a dread of letting it be seen, but left things as they were. Mary and the cook made my bed, and must have seen it. Servants see funny things on beds often. I wonder what they say, and what they think about it. It can't be easy for a young woman to see sheets, and night-gowns, spunk-stained, without its affecting her imagination baudily, and paving the way for somebody to stain sheets and linen with herself.

I gave up all idea of attacking Mary, but "cock and cunt will try to get together." There is no use in resisting it. So again with no fixed intention, but simply from pleasure for the time being, and impelled by desire (all my silk handkerchiefs were gone and I was again without money), and by opportunity, I got to courting, and we soon kissed. I had pressed her belly against mine, got my hand on to the calf of her leg, and was on the high road to the snatch at her cunt, which my experience now told me was the right thing to do, when all came to an end.

I went daily to the W°°°-Office returning about half-past four. One day when about half-a-mile from home, a lady in black silk and with a dark veil approached me; but as if she had made a mistake, when close to me, turned on one side and passed on. I looked back and saw she was standing still, then on she went, and so did I, and had nearly forgotten her, when I heard quick footsteps in the rear, and some one saying, "Master Walter, don't you know me?" I turned round, stopped, and tried to see who it was, but the veil prevented it. She hesitated an instant, then lifted it, and I saw Charlotte.

With flushed face, bright eyes, and a gentle smile, she looked exquisite. My heart beat tumultuously, my love returned in an instant. I put my arm round her, and regardless of the publicity of the place, gave a kiss. There was, it is true, scarcely anyone about, but she as well as me when I had done it, saw the impropriety. "Don't for God's sake," said she, "what will people think?" "Let us walk," said I, and pulling her arm through mine, on we went; I looking into her face all the way, noticing how much the time which had passed had improved her and overwhelming her with questions. I felt overjoyed, as if again I should possess her, and old times had returned. She for a few minutes seemed to give way to similar elation. Just then I saw a gentleman named Courtauld approaching, he was our next-door neighbour. We nodded as we passed, but the incident altered the current of our thoughts. I led her down a turning where there were scarcely any people, and saying, "I am so glad old Courtauld did not see me, for his brother lives just by us, and his old servant is often there and knows me." She relapsed into silence. I went on chatting of the happy times we had had, and the pleasures we had tasted together. She remarked, "Oh! pray don't talk of that any more, recollect I am married, let me say what I have come to say, and then I must go."

"To say to me?" said I. "Pray don't misunderstand me, I thought you would excuse it," said she getting confused, "besides, it is my duty, and of course knowing what I do about you, I was so afraid of something." "What do you mean?" "Well, if I had known where she was going to I would have made mother stop it, now I come at once to ask you not to hurt her." I proposed going into a small half-country ale-house close by, but she refused, saying that, if seen to do so, and it became known to her husband, it might cause much harm.

"Oh! no," said she in a hurry again, "I must go, I must get back, I came to ask you not to hurt her, promise you won't, for my sake." All this time I was in a fog. "Who — who, — what do you mean?" said I. "Oh, you know, — Mary, I mean Mary, she is my favourite sister, pray don't harm her." The whole affair was clear to me at once. "Is that what you came about?" I asked, disappointed. "Yes, I have been coming for a fortnight, but could not make up my mind; her last letter made me determine at any risk to do so, and now, dear, promise me not to hurt her, and I will go."

I was annoyed and wounded in vanity, for I had almost brought myself to think she had come for the pleasure of meeting me. I had no intention of quitting her so soon, felt as if I could not, so chaffed her. "What do you mean by hurting her?" "Don't talk nonsense, you know what I mean." "Another case of cock and cunt coming together." "If you talk like that, you insult me, and I did not think you would." "Well, I love you and would not like to hurt your feelings, what you really mean is that I am not to try to do it to her." "Why of course, don't ruin her, that is what I mean."

We had walked without any intention on my part to the outskirts of our village, where the pew-opener's house was in which Charlotte and I had spent many an hour in love's frolics. The house was in sight, the hope of again having her came to my mind. In her excitement, which was as great if not greater than mine, she had not noticed where we were, until quite at the angle. The pew-opener was at the door, gave me a nod, and thinking it possible I might be coming in, I suppose, left the door ajar. "Come in," said I. "Never! oh! no, you have brought me here purposely." I saw there would be difficulty. "Here is that old Courtauld's housemaid, damn her," said I. "Where? — where? — which way?" said she, looking in alarm in all directions, but unable to see clearly through her veil. "There, — there, just step inside the door till she has passed." She stepped in quickly, the next instant I half pulled, half hustled her through the little door into the bed-room, slammed the door, locked it, and stood still, half afraid of my own boldness. She went to the window and began to peer through the blinds to see the old housemaid.

"I can't see her," said she, "she must have passed, tell me which way she went, and let me go." "Not yet. What do you want about Mary?" "Promise for my sake, you won't try to ruin her." "Well, let us have a longer talk, how do you know I want to do so?" "I know you do." "Sit down." "I cannot." "Then I won't promise, why should I?" "Oh! don't be a blackguard, don't, oh! don't, — you shan't have her, I will take care," and then she burst out crying.

I loved her so that I felt I would do anything to please her; but wanted her so much that I could be cruel enough to do or say anything to have her again. Desire was the stronger. The sofa, the bed, the room, her beauty, all made me feel savage with lust, so I temporized. "I am so excited," said I, "I scarcely know what to say, what to do, tell me more, what you know, what you want, for all this seems so strange to me, — sit down." "No." "Sit down only while you tell me." "No." But I laid hold of her and pushed her on to the sofa, and there I held her, and after beseeching her to be quiet and kiss me, she did so. Then she sat for a minute, drying her tears, and began her tale and her request.

"Mary is my favorite sister, she lived with us for a year after I married, but mother wanted her, and she went home. She grew tired of being at home, went to service, did not like it, and went home again; again grew weary; and, to my astonishment, the last time I went to see the old people found she had gone to live with your mother. I was frightened for her sake, for I love her dearly." "Why frightened?" I asked. "Why frightened? don't I know you, do you think I have forgotten all?" "I never thought of doing her harm." "Perhaps not," she replied, "but I would not trust my sister near you, if she had the least liking for you, or you for her." I protested I was indifferent to her. "Why kiss her and squeeze her so?" I began denying it, when she stopped me, saying vehemently, "Now don't tell stories, you never did to me, I know all, I know you do, you mean her harm, or if you don't, harm will come of it. Look, here is her letter," and she put it into my hands. To my astonishment, I found Mary had told her sister all, mixed with warm encomiums of me. I was shut up, and could only say I meant no harm. "Perhaps! but harm must come of it. It nearly brought me to ruin for I would have done anything, lived anyhow, to keep near you; but I have escaped it. Poor Mary may not, for you are older now and may do more harm; she is a different temper from me, and in despair will go wrong altogether; so I pray you, if you ever loved me, not to injure her, for my sake. If she came to harm, I should break my heart," and she broke again into tears, getting up at the same time to go.

I pulled her back and kissed her tears away. "Charlotte, we cannot meet and part like this, I love you still, I have never ceased to love and think of you, oh! let me." I could say no more, for in my eyes then there was a sanctity about a married woman which stilled my tongue. "Oh! let me," was all I could say.

She understood what I wanted, and replied, "I am married and cannot, let me go." At my entreaties she kissed me freely, yet all the time struggled to get up.

I thought to myself, "You have had her. She loves you still. Think of the pleasure you have had with her. Here she is in your power, and cannot escape without a riot, which she will fear." Kissing her fiercely, stifling her voice with my mouth, "I must, I will have you again," I pulled her violently back on the sofa, and had my hand on her thighs in an instant.

"Oh! don't, for the love of God, think, I am married, don't make me afraid of myself; oh! take care, you crush my bonnet, what shall I do, how shall I get home?" Holding her tight, I dragged the bonnet off her head, and recommenced. We made such a noise, that the old pew-opener knocked at the door and asked if anything was the matter.

"By God," said I, "either I will have you, or you shan't go out of this house this night," and so I struggled on through tears and entreaties, threats, kissings and promises, till with broken voice her head sunk back, her struggles ceased, her legs opened, my hand slipped over her smooth thighs, and nestled in the warm moist slit it had so often toyed with in time gone by. It is nigh fifteen years since that delicious afternoon, but I recollect my sensations, as I touched her cunt, as well as if it had been but yesterday.

Resistance had ceased; for a moment in silent enjoyment I laid with my fingers in their warm lodging, then too impatient to get to the bed, or take the full luxury of my fortune, I arranged her on the sofa as well as its size permitted, with her petticoats up in a heap, and with my trousers half unbuttoned, flung myself upon her, and entered the smooth channel in which I first had spent my virginity. Frantic with excitement, the pleasure came on ere I was full up her. She, excited and loving, clutched me tightly in her arms, whilst her cunt and belly moved sympathetically. In too short a time we spent together.

My position was a fatiguing one, I was half on, half off the sofa; hers was but little less so, yet as long as our privates would keep together, we kept them so. I poured out my love to her, and joyed to hear from her that she loved me still. But our position could not last for ever; gradually I slipped off. My prolonged embrace, my sensuous imagination, and my love for her had told so upon me, that I was already contemplating the pleasure of another poke, a desire to see her charms came over me, I went on to my knees and had a glimpse, between the open thighs, of the half open cunt, from which a love-drop was rolling. She pushed down her clothes, and sat up, looking at me and blushing like the most modest of maidens.

It is extraordinary what objection so many women have to a man's looking closely at their cunts. A woman will stand naked, lay naked on her belly or bum, stand with one leg on a chair, kneel with one leg on the bed, be looked at frontways, backways, sideways, and be pleased with the admiration. You may lay and kiss the outside, put your fingers up and probe it, rub your knuckles into it, tickle or frig it; but directly you want to pull the lips open, to see the hole which lays hidden by the hairy outer lips, to see where your prick is longing to hide his head; they object, put their thighs together, say, "No, it is not to be looked at." Or if angrily pressed, reluctantly half yield, throw themselves down, so as to put their back to the light, lifting one leg so as to hide the light, and using every maneuver to prevent you looking closely at it; and if you desire to look when it's laden with the efforts of your love, they will struggle to prevent you. Gay or modest, it is the same among the English, although a gay lady will yield to please her friend. With the French the objection is less, a French gay woman will pull open her cunt with her own hands and let you pull open her arse-hole if you can, and like it. I have known a few women of other nations, and even of my own, as free and easy, but the rule is as I say. This cannot be modesty. I rather imagine it results from a fear that some discharge will show itself, and sicken the man's appetite.

Up jumped Charlotte, and went into the adjoining room. I heard her splashing away a long time at her cunt, and went to her. I had no desire to wash away from my person anything which had come from hers. She pushed me back. I had a glimpse of her, naked to her waist, washing something. She said, "My linen is in such a mess I have been obliged to wash it." She had found much spunk upon it and washed it for fear of being found out. She put a petticoat over her neck to hide her charms, the chemise was so wet that it was almost impossible for her to put it on, and she did not know what to do.

"Good God, you will catch your death of cold." I rang the bell and gave it to the old woman to dry. "Now," said I, "you cannot go, it is of no use, I must have you again, and will see all your charms, I had you first, I have had you again, and again I will have you; don't be foolish, all harm is done."

Crying, entreating and saying she was married, I got her on to the bed, and stripping myself was soon folded in her arms. My prick was ready, she had struggled hard, now saw it was useless, and lay in all her beauty before me, her hand on the pillow and her eyes closed, leaving me to work my will.

I saw her as leisurely as my throbbing prick would let me, from head to foot, that she had grown stouter, taller, and was now a splendid woman. Her breasts were full and hard, her buttocks large and solid, her thighs more rounded, the hair of her cunt thicker. Curiously I opened its lips and put my finger in, to see if marriage had made any difference, but was far too young and inexperienced to find it out, if there had been any. It seemed the dear old split which had so often given me pleasure before; that look and feel finished me, in another second my ballocks were banging away against her bum, and she met my embraces with fervour which too soon came to an end. Repose followed, the luscious tongue-kisses ceased, our sighs stopped, and we fell asleep.

But not for long. The wet chemise was brought back. That off her mind, into bed I got with her. The coach by which she now could go home did not leave until eight o'clock, hurry was of no use; with my finger in her quim, side by side, mouth to mouth, we laid and talked.

Her anxiety was about her sister, whom I swore I never would attempt. That settled her. She wanted to know all about me, that was soon told. I never mentioned Mary's name, although she asked after her. Then I was curious about her married life, how she got over her marriage night, how often he poked her, and so on. I got but little out of her, beyond that he had not discovered that she had been fucked before, and that he was a good husband to her; my other questions she said were disgraceful. I felt mad to think that another man should put his prick where my fingers then were, so I asked if she enjoyed it with him, whereupon she burst into a passionate flood of tears, and it closed with her saying, "Whether I love him or not, he is a good fellow to me, and if I am found out and disgraced it will serve me right." Would she meet me again? "Never, never, I love you still, but never again." It ended in another fuck.

And so it went on till the time for going. Never in my life up to that time had desire been so strong in me. When I knew she must go, I insisted on again doing it, but could not come up to the scratch, until with a sharp frig it stiffened and again it was put up her. What a long hard poke it was, what a test of my manhood, how proud was I when with a sharp and sudden pleasure I felt my spunk squirting up her dear quim, and a spasmodic clutch, a sharp sob and "dear Walter," escaping from her told me she had spent with me.

She washed, I dressed, swearing I would never wash my prick again till I saw her. "I have poked you, darling, five times," said I in triumph. It was the first time I think I ever had done so, but am not sure, and proud enough I felt. We soon relapsed into sadness and tears, and telling our love to each other, parted at the coach-stand.

I was mad again for her; had now money, and twice went down to the place to get a glimpse at her and failed, but saw her husband in the shop. We stared at each other. I wonder if he felt that I should have liked to throttle him, for so I did. I wrote and got no reply. I pumped her sister, to see if I could learn where she walked or went, and got no information; indeed soon lost opportunity, for suddenly her sister left us. Her father came to ask my mother to excuse her on account of his wife's illness, and she never came back. I have but little doubt it was only to get her away from our house, and that it was Charlotte's doings. I never saw Charlotte again, though I still may do so; but to this day I have an affection for her, and although she must be forty, should like to poke her.

Next year, one day my mother opened a letter, it was from the E*** family; and read aloud little scraps of it to me and my sisters who were in the room. "That family is all doing very well," said she; "Mary, who was with us but three months last year, is married." She went on reading, "And Charlotte's husband has taken a large shop and is making money. — Ah! I am very glad of it, for she was a nice, respectable girl. Oh! here, — and has just been confined with a fine boy. — I am very glad," said mother. I looked and found it was nine months after Tom's birthday, and that that day nine months some one had fucked Charlotte five times. I was delighted.

My appointment now made it needful to dine late, so we reverted to a six o'clock dinner. This neither suited the cook nor housemaid; both left, and two new servants came. I was about nineteen years old.

The cook, whose name was Brown, was clean, fat, and wholesome to look at, and, I should say, forty-five years old. She must
have weighed sixteen stone. The width across her arse, as I eyed
it outside her dress, looked greater than that of Mary the cook;
there was a roguish twinkle in her eye, which made her look like
a good-tempered monthly nurse, her eyes were blue and her hair
brown.

Harriet the housemaid was very tall and very sallow, had jet-
black hair and black eyes, with the expression of a serpent in them.
She showed splendid teeth when she laughed, and then looked half
cat, half hyena. She never looked you in the face long, was so quiet
in her movements that the cat moved less noiselessly; she startled
you by being close to you when you did not know she was near,
and had a sneering laugh. After a day or two my mother remarked
she did not like the pair, and was sorry she had engaged them.

Up to this time I had only poked two servants, Charlotte and
Mary. Others had not been to my taste. With one I tried it on and
failed, and when randy now could not help thinking at the couple
in the house. I tried it on with Harriet, but she so snubbed me that
I set her down as an impregnable virgin. Then I turned my eyes to
Brown, though it seemed absurd to think of such a fat, middle-aged
woman; but I one day chanced to see that she had a very fat pair of
calves, and I knew she must have a big arse; and as fat legs had an
irresistible attraction for me, I tried to see more of them, but without the thought of taking liberties with their owner.

I saw her legs again; from thinking of them and her rump, my
mind naturally went to her cunt, which I pictured must be very
thick-lipped and hairy like that of Sarah, whose cunt had made a
great impression on me. Her age then seemed to fade from my
mind, and I used to follow her when going upstairs, trying to see
her legs, and flattering myself she did not see what I was after, but
she knew it as well as I did.

One day going upstairs she stumbled upon her dress, and as if
to prevent doing it again, held it up, so as to show nearly to her
knees. When she got on the top stair she turned round, and as if
she had only just seen me, dropped her dress quickly. Another time
she stooped and jutted out her bum, so that I saw a good deal up
the clothes, whilst she pretended to be doing something to her
boot. It seemed to me accidental, but it was all intentional.

Then my prick used to stand when I saw her. About nine o'clock one morning she came into the garden when I was there, and gathered some herbs. Her stooping posture gave me a cock-stand, and under its influence I joked her about her legs and my seeing them. She gave a suppressed laugh and saying, "Lawk! did you sir?" went down into the kitchen. What made me go down I do not know, but five minutes afterwards I did so; and, just by the kitchen door, saw her with one leg on a chair, putting up her garter.

I stood stock still and silent. She adjusted one garter neatly, then put up her other leg, unrolled the garter, pulled up the stocking and put on the garter quite deliberately. I saw the flesh of her large thighs, for her garters were tied above her knees, and she pulled up her petticoats freely. Putting down her clothes she turned round, saw me, then with a grin said, "Lawk sir, how you startled me."

Bursting with randiness I lost all prudence. Mother, sister, Tom, and the other servant were about the house, but up to the cook I went, whispering, "I saw your legs, what jolly ones, what thighs, what a cunt you must have, let's have a feel," and got one hand up her clothes. She pushed me away saying, "Hish! here is missis." It was a lie, but it frightened me away.

The same evening I went downstairs after our dinner. The housemaid had been sent to the circulating library. Mother, sister, and Tom were, as they usually were after dinner, when the weather was warm, sitting in the summer-house at the bottom of the garden. I usually sat with them, but slinked into the house, and down into the kitchen, which, being underground, was darkish, although then it was light till eight o'clock. Cook when she saw me, grinned and became familiar, for she was a regular old stager and knew well that when a man wanted to take liberties with her, she might safely take them with him. "What do you want?" "To feel your cunt," said I, "see your legs, feel that crummy rump of yours, cookey." "Then you won't," said she, laughing, and lifting a heavy saucepan off the fire with both hands, she carried it towards the sink in the back kitchen. Randy and ready, I saw my opportunity; and as she neared the sink, thrust both hands up her clothes, grasped her arse, and was fumbling for her slit; when putting down the saucepan with a bang, she flung round, and hit me such a slap on the head as knocked me over, saying, "Why, you young devilskin, it would serve you right to tell your mother of your capers," and then she stood and laughed at me.

I persisted, kissed the old party, and told her how I wanted her, for indeed at that moment I would have fucked her, if she had been eighty. She repulsed me saying in a whisper, "Harriet is upstairs." "She is going out," said I. "Wait till she has, if she hears you, she will make mischief." As I felt this might be true, I desisted.

I went back to the garden, thinking and hoping mother and sister would not go indoors. When Harriet had gone off, I went back into the garden parlour quite leisurely (for mother could see me do that), then down to the cook. It was nearly dark. In a minute I had pushed her up against the dresser, was groping her, and she was feeling my prick and ballocks with seemingly hearty enjoyment. She opened her legs to give me every facility. I attempted to get into her, but her clothes and big belly prevented me. She held my prick against her cunt, so that it pushed against her orifice, but did not go up it; and such was my state, that I spent against it. She kept hold of the prick, rubbing it, and gently squeezing it, until not a drop of sperm was left in it. Then for fear of being found out, upstairs I went again. The whole business had not occupied five minutes.

I had once spent by accident in Mary's hand, and had fear lest it should disgust her. There was something about this affair which seemed quite different. I could scarcely make out how, with a cunt close to my prick, I had spent as I had done. The next night came, I tried it on at the same hour with the same result. She not only let me feel her, but put my fingers to her cunt, at a place where she wished me to rub her, she meanwhile frigging away at my prick. But I wanted more than this, and just as it was too late, she let me put my prick in. At the first spurt of my spunk, she by a twist threw my prick out, caught hold of it with her fingers, letting me spend over her thighs and linen, but squeezing and frigging at my doodle until it had shrunk thoroughly down.

For a month the same thing occasionally happened. She would let me finger, feel, rub her (in the nearly darkened kitchen), putting one leg on a chair, or stooping down, or any way to let me feel both inside and outside well. When I got my prick out, she immediately began to frig it. I used to have quiet rows with her for not letting me put it into her; and when at length she did, I was always near spending; and do not think that more than once, I spent up her completely, so did she manage to throw me out just as my sperm began to flow. All was done standing up.

She treated me like some one she had known for years, did everything before me, talked both baudily and beastly, called my balls my cods, and used to say, "Hish! let me piss first." Then she would sit down on a pail in the back-kitchen and piss, sometimes farting, and saying, "Oh!" with a laugh, when she did so. She would belch without ceremony, blow her nose through her fingers, and I noticed she never washed her hands (whilst I was present at all events), when I had spent upon them. She would say, "How are your cods off for starch to-night?" She was complaisant enough in letting me feel, would turn her backside round and let me fumble about it anyhow, but although want made me do what I did, it never seemed quite pleasant to me, and I disliked her. I never got a glimpse of her belly or cunt. If the front-kitchen was not dark enough, she moved to the back, before we began our pranks, and scrupulously avoided light. Her cunt I felt was a large one, but, so far from having the quantity of hair I expected, she seemed scarcely to have any. One thing she did which annoyed me. After feeling my cock, she would slide her hands under the balls to my arse-hole which she would press hard with her middle-finger, giving a "tchick" with her tongue, at the same time.

All this took place in about six weeks. "Hush!" said she one night, "some one is listening." I could hear nothing, but she whispered, "Go up to the garden." I did. It was dusk, and I thought I saw a figure enter the garden parlour, just as I got up the garden stairs. All were out but me and the two servants. Cook at the same time went up the kitchen-stairs, calling out loudly, "Harriet, is Master at home, do you know?"

A few days afterwards when at our fun, we stood in the door jamb; Harriet was at the top of the house. Said cook, "If I push you hard by the shoulders, go out into the garden at once, without saying a word." It was nearly dark. The kitchen garden-door was shut, but she opened it wide, before we went to work. I had my prick against her cunt when a push came; off I went, buttoning up, and, after a time, across the garden, into the parlour. Afterwards Harriet brought up lights, her eyes cast down as usual. The next day the cook whispered to me, "It was that bitch Harriet watching, I found her coming downstairs with her shoes off, saying she wanted a candle; — but I will be even with her."

I never had the cook but once after that. She would not let me. The two servants quarrelled so that my mother threatened to dismiss both. When I tried it on with Brown, she said, "Why don't you ask Harriet, you young devilskin?" I told her there was no chance. She said she was quite sure that I should not be the first. Another day she repeated it, saying, "I bet she will let you, the baker has had her I believe." Then she put me up to watching the baker with Harriet. The man came in the afternoon. Just when I returned one afternoon, I posted myself at the garden entrance-gate from the fore-court, from which door ajar I could see the street-door. The baker after giving her a kiss, made a poke at her quim outside her clothes, which she returned by knocking a loaf against his trousers just by his tool, and laughing. This I told the cook, who said, "She will let you, if you try, young devilskin, she has seen you and your cods naked." "Seen me naked?" "Both of us have," and then she told me how.

Opposite my bed-room door, at the end of the room, was a cheval-glass; between it and the door was my sponging bath, then a big tub. Any one looking through the key-hole could see me naked when I was in it. I took the bath directly I was up, which was at about the time the servants went down. Many a time have I looked at myself naked in the glass, making my prick stand, to see how I looked in that condition. Both servants had seen me so. They had sometimes arranged the key so as to leave the hole clear. Never had it occurred to me that I should be so looked at, although I had often looked through a key-hole myself, at women. The cook made this clear to me, by standing in the tub and requesting me to look at her through the key-hole.

We arranged that I should bathe the next morning and suddenly open the door. "Pull your cods about well, and I warrant Harriet will look as long as she can," she said. I did so, heard the servants' door carefully open, and then frigged my cock, till it was as stiff as a poker. Stepping out of the bath with a towel, as if to dry myself, I opened the door suddenly, and found Harriet just rising from a stooping position. She rushed downstairs, but quietly, for fear of awaking my mother. For all that I could not make up my mind to try Harriet, but tried to get Brown again. "No thank you, young devilskin," said she, "not with that bitch of Harriet about."

Then I had a stronge erotic fancy. Randy with abstinence and fearful of Harriet, I took to frigging and spending against a piece of paper pinned against the wall of my room, opposite to the glass, and when standing in the tub.

Autumn was coming. As I could not then get leave of absence, my mother, with my sister from school and little brother, went without me on a visit to my aunt in H°°°f°°°d-shire, leaving an old female relative, who was very deaf, to take charge in her absence. Cautioning her specially to make me comfortable, and look sharp after the servants, she said that she could not bear them and would perhaps dismiss them on her return; for she had heard them using foul language to each other. I heard this.

Cook gave me unasked her opinion that Harriet would let me sleep with her. Instigated by her, I asked Harriet how I looked naked. She did not reply, and went downstairs. I overheard them quarrelling. Afterwards I asked her before the cook. She did not know what I meant, she said. I then asked the cook if she had not been looking at me through the key-hole. Cook laughed, saying, "He caught you, Harriet, once he caught you." "You are a liar," said Harriet. "Oh! if it comes to that," said cook, "we have both seen you naked a dozen times." There was a row, interrupted by my deaf relative coming home. The same afternoon cook whispered to me, "Come to our room when we are both in bed."

That night, with candle in my hand and in my night-shirt, I crept stealthily into their room; both were awake; Harriet sat up in bed, staring at me. When I entered, cook asked me what I wanted. I replied, "To see as much of them as they had seen of me," and pulled up my night-gown to my waist. Cook laughed; Harriet said, "Now leave the room." "If you are a fool and make a row," said cook, "we shall be both sent off." Just then we did hear some sort of noise, cook sat up and listened. "It is nothing," said she, and with a grin laid down. I drew off my night-shirt, standing then naked, and Harriet laying down with a modest look; I felt encouraged, extinguished the light, and jumped into bed by the side of Harriet. The bed was so small I was obliged to hold on to her, to prevent myself falling out. She turned round her bum towards me and got close to the cook, which gave me more room; and for a minute we all three lay as close as three herrings in a barrel.

Darkness encourages baudiness. Harriet had tucked her clothes tight round her, but I could feel her bum outside, and there did not seem much of it. I tried to push my fingers between its cheeks, and there was much struggling and quiet complaining on her part, and joking on mine. Harriet appealed to the cook to help her, but she only chaffed and chuckled. At length putting my hand towards the bottom of the bed, I got hold of her night-gown end, gave it a pull, and it came clean up, the next moment my naked body met hers from her heels to her waist. She gave a howl, cook said, "I'll go into young devilskin's room, and leave you to take care of him," got up and went across to my room and into my bed; and there was Harriet and I in bed alone.

She seemed furious, I felt her over, she was powerless, I dared her to call out, and at last in one of her writhings to escape my fingers, getting on her back; I rolled on to her and pinned her under me with my weight; but her legs were tightly closed, and so for a moment I laid my stiff prick between the shelving of her thighs, the tip just laying buried in the hair of her cunt.

"I can feel your cunt with my prick, I am on it, let me do it," said I, and struggled to force her limbs open with my knees.

"No," said she. Again I asked and got a request to get off. "Not if I lay here all night," said I. I did lay for some minutes, she complaining of my being heavy, and hot, I every minute trying to wriggle my prick between her legs, coaxing and kissing and begging. "What made you think of coming here with both of us in bed?" said she at length. "Wanting you." "It's funny," said she, "and Mrs. °°° downstairs." "You know," said I, "that unless you bawl she cannot hear." At length I told her that if I did not do it inside, I must do it outside, and began shoving my prick up and down, which made her restless. She asked me if I would tell the cook. "No." Gradually her thighs opened, I slipped down between them, and felt my prick at the portals of her cunt.

The rest was quick enough. I felt my way through a mass of hair to a low-down slit, a hole which seemed tight, and as I guided my tool, fancied for an instant I was again going to have a virgin. I was mistaken, but the entry needed a hard, sharp, and painful push to me, and a comparatively easy passage followed. No sooner did

I feel up than all came to an end; spending copiously, I sank on her, long before the strokes could have told on her sensations, for in a savage voice she said, "Now, get off, I hope you are satisfied, and that beast Brown has got me as she thinks. Now, I suppose you are going."

I rolled off, but let her know I meant to stay. There seemed something odd about her which awakened my curiosity. The knob of my tool seemed to catch as it came out and hurt me, so I began feeling, which I had not done before nor did she want much solicitation to feel me, and as she did so, it struck me she was not unaccustomed to the feel; but her cunt was a wonder, it was so small and tight on the outside. The feeling had a good effect, and in half-an-hour I got up her again. And what a difference! After a few thrusts she gripped me like a vise, she did not heave, but writhed and wriggled in a way which in my young experience I never had noticed before; she threw her long legs round me, and with her equally long arms tried to feel my balls from behind. Then a certain feeling of constriction in her cunt seemed to hurt, but it brought me to the crisis just as, with a last wriggle and sigh, her limbs relaxed, and she became quiet. I laid for some time in her, but although gradually reducing, my prick did not come out. I attempted to withdraw it, and it seemed sore and as if something caught the knob and kept it back. At length out it came, and we both fell asleep.

Some one pushed me. It was the cook. "Now, young devilskin," said she, "be off, or you will be found out." It was broad daylight. She pulled the clothes off us. I was on my back with my privates visible. There lay Harriet on her back asleep also, with everything visible from her knees to her breasts, and I saw for the first time her black cunt-fringe. The cook grinned and awakened her. Up she got, off I went to my room, and found my prepuce torn at the top, raw and all but bleeding.

When I saw them the next day, Harriet was savage, for the cook was chaffing her. The next night I again turned the cook out and had Harriet. On the third night the cook was restive. "You may do what you like together, I shan't take any notice of you," said she, "but I am not going to be turned out of my own bed." When I began to fumble about her, with the view to annoy her into leaving, she struck out right at my ballocks, saying, "If you annoy me,

I will soon settle you for the night," and it ended in Harriet coming into my bed-room.

I examined every part of her body much against her will, nor did she fail, when she warmed under my overhauling, to look at me. But a woman is soon satisfied, and when she has squeezed the balls and looked at the tip, she has done. Some men — and I am one — are insatiable and could look at a cunt without taking their eyes off it for a month. So I satisfied myself well, and at times afterwards, — for she was a peculiar and an unpleasant woman in every way, one of the out-of-the-way ones not often met with, and one I never want to meet again.

She was quite five feet ten high, her face was sallow and nearly white, her eyes sloe black, but with the look of a dull serpent in them, her mouth large, long, and straight, teeth white and large, and the whole were shown when she laughed, and then she had half the look of a wild beast. Whenever she smiled baudily, her look was still more unpleasant; when thoroughly lewed, her eyes opened on you with a still worse stare; often, just before she spent, I have seen them, and they startled me.

Her hair was jet black and magnificent, it fell nearly to her waist; her shoulders were broad, but there was scarcely more breast than on a girl of fourteen, and seen sideways she looked more like a man than a woman. Her ribs you could count as she lay; she was very wide across her hips, but she had almost as little flesh on her buttocks, as on her shoulders; her belly was flat, and as she laid down seemed to fall in, and the sides rose to the two projecting hip-bones; in fact she seemed to want filling up all over, and yet she was not a skeleton.

Her legs were thin, her thighs seemed closer than in other women's. I used to say when fucking her, "Open your thighs." "They are open," she'd reply, "they are the same as other women's." She had a huge conceit of herself, and if I said other women's seem to open more, used to reply, "What do you know about it?"

Her cunt was set in a quantity of longish black hair, strong but not very curly. I didn't much like the look of that. The slit quite hidden by the hair was long and the lips thin; of inner lips she had none, and the first idea as I pulled aside the hair was that the cunt was large; instead of that, low down, and near to her arse-hole was a hole not bigger than that of a girl's of ten years;

you saw both holes quite close together. Her cunt was in fact a study. Something seemed to bar the passage; for about an inch further up it seemed smaller. The whole thing seemed out of proportion, yet I could not say how, or where that deformity was, with the experience I then had.

Her arse being so flat, her cunt-hole so low, and her thighs so close, my prick as it entered seemed to bend under in some way and hurt me; my tight prepuce was often torn rudely down, and frequently bled. When I probed her cunt with my finger, it never seemed to have the soft buttery feel I had been accustomed to, but to be harsh; so I found it best to wet my prick copiously with spittle when I had her. Then off we used to go; she raising her long legs until her heels were above my buttocks, writhing and wriggling under me and finishing her pleasure with a sort of snort. Then my prick would be up her until quite small, when with pain at the knob, I pulled it out, making a sucking noise as it came away; nor do I think till pulled out, that any spunk left her, such a fit it was at the mouth.

I had much opportunity with her for a few weeks, and she took good care that she would have her fill of me. She took sleeping with me as a matter of course. I used to awaken and find her twiddling it up. If I went up to my room in the middle of the day and Mrs. *** was out, she came up directly, and I had her, for I felt ashamed to say I did not want it. I am not sure, and at that time did not know much about the thing, and how little a woman really lascivious will stop at, but believe that in the night when I was asleep, she used to suck me up; for I have awakened and found her with her face upon my doodle, kissing it. She asked me to kiss her black pussy, and now think she must have wanted me to lick it, but did not then see what she wanted. There was one thing I did with her which I had not done before and which the flatness of her backside favored doing, fuck her from behind, both laying on our sides, and it became my favorite way. I used to go to sleep after my spend with my prick up her in that fashion; she with her long arm put between her thighs clutching my balls.

I was constantly at her, and more by her randiness than mine. The cook used to grin and say, "Well, young devilskin, you seem jolly well knocked up," and made Harriet savage by saying, "Have a little mercy on him." The cook now took no notice of me, she was a coarse beast, would go to the servants' closet leaving the door wide open, and begin to talk with me as I passed; Harriet called her a beast one day for doing so.

I found that the cook, after going to my room, used to go down again. Harriet would let her out, and she stayed out all night, Harriet letting her in in the morning. One night Harriet did the same, saying her mother was ill. I spoke to the cook about it; she said, "Her mother! pugh — she goes to see the baker." I began to feel very uncomfortable about these tricks, in case it came to my mother's ears, and that I knew of them.

The cook asked me to look carefully at Harriet's belly, and explained to me that I should find certain marks of her having had a child, and to tell her (cook) if I did. I could not find them. "I am sure she had had one for all that," said cook. I never told Harriet what I had looked for. The cook one day said, "If you tell Harriet what we have done together I will split on you both and tell your mother, I don't care a damn for the place and am tired of service," so I held my tongue. Harriet always declared she was a virgin until she had me, and that the cook had had two or three children. I did not tell Brown that, for fear of a row between them. Another night that Harriet stopped out, the cook said, "You may come to me if you are frightened to sleep alone." I went. She undressed, pissed, and farted; but seeing her fat form, into the bed I got. When I was stiff she said if I would tell all about my doings with Harriet I might poke her as I liked. I told her most that she asked me; but she threw my prick out just as I spent for all that.

Things were now uncomfortable, they quarrelled so. One night I asked Harriet, who was frigging me up, whether the baker did not do it enough to her. She dropped my tool, rushed across to the cook, said that she had been telling about her, and made such a row, that even my deaf relative was awakened, and came out of her bed-room asking from below if anything was the matter. I was on the landing when I saw the light and hopped across to my own room in a fright. Up came the old lady, the cook came out and said, "Harriet is very unwell Ma'am, can you give her a little brandy?" I had no fuck that night. The next night she began about the baker. I would answer nothing. She said, "If I have had him it's my affair; at all events it's an insult to a woman whom you never gave the slightest present to yet."

I was struck with that. My allowance was due, and I took her home some article of jewelry. She made me for the ensuing week fuck her till I was as dry as a bone, and my very arse-hole ached the last time I did it, — it was the day before my mother returned. She sat on the side of my bed and frigged me for a quarter of an hour before she got it stiff, saying that I did not seem to like her as I used to.

My mother and sister came back. I never got a poke for a fort-night. When mother returned, nothing would get it out of her head that I had not been out late of night; it never *could* be got out of her head that it was late at night that did the harm. Not being able to get Harriet now, I waited for her one night as she went to the library. As I got near a wall by our house, I saw a man and a woman standing close up against it together; the man went away directly I approached, and I saw Harriet. "There was a man with you?" said I, "Yes," said she, "it was the baker, whom you have heard such stories about, I am going to marry him." I pulled up her clothes, and to my surprise she resisted, for the first time, saying, "I want to piddle," which she did, and then I had her. Her height made an uprighter easy, her quim did not seem to need so much wetting as usual.

A day or two after this event, I came home; my deaf relative opened the door. Finding that she was laying the cloth, I asked, "Where is the servant?" My mother said, she had turned both the hussies away, and the people who gave their characters ought to be prosecuted. With heart beating, I asked what was the matter. "It's not needful for you to know," she replied, "they are a bad couple." I saw at once I was not implicated, so asked no more, nor did I ever see them again, though, about ten years after, I met in the streets a tall, gaunt, haggard woman who stared at me, and I think it was Harriet.

For some years this episode seemed a funny one, especially the cook's uncunting me just as I began to spend, but of course I know now why she did it, or fancy I do.

Her inciting me to get Harriet also astonished me, but I have since found girls anxious to get others into the same way as them-selves. Many I am sure like doing that, and all girls who have been fucked illicitly like other girls to do the same.

Harriet was a lewed bitch. I never liked her, and her cunt al-

ways gave me pain as well as pleasure, but she was at hand, and so
I got into her of course. I can't even now make out what was the
matter with her cunt; for though she would let me look at it at
times, she always hindered a quiet inspection; besides, I could not
at that time of life look at a cunt for a minute without my cock
standing. Then I rushed it up the machine and had done for a time.
I had seen one virginity, but that was but for a minute, for I pricked
it directly. All I recollect afterwards was that it did not look as open
as other cunts, I could not describe it. I did not care about virginities and never thought about them. I liked best a good, large, fat-
lipped, hairy hole into which my prick glided easily. When Harriet
said I took her virginity, somehow I felt sure she was lying, but had
it been true I should not have noticed it, as far as my pleasure was
concerned.

CHAPTER XI

Charwoman and daughter. — At a key-hole. — Cutting corns. — A shower and a barn. — A fat rumped Devonian. — Suggestive pictures. — A bum-hole offered. — Erotic madness. — Remorse.

We could not get servants for some time. A middle-aged charwoman came to assist, and one of her daughters came from time to time, stopping generally the night. Their cottage was not far off, I had seen the girl from an infant, she was then about eighteen years old. I had often smiled when I met her, of course I smiled now. She was quite a slim little girl, there was nothing of her, but I was at an age when anything having a cunt attracted me.

Profiting by experience, I now used key-holes; fortune favoured me, for, for some reason, instead of one large bed, two small ones were put into the servants' room; between them a wash-stand and a chair on each side of it were nearly opposite the key-hole. How I chuckled at this, for unless the key-hole was covered, I could see nearly all one bed and both chairs and wash-stand. I saw the old woman wash and use the pot, put on her stockings and other things; the other bed was a little out of range. I could not so often see the girl, but did at times.

One evening the girl only stopped. So soon as I heard mother's door closed, out I went in my night-shirt, and through the key-hole saw the girl naked. She put the light on the floor, one leg on the chair, and with a small handglass looked at her quim, her bum was towards me. Not satisfied she turned round, sat down facing me, putting the candle on the floor and with legs as wide open as she could went on with her investigation. I had a reasonably good look at her, and her cunt. As said, she was nothing to look at, but I got in a fearfully excited state and made some noise at the door which alarmed her, for up she got and stood still listening. I went to my room, looking through the half-closed door, hers opened and out came her head. I nodded and back she went.

The next day she was going home, and as I now (although having rows with mother about it) went out when I liked, just before she left I went out and walked. It was dark. In two or three minutes out she came. After walking by her side for a time I asked her point blank how she liked the look of it last night. "What do you mean?" I told her all I had done. "Oh!" she said with intense surprise, "what a mean thing to do." I told her how one of our former servants used to look at me naked. After a minute she did not appear to be at all disconcerted at having been seen naked; from my description she could have had no doubt whatever that I had seen all. "What did you look at your quim for?" asked I. "Ah! that's my business; what did you look at me for?" "To see your cunt." Being at a dark part of the road I began kissing her, and got my fingers on to her belly. She made no row, but crossed her legs; and small and seemingly weak as she was, succeeded in preventing me feeling. I was out with her an hour, kissing, coaxing, attempting; I got my fingers and hand over her bum and belly, but not on to her slit. At each failure she laughed and said, "Done again." I swore I would some day. "No you won't, you're not the first that has tried," said she, and I went home without having felt her quim properly.

I attempted it the next day and at every opportunity in the house and out of it, till new servants came. She felt my prick, would look at it, squeeze the balls, talk about fucking and baudiness to any extent, tell me what she had seen and what she had heard about such matters. She at length scarcely resisted my feeling her bum, belly, and legs, yet I never got my finger on to her slit, so as to feel the moisture; for she closed her little legs and wriggled, or got away from me somehow. Once or twice when I got a little rough, she set up a squeal, and I desisted. I offered her money. She replied, "No thank you, I am not going to spoil my chance that way." Our conversation used to begin by my saying, "How is your duff?" "Oh! nicely, thank you; how is your jock?" "All right, and stiff, waiting for your duff." "Then it will wait a long time," and so on. It always ending in my trying to feel her, and getting no further. At length they left, new servants coming.

I frequently saw her afterwards, and always began the same

game. My mother was told I had been seen talking to her, so after that I only spoke to her at dusk. Some time afterwards she married a gardener, and I occasionally saw her, but recognition came to a knowing nod and smile, which she always returned. Meanwhile I had got my fortune, as I shall tell, had no end of women, and had forgotten her when, walking across a field not far from our house, I overtook a short woman with a little child, and it was she. A shower came on, and we went into a barn, no one was in it. She told me I was said to be a "dreadful chap after the gals." "You know all about that now," said I. "Yes," she replied with a grin, and gradually talking baudier, we went on, until in a few minutes I had laid her down and fucked her on the hay. "I told you I would do it," said I. "But you didn't when you said you would, — now it won't matter." That was her notion. The rain continuing, she said she must go, whether wet or dry. Neither of us had an umbrella. She pulled her gown over her head, and saying, "You won't tell anyone, will you?" took the child by the hand and was going, when my appetite came again. I pulled her back, and with little persuasion, again went up her. She enjoyed the fuck greatly. As I lay on the top of her we heard a bang, and the barn grew dark; a man was shutting the door. "Ulloh!" said he, "I didn't know any one was there; I hope I ain't disturbed you." We made no reply, but out we went. "You will have a boy out of this," said I. "I hope I shall," said she. That was the end of my adventure, for I never had her again, and she soon left the neighborhood. It was her own little child that was with her.

Though I have (as I shall in other cases) told all I had to do with her consecutively, yet between the time when she was in our house and the time of meeting her at the barn, three or four years must have elapsed; and didn't we talk baudy in the barn before I got into her. That may have warmed her up, yet I believe she wanted me, as soon as she found herself alone with me. Her little child witnessed the business.

Just at this time or a little later, an adventure of a serious kind occurred to me.

The streets leading out of the Waterloo Road were then occupied much by gay women. Some were absolutely full of them; they were mostly of a class to be had for a few shillings if they could not get more (my Granby Street adventure has been already told), but many a swell I have noticed lingering about there. My mother now took nearly all my money for my board, but with the little remaining I had a knock off occasionally. It was one of my pleasures to walk up these streets when dark and talk with the women at the windows, which were always open whatever the weather, unless some one was within engaged with the ladies.

Each woman had generally but one room, but two or three used to sit together in the front room in their chemises. There was the bed, wash-stand, chamber-pot and all complete. Perhaps one lolled out of the window, showing her breasts, and if you gave such a one a shilling, she would stoop so that you could see right down past her belly to her knees, and have a glimpse of her cunt-fringe. Sometimes one would pull up her garter, or another sit down and piddle, or pretend to do so, or have recourse to other exciting devices when men peeped in.

I used to look in and long. Sometimes had a shilling peep and then bashfully asked for a feel of the cunt for it. I so often succeeded that, ever since when I wanted that amusement, have offered a shilling for a feel and met with but few refusals in any part of London. Sometimes it ended in a fuck. Once or twice to my astonishment they took mere trifles, and, as I think of it, there is wonderfully little difference between the woman you have for five shillings, and the one you pay five pounds, excepting in the silk, linen, and manners.

One night I saw a woman with very fat breasts looking out of the window (I was then fond of stout women); and, after talking a minute, asked her if she would let me feel her cunt for a shilling. "Yes," said she. In I went, down she shut the window, and in another minute I was groping her. She did not let me feel her long. I had not felt such a bum since Mary's (already told of), and it so wetted my appetite that I struck a bargain for a fuck. She was soon stripped, and all I now recollect about her is that her cunt was large and covered with hair of a brownish colour; that her eyes were dark; and that she seemed full twenty-five years of age. I fucked her on a sofa.

When I had buttoned up, she produced a book full of baudy pictures, of which I then had seen but few; and I went a second time, to see the book rather than her. Looking over it, she pointed out to me, with a laugh, several pictures of men putting their pricks into women's arse-holes, and into the rumps of other men. Having never before seen such pictures, and having no idea of the operation, I felt modest and turned to others; but she so regularly, as we turned over the leaves, pointed out this class that my sense of shame gave way to curiosity; and, not believing, asked if it was possible to do it so. "Lord yes," said she. "Does it not hurt?" said I. "Not if properly done," she replied, and went on to say it was delicious, some men thought; and she talked altogether in a very knowing way about it; told me how it was best to grease the hole first, then the prick, and to shove gently, and went on so that I said on a sudden, "Why, you have done it, I think." "Yes, but only with a particular friend of mine who is very fond of it, — and so am I; it is better than the other."

I felt shocked, bewildered, and excited. The subject dropped, but she sat feeling me, slipping her finger under my balls, and pressing my arse-hole with her finger. I prepared to fuck. She suggested she should kneel with her buttocks towards me, so that she could feel my balls when my prick was up her. I assented, and her bumcheeks were presented to me. Excited by her conversation and her hints, I looked curiously at her large slit, and then at her bum-hole; I touched the latter, and she drove her bum back upon my finger with a laugh. I did not take her hint, but drove my prick into her quim and pushed in the regular fashion. Thinking of the pictures excited me, and without knowing what I said, I suddenly pulled it out, saying, "Let me put it into the other." "Not tonight," said she, "put your thumb a little way in, your nail is quite short (she had noticed that I used to bite my thumb-nails short)." I instantly did, the next moment spent, and dropped over her back, waiting for the last drop of sperm to run off into her.

Her hints, her pictures, of which she had actually scores, stirred my curiosity; her manner disgusted me, yet my brain seemed affected. Is it possible, thought I, that a man's prick can go in there? — Impossible. And yet she says she has had it done to her, and my thumb went in easily enough. The more I thought and the more I reflected how a hard turd hurt me sometimes in passing it, the more I was puzzled about the intense pleasure which she said the operation gave! To solve my doubts (although I had determined not), I went to her again, and saw the pictures. She again talked about them, until, scarcely knowing what I was doing, "Will you let me?" I asked. "Yes, if you do what I tell you." I consented. "Don't talk loud," said she, "it will never do to let any one know what we are at." Our voices dropped to a whisper, whilst by her advice I pulled off trousers and drawers, and she stripped stark naked.

Then she carefully greased my prick with pomatum, and put some on her arse-hole; it was the work of a minute, not a word was said. She then, start naked, sat by the side of me on the sofa, began fondling and kissing me, took my hands in hers and rubbed my fingers on her clitoris, half frigged herself with my fingers, I let her do what she liked. Then she turned round. "Put it in," she said when her rump was towards me, "then give me your hand, and don't push till I tell you." Her arse-hole was at the level of my prick as I stood by the side of the sofa, my machine was like a rod of iron, my brains seemed on fire, I felt I was going to do something wrong, dreaded it, yet determined to do it. "Put it in, slowly," said she in a whisper. The hole opened, felt tight, but to my astonishment almost directly my whole prick was hidden in it without pain to me or any difficulty. "Give me your hand." I did. Again she began frigging herself with my fingers. "Rub, rub, push gently," she said, and I tried, but was getting past myself. "Now," said she with a spasmodic sort of half cry, half grunt. I felt my prick squeezed as in a vise, I shoved or rather scarcely began to do so when I discharged a week's reserve up her rectum. My brain whirled with excitement, whilst she, leaning over the pillows on the sofa, kept breathing hard and half snorting like a pig, still frigging herself with my fingers.

As my senses returned, I could scarcely believe where my prick was; excitement still kept it stiff, but desire had left me. I pulled it out with an indescribable horror of myself.

"Wasn't it delicious?" said she. "I like it, don't you? you may always do it so." What I replied I know not; I washed, dressed and got out of the house as soon as I could. When in the street, I was sick. I ran off, fearing some one would see me, got into a Hackney-coach and drove in the wrong direction; then got out and went a round-about way home, fearing some one was following to upbraid or expose me. I scarcely slept that night for horror of myself, never went up the street again for years, and never passed its end without shuddering, have no recollection of having had pleasure, or of any sensation whatever; all was dread to me. And so ended that debauch; one I was deliberately led into by that woman, having never thought of such doings before as possible, or at all, as far as I can recollect.

CHAPTER XII

Sarah and Susan. — At the key-hole. — A village fair. — Up against a wall. — An unknown woman. — Clapped again. — My deaf relative. — Some weeks' felicity. — Sarah's secret. — Susan's history. — Sarah with child. — Amidst black-beetles. — Susan's virginity. — Susan with child. — Sisters' disclosures. — A row. — A child born. — Emigration.

I had now passed my twentieth year. The new servants were sisters (how many times have sisters fallen to me!); the eldest, who was cook, was named Sarah; the youngest, Susan. Sarah was about twenty-six, Susan nineteen or twenty. I carefully arranged the key in the key-hole of their door the first night, but saw nothing for two or three nights. Then, oh! fortune again. They rose later than my mother liked; she came up to their room one morning and found them locked in, so she took away the key. Now I had, as far as the key-hole permitted, a fair field, but then clothes hanging upon pegs on the door were often in my way; yet I was so persistent in looking when they went to bed, and arose, that I saw a great deal. How cunning I had got; I had filed and oiled the lock and hinges of my door and theirs so that I could close and open them noiselessly, used to stoop daily with my eye to their key-hole, stepping from my room with naked feet. I was nearly caught several times, but never quite. It now seems wonderful that I was not. I was so demure and quiet in talk about women always, and had kept myself so circumspectly, that my mother never had the least suspicion of me, — but in all matters of love and intrigue, mother always seemed to me as innocent as the babe unborn.

For all that, my mother just then, and to my dismay, seeing that my little games would be much interfered with, said I had better change my room, and have one on the first floor. Mrs. * * * had remarked that, being a man now, I ought not to sleep on the servants' floor. "As you please, — it's one flight of stairs less for me, but Mrs. * * * is a fool," I said. "And which room?" "Your sister's. Annie will always be with her aunt (adopted), and Jane is only at home on the holidays." But I would not be pushed into a small room; where was my tub to stand? where my books? I must have the spare room. There was much altercation, I made my mother cry by saying that when of age I would get chambers away from her, and into the spare room I moved.

It was next to my mother's. Installed there, I did nothing but complain of its inconvenience. I smoked incessantly in it. The smell got into mother's bed-room, and she could not bear tobacco smoke. I made a noise when she was in bed, — that annoyed her. I did all in a quiet way to make her as uncomfortable as possible. An uncle and aunt, who stopped with us when in town, just then came from the country; and, not liking my sister's room, went to an hotel, which wounded mother considerably, so she said I had better go upstairs again. I refused point blank; being down there I would remain, and so managed that she thought I went back as a favour to her and much against my will; but was I not glad! — and got to my spying immediately.

Within a month I had seen them both start naked, for being sisters they had not hesitated to strip. I had seen the cook piddle, wash her cunt, and put on her napkin. Susan's bed was not on the right side for me, but nevertheless I saw enough of her to compare her with her sister. Sarah was demure in manner, stout, with a splendid bum, and with little hair of a lightish brown at the bottom of her belly; she wore black stockings, of which I then had a horror. Susan had a wicked, merry face, and splendid bunch of dark hair on her motte which attracted me largely. It struck me that I should have a better chance with her than with her sister, and began making approaches, when one Saturday night, seeing Sarah wash herself from head to foot, I got such glimpses of her round, fine haunches, and the split between them, that I fell into a fit of randy adoration, which settled the direction of my attentions to her instead of Susan.

I feared to go on with either, because they were sisters, but lust got the better of my fears. I began kissing cook Sarah; who returned it, saying she would not have her sister know it on any ac-

count. Shortly after I kissed Susan, who made nearly the same remark; and I found that each was careful not to tell the other; which
was just what had occurred with two sisters of whom I have already
written. This was very jolly. Meanwhile I once or twice had a cheap
poke on the road, but always with fear of disease.

I had but little chance of the cook having now no pretext for
going into the kitchen, and the sisters were not much separated;
but I looked up my chances indefatigably, and finding Sunday favorable, to the horror of my mother, left off going to church in the
morning because the cook was then alone. After our early Sunday
dinner, I used to go to my bed-room, nominally to lay down but
really to look through the key-hole at cook who, on that day only,
dressed and washed herself in the middle of the day, her sister
being downstairs. I got on but slowly, in two months only having
taken outside liberties; till, meeting Susan coming away from the
privy one day, I saw her press her clothes against her belly to dry
her cunt, and she saw me. Whenever I met her afterwards I used to
tuck my frock-coat between my legs and smile at her. It was an old
dodge.

I had then bought a *Fanny Hill*, which I kept in my bed-room
locked up. One morning I forgot to put it by, thought of it and
rushed upstairs, entered the room where the servants had been making the bed, and saw Sarah intently looking at the book. I had
feared that my mother had entered my room and seen the book. I
stood for an instant motionless, she turned round, gave a cry,
dropped the book, and rushed out of the room, her face like blood.
I locked the book up, feeling somewhat uneasy, but afterwards
joked her about it and the smutty pictures, and this took effect.

There was a fair held not far from us at that time, the girls
were to go there each on separate evenings. Before Sarah went out,
I went out, she had agreed to meet me at the fair; it was dusk,
she had a female friend with her. We went into a dancing booth
and had drink, then into the long rows of stalls in which was a dense
mob, shouting, crying, pushing each other, scratching backs, blowing trumpets, and speaking baudily to the women. As it got later,
the men used to feel outside the women's cunts, and many a so-
called modest girl felt a man's prick outside, and passing in the mob
without being found out. Many a grab have I had at my prick

which could only have been done by a woman, who looked quite demure whilst she did it. I got excited, put Sarah in front of me, and in the first rush, put my hand round and gave her cunt outside her clothes a grab. She upbraided me, rushed out of the crowd at the side to escape me, I after her, into a dark passage between the backs of the booths, where men were pissing. They hailed her with laughter, asking her if she had come to piddle. Back into the crowd she rushed, I with her, and did the same thing, talking baudily, and kept this up until it was time for her to go home.

I said I should walk home with her. The village-road had but occasional oil-lamps; at places it was quite dark, loving couples were walking or turning off into dark bye-places by hedges and fences to satisfy their amatory wants. This I pointed out to her, and talked of the prints she had seen in *Fanny Hill* that morning. Altogether she had gone through enough that day and night to make a female randy. Suddenly a girl in the dark squealed, and a masculine voice in the dark shouted out, "That's right, shove your prick well up her, old boy." I tried it on with Sarah on the way home, but it was no go, I felt her bum and thighs, got her hand on to my prick, but she would not let me have her.

Next night I was at the fair and met her sister Susan there by chance. I got excited and tried the same dodge with her, she had also a female friend with her. I pressed their bellies and pinched their bums when in the crowd; her friend went off with her young man, then I had Susan alone and tried pushing my hand against her belly, more than ever; she took no notice. Her friend and we then met again face to face in the mob. I had an impression that a feel at my balls must have come from her friend. We all went to a public-house and had drink; there suddenly she bid me good-bye, saying it was late and she must get home, set off running, and was out of sight in a minute.

I had no intention of going home, but after thinking an instant ran after her, saw a woman squatting who got up as I neared her; it was she. "You have been piddling," said I. There was some joking on this. The same sort of couples were to be seen cuddling about as on the previous night; the same whispering, squealing, and scuffling a little way off in the dark lanes. She was more frisky than her sister, and more talkative. "Ain't they larking!" said she as a girl gave a half giggle, half cry in the dark. Said I, "They are fucking." She stood stock still for a minute, and then walked on quietly without saying another word. I had not before said a baudy word to her.

Having got the word "fuck" out, I was game for anything, rattled on baudily; at last, after a long silence, something I said made her laugh. I began kissing her, at length she returned it, the next instant I thrust her up against a wall, pushed my hand up her clothes, and my fingers on to her slit, which was as wet as a slop-pail. She cried, "Oh! you vagabond," got my hand away, took to her heels, and ran off, I after her, till we both stopped breathless.

I tried again, her resistance grew feebler, she was silent, I had her against a wall, one hand holding her cunt, with the other I was guiding my prick to it, it was sliding in, in an instant it would have been up her, when putting down both hands she pushed it away saying, "Oh! gracious God, what am I about again," ran off, and never stopped until she had rang our house-bell.

I went back to the fair and later on met outside it a very short girl, who seemed too respectable to be by herself and had her veil down. I spoke with her, found she was going my way, and walked with her. She knew my name, and where I lived. Two nights scrambling had not got me a poke, that I suppose made me bold enough to make advances to this modest, quiet, girl; I stole a kiss, then another, then a hug, then a feel, and finally, with scarcely any hindrance, fucked her. We walked and talked when it was over, she would not tell me her name or address, nor give me a glimpse of her face; I fucked her again up against our own garden-wall, insisted on knowing where she lived, said I would walk till I saw, and did walk with her for about an hour. She said, "If you walk about all night you shall never know where I live, but you may do it again if you like, or I will meet you to-morrow, but I dare not let you see where I go." I feared I could not poke again, so stopped to piss. She modestly walked on a little; I frigged my prick until the steam was up, then in her well-moistened cunt consummated, and parted, promising to meet her the next night.

I looked at Sarah and Susan the next morning, took opportunity of reminding each of them that I had felt their cunts, bragged to each that a young lady who lived close by had let me do it to her. The next night came, the unknown girl did not keep her appointment, and the following morning found I had the clap. I never saw or heard of her again, nor knew who the young lady was who gave it to me. She was not a common domestic, I am sure.

This stopped me for a month, but the time was not all lost, for I indulged in baudy talk, and familiarized both servants with it, and the fact that they had felt me, and I them. The eldest used to look uncomfortable, Susan used to brazen it out with such a bright, roguish eye that I then almost turned to her, especially as Sarah still wore black stockings; but then Sarah had such fat white thighs, and a larger bum.

When better, and I was again alone with Sarah on a Sunday morning, I got her on to a chair, pulled up her clothes all round, exposed her legs, showed her my prick, showed her the pictures in *Fanny Hill*, got her excited, but did nothing more. Another Sunday I tried it on unsuccessfully. The third Sunday, going upstairs, just after mother and Tom had gone to church, she said she was not going to be worried with me, and Susan would be at home. Susan had not, I found, gone to church as usual. Baulked, I was going out, but, catching her in the hall, tried to pull up her clothes. She said, "For God's sake don't, I would not let Susan hear for the world." This confirmed me in what I had felt nearly certain of; the sisters did not tell each other of my games. I heard Susan say to her sister, who had gone to the top of the house, "I shan't lose my outing, there is nothing the matter with you," and out she went. The next minute down came Sarah; I stopped her on the landing, by my mother's room.

"Now don't," she began in a coaxing way, but I had not spent for weeks, and as I looked into her bright eyes and flushed face, meant that day to do so if I could. She must herself have wanted it, there was such a soft look about her. My reply was to try to pull up her clothes. We struggled, pushed against the door of mother's bed-room, and staggered into the room together. Nothing could have been more favourable. I got her up against the bed, her clothes up, my prick against her belly, and there for a minute we struggled.

Opposite my mother's was a small, low sort of bedstead called a child's, I don't know why. It was covered with a large skin on a mattress. Mother used it as a sofa. My prick was actually up against Sarah's belly, my balls nestling in the hair of her cunt, my hands tightly round her bum, but her legs were so close together, that I could not get into her; I put one hand down to open the road to her cunt, but could not manage it, though her resistance was growing less. She ceased praying me to leave off, but tried, by putting her hands down, to dislodge me from her belly, withdrawing her hands as they touched my prick. The blinds were down, no one but us in the house, I saw the child's bed, pulled her towards it, I going backwards. We fell on it together, she more than half on the top of me; another struggle, and her petticoats were flung up as I rolled her round on to her back. She tried to pull them down, bringing her knees half up to meet them; I saw her buttocks beneath and recklessly pushing with my hand, a finger went half-way up her cunt. Down went her legs quite straight, the next instant I was on the top of her.

I weighted her down, she lay panting. "Now do, Sarah dear, be quiet." She said not a word, nor looked at me. I pressed my knees, and with difficulty opened her thighs, and we were belly to belly; with one or two vigorous shoves, in went my prick without difficulty, and spending as it entered. So did abstinence, desire, and excitement tell on me. It has often behaved in the same way.

I was now at a time of life when I could do more fucking, and after long abstinence, if I liked a woman, could sometimes do it twice before withdrawing. The first words she uttered were, "Oh! let me go downstairs, the dinner will be spoiled." But what did that matter to a man whose prick was stiff up a cunt! So I waited my second enjoyment; and if I know anything about the matter, you, my dear Sarah, brought your liquor out to mix with mine.

Scarcely was my prick out of her, before the street bell rang; downstairs she ran, I went upstairs. I recollect how wet my hair and my balls were as I ran, wrapping them up. It was her sister. Directly afterwards, home came mother. Dinner was served, what a row there was, the meat was not done, the vegetables smashed. "It is disgraceful," said mother, "has she been upstairs, Walter?" How queer I felt at that question, and wonder my confusion was not noticed. I said I did not know. "I will be bound she has," said mother, "and been trying on her finery before going out to-night. Sundays and dress are the ruin of servants now-a-days." "I have been out," said I to mother. "You would have done yourself more good had you been at church," said she.

After dinner mother went up to her bed-room as was her custom, to doze on the small bed; the next minute her bell rang violently. "Send up Sarah," said she angrily to Susan, and up she went. I went into the hall, listening, in a funk. "Why don't you keep my bed-room door closed?" said she, "as I tell you." "I am almost sure it was closed when I went out." "Have you been in here?" "No m'am," stammered the poor woman, "the nasty cat has been up here on this bed (luckily the cat had done that once before) and been scratching up the skins. "You must have opened the door, — and oh! the beast has made some mess upon it." Mother told Sarah to wipe up the place; it was only marks of what Sarah's overflowing cunt and my prick had dropped in our hurry. A little more blowing up, and mother's anger was over. Sarah came down, looking more dead than alive, when I saw her in the hall.

In the evening Sarah went out, and I to church, — so mother thought, — but in reality to meet Sarah. For an hour we walked about, then as it grew dark began kissing. What a difference the morning had made. No resistance now, my hand roved over the smooth bum and belly, a slight objection on the part of the thighs as my hand touched the hairy covering, but for an instant only, then as of a right the fingers felt the moist lapels, which were soon opened by my prick, as I fucked her up against the wall of the garden, at the very spot where, some weeks previously, I had fucked the unknown lady and caught the clap.

Good and bad luck come in heaps. I was now in for the good. Next Sunday, and others afterwards, we had a nice half-hour on her bed, or my bed, or on the sofa in the parlour; but we left no signs of the cat anywhere.

My mother then went on a long visit to my aunt in H°°tf°°d-shire, wanted me to go, but I could not get away, so she took my sister from my aunt's, and Tom, and to my delight took Susan. Sarah was left as servant, the deaf female relative came again to take charge of the house, and we three were alone in it. My deaf relative slept in my mother's room. My mother's last words were, "Give as little trouble as you can, and I hope, Walter, you will keep out of bad society and not be out late." I was mostly to dine with my guardian's executor, an old family friend.

That night, and for several weeks, Sarah and I slept together; it was a honey-moon. My old relative, deaf and timid, used to lock her door; I used to go across to Sarah's and lock it, mother having put back the key. We had fear of being found out, but not much. In those weeks we gave way so to our passions that we were worn out. I taught her all I knew; she was willing, docile, and did all I told her; love's amusements in every variety which I then knew of did we try; never had I had such continuous fucking. The first thing mother on her return noticed was that I was pale, and then great was her astonishment when told by my old deaf relative that I had scarcely been out one night after seven o'clock, and up early most days; so my mother put it down to close attention to my studies, for I was preparing.

I told Sarah in confidence I had had a virgin, and that there had been difficulty with her, but none in getting into Sarah. She swore by all that was solemn that she never had had a man, that although she had been kissed and tried, no man had put his hands on her naked thighs until I had. From what she had heard of girls' virginities, she thought she must have been different from them; she could always easily put a finger up her cunt, and I believed her. She spent the second time I did it to her.

Talking excitedly about her virginity and her not having bled when first pierced, she remarked, "Susan told me that when she — " Then she stopped and turned the conversation, but my curiosity was whetted. I pressed her to tell more, she got confused, said it was her cousin Susan, would not go on to say what Susan had said, at last refused to say more. I did not forget it, and one night as I lay kissing her and fingering her clitoris, she told me, under promise of the greatest secrecy, that her sister Susan bled when her young man first put it up her, and with this, that Susan had been seduced and had a child; so her father had sent her to service in London, and, the better to get her taken care of, had arranged that her sister Sarah should always take service in the same house with her; hence at my mother's. "And, oh!" she concluded, "if Susan or father should ever know what I have done, I should die." The family trusted her.

This accounted for the somewhat forward manner of Susan, for her exclamation when I got up against her belly on the night of the fair, "Gracious God, what am I about again!" Sarah believed Susan could have had no one else but her first sweetheart, and that was more than a year before. All this set me thinking, and more than once, when twiddling Sarah's cunt, I thought of Susan's with the thicker and darker hair and wondered in what other respects it differed from that of her sister.

Now came trouble. Sarah said she was two months gone with child; she had kept it to herself, hoping her courses might come on. She got with child she thought the first day I fucked her. We were both in great anxiety, but did nothing to help it. Sunday morning usually passed this way. Directly they had all gone to church, up came Sarah to mother's room or into the garden parlour, there I looked at her belly to see if it was bigger, then she had a crying fit, then we fucked, then she went down to see after the meat roasting, then generally we had another fuck, and all was over for that day; for my prick usually came out of her not long before Susan rang the bell to be let in.

At length her state began to show, her mother just then was very ill and wrote to her, she made this an excuse for asking to go home, intending to try when there to get rid of her encumbrance. My mother with great objection let her go, for she liked her. For one or two weeks before she left, someone or other had stopped at home on Sundays, so I was baulked in getting at her, and only did it once to her in nearly a month. I gave her what money I could to help her; a charwoman came to work in her absence; it was arranged that her sister should do most of her work as well as her own, as far she could.

My mind reverted to what Sarah had told me about her sister. Would she not like a doodle up her again? how she must long for a man, I used to think. She nearly let me coming from the fair; what if I tried again? Then I thought how wrong it was, seeing what I had done to her sister. But back again the desire came; I grew randier. "I won't try her on account of her sister," thought I, "but there will be no harm in larking with her."

So I began and reminded her of the night of the fair, told her I knew that the hair of her motte was dark, by degrees got her to kiss me, to leave off chaffing her, felt her outside, but went no further. About the fourth day after her sister had left I got my hands on her thigh. On Sunday, when all were at church, to blind my mother I had gone out, but went home directly and into the kitchen to resume my baudy chaff, I forgot all about her sister, got to kissing and trying to feel her. I was long in the kitchen with my prick out, sometimes hanging, sometimes standing stiff, trying to induce her to let me, but it was of no use. Her cap was off, her hair dishevelled. I had got her clothes once up to her hips, had seen her motte, felt it, got my prick up against it, knocked it about all over her belly, but no more; time was short, and at last with a sort of guilty fear I went out before church was over, and came back in time for our early dinner, telling my mother I had been to °°° church. Then I reflected and thought it was as well I had not done it to Susan.

When mother returned, she left my sister and little brother in the country. My old deaf relative remained with us and slept in the room adjoining my mother's. That same Sunday night, I waited until Susan came up to bed, pounced upon her on the top landing and tried to feel her; she dropped her candle-stick and made such a noise that back I sneaked to bed, and was asleep when I heard the bell ringing violently in the servants' room. Out I rushed, saw Susan on the landing with but a petticoat over her night-dress, and old Mrs. °°° going into my mother's room, who was taken very ill.

Down to the kitchen went Susan and I to get boiling water, I heaped wood and coals on the fire, she blew it with the bellows, old Mrs.°°° was upstairs getting brandy and other things ready. What followed I recollect as well as if it were yesterday. Susan was half squatting, half kneeling and blowing the fire furiously. Standing by her my randiness came on, I pulled out my prick, and pushed it right in her face. "For shame!" said she, "I will hit you with the bellows, think of your mother." It did shame me for a moment, I hid my prick, and knelt by her side, stirring the blazing wood. But just then I saw her breasts through the half-tied night-gown; it was too much for me; that, and the attitude she was in together; losing all prudence, I pushed one hand on to her breast, and the other up her clothes, between her legs, — which were very conveniently opened quite wide, — and on the slit of her cunt. With a suppressed cry she dropped the bellows, attempted to rise and repulse my hand, and in doing so we both rolled backwards (for I had stooped) on to the floor among the black-beetles, of which there were dozens about. "You wretch," she cried in a suppressed voice, "Oh! don't, — and your poor mother so ill, — oh! don't, — you shan't! — and wanting hot water, — you shan't!" in a still louder tone as I got my hand full on her cunt. "Oh! my God, here is Mrs. °°°." Had Mrs. °°° not been as deaf as a post, she must have heard our scuffling, as she neared the kitchen.

In an hour or so my mother was better, and Mrs. °°° stopped in the room with her for the night. My mother was asleep when I left, Mrs. °°° had had a good dose of brandy and water, and I knew she would sleep well enough. I went to my room, excited by the continual trying it on with Susan; Mrs. °°° had given her a glass of brandy and water, "to keep the cold out," as she said, and she went to her room. I listened, heard her moving about longer then I expected. I had come up some minutes before to deceive all, and was shivering in my night-shirt. I thought how unfair it was to her sister, who was in the family way by me, of the risk I ran with my mother in the house; but a standing prick stifles all conscience. I crossed the landing, opened her door, shut it rapidly, and there I was in the room with her, both of us in our night-dresses. She was doing up her hair as I entered, she wore a night-cap.

"I won't let you come in here." "Hush! mother will hear you," said I. Her voice dropped to a whining, "Pray go, I shall lose my character, if any one supposes anything of this; it's very hard on me." Such was my state that I believe if my mother had come in just then I should have tried Susan. My reply was to strip my nightgown right off and stand naked; then I caught her in my arms and forced her into a sitting posture on the bed-side, sitting myself down beside her. "Let me do it, — let us fuck, I have felt your cunt, — seen it; — look at my prick, — let me put it in, — let me do it, — you did nearly once, — let me now." "For God's sake, go!" "I won't." "Oh! don't, — oh! go, — if Missus should hear us, what will become of me?" "Don't make a noise, then, or she will." "Well go, there is a dear, — not now, — perhaps some other day I will. She was defenceless, I hitched up her night-gown, saw a pair of nice white thighs. "You shan't, — you shan't," she cried in a louder tone, pushing down her night-gown. I gave it a violent tug and pulled it up to her belly, saw thighs, navel, and dark brown hair between her thighs, that I had looked at in glimpses through the key-hole. There was my thigh close to hers, my stiff prick within a few inches of her cunt; considering all she had gone through that day with me, it was a position which would have upset the frigidity of an angel, had she not frigged away some of her passion in the interim.

But her passions were conquering on my behalf, for she was a woman who had known love's pleasures; her voice was quiet as she said, "Oh! pray don't, oh! pray now." I pulled her back and slid my naked limbs between her thighs, then in a moment I was on her, but in an uncomfortable position; two of our legs on the bed, two off, my belly touched hers and pressed her down; with my right hand I guided my prick to her slit. Her hour had come, "Oh! for God's sake, leave me, I will let you another day, — I will, — not now, — oh! if you knew! — oh! now! — oh! . . ."

It was all but over, my fingers were feeling their way, my prick between them, every motion she made to help herself, helped me; I held her down with force until I felt my penis was on the notch, but as it touched the slippery sides of the red orifice, the first pang of pleasure came and my sperm spat on to it. With a furious thrust I plunged up her and threw my whole body over her, grasping her bum, quivering, wriggling, and pushing. The deed was done, she knew it, and was as quiet as the grave.

The position was painful to both of us, I felt it in both my legs; she moved uneasily saying, "I hope you will go." I had no such intention, kept her down, and my prick in her as long as I could; then got up quickly, hoping to see her spunk-trap whilst her thighs were open. A woman seems always up to this, how quickly they shut them. She did, but the light, though feeble, was close by, and I saw sperm outside; then she sat at the side of the bed with her limbs uncovered, I stood naked with doodle wet, flabby, and shrunken, not a pretty picture at all. She begged me to go, was tranquil, sat twisting up her hair, scarcely made attempt to hide her limbs, all her anxiety was about her mistress finding me in her room; but after a few minutes' altercation, I was in bed with her, cuddling and promising to leave directly I had fucked again.

I got into bed without my night-gown, hers was rolled up so that she was all but naked, our naked bodies touched at all points, my hands were free to rove everywhere. How she must have wanted it, only a woman with twelve months abstinence from cock can tell; and then, after feeling her cunt well and putting her unresisting hands round my pego, I pushed her on to her back, there was no difficulty about her thighs, they opened at once as I turned on to her, her frame thrilled, her tongue sought mine, her hand clutched my naked back; she spent I verily believe before I had begun, and finished again with me a few minutes afterwards. About daybreak, neither of us having closed our eyes, I went back to my room, tired out.

My mother kept her bed the next day, so Susan and I had time to talk. "I don't know what to do," said she, "we have made the sheet in such a dreadful mess," and that night, before she went to bed, she took it down and did something to it. I fucked her that day on the kitchen table.

Her sister did not return for a fortnight, and during that time we had plenty of fucking; a few nights after I first had her, she was excessively quiet; on questioning her she said, "I think I got in the family way last night." "Nonsense," but she told me she had heard that women sometimes had a sort of consciousness of getting with child, and added, "I somehow feel certain that I shall have a child from last Sunday." This will be a pretty go, thought I, and asked, "Did you ever have your belly up before, for I don't think you were a virgin when I had you." She denied it, and there the matter ended, but I never could get to see the lower part of her belly; she would let me see up to her cunt, and down to her navel, but never more. My experience might not have taught me much if I had, but I guessed something from what old Brown had told me, and knew that women had marks of some sort on their bellies after child-birth.

As the time came for Sarah's return I felt trouble could come with her. The day before she did, Susan cried, said she was certain she was in the family way, and expressed great dread of her sister knowing it. "Surely you don't mind your own sister." "Oh! you don't know how hard she is upon poor girls who get into trouble," she replied. "Here is a mess!" I thought.

Sarah returned, had tried to get a miscarriage and failed; she grew bigger, all her fear was lest Susan should find it out before she left, and on plea of her mother's health, she gave notice. Both girls were afraid of each other, both seemed determined to get as much fucking as possible. Sarah got hers on Sundays, and sometimes on week days. Susan who was more about and could often get five minutes with me slyly, threw herself in my way, got it when and where she could, and had it once or twice daily. I was not loth. The excitement of two cunts and a certain pungency in the position stimulated me. I have seen the two standing side by side, each at the same moment with my spunk in them, yet neither knowing the other's condition. At times before I had washed my prick after one sister, I was wetting it in the cunt of the other, which delighted me.

Things got desperate. Sarah said I ought to marry her, spoke of committing suicide, and, at length, unable to hide her belly, left. I was anxious to do what I could to help her, so disclosed my case to a friend, who advised me to borrow, as I was so near coming into my property. I borrowed fifty pounds of a Jew, promising to pay him a hundred pounds for it six months afterwards, and got her lodgings a few miles from our house. Susan also got bigger, and made no disguise of her intention of getting abortion.

No disclosure of the sisters to each other had yet taken place, yet I felt it would be done. One morning Susan's eyes followed me whilst waiting at table in a most unpleasant manner. I felt all was found out, so, to face it and get the worst over, threw myself in her way. "You wretch, you scoundrel, you blackguard," she whispered to me on the staircase, "it is you who have seduced my poor sister?" Soon a better opportunity was found, and we had a scene; it took place in my bed-room, when the other servant who had replaced Sarah, and my mother, were out. I could only say I was sorry. She blazed out worse than ever then, and spoke so violently about my behaviour to herself that I told her, whatever her sister had to complain of, I thought she had but little, for that mine was not the first prick which had been up her, I was sure. My words and manner staggered and quieted her; and, after making me take a solemn oath (which I did holding a Bible) I would never tell her sister that she was in the family way by me, she got tranquil, and I fucked her before she left the room.

Susan was dreadfully ill a few days afterwards, she had got a miscarriage; my mother attended to her, thinking she had inflammation of her bowels. I went to see Sarah, who told me some fellow had got her sister Susan in the family way, she could not tell who, for Susan quite refused to say. She was soon after confined with a fine child. Troubles then came apace, the mother of the two women died, Susan left my mother at once to take charge of the old man's house, and never let me have her again after her miscarriage. Then the father came to grief, failed, and was sold up. Sarah went home with her child, and after a time, acting on the advice of a friend, I advanced money out of my property which I had then come into, and sent the whole lot to Canada. After a year my child died, and Susan got married. What became of Sarah, I don't know, for all letters soon after ceased; but to the last I believe that Sarah never knew that I had had her sister as well as herself, although Susan knew I had had both of them and was father of both children, or what would have been both children.

This ended my intrigues with servants for some time, for my fucking took quite another direction. Harlots of small degrees amused me till I came into what was a pretty fortune in those days.

CHAPTER XIII

Of age. — Camille my first French woman. — Lascivious delights. — Harlots by the dozen. — Baudy books. — Tribades. — A grey-haired cunt.

I came into my property, and, to the great horror of my mother and family, soon gave up my post at the °°° and my intended career, and determined to live and enjoy myself. I had been all but posted to a regiment; that commission I resigned, though all my youth desiring it. I lost much money by doing so. What I did between the time that I had the two sisters until I went regularly on the town is not worth telling of more than already done. Frig myself I did not; gay women since my last clap I was shy of, but I used to shag a servant of a family close by, and rather think one of our own servants; but, if so, all circumstances made small impression on me, and nearly escaped my mind, excepting those of a comely woman of about thirty, with black curls, of a wall not far from a church and of fucking her up against it, of her being so anxious to get indoors by nine o'clock, and scuffling off with her wetted cunt directly she had finished with me. Her name, or who she was, I quite forget.

This I know, that I had no other woman at home and had no liking for gay women, nor is it to be wondered at, since my experience with them was confined to one I had with my cousin Fred, women by the road-side who would take a shilling, and others of a queer class in the confines of the Waterloo Road (two debauches there told of) then filled me with horror, and three claps; yet I was to leave off giving my passion to quiet women and bestow all my attention for a time on gay women.

Walking up Waterloo Place one evening, with plenty of money in my purse and lust in my body, I met a fine, clear-complexioned woman, full twenty-five years of age, who addressed me in French, and then in broken English. She had an eye and manner which fascinated me, her dress was quiet yet elegant, as unlike the French woman of Regent Street of the present day as a duchess is to a milkmaid; but she was the ordinary French whore of the day, of whom there were then but few in London (there was no railway to Paris), and who were exclusively supported by gentlemen at the West End. I went home with her to a house at the corner of G°l°°n Square, after fearing and hesitating.

As I got to the door my fear returned, and, but for shame, I would not have gone in. "I have but little money," said I, "have you not a Victoria?" said she. "No." "You will find one, I am sure." By that time the door was opened, and in I went. "You will find one Victoria," said she in broken English as she closed the room-door, "but if not, shall you not give me what you shall find." The room was nicely furnished, out of it was a nice large bed-room and a smaller one (she paid twenty shillings a week for all, as you will soon hear). Four wax candles were lighted, down she sat, so did I, and we looked at each other. I could say nothing.

"Shall I undress?" said she at length. "Yes," I replied, and she began. Never had I seen a woman take off such fine linen before, never such legs in handsome silk stockings and beautiful boots. I had had the cleanest, nicest women, but they were servants, with the dress and manners of servants. This woman seemed elegance itself compared to them. A fine pair of arms were disclosed, a big pair of breasts flashed out, a glimpse of a fine thigh was shown, and as her things dropped off, and she stooped to pick them up, with her face towards me, her laced chemise dropped, opened, and I saw darkness at the end of the vista between her two breasts.

A pull up of the stockings and garters disclosed other glimpses of the thighs and surroundings. Then she sat on the pot, pissed and looked at me, whilst I sat in fear, saying nothing, doing nothing, my cock shrivelled to the size of a gooseberry, and longing to go away. The whole affair was unlike anything I had seen or dreamed off; a quiet, businesslike, yet voluptuous air was about it, which confused me; it affected my senses deliciously in one way, but all the horrors about gay women were conjured up in my imagination at the same time. I was intensely nervous.

She, seeing me so quiet, sat herself on my knee and began unbuttoning my trowsers. I declined it. "Are you ill?" said she. I told her no, scarcely knowing what she meant. Then she unbuttoned me in spite of my objection, laid hold of my little doodle, and satisfied herself that it was all right I suppose; for she hurt me; I could not tell why she squeezed it, for I did not know then the ways of gay women. The squeeze gave me a voluptuous sensation, although fear had still hold of me; then she kissed and fondled me, but it was useless. Then she said, "You have never had a woman before, I see." My pride was wounded, and I told her I had had many. "Are always you like this with them?" she asked. "No, but I really did not want it." "Oh! yes you shall. Come to the bed." She got off my knee, went to the bed, laid down on one side, one leg on, one dropping down to the floor, drew up her chemise above her navel, and lay with beautiful, large limbs clad in stainless stockings and boots, her thighs of the slightly brown color seen in Southern women, between them a wide thicket of jet-black hair, through which a carmine streak just showed. She raised one of her naked arms above her head, and under a laced chemise showed the jet-black hair in the armpit. I had never seen such a luscious sight, nor any woman put herself unasked into such a seductive attitude.

"Come," she said. I obeyed and went to the side of the bed, my prick not yet standing. She took my hand and put the finger on to her clitoris, pulled my prick towards her and kissed it, and at the double touch up it rose like a horn. "Ah!" said she, moving on to the middle of the bed, "take off your clothes." I was on to her without uttering a word and had plugged her almost before I had said "no," which I had meant to say.

What a cunt! what movement! what manner! I had till then never known what a high-class, well practised professional fucker could do. How well they understand the nature and wants of the man who is up them; hers was the manner of a quiet woman, who had been some time without a prick, it was so like baudy nature in a lady that I was in the seventh Heaven. My crisis came whilst she kept murmuring, "Don't hurry"; but the wriggle and heave, and the tightening of the cunt, kept hurrying me, as well she knew.

I had scarcely finished my spend when curiosity took possession of me. She yielded in the way a French woman does to all a man wishes, almost anticipating them. The black hair under her arm-pits first came in for my admiration, then her eyes, her bubbies came in for their share, as raising myself on an elbow, my prick still up her, I looked and felt all over her, I even opened her mouth and felt her teeth, which were splendid. Then, rising on my knees, I looked between her legs, at the splendid thicket of black hair. Far from attempting to get up, or prevent me, she opened her thighs wider, I pulled aside the cunt-lips, there rolling out from a dark carmine orifice was my essence. At the sight of it, up came my prick, still dripping, and up it went into the sperm-lined passage.

My second fuck over, she washed. No sooner was that done than I wanted to see it all over again. "You are very fond of women," she said, "I thought you had never had a woman before." Then I explained, gave her the Victoria, and, scarcely daring, said (for she was dressed again), "How I should like to do it again." "You take up much time of me, but you may, if you like, at side of de bed." Out came my prick, up it went, her duff and belly in sight now, till I spent in her, and, promising to see her again, I left. One does not get silk stockings, laced chemise, four wax lights, and three fucks for a pound now, if rooms be well furnished or not.

I saw her the next day, then saw her almost daily. Little by little I took to calling at all times, and sleeping with her. The more I had her, the more I liked her. She was a very nice woman in most ways, I scarcely ever found her untidy, dirty, or slammerkin. If not dressed, she had a clean wrapper on, had nearly always silk stockings on, and a clean chemise; and therefore, call when I might, she was ready to be fucked at a minute's notice. She was a good cook, and would cook omelettes and nice things in her room. I used to fuck, get out of the bed, eat, and fuck again with the food almost in my mouth. I used to have little dinners in her room, sent in by a French cook, which were excellent, and then, with stomach full and with nice wine, would spend the evening in baudy joys.

What astonished and delighted me at the same time was the freedom and the way she lent herself to all my voluptuous inclinations. The gay women I had had I had fucked as fast and got away from them as soon as I could; my spend even scarcely finished at times. With my mother's servants (my first love Charlotte excepted, and for a time with Susan), my enjoyments were mostly hurried, a fingerstink, a frig on their cunt, and a hurried look were all my amatory preliminaries for the most part; because I was too impatient for the spend, was mostly obliged to seize opportunities in a hurry, or because the girls were impatient at being pulled about. When I had tried with them some of the little amatory amusements which were beginning to suggest themselves to my voluptuous imagination, they resisted, or only half lent themselves to my will. With Susan I had tried the most, because I knew she had had a bumbasting before, and she had been more willing; she liked pulling my prick about, but even she made a fuss one night when I wanted to fuck her with her bum towards my belly, and never let me look at her belly. Thus my baudy longings had never been satisfied. With Charlotte I did a little variety, from curiosity; now I began to want it from voluptuousness. The natural impatience of my age, and my few opportunities, had led me to bring my women to the bed, throw up their clothes, pull open their legs, give a rapid glance at their thighs, belly and cunt-fringe, by which time my prick was nodding and throbbing. Then followed a grope, and the next minute I was fucking as hard as I could.

With Camille all came like new to me. She even anticipated me. If I pushed her to the side of the bed, she fell on her back and opened her legs gently, disclosing her slit in the most voluptuous manner, without speaking. If I strove to open her thighs, open they went as wide as she could make them, leaving me to open, shut, pinch, frig, or probe her cunt, as I listed. At a hint, she with two fingers would spread open the lips to enable the fullest inspection. If I turned her round, she would fall on the bed arse upwards, like a tumbler. If I cocked up a leg, there she kept it till I pulled it down. I scarcely ever said what I wanted, she guessed my desires from the way I turned her about. It was only at a later time, when my baudiness grew whimsical and invented strange attitudes, or singular caprices of love, that I had to tell her what I wanted; but at first I was too timid for that. She once said to me, laughing, "I am a born whore, for I like it, and like to see a man amuse himself with me."

Her every movement, even when I was tranquil, was exciting. If she sat down, her limbs were in some position which by contemplation stirred my lust and made me rush to stroke her, and was gratified in any form and manner I liked. With her, all forms of copulation were wholesome and natural, so that I had enough variety.

I was constantly with her until pretty well fucked out, then I stayed away a while. When I recommenced she, I expect, thought I was weary of her and set to work to keep me, by putting into my head things I had not heard or thought of, asking if I would like to sate my lust in such and such ways; and then procuring for me what she had suggested.

I was indeed worth treating so, for though I only gave her a sovereign at first, my money quickly began to go into her pocket from mine. The more variety I had, the more I paid, which was but natural and fair.

She had a book full of the baudiest French pictures; there was not an attitude depicted in it that I did not fuck her in. That done, she asked me one day if I would like another woman to feel whilst I had her. She came, and I fucked Camille feeling the other's cunt, longing to fuck it, but fearing to propose it. Camille guessed what I wanted and proposed it herself. With what joy my prick entered the stranger's split, Camille looking on, holding her cunt open for inspection at the same time and going through the motions of frigging herself whilst I was shoving. Then came endless variety. I had two other French ladies and fingered their cunts whilst I fucked a third, then two more, laying cunt upwards, legs in the air, and arses meeting over Camille's head. At last I had six altogether at once, and spent the evening with them naked, fucking, frigging, spending up or over them, making them feel each other's cunts, shove up dildoes, and play the devil's delight with their organs of generation, as they are modestly called.

Then came other suggestions. "I know such a little girl, not above this high," she said. I ballocked that little girl. Then she knew one six feet high. She also I had. Then she knew one with an immense duff of hair on her cunt. Of course I had her. Then one with none at all; and mightily pleased was I, as my doodle rubbed in and out of that hairless cunt, the owner laying at the side of the bed, I standing up, and Camille holding a candle over the hairless quim, to enable me fully to see and enjoy the novelty, I was pushing up.

At intervals, when worn out with spending, or disinclined to find the money needed for this endless variety of women and cunt-hunting, I frequently spent evenings quietly in Camille's society. I got from her information about habits of women in a way which is not often given to young men by gay women; learned that women thrust sponges up their cunts, to prevent men finding out they had their courses on. For the first time with her, I understood that women could, and did, frig themselves; and on her own cunt, placing herself my finger there, I first knew the exact spot where a woman rubs for her solitary pleasure. She told me of women rubbing their clitorises together so as to spend, — what the French call tribadism, — and two women of her acquaintance did this. All of us half spoony with champagne after a jolly little supper; she set the two girls rubbing their cunts together. The two girls on the top of each other I thought a baudy amusement, and did not believe until after years that flat fucking was practicable, and practised, with sexual pleasure.

Then should I like to see a man? Now it was not many years since I had frigged two or three, and seen a frigging match, which did not please me, so I declined it. Yet one night she expatiated so much about the wonderful size of a young man's prick, and what a lot he spent, and how respectable he was, and what gentlemen had him, etc.; that I, who had a dislike to men being near me, consented, and a fine young Frenchman came. I could not for half-an-hour go near him, but my temptress meant I should, and I frigged one of the largest pricks I have ever seen, and saw his spunk squirt over Camille's arse, which the Frenchman requested her to turn upwards for him to spend on; indeed he said he could not make his cock stand until he saw her arse. Directly afterwards I had the most ineffable disgust at him, myself and all, and never saw him again.

I would not again be in the room with a man, but she arranged to let me see, through a hole made in the door, herself fucked by another man, which I immensely enjoyed, but had not the sight repeated. I even used to hate the idea of her being fucked by any one but myself; not that I had anything in the way of love or liking for her, which might have been termed affection.

So time went on, I paying handsomely, trying to see and do anything she suggested, and glorifying myself at being in the lucky way of doing and knowing everything. I told much to some special friends, some of whom wanted to find out my sources of such enjoyments; others thought I was a mere braggart.

Nearly a year ran away, and four thousand pounds, leaving me with infinite knowledge and a frame pretty well worn; but I never had a love ailment, nor have I ever taken one from a French woman yet.

She never suggested arse-hole work. In her book were pictures of buggering, and she asked me if I would like such a thing. I frightened at what I knew, which seemed like a horrible dream, said, "certainly not," and asked if it was possible. She told me it was, but was "*villaine*," and the matter was never again referred to.

With much fucking I got done up, and one night could get no cock-stand. She asked me if I had ever played at minette. I did not know what it meant. She told me it was having my prick sucked. I told her no. I have already narrated my licking the slightly haired cunt of young Martha, and how when doing so, she having my prick in her hand close to her mouth, and was playing with it, when scarce thinking of consequences, "Kiss it," I said, "put it in your mouth"; and that the young girl randy with my licking, put it to her mouth or tongue, and that I immediately shot out my spunk without meaning it. That remained in my recollection as a nasty subject. The big-cunted woman also sucked me against my will. So when Camille suggested it I refused. There was another French woman with her; they were both naked on the bed, and I had been fumbling both, and baudily amusing myself, with no cock-stiff or fucking desire about me. After a while I laid down on the bed with them, the other French woman told me, that some men never did anything else and that she would like doing it to me. She had found out I was pretty liberal, and I dare say counted on my being so now, if I could get by her a new sensation; but I declined. The two women were laying in the reverse direction to me on the bed, so that I could see and play with both their cunts, a favorite posture with me then. After extolling the sensation of minette, she without my consent turned over me, and getting me between her knees back up, and so that her bum-hole and cunt were within a few inches of my nose, she began; whilst Camille who knew what would fetch me better than I knew myself, moved up her backside, so that I might grope her more freely. The double cunt feeling, the suction and sight generally, was too much for me, and the mouth soon drew my sperm with long lingering and half painful pleasure. My tender-tipped prick suffered, as it often did indeed when in the proper receptacle.

The act made some impression on me, for I soon after had it repeated by the same woman, and she did it that time so that I saw the prick in her mouth. I expect it upset me instead of giving me pleasure, for I stopped her, and my doodle dropped; but I permitted her to recommence; then I felt something press my arse-hole, it tickled and hurt me, I called out, "What are you doing?" At the same instant spent. "What have you done?" said I. "Nothing," said she winking at me, for Camille was in the room. I did not like the business; she had shoved her finger or thumb up my bum-hole. I was too young to appreciate that luxury, took a horror at her, and never would have her again, nor would I have my prick sucked any more. Many years elapsed before I either had my arse-hole felt or felt a woman's, after that night.

Then I had an old woman. Those she had brought me had mostly dark-haired cunts, and her own was black. As cunt was an inexhaustible subject with me, we were always talking about it. She said she knew a woman whose hair was quite grey. "Is she very old?" "No not above fifty." That was older than my mother, and I could not think of it; but the conversation was renewed. "She has got as much hair as me, but quite grey, nearly white, and she is a nice clean woman; have us both, and you can see the black and white together."

So a fattish middle-aged woman, certainly fifty and who seemed to me sixty, came; her hair was nearly white, Camille lent her stockings and chemise, to make her decent I suppose, and the old woman, who spoke scarcely a word, but drank furiously, turned up to me. She made some objection to showing her grummit, re-marking she did not know it was to such a young man, but being told if she did not, she might go without pay, the sight came off; the cunt-fringe was nearly white. She was an English woman. Camille suggested I should have her; the old woman demurred, but Camille settled (and I really used to do almost what she advised), that I should have her and look at the grey cunt at the time. So it came about; but when half up to spunking time, Camille said, "Take it out of me and put it into her." When a prick stands and novelty is in the way it rushes at it. Out I pulled my prick, and put it up the grey cunt, spent in it, and pulled it out almost before I had finished. I never saw the old lady again.

CHAPTER XIV

Piddlings. — Posturings. — Breast and arm-pit. — A turn over. — Used up. — Wanting a virgin. — Camille departs. — The Major's opinion. — Camille returns. — Louise.

I have told the most novel fucking bouts I had with, or through, Camille, excepting the final one; but should say that whatever women she got me I turned to her with pleasure again. Sometimes, when I had one or two to amuse me, I used to give her the preference for the fuck, and she always had one of the gruellings, for she was very handsome, understood everything, was sensuousness itself, but not vulgar. When I had a fit of extra lewedness she got me other women. Of course she got profit out of all, a thing I knew nothing about then. Often I had no want but for her, and she used to strip herself, or dress just as I wished, put her body into some attitude, then lay and read the paper whilst I used to sit and read as well, looking up from time to time at her. Then I would put her in a new attitude, and go on so for a time; then would make her piss, catch it in the pot, piss at the same time in it, stick a dildo up her cunt, and have every variety of amusement I could think of. She was always willing, never in a hurry, never refused. A charming harlot.

Making her piss was a favorite amusement with me, I would keep her a whole day without doing it, so that I might have a good long stream out of her when looking on.

I was most curious about the way a cunt opened and shut in squatting, it was the subject of my earnest investigation. I used to put two chairs so that they would not slip, nearly close together, and lay down with my head between them. Then Camille, naked all but boots and stockings, would stand up on the chairs, one foot on each; the legs, naturally a little open as the chairs were a little apart, just disclosed the cunt. Then she would sit down slowly, so that I could gradually see the gap widen, the red nymphœ show, the clitoris jut out, and at length the whole cunt-gape ready for the piss. Then she would rise slowly and repeat it till I was tired; then, still laying down, I used to hold a large basin on my breast and belly, and, squatting above my head, she would piss into the basin. I would feel the cunt, and if very wet, dry it. In all this she was obedience itself; she never moved from one posture till I told her to get to another, would answer any question with frankness.

I have never lost this pleasure in seeing a woman piss, but at that time was too impatient to vary the amusements which a man and a woman can have with their piddle. It was reserved to me with other women, notably a French woman named Gabrielle, and Sarah F**r, to have the fullest variety and enjoyment in that particular.

I had fucked Camille in every way excepting her arse-hole, I had spent between her bum-cheeks, but without the slightest intention of invading the bum-hole between them, — indeed then had a great dislike to looking at a woman's arse-hole. At last fucked her arm-pits; she had a splendid arm, and an unusually large quantity of black hair beneath it which I much admired. One day she was poorly, I began fucking between her breasts, she suggested another woman, I would not have one; from her breasts I got to shoving between her arm and her breasts; then she wetted her arm-pit with Castile soap, which is of a soft slimy nature, and I fucked and spent between it. After a time we improved on this; she would lie in a convenient posture, I would lay a sheet of clean white paper on the bed, and just as I was coming, protrude the tip of my prick so as to free the pit, and shoot my spunk on to the sheet of white paper; or would catch the spunk in my own hand, and before my frenzy of pleasure was over rub it on her cunt, then fling myself on the bed and go to sleep.

I used to have her at the side of the bed with her bum towards me; then she would gradually twist herself round, and cocking one leg over my head, get herself with her back on the bed without uncunting my prick. This had to be done very gradually, for a jerk, and my prick used to slip out. I used to bet with her about this, and she generally managed to twist round and win. "Now push, — keep it well in, — hold on, I am going to lift my leg," she would cry

at the difficult point, which was when she had got her bum sideways to me, and was about to lift her leg; then, putting my hands
well on her hips, I used to draw my belly to her, and prick into her,
as tightly as I could, whilst she gradually raised a leg, and, pressing
her bum up to meet my pressure, gradually got on to her back,
with her limbs in a natural, easy posture on either side of my
hips. By that time I had got steam well up, and a shove or two
usually let me off.

At last having done as great a variety of ballocking, and learnt
more baudiness than most men of my age, I was knocked up, fucked
out. My mother with whom I still nominally lived, was in despair.
My guardian, alarmed at the rate I was spending my money, re-
monstrated, so I left Camille and her bevy of women, and went to
the sea-side. There I renovated, and then spent my time on the
sands, trying to see the women in the water. As I grew better my
randiness returned, I got hold of gay women, but my old timidity
clung to me, I used to pay them to piss, and had a grope up them;
but do not recollect having anything more. I came back to London,
and for two or three days afterwards Camille's cunt had no rest.
Then I temporarily got into another servant, and ceased to see
Camille much. She tried all sorts of inducements to continue it on
the old footing.

Then although she knew every incident of my life, she took
to asking if I had ever had a virgin, saying, "Are you sure, did you
see her cunt before you had her? Would you not like one again, if
I can get you one, a young virgin French girl, one sure to be a
virgin?" — and so on until she made me doubt if I had ever had one.
At last I thought that I should like to have another. Well, she could
get me a young French girl, but would have to go to France, it
would cost a large sum of money. This talk went on for some time,
and little by little I agreed to give her fifty pounds to pay her journey, and also to keep her lodgings on. She postponed the journey
for a long time, but at length she went. She made me promise to
do something for the girl besides paying her, — which meant something or nothing, — but I promised to pay the journey of the virgin
back to France, should she want to go; and also whenever I had the
girl, to pay Camille a Victoria, "because," said she, "you will have
my rooms and prevent my bringing friends home."

So I came down with fifty pounds. Off she went in quiet dress, and looked a quiet lady or middle-class woman. She advised me to keep myself steady, and the very moment before she left, whilst the cab was at the door, I turned her with bonnet and travelling dress on, bum outwards, and fucked her; she hurrying me all the time for fear she should loose the coach, she had not time to piss, or wipe, or wash. "It will give me good fortune perhaps," said she, laughing, "or make you wish me back, it is lucky for me."

There was but a slow rail to Dover then, nothing but tidal boats, and to Paris, the way I thought she was going, no rail at all, and it was a long journey. Whether she went to Paris or not I don't know, but from later experience think not, that she was a Southern woman, and went straight home. She was to be back in a month. It came, but not she; another week, another, and I began to think I had been sold; another, and I gave her up altogether, and experienced a little relief, for the habit of seeing her had so got hold of me that I could not shake it off, and yet I was tired of her, but I wanted the virgin.

There was a middle-aged man with whom I chummed much at my Club, a major retired, and a most debauched individual. He borrowed money of me, and did not repay it. His freedom of talk about women made him much liked by the younger men; the older said it was discreditable to help younger men to ruin. Ordinarily very careful how I spoke about women (for my loves having lain much in my mother's house, caution had become habitual to me), I one night talked about virgins and of getting them. He said such things were done; that Harridans got a young lass, if well paid for it, but that they generally sold the girl half-a-dozen times over, "and," said he, "they train the young bitches so, there is no finding them out; you may pay for one who was first fucked by a butcher boy, and then her virginity sold to a dandy; you may pay for it, my boy, and not find out you have been done." I pondered much over this, and the next night returned to the subject. His opinion was that an old stager like him was not to be done; but that any randy young beggar would go up the girl, and flatter himself he had had a virgin, if the girl was cunning. "When you see the tight covered hole with your eye, find it tight to your little finger, and then tight to your cock my boy; when you have satisfied your eye, your finger, and your cucumber, and seen blood on it, you may be sure you have had one, — and not otherwise."

Thought I, "I am going to be humbugged." Another week, no letter, I went to her lodgings, and found she had taken away everything she had with her. That night I told a little of my hopes to the Major, not telling him who the kind lady was, or where she was gone; but it made him laugh. "You are done brown my boy, done brown; that woman will never turn up again." He joked me so that I avoided him, and kept the subject to myself afterwards.

Again to the lodgings; the landlady could not keep them vacant any longer; I paid the rent, but she got no perquisites; I increased the allowance. Then again I went; the landlady said she did not expect to see her again. I had now set my heart on having this virgin; ten weeks nearly had gone; I said if Camille was not back next week she might let the rooms. It passed; a bill was put up in the window, and the next morning calling as a forlorn hope, there was a letter for me, — she would be back in a week. I was in a state of excitement that week and kept myself chaste, with the idea of the virgin cunt, and Camille's well paced rogering in anticipation.

The day came. I was so impatient that I was there quite early; she arrived some hours earlier than she had said, and seemed surprized at finding me; my impression is that she did not want me to be there when she came back. She came in a hackney-coach; a stoutish full-sized young woman with a funny bonnet and long cloak on, got out of the coach with her, and in a free-and-easy way helped the things upstairs. She called her Louise. The wench put down a big box, and, on my turning round after giving Camille a kiss, I saw she had seated herself on it and, hands on her knees, was looking at me. "Uncord the box," said Camille. Said the girl, "I am tired." She uncorded it, again sitting down and looking at me said, "Is that your young man? — He's a good-looking fellow." Camille told her to hold her tongue, to go on unpacking, and that I understood French, eyeing her at the same time in a savage way and looking at me at times very uneasily. She was a rough sort of girl, she said, a relative of a friend of hers, had come as her servant, and in a short time would understand her place; smiling at me in a knowing way as she said that. Camille always addressed her servant in French, me in English; but I understood French tolerably well.

Louise did as she was told, but bounced about in an independent way, threw off her cloak and bonnet and, putting her hands on her hips, stared at me again. I stared at her, thinking of the virginity I was destined to break up. Certainly she was appetizing; her cloak off showed a thick woollen dress of dark brown, striped with blue, a fine big figure, a couple of big breasts; her arms naked nearly to her shoulders, as French peasants usually wore them, were large, fleshy, and brown; the petticoats were half-way up to her knees, and showed the thickest woollen black stockings on a stout pair of legs, and feet in thick shoes with brass buckles; she had immense gilt earrings, and was in fact in the dress of a Bordeaux peasant woman.

I did nothing but stare at her, Camille nothing but scold her, talking to me at intervals. The girl got the boxes ready for opening, then walked about, taking up poker and tongs, chimney ornaments, and everything in the room with curiosity. Camille and I had so much to say that we took little notice of her; then she threw up the window and looked out. As she bent forward, her short petticoats showed her legs up to her knee-backs; Camille was about to stop her looking out when I winked and, stooping, saw a thick roll of stockings just beneath the knees, and the flesh just above. Camille understood. "Madame, madame," said the girl, "come here, here is fun." I heard Punch squeaking in the streets; she was delighted; her mistress went to the window, giving me a knowing look, and, looking out of the window with the girl, put her hands over the girl's petticoats and lifted them up slightly. Louise took no heed of this, being so engrossed with Punch; I dropped on my knees and saw half-way up the girl's thighs. I had been chaste for a few weeks, or nearly so; the sight of Camille had fired me, the thighs finished me; I shoved my hands up Camille's petticoats on to her arse, got her into her bed-room, and with her clothes in a lump on her belly, drove up my prick, spending directly I got up her cunt.

With half my spendings outside, half inside I lay with throbbing prick, which only came out when it had spent again. Camille vowed she had not had a man for weeks, and took it out of me, perhaps fearing if I went away with stiffening left, some other cunt would take it out. The ballocking over, I went home.

I was early there the next day; Louise had been installed in the little room leading out of the sitting-room. Camille told me a great deal about the distance she had gone, and the trouble and expense she had been put to in getting the girl's relatives to let her come; she hoped I would pay the additional expenses; and that

I did at a cost of about twenty pounds. What with that and paying for her journey, and for lodgings while absent, Louise had cost me nearly ninety pounds already. Then I undertook to pay for the additional room, in which a bed having been put, an extra was charged; cooking now being done downstairs. Then Louise must have a new gown; then Camille thought I ought to give her something for herself, because whilst away for me she had made no money. That I refused and blazed up about it; for all that agreed to pay for a new silk dress for her, and a lot of little odds and ends on the second day of Camille's return, for all of which outlays I had only had a peep up the girl's petticoats.

Then I had talk about her. The girl was the daughter of a small grape-grower, a friend of Camille's; they thought Camille was in London as a dressmaker, making a lot of money, because she sent money home to her father. Camille offered to take her, saying she would be sure to get on, if not in one way, then in another; that good-looking girls always did well in London. The girl was mad to come and persuaded her parents to let her do so, believing that Camille got her living honestly; she was to be her servant until she could be put in the way of doing well.

"What are you going to tell her now? What are you going to do with her? What will she say when she finds out?" I asked.

Camille did not know. The girl would find out, and then she must excuse herself as well as she could, would say it was better, and jollier, and more money making than to make dresses. Besides, the girl could not help herself and would have to make the best of it.

When was I to have her? I asked. As soon as I could get her; there she was, and I might try when and how I liked; help me more she could not, she could not insist on Louise letting me; but no doubt she would in time, no one else should have her.

I was not so sure of that. Camille was gay, and although I had for more than a year excluded most men from the house, yet she did have other men there, and I knew they would see the girl, might like her, might pay Camille; all the remarks of the retired major came strongly before me, and I thought I was going to be sold, and said so.

She replied that I was not; she would leave me with the girl when I liked; if the girl spoke to her she would advise her to let me, but would have nothing to do with influencing her beyond that; and when the event came off, she meant to be out, so that Louise's friends could not say anything. If she went gay it was no fault of hers, young women would have it done to them, it was natural. That was the game she meant to play.

I saw that I had paid her only for bringing a girl, and must take my chance of getting into her; all she would do was to keep the coast clear. I don't know what I really did expect Camille to do, but think I imagined that she would have got the girl in bed with her some night, let me get into bed with them, and helped to make her fuck, if she would not. This was dissipated; I was to have the chance I should have had with a servant in my mother's house, or less, for this girl I should not see so often, and could not be sure she would be so well looked after.

So Camille went out, leaving me alone with the servant whenever I wished. I expect she went with other men at houses of friends, and so got her time paid for twice over and made a good thing of it; perhaps she thought the longer this lasted the better it would be for her. I think now that that was her game.

END OF VOLUME FIRST.

MY
SECRET LIFE

BOOK TWO

'WALTER'

CONTENTS

CHAPTER I

Louise sapped. — Suspicions. — Lectures on virginity with live illus-
trations. — Drugged for inspection. — Camille's hesitation. — Absents
herself. — The house in G°°d°n Sq°°°e. — Baudy prints. — A feel,
a sniff and a kiss. — Out shopping. — Garters. — Dinner and after.

I went to work to get into Louise; having no compunctions it
seemed to me the most natural thing in the world. I had read about
the naughtiness of seduction, but my associates had taught me that
every girl wanted fucking and was longing secretly for it, high or
low, rich or poor, it was the same. As to servants, and women of the
humbler class, that they all took cock on the quiet, and were proud
of having a gentleman to cover them. Such was the opinion of men
in my class of life and of my age. My experience with my mother's
servants corroborated it; and so to get into Louise seemed both
natural and proper.

I suppose there is but one way ordinarily of beginning with a
woman. A man must first make himself agreeable, then successively
familiar, endearing, coaxing, loose, bold, baudy, determined, then
if needs be fierce, or even violent. This order comes naturally to
men cunt-hunting, and ends in fucking. It does not follow that if
the early stages pass easily, that the last shall ensure success. Occasionally the woman is scared, put on her guard against herself
and the man, and the chance is lost.

This course had become familiar to me at home, and I began.
No person in the house except Camille and Madame Boileau spoke
French; there was no other to speak at all, so my conversation was
acceptable. At the end of a week I had kissed her to her contentment. No strong, healthy woman of eighteen is otherwise than
gratified by the kisses of a young man. Money I knew now told

much, and I gave some to her who had never perhaps had five shillings to call her own. She gave me a kiss in the dark passage, I hugged her and pushed outside at her cunt, she ran upstairs angry, but had forgot it the next day.

Looking at her and longing used to make me randy, then, if near, Camille's cunt got the benefit of it. The girl used to eye us when we went into the bed-room. She had a quarrel with her mistress, and said she should go home. Camille said she might; but speaking only French, and without money, how could she? Just then, through change of climate and living, she fell ill.

We were very kind to her. I got her everything. When asleep one day, Camille partly uncovered her, and showed me her limbs naked; they were so fine, and so excited me, that but for Camille, I think I should have ravished her. She soon got well, and I said, that if I did not soon have her, I should cease seeing her. "Who hindered?" Camille asked. There she was, I might have her.

Then I had a suspicious fit. All the old Major had told me about fellows being sold, and taken in by women who were not virgins came to my mind. The girl was never out but for a few minutes at a time to fetch things, yet other men saw Camille, and some might have seen and had the girl. Camille had once taken her out in a cab; she might have been to some man's. So I said I would not give the money unless I saw her virgin cunt first. After a day or two, Camille agreed to it if I would give her ten pounds down, and would swear never to disclose it to the girl.

I thought still I was to be fooled, so I called upon my old schoolfellow, who used to say, "Snatch at her cunt, and show her your cucumber." He had been one at the frigging match, and had just been appointed assistant surgeon at a hospital; he was a bachelor and baudy-minded as ever. "M°°°°," said I, "have you ever seen a virginity?" "Many," he replied, "I have dissected them, and if girls have anything the matter with their wombs, or cunts, we get a look, they don't mind a doctor. If a girl has piles, I make her turn up, and have opened several fine women's virgin cunts, asking questions all the while, if they feel this or feel that. They say yes or no, which of course I knew they would say, but they think I am very clever for asking. Some like a young doctor's fingers on their privates, though they say they object. Assistants only get the chance with the poor, the better classes have older married men."

I asked him to explain one to me on a woman, and he did. We went home with the same women; they were astonished, for instead of pulling our pricks out, we both merely felt and looked at them, and he gave me a full lecture. It was an odd sight to see him explaining the situation of a virginity, I holding a candle to see better. One of the girls roared with laughter, the other fancied they had some ailments, when they found out he was a doctor, and he gave them advice. I don't mean ailments of their cunts. We did not fuck either of the women.

From reading, his descriptions, his sketches and what he pointed out on three different cunts, I felt satisfied that I should know a virgin, and told Camille what I had done. She was then good enough to point out to me on her own cunt, where her virginity had been, as far as she could recollect it. She was quite sure about Louise, and explained that girls being with their parents in France were well watched; that the loose pricks about a town were all taken by the married women, — which I did not believe.

One night I was to see it, I waited for a signal from a window, of two lights, rushed across the road and was let in by Camille. We went into Louise's bed-room. There the girl lay in her night-dress on the bed, insensible. "We must be quick," said Camille. Then she threw the girl's clothes rapidly up above her navel, gently pulled apart her legs, and held open the lips of the girl's cunt. It was such as had been described to me. My excitement was fearful. She was a splendid limbed woman, looked twenty-five instead of eighteen years old. Her cunt-hair was jet-black, crisp and thick as on a Negress's head, grew up her mons and down beside the lips. The vermillion stripe in the midst of it was enough to drive any man mad. I put out my hand to touch it, but Camille pulled it back. "No, no," she said in a suppressed voice, "you must go, you promised me." "Let me fuck you then." "No, go at once." She pulled me towards the door, the girl was breathing heavily. Wild with lust, I pulled out my prick. "Come away, you promised, she must see neither of us." "One look more then." Again Camille opened the cunt lips. As she did so, Louise gave a groan, and turned round on one side opening her eyes wide. Camille blew out the light, and pulled me into the sitting room. "You must go," she said. I wanted to fuck her, but she would not let me.

I met a woman in Regent Street, it was raining hard. Much as

I still hesitated at going with strange gay women, I went home with her, threw her down with her clothes on. The instant I saw her cunt, and almost before I could get my prick out I spent over her bum and thighs. She remarked, "You did want it, and no mistake." I left, got down to the Italian Opera. Crowds of women walked under the colonnade, they often then wore low dresses walking. I went to a baudy house with one, and fucked her thinking of the black-haired motte and lips between the thighs of the unconscious Louise.

I never knew what Camille had given the girl. She said she had made her drunk with champagne. Louise on a subsequent day said she had got drunk with champagne, but she never knew that I had seen her on that night. I believe that something else had been given to make her insensible. There was a convulsive movement in her body as she turned round; her limbs before she did so seemed dead, her breathing resembled a groan, her breast heaved distressingly, she opened her eyes, but saw nothing. The more I reflected, the less I understood the agitation of Camille, who usually was so calm.

I had seen the girl's virgin cunt, and recollect the look of pussy, belly, thighs, and slit. The cunt-hole as I held the candle near it seemed to be covered, excepting a little perforation just big enough to put a little finger through, corresponding with my surgical friend's description; yet I seemed to have less recollection of it than of all the rest of her body. It was confused, strange, like the remains of a dream on my mind. So much had suspicion taken possession of me, that I was by no means now sure I was not being done. I paid Camille the ten pounds. When she had got them, she said she expected the fifty pounds all the same, that the cunt inspection was a preliminary she had not bargained for. I thought I was being cheated, and said so. We had a row, but such a fool was I, so much desire had I to get into this girl, — simply because she was a virgin, — that at last I agreed to it.

The girl could not get up the next day. I saw her in her bed by myself; she said she had been ill through eating something, and had had champagne. I caressed her, and spite of her struggle, got my hands on her breasts and half-way down her belly, spoke baudy, pulled out my prick, was repulsed, and gave her a sovereign. Camille came back and I fucked her. I recollect telling Camille, that there was a wonderful likeness in face, colour of hair, eyes, limbs, and even in cunt, between her and her servant. Camille laughed and said, the two families had always been thought to be much alike, and were related.

Louise became inquisitive about my intimacy with Camille. "Was I her lover? Was I fond of her?" "Yes I had been, but was not now." "Why did I come there?" "To see you, my dear."

When Louise first arrived Camille was particular in not exposing her own legs or breast to me. Before that she used in warm weather to be with naked breasts, a chemise and slippers often being her only garments. Now she got into slipshod dressing again, and began to talk baudy. She had told Louise how she got her living, and talked about making money by fucking, so she told me; but she would not let me take any liberties with her before Louise. She went out leaving me alone with her, taking my money when she returned. It is a wonder to me now how I stood all this, felt I was being humbugged, played with, and yet things went on as I describe. Three weeks had elapsed, or more, and yet I had never felt Louise's cunt. So I told Camille she was humbugging me. Louise got funny in her behaviour to Camille, said she would or wouldn't, and one day they had a quarrel, in which Louise insolently remarked about something she wanted, that Camille would do well not to show the point of her nose in the village any more. When alone I said to Camille, I was not to have the girl I supposed. Who hindered me? "Help me." "How?" Being in a blackguard humour I said, "Make her drunk, and then I will have her." No, it should never be said that that happened in her rooms; if a woman let a man of her own free will, well and good; if he got into her fair and square, good: a woman might do what she liked, — it was natural to have a man; — if Louise liked it, it was not her business; but she would not have her made drunk.

I said she was always in the way. She said she must live there. "You would like me to go out of town for a fortnight." Said I, "That is the best thing you can do." She said she could not.

I insisted, and at length she agreed to go for ten days, I paying her I think fifteen pounds and her lodgings. Off she went, and I dare say went to a friend's close by, I never knew. She said she was sorry she had brought the girl to London. Louise was not to know that I was aware of her departure. The last words she said to me were, "I suppose when you have had her you will leave me." I replied I had no such intention, nor had I; but a gay woman is a good judge of the future.

I must now describe the lodging more closely. The ground-floor was occupied by a cloth merchant; there was no shop, but in the windows were some bales of cloth, a brass name-plate was on the inner door, the top of the house was the cloth-dealer's store. The man was rarely in England, the entrance to the shop from the hall was always locked, and I never saw more than one man enter it.

The first floor Camille had. On the second floor was a grumpy old woman named Boileau; she took charge of the house. I scarcely ever saw the old woman excepting when she opened the door, and then she neither spoke or looked at me. Until Louise came, Camille had had a French servant. Some years afterwards it turned out that the woollen shop was used by foreigners for forging foreign notes: the cloth business was but a mask. Camille had been there two years.

Off Camille went. That same day I was at the house. Madame, Louise said, had gone for ten days into the country, and had left word that no one was to be let in. I went upstairs saying I should come when I liked, that as Camille had gone, we could do as we liked. She looked hard at me.

"I expect Madame has gone off with some man," said I, "she will get a good lot of fucking." She had heard me talking baudy, and knew that word in English and French. Then we had breakfast together, and I made love to her.

Louise was as vain as a peacock, and excessively fond of her stomach. When she had a glass of champagne, she used to swallow it as fast as she could. This weakness and inclination in any woman places her at the mercy of a man who will spend his money; and though I did not then see the advantage of money as plainly as I see it now, I instinctively used it.

"This is jolly," said I. "We will go and have dinner, then go to the theatre, do what we like afterwards." Her eyes sparkled, but she feared to go, for "Madame was such a demon when offended." "Who would know? The people in the house would not know what we did," I replied.

It was yet only mid-day. "Nobody can interrupt us, let's have luncheon here, I will get the wine." A French restaurateur sent in a hot luncheon. I fetched champagne, then bethought myself of something which had not occurred to me before.

Camille had as said a big album full of voluptuous pictures. When she went to fetch Louise I asked her to leave it with me till ner return. She said, "I will pawn it to you for ten pounds." I lent that sum. Since her return she had not asked for it, maybe thinking I would ask for my ten pounds. I knew now well the effect of baudy pictures in exciting lust, so I fetched it. We had luncheon and champagne, she laughed, talked, objected to sit down with me, but at last was thoroughly at home with me, and for the first time talked freely of her mistress, whom she feared. She disclosed a deal of simplicity and a very great deal of vulgarity, for she was an utterly vulgar peasant girl; but I didn't mind anything to get up her cunt.

Good living heats the body and stimulates randiness; there is fifty times as much danger in leaving a young couple together with their stomachs full of good food, than when they are empty. A gentle heat, a sense of fullness, a gentle swelling, creeps up the stem of the man's prick, the knob feels tender and voluptuous; a gentle moisture distills in the woman's cunt, heat and an all-overish feeling, from clitoris to arse-hole overcomes her. Both are then ready for fucking, and only restrained from going at it by various social reasons, which determine our actions in every-day life. Such was our state when kissing and laughing we put away the things. Then we sat side by side on the sofa, with my arm round her waist.

I produced the book, which I had brought with me. I recollected how, poring over it with Sarah or Susan, the pictures in my "Fanny Hill" used to throw them into a state of randiness which it was left me to appease. Susan used to say, that she only had to look at the pictures for a minute, to make her want "to forget herself." I took the book out of the paper; it was a large square book, which immediately attracted her attention. "What is that?" she asked. "Pictures." "Oh! show me." "Come on then." She sat on my knee, I put my left arm round her waist. "Give me a kiss." She gave it. "Now let me look." I had placed my right hand on her thigh outside her clothes, and was thinking, what a nice chance I had for throwing her back on the sofa, but I opened the first page. It was a fine, large coloured print (how well I remember it) of a bed-room. On the bed knelt two young women side by side, their petticoats thrown over their backs, and showing their backsides to their waists. Close by stood a middle-aged woman looking at them; through the door were the heads of two men peeping at the posteriors, lust was on their faces. One of the girls had a much fatter bum than the other, both cunts were visible, the hair of one black, the other, light. It was a bet as to who had the handsomest posterior, the woman to decide was saying, "Marie a gagné, elle a la plus ronde et la plus belle."

Louise gave a loud "oh!" as if taken by surprize, her face changed blood-red, she turned the cover over and burst into a fit of laughter, tried to get away from me, but I held her fast, so she put her head over my shoulder and laughed, I laughing with her. "You have as nice a bum as the dark one," said I. "There is nothing more like that, look through it." I opened the book again; under her eyes was a picture of a woman undressed, laying at the edge of the bed, her legs open, her middle finger on her cunt; by her side a man with trowsers down, his prick out stiff and crimson-tipped, one hand on the woman's thigh, and intensely looking at her cunt.

"I want to do that with you," I said. "Fie donc! C'est villain," said she, and pushed the book violently away. It fell on the floor, and at the same instant she attempted to rise. I held her tightly, and pulling her back on to the big sofa, her legs flying up, I threw up her clothes in front, showing her fine pair of thighs, and the next minute I had my mouth and nose buried in the hair, kissing and sniffing it, my hands roving about wherever I could feel warm flesh.

With a shriek, — then another, — she twisted round (in doing so my nose rubbed on her clitoris), her petticoats fell down, she got across the room to her bed-room, and bolted the door.

I stood shouting, "What a beautiful form, what thighs, how dark the hair on your cunt, how lovely my nose has rubbed on it; let me see it again, let me fuck you, have pity on me." All that suggested itself to a man whose prick was ready to discharge in his breeches did I say, but fruitlessly, she made no reply. I went back to the sofa and considered what to do. Soon I heard her moving, crept to the door, and heard the rattle of piddle. "You're piddling out of that dear cunt," said I, "How I wish I could feel it." The rattle stopped, and again I went back to the sofa.

I had told her that I would take her out, and called to her to get ready, she never answered. A few minutes afterwards I wanted to shit; it was needful to go downstairs into a yard. Thought I, "If she hears me go down she will come out; — Ah! if she does, there is the book, I wonder if she will look at it." I opened it at a picture she had not seen, tearing up little bits of newspaper, I placed them between adjoining pages, so that if opened the bits must fall out, then said, "I am going downstairs; if you won't go out, I will go without you."

I stayed at the shit-house some time, went up quietly, and heard her door close as I went up the stairs. When I entered the room I looked at the book: it was just as I had placed it, but two of the bits of paper had dropped out. "Louise, Louise, you have been looking at the book." "You lie," said she quickly. "You have, I put bits of paper in, and they have fallen out, so must have." "I have not," said she.

"I wanted to take you to see the shops, to the theatre, if you won't answer I shall go alone, and dine alone." "I shan't come then." "Don't," said I in a huff, then went to Camille's bed-room and washed. "I am going, will you come? In another minute I shall be gone without you."

"Will you promise not to be méchant?" (The French term.) "I have not been wicked," said I. She was yielding; I knew she was wild to go out with me. "Will you promise to leave off talking so." "Not forever; how can I when I have seen what I have." "I have no boots, only my thick shoes." "Come in those." "Camille has left a pair; they are too big, and there is a hole in them." But it ended in her putting them on. Dressed, she looked an odd mixture of a peasant and a servant, who had got on some of her mistress's things. I was ashamed to walk out with her; she saw something in the expression of my face which wounded her pride. "You don't like walking out with me," she said, and sitting down, big tears came into her eyes, "but I am handsomer than Madame, my feet are smaller although my leg is bigger; my shoes are shameful, she would not let me have boots like hers, she said she would send me home; *she* won't go home again, if I tell them about her." Thus she jabbered on in a fume, till she had exhausted herself, her pride wounded, excited much by feasting, by the baudy book and my kiss on her cunt. She talked so fast in her provincial French, that I could scarcely understand what she said.

I did not care what I spent, so that I could spend up Louise. "I am proud to walk with you, and I will buy you a pair of boots." She jumped up with delight. "But you shall let me do one thing." "What?" "Let me feel your leg, which you say is so big." "Volontiers," said she, "there is no harm in feeling a leg; in my country our clothes only just come below our knees," and so with joking, kissing, and a promise to let me put the boots on, out we went in a cab.

I took her to a boot-maker's, and fitted her to perfection; she was delighted, and in the cab did nothing but put up her feet to look at them. She let me feel her legs, after she had pulled her petticoats tight round the knee; I wanted to go higher, "No, no," she said; but I pushed up, on to her thighs.

I bought her a bonnet, but it had to be altered and was to be sent home in the evening; I got out of the cab and going into a shop without her, bought (guessing the size) white silk stockings and showy garters, without telling her. Then I bought her gloves, a collar, and one or two other things, and then we went to dine.

As I bought each successive article I told my wants coarsely enough. I felt her in the cab, and got so excited, that I pulled my cock out, keeping it covered with my handkerchief, removing it from time to time as I thought the sight of the cock would excite her. "The omnibus, the omnibus," she cried out suddenly. Forgetting myself and all but my wants, I had exposed my randy doodle just as an omnibus passed, and as I looked up, there was the conductor laughing at me. I went to the N****n hotel, then just opened, and ordered a dinner; there the collars, cuffs, gloves, and other things, she fitted on and looked at, and laid them down, so that she could see them when dining. Gloves she had never put on in her life before. The anticipation of the bonnet filled her with delight; it was handsomer, she was sure, than any one she ever saw Madame wear; did I not think she would be handsomer than Madame, if as well dressed? She was wild with conceit, and told me again how Madame had refused to buy her the things she wished; saying that a servant could not be allowed to wear them. This grievance had sunk deeply into her mind. Meanwhile talking, laughing, joking, sometimes saying, "Fie! fie! donc," sometimes, "Oh! villain!" sometimes giving me a kiss, sometimes saying, "Be quiet," she eat a good dinner, drank more champagne than she was aware of, got more and more talkative, whilst I got more and more lewed.

CHAPTER II

Undressing. — Silk stockings and garters. — The attack. — Foiled on the outside. — A battery. — A breech. — A tough virginity. — Triumphant. — Sanguinary proofs. — The second entry. — My foreskin. — Twenty-four hours fucking. — Gamahuching. — Six days' pleasure. — Camille returns.

"The bonnet will be home," said I, "let us go." "Allons, allons," so off we went. It was dusk when we got in the cab. "I am to put on the stockings if I give you a pair, and to feel," I said. "No man has, c'est trop fort, you ask too much; you may put on garters below the knee." "Why not above?" "Oh! quite different," said she, "in the fields no girl minds putting her garter on before all the world below knee; but above, ah! that is disgrace." Such is fashion, I have seen an Italian market-woman stoop forward and piss whilst talking to a man (a neighbouring stall-keeper): she saw no harm. An English woman would burst first, yet if the Italian had put his hand rudely up her legs, that man might have been stabbed by the woman. Louise saw no indecency up to the knees, but above was a disgrace. "Put your boots up," I said, up they went. "I may garter to there?" said I, feeling outside. "Yes." I shoved my hand up her petticoats on to her thighs, they closed, and down went the legs: a squeal, a struggle, but on her thighs I kept it until I got to the house.

We let ourselves in, the bonnet had not come, Louise opened the window to look out for it, although it was dark. A ring came, it was the bonnet; down she rushed for it. "Bring lights, bring lights," said she, taking one in her hand herself, the bonnet in the other; and rushing into Camille's room where there were large glasses she put on the bonnet, clapped her hands for joy, and kissed me saying, I was so good. She put on her gloves and collar, turning round to me each time, and asking how she looked. "Let me sleep with you, and I will buy you a dress tomorrow morning," said I. "Impossible, impossible, was I not going now," said she thoughtfully on a sudden. "No," I meant to sleep there; and as I had fetched a valise, I pulled out my things, took off my boots, put on a dressing-gown. "There," said I, "I shall sleep here till Camille comes home." "There will be a row then, and what will I do? Madame Boileau (the old woman upstairs) must know, and will tell Madame," and she looked hard at me.

Then she was attracted by my dressing-gown, which was showy, but soon began looking at herself again, and took off all her finery with a sigh. "I am so hot and thirsty," said she. It was not wonderful, for she had fed twice heavily, and been champagning off and on for hours, her hands were burning, heat was throughout her frame. "Let's have some more champagne," said I, and opened a bottle; I pulled my trowsers off, — it was so hot, — being then in dressing-gown, drawers, and slippers, I made up my mind to force her, if I could do it no other way. Then my eye caught sight of a white muslin wrapper which Camille wore, it was tied down the front with blue bows.

"Put on Madame's wrapper, if you are hot, you will look hand-somer than she does." She went into Camille's room, bolted herself in, and came out looking splendid, and had only on beneath the wrapper, her coarse chemise which I could see (as indeed I knew before) just reached below her knee. My heart palpitated, I was in my dressing-gown, she with but thinnest garments on.

The champagne was before us, we were on the sofa, my arm was round her waist; through the thin folds of her light dress I could feel her firm haunches and well-moulded body; I talked baudy, squeezed her to me, pressed her thighs with one hand, and put the other down her bosom. Every now and then there was a scuffle, a cry, and forgiveness; then resistance grew fainter, another glass of champagne, and her head dropped on my shoulder, subdued by amourousness, and when I asked her to let me sleep with her, she only said, "Oh! I dare not. I must not." I slipped my hand up to her thighs, she put her hand down stopping its progress. "If I could only get her into the bed-room, and on to the bed," I thought, and went to Camille's room, the candles were still burning. "Would you like silk stockings? Here they are." "Is it so?" said she, bounding up. I held them up before her. "Let me put them on." "The garters above knee, mind." "Yes, yes," said she impatiently, "give them me."

She sat down on the side of the bed, and let me put them on, putting one leg up after the other, I pulled off her new boots and old stockings, I saw her thighs, but she never heeded, so anxious was she to get the silk stockings on. I had thrown off my dressing-gown, and knelt in front of her as a bootmaker does in fitting on boots. I was so slow, that impatiently she said, "Give it me, give it me," pulled it on herself, and then put on the boot. I sat down on the floor, lowering my head and looking. Her silks and boots engrossed her. My prick came out from under my shirt, stiff, standing, and pointing up to her; she never saw it, but got up directly one garter was on, contemplated one leg in the cheval-glass, laughed with delight, turned round, kissed me; then on went the other. As I put that garter on, I kissed the thigh just above it, up she got, lifted her robe to see her legs, strutted up and down in front of the glass until tired of looking. Her fine limbs looked exquisite in the silks and boots.

I cuddled and kissed her, put my arm round her. "Do let me, dear," I said. I got my hand up her clothes and between her thighs, she crossed her legs without replying. "I will fuck you, I swear I will," said I as I forced my hand still closer in. "Oh! oh!" she said, and nothing more. I pulled her backwards on the bed, my cock stiff, standing, was under her eyes, drew her lips close to mine kissing rapidly; my finger rubbed the warm slit, her bum began to move uneasily, her breathing was short, her thighs unclosed, my finger slipped further. "Oh! don't hurt me," she said sharply. Pressing her backwards on the bed, I lifted her limbs, she was yielding, meant fucking. I ripped open at once the slight blue bows which fastened the muslin gown, threw up the chemise, saw the well-rounded limbs in silk, the bright red garters, the thighs above, the black hair of her cunt, rolled on to her, was between her thighs, my naked belly on hers, my prick touching the cunt-lips.

The accumulators of my ballocks must have been gorged with sperm. Off and on all day my prick had been on the stand, I had feared to touch it lest it should go off, nor had I put the girl's hand on to it; the last half-hour my prick had been erect without subsiding. As my belly met hers a tremor shook my whole frame. "My God, shall I spend outside?" thought I; my prick like an iron rod touched the top of the wet slit and slid right down on its passage.

Is she virgin? A sharp cry, "Oh! don't hurt me!" I felt an obstacle, pushed violently again and again, "Oh! oh! don't," and then throb, throb, throb, with each throb a jet of sperm shot out against the mouth of the orifice I had not penetrated, I lost my power in the contentment of a copious emission, and the pleasurable certainty, that no prick had yet been up the hole against which mine had been battering.

Next was fear lest she should get up, so rapid had the spend overtaken me, that I had not got my hands under her, they were on the side of her smooth haunches. To keep her under me until my powers returned, I slid one hand under her bum, the other under her waist, and squeezed her to me, then gently loosening my belly a little from hers I pushed again where my prick laid. With what delight I found it still stiff, with an obstacle in its front; I nestled gently in the spermy lips, the heat, the smoothness gave me a titillation as if a spend was again not far off, and that I need not have feared my manhood. With pride and power I clasped her, feeling sure she was virgin. There she lay in all her beauty, submitting to my will, I enjoying my sense of power, wriggling gently for a minute, till my prick demanded its right of entry. I pushed, a sharp "Oh!" a harder push, a louder cry, the obstacle was tight and hard indeed, I had never had such difficulty before; my lust grew fierce, her cry of pain gave me inexpressible pleasure, and saying I would not hurt, yet wishing to hurt her and glorying in it, I thrust with all the violence my buttocks could give, till my prick seemed to bend, and pained me. "Oh! mon Dieu! Ne faites pas ça, get away, you shan't," she cried, "Oh! o — o — oh!" My prick moved forward, something which had tightened round, and clipped it gave way; suddenly it glided up her cunt, still tighter I clasped her, as she moved with pain beneath me, my balls were dangling on her bum, my sperm shooting against the neck of her womb, and I had finished the toughest virginity I ever had yet.

The job was done, months of anticipation, hopes, fears, and desire, were over; my prick was in the cunt of a French virgin, at a cost of two hundred pounds. After my second poke, I had a feeling of pleasure and tranquility, a weight off my mind, a future of voluptuousness before me. My cock still lingered in her cunt, I moved it about, excited and full of lusty vigor I could have gone on fucking; but letting my penis withdraw, I lay thinking about her cunt, then with a kiss lifted myself off the beautiful creature who lay under me with eyes closed. I saw the gauzy dressing-gown lying open, the blue bows torn, a coarse white chemise in a well pressed heap, above a navel, an ample belly, finely formed thighs, of a slightly brown tint, and on the chemise beneath large spots of sperm, patches of blood, and spunk streaked with blood in quantity filling and covering the space between the cunt-hole. Getting off I seated myself by the side of the bed; Louise seemed to awaken to consciousness, and with the instinct of a modest woman covered herself by drawing down her chemise, carelessly, half-sleepily and unconsciously; more as if from habit than of thought to hide her charms. Then she drew herself to the edge of the bed, put one leg higher up than the other, resting her elbow on it, her head upon her hand, she looked at me wistfully without uttering a word.

A newly fucked woman rarely looks at the man, sometimes turns away, rarely speaks, but avoids a man's eyes. Louise did not speak, but she looked as if she was collecting her senses, looked so long and in such manner, that it made me uncomfortable, until her fine legs, in an attitude I had not yet seen them in recalled me to myself. "What lovely legs," said I. She pulled the chemise down lower, but the chemise was short, and she was sitting on it; she never took her dark eyes off of me, but with her head still leaning on her hand, said slowly, "You have promised me never to go into the bed-room with my sister again!"

"Your sister!" What a revelation! The likeness to Camille. I wondered it had not struck me more completely before, the hesitation of Camille to let me get the girl, her wish that she had never fetched her, her half intention to send her home, the oath she made me take not to disclose my having seen Louise's cunt when she was insensible: all struck me at once.

Louise jumped off the bed in a fright, "No, no, no," she said. "Not my sister, my mistress: did I say sister? I didn't mean it, it's my mistress, don't say I said sister."

I was certain she had spoken the truth: the likeness, Camille's anger when I suggested making Louise drunk, her desire to be out of the house when her virginity was taken, and other things crowded on my mind. "Deny it as you like, *ma chère*, but you *are* her sister, the very image of her."

Don't say so." I swore I would never tell. "She will murder me if she knows. She is a demon, you don't know her — mon Dieu! mon Dieu! What shall I do? I must run away."

I calmed her, told her no one need know, I would never tell. She believed me, seemed comforted, but still kept assuring me she had made a mistake: she meant to say mistress.

This was a funny episode, a funny conversation between a woman carrying her first male spunk in a bloody cunt, and a man with a cock still dripping with cunt-juices on to his shirt, sitting by her side.

We talked by the side of the bed; then for a minute she put her head on my shoulder and cried: it was over-excitement, nothing else, no regret.

Was I going? My reply was to put on my night-gown, say I meant to sleep all night with her; I showed her my shirt, dabbed with bloody semen, and gloried in it, told her her chemise was in the same state. She begged me to leave her, and pushed me into the sitting-room, wiped her bloody quim, and changed her things. She could not find Camille's night-gowns, her own were dirty, so she put on one of Camille's beautiful chemises, and over it the white robe. What a difference that entry of my prick had made: twelve hours before, a refusal to let me put on a garter, a struggle, a fight to do it; now my hand rested tranquilly on the smooth thighs, whilst she listened to the pleasures I meant to have with her. I drew her towards the bed-room, pulled off her boots and stockings, her robe, then her chemise, and she got into bed naked, and I with her. It was a hot night, cuddling was close work; lying by her side, my mouth to hers, my belly to hers, my doodle pressed close into her thighs, my hand on her bum, our legs touching their whole length, I was talking of fucking, and she listened lewdly. What a difference! I guided her hand to my prick; oh! my delight in that. and hers! How quietly it laid where I placed it, — then under my balls, her hand was quite full of them, and there it lay, then again round my pego. Again it was beginning to swell, she lay with her long black hair floating on the pillow, her eyes closed in bawdy reverie. "You have got my prick in your hand, it has been in your cunt and spent in it." She moved her head close to mine and kissed, my cock stood stiff at once.

I closed to her, feeling every part of her body, excepting that which I had just injured. That came in now for its share: thrusting one knee between her legs I lifted hers so as to leave room for my hand between them. She prayed me not, she was sore, ill, it hurt her. Hurt her? I longed to hurt her, knew I was going to give her pain whilst I lied saying that no pain more would she feel, and then with a little gentle force, my finger slipping over her clitoris, I felt the cunt hole gently, went up it, she wincing and moving her bum in an inciting manner, then up her orifice went my cock again, amidst murmurs and prayers to leave her alone, a glorious fuck.

Then I dozed, dropping off on one side from her sweet firm body; but excitement would not let me sleep, I kept awaking as fast as I fell asleep, a burning heat pervaded my penis, my mind dwelt on the day's work, her limbs were close to mine, cunt in reach of my fingers, smell of her body in my nostrils. The lights were out, she was slumbering with quiet regular breath. Up came my prick again, my fingers slid between the cunt-lips, felt the signs of my last pleasure, she awakened. "Oh! don't." She was ill, sore, very sore, I was unkind; but what women can refuse the cock which has just wetted her. Now was a prolonged fuck; then overcome with fucking, worn with excitement, I fell sound asleep.

When I awakened the sun-light struggling through the red curtains cast a pink tint over everything. We had slept eight hours, were laying rump to rump, naked and touching, for after much fucking, the fondest lovers turn their arses to each other. What a sight she was as she lay on one side, as sound asleep as a top, there had been but a sheet over us, that was off, and she was naked. She had a pretty foot, the leg was perfect, thighs and bum thinner than Camille's, backside and thighs take on fullness at later age, or after one or two years' good fucking which serves quite as well; her breasts were superb, firmer and handsomer than Camille's. On one side I saw the black crisp hair which shaded her seat of pleasure; on the other I could, by putting my head on the bed, just see the dark hair creeping between her bum-cheeks, her flesh had the slightly brown tint common to French women; on the bed lay rounds of spunk mixed with blood, a smear of it was on her thigh on the bum-side. My prick rose again to stiffness at the sight, I wanted to piss violently, but could scarcely accomplish it. I looked at my shirt tail. Spunk and blood were thick on it. I found under the bed her chemise; on it profusely were the bloody seminal marks of her virginity. I felt a pain in my prick, and found the foreskin a little raw. I had paid for hurting her by hurting myself; but what did that matter; I was the first that had been up that cunt, had torn it open, my spunk was in her then, the bloody indications were all around me. I awakened her.

She looked at me, then conscious that she was naked, clawed up the sheet; in a minute I was close to her. She went across to her own room to piddle, then into bed again she got, and then spite of her I put it into her. I felt the cunt tightening, looked at her: her manner was different, I felt her clasping me, she was doing it involuntarily, her breath came quickly, she was spending as my spunk came, her first pleasure with me; all before had been pain, — I knew that.

Then was more fucking, then she made coffee, we had eggs, bread and butter, again to bed, and more fucking. We went without luncheon, spending the entire day in bed, feeling, kissing, cuddling, fucking, and sleeping. We were both worn out, and perhaps might not have got up, excepting that I had to dress, to go downstairs, and then felt hungry, so we both dressed, went to the same place as the day previously, had a jolly good dinner as fast as we could and directly it was over went back. I kept my finger on her cunt when in the cab, both going and coming; the instant we returned we went to bed (it had not been made), and fucked, and fucked, and fucked, and then slept a dozen hours without awaking. A lovely time it was.

Next day I was used up, I never could accomplish the wonderful fucking bouts I have heard men brag about, but dare say in those thirty hours I had fucked her twelve times. She was very tired with it, and was so sore; I was also sore, my prick had slightly bled, the foreskin was torn, and through that fucking bout my prepuce was easier ever afterwards, I could pull it down better than I could before I had torn open her virginity.

The difference between the ways of a woman and man towards each other after they have fucked is wonderful. On a previous night a woman may have refused his kisses, and his embraces, and revolted at his hands touching her quim. He, although longing for her, eager to join his body to hers, may have been timid, cautious in his language, hesitating in action, and until passion got full sway, might as soon of thought of putting out his doodle, and attempting to force it up her, as of trying it on his aunt. But what a change a night has made: they sit at breakfast, he with satisfaction on his face as he looks at her and thinks that her most secret parts have not been strangers to him, has felt between her thighs, the lips hitherto untouched by man, has been up her cunt, and spent inside it the essence of his blood. "She has given me pleasure, I have given her pleasure." She looks at him wondering how she came to allow it, how she forgot her resolves, there need be no more disguise, nor hinderance in the way of their pleasures, of the pleasures she first tasted with him; all that she has been taught to hold most sacred from man he has seen, felt, kissed, pierced, violated, and wetted in. The virginity she prided herself on he has destroyed, she no longer shuns him, but is ready to comply with all his wishes, hopes he will compel her soon to yield again. This is the work of a few hours, and as she sits drinking her coffee opposite to him she thinks with him, what a change has taken place.

That was my state of mind with Louise. I had had virgins before without pride in having them, they came in my way, but never had I sought them. Two certainly had never been broached before, but it gave me no pride nor special gratification. This woman I had thought and thought about for months, coveted and paid for the sole pleasure of piercing her hymen. I had now the delight of experience, of leaving my sperm where man had never left it before. This girl of sufficient age, growth, and form, I had bored with difficulty and pain to her and myself, she had bled, I had bled, I had torn up her cuntal diaphragm, had given her sexual pleasure, had revelled in her body. Shirt, and chemise, spunk and blood slobbered lay there. I was rested, she was fresh, and I sat at breakfast with as much complacency and jollity as a man could; yet beyond fucking, I felt that I did not care one damn about her, and even felt sorry. I cannot explain why I felt that, but recollect it.

We had seven days before Camille would return, in those days I more than fulfilled my word to the girl, bought dresses, a ring, brooch, umbrella, parasol, in fact I don't know what I did not give, and must have paid fifty pounds; we dined out, went to theatres, eat, drank and fucked like blazes.

French women when they have given themselves up to a man, do so with all their heart and soul. One day as luncheon began to operate on her, she nothing loth, she strong, healthy, and with passions roused, feeding daily in a way she had been unaccustomed to, yielded freely to my wishes. I placed her on the bed-side, threw up her chemise, kissed the dark crisp hair of her motte; her thighs separated, her limbs went up, and I saw the adorable vermillion gap, the ragged tear my penis had made. It was a small cunt for so fine a woman. What enticed, and incited me I don't know, I never shall know why dozens of women I have had I never have done it to, but I was taken with the feeling now. I looked, fingered, titillated, kissed it, out went my tongue; it played lightly over the clitoris, then baudy frenzy seized me, and I licked and sucked her cunt. She wriggled, scarce knowing what I was about, when pushing my head away she cried out, "Oh! Mon Dieu, ah! quelle bête! Aho!"

I had never done it willingly but to Martha, now the letch seized me furiously, every day afterwards I had my mouth to her, and when I was so fucked out, that I could come no more, would lay and lick her till she was worn out too with spending.

We had indeed no other amusement than fucking, talking about it, eating, drinking, and sleeping, which was to us all the charm of a honey-moon. I think I see her now, making my cock stiff under my direction, her amusement at pulling the prepuce up and down was great, I almost feel her bum now as she used to sit on my knee, looking at the pictures in the baudy book; we used to talk it over until we went to bed, and eased our passions; what fun when we did not mind washing each other's privates, as we did.

We used to lay on the bed with my head between her thighs, licking her quim, she playing with my prick, but I never put my pego into her mouth, nor did she ever do more than kiss it.

On the day but one before Camille returned, we went to bed, had a fuck, then a second, her cunt felt funny, and I found her courses had come on, or as she called them, her periods. There was an end of my fun, nor was I sorry. Not having left her day or night, nor been to my lodgings, nor to my mother's. I was fucked out, and so was she, — so that her reds came on most opportunely.

Next day we were duller, there was nothing in her to make her a companion when not in amorous amusements. She became tiresome, and annoyed me by putting on her things one after the other, all day long, and asking me, how she looked in them, if she did not look better than Madame. Then how tell her mistress she had got the things? What to do, if her mistress refused to let her wear them?

How was I to see her again? At length we resolved to tell rousing lies about everything, — my behaviour was in fact most absurd.

The following day, a letter came to say Camille would be home that night. I took away my trunk and clothes, went to my virtuous lodgings; it was a relief to be away from cunt for twenty-four hours, and I could not bear a woman with her courses on.

CHAPTER III

Camille at home. — Her little game. — My greenness. — The house in O°°°d°n Street. — The glove shop. — Louise fatigues me. — Fred on the scent. — A cigar-shop. — Three into one. — A clap. — Serious reflexions. — The sisters disappear.

A day or two recruited me, I wrote to Camille who met me in the street, she had sent the girl to the theatre with a friend, so I went indoors with her. "Have you done it to her?" was the first question, as if she did not know, I told her all. She questioned me with strong interest. I gave her the fifty pounds. Then she asked me if Louise had told me where she came from, and other questions, which I saw were to put to see if Louise had told about their relationship. As we talked I looked at her, comparing her with Louise, and saw the likeness stronger than ever. "Why stare so?" she asked. When she had heard of all our bum frolics she gave a sigh and said, "Well, if I had not brought her to London, she would have gone to Paris with A°°° (mentioning some French name), and have had it done to her there, — so it comes to the same thing."

Then suddenly, "Are you never going to have me again?" "No," I had promised Louise. She looked amorously fascinating. "She won't know it, I have never had it since I left." She was half reclining on the sofa, by intention or chance her legs raised up on the sofa, one flat, the other foot on its heel, exposing the recumbent limb from foot to knee. "Do now," said she. "No," but I moved from the chair to the end of the sofa, and began stroking her leg with my hand.

She lifted the clothes just above the knee, I saw the large thigh nearly up to her quim, my hand involuntarily slipped higher, and began smoothing the flesh just above the garter. "Do it now," said she, falling right on to her back.

240

I thought of Louise, of my promise; I knew the look of both their cunts, — of Camille's the best, — desired to see, to compare it. I had been feeling Louise's cunt eight days, now thought I should like to feel Camille's, to feel the difference. I knew her cunt was looser and more hairy, her bum and thighs bigger, yet was I right in my comparison? My cock got uneasy, I helped it to rise in my trowsers by giving it a push outside.

"I won't have her," I thought, "but there is no harm in feeling," and began playing with the hair of her motte. "Your hair is longer than Louise's." She laughed, "Do it, baisez-moi," said she.

My fingers touched the slippery, it was irresistible, the next instant they were groping and feeling. "Your bum is bigger than Louise's," I said. She laughed again.

Sitting where I was, and playing at stink-finger, my position was inconvenient. "Come up closer," said she. Then I sat by her hips, on the sofa edge, she lifted her clothes right up: there was the quim, the jet-black bush, the fine round thighs, my cock was restive, my hands wandering, she unbuttoned my trowsers, gave my prick a squeeze, sending up the blood, and completed my randiness.

"Louise won't know, you shall kiss me," and she raised herself to throw her arm over my shoulder. Like a young virgin who says, "No, no," whilst she yields, I kept repeating "no, no." The thighs had opened, I was pulling open the lips, and trying to see the red inside, and still saying "No," slid on to her, on to it, up it, and spent before I well knew what I was about. "Oh! You are so quick," said she, "you have spoiled me, I was just coming."

She did not mean to be spoiled, trying her most baudy endearments, she held me tight, caressed me, as a French woman knows how, — better than any other. Forgetting Louise, my mind fell into its baudy dreams, I fucked her again, and then she let me get up.

And then to business. "What are you going to do for the girl?" she asked. "Nothing, I have given her money and things worth about a hundred pounds, and have paid you, when I have her again I shall give her money." "You promised to do something more, if not what will become of her?" I did then recollect, that she had made me promise, but had attached no definite ideas to it.

"I relied on you, or would never have brought her; are you going to keep her, or let her be gay like me?"

I did not like either; to keep her I had no intention, did not even like the girl, though I liked plugging her. Said Camille, "We have had a row already, she won't work, and says she will wear the clothes she has got, although I have only seen a few of them." "What do you expect?" I asked. "Set her up in business, selling gloves or perfumes, a small shop somewhere."

Not liking the aspect of affairs I left, it was the first time such propositions had been made to me. I felt inclined never to go near the house again, but had promised Louise to be with her soon, and always kept my word, so thought over the matter.

Keeping her was out of the question, I had heard that men who kept women did so for other men; besides I had no idea of tying myself up that way. I was not pleased with her: a fine girl, a fine fuck, a fresh woman who shivered with delight the instant the prick entered her, who was randy-arsed enough to learn anything in the way of copulation; she had been delightful to me eight days, and might for more; but she was coarse, vulgar, and had not two ideas in her head, was evidently violent tempered, and excessively vain. Set her up in business! Why she had cost me hundreds to get her, why should I?

I could not make up my mind, and resolved never to go near again; but two days afterwards, that funny sense of fullness came over my cock-knob, then the tingling, then the desire for cunt, then for Louise's cunt, the ragged slit made by my cock was before my eyes, and instead of quenching my wants in the channel of some other woman, I went there. Camille was just outside the door, and we conversed together in G°°d°n Sq°°°.

She suggested my seeing Louise alone, and paying her (Camille) as I had done before. I did not mean to submit to that restraint, nor to keep her, but let her go her own way. "What does it matter, she must know you will find it all out, so why not at once?" I said.

"If she knows that I know it, I must turn her out ("I don't think you will turn your sister out," I thought), then I must put her into lodgings, and she will be gay." "I can't help that." We came to no conclusion, I left her, went to the door, rang, and Louise opened it. She kissed and hugged me in the passage, a minute afterwards she was on my knee grasping my prick, my fingers were on her cunt, our lips together; in another with tongues lapping together I was up her; in two or three minutes more we were quiet.

(I should so like to experience the feeling a woman has as she sits and talks with her cunt full of sperm, does it feel so very pleasant sitting so?) She poured out her griefs, Camille had asked questions, who had been? how did she get the bonnet, the new boots? she had refused to tell anything, Camille had said she had better go. "Why not tell Camille?" I said. "If she did not like it she might lump it, as far as I was concerned"; but the girl was evidently afraid, — or was it sham?

Next day I wrote to Louise who met me, and I took her to a house into which I had never been before. For three weeks I met her on writing to her, and we spent hours together. She now had frequent rows with Camille, each time she came to meet me she put on more of her new things; at first she only came with a dress, then with the bonnet and something else, and at last with all the finery; she looked a handsome swell, but a vulgar one. I ceased paying Camille.

One night she said Madame had had no one visit her for a long time, nor was she much out but often was all night, where she went she did not know; there was one man who came, a gentleman, she thought he was a lover of Camille's.

We came out of the house in *** Street one night after a surfeit of voluptuous pleasures, when a woman stepped across the road, and lifted up her veil. "Oh! My God, it's Madame," said Louise, and she got right at the back of me where I stood. "So," said Camille, "I have found you out, you have been in a baudy house with my old friend." She burst into a laugh, turned, and went away without saying another word.

I don't know what actuated me in my course of conduct, at that time I know well what I did, but my reasons are not so clear, I cared nothing whether Louise knew that her mistress or sister knew I had had her, yet I did not go to the house, firstly because Camille wished me not, unless she was out, and it did not suit me to be waiting for a girl who was burning to let me have her, and also because Louise was in a funk when I was with her in the house, and Camille was out. I was convinced they were sisters, and had a glimmering, that Camille would not like Louise to know she had been got for me by her; yet I thought that it must be found out.

As Camille walked away Louise began to cry, I could not get a word from her; we walked up and down A*** Street, she was frightened to go home, we went back to the baudy house, and there we slept. The next day we stopped there, then I went home with her, — Camille was within.

"So you have been to a baudy house?" said she. "So you have been fucked, fucked by my friend; you are a nice one to speak ill of other people." "I am not a whore," said Louise, taking cheek. "Ain't you?" said Camille, "I don't know that." "Say I am a whore, and I'll hit you," said Louise, going up to her. "Have it out by your-selves, I am not going to stop for a row," said I, "Camille, be good to the girl." "If I had not brought her from France she would not be what she is." What was I going to do with her? "Nothing." Then the sooner Louise went out the better.

Louise sat down, and began silently crying. I hate to see a woman cry, and always had one remedy, — could champagne be fetched? Mother Boileau condescended to fetch some. We drank, I got communicative, and began to tell Camille. She cut me short, wanted to know nothing, we had been in a baudy house together, it was enough. What was I going to do? The girl would no longer work, and she was going into other lodgings; I might take hers for Louise if I liked.

It gradually shaped itself to this: I was to take the lodgings, Camille to stay rent free, a servant to be got, but one particular friend only was ever to visit Camille there; Louise took Camille's bed-room, Camille Louise's, I had in fact the pleasure of keeping both. The next night I slept with Louise in Camille's bed, slept there several times, and one morning Camille said, "You have got the girl with child, I quite expected it."

This annoyed me. I had been getting tired for some time, did not like the girl, who became so jealous of Camille, wanted so much admiration, that she quite fatigued me. She wanted to walk in the streets to be admired. I had given her more clothes, she got careless, wanted to go to theatres, and I took her. The Argyle was just opened, and I took her there, she wanted me to go there often. I had seen one or two other women I lusted for, but above all wanted to go to France with Fred who had returned from India; so her being in the family way bothered me. I got it into my head, that it was a plant, and took her to my friend the doctor who said it was a fact.

Camille asked me to meet her in G°°d°n Sq°°°e, for con-venience I took her to the baudy house; she had got mighty par-ticular, made me go in first, and came in afterwards with her veil down — she always now wore a veil. She again asked me what I was going to do. She had got the girl, and was sorry for it, at length she said, "I am going to be married, go into business, and will take her with me, if you will help, or I will get her home again to France, if you will give her money." I agreed to think of it.

We sat on a sofa. As I looked at her I began to feel a desire for her. "Let us have a kiss," said I, "for old acquaintance' sake." "No," said she, "I am going to be married, am perhaps watched, am frightened of being here. I expect my friend back from abroad daily, he may have come back now. Madame Boileau knows him, I must be careful."

But how can a woman resist a man who has had her often, who knows every crack and cranny of her body, has looked at her motte long enough to count every hair on it, a few rubs on her clitoris, and back she fell on the sofa. We were both dressed, but plunging up her, and grasping her ample rump, I was soon enjoying her; when thinking of Louise, and I suppose comparing her mentally, I said in the height of my pleasure, "Oh! I like fucking you better than your sister after all," or something to that effect.

"What?" said she with a start as her cunt clipped, and jerked my prick out. Cursing, and damning at my interruption I drove it up again, and consummated.

"What did you say about being like my sister?" said she as I still lay with my doodle up her, "What sister?" I replied she looked so like Louise, that she must be her sister. "But she is not, although she is like me." Then the matter dropped, and she slopped her cunt clean. I used to like a woman whom I knew not to wash it, when I was going to fuck her again, Camille had humoured me in this, and as my lust came on for my second poke, used to begin my amatory pastime by looking at the cunt with my pleasure signs on it. So Camille washing astonished me. "I am going to be married, and must," said she.

We had more fucking before we left. She was all anxiety about Louise, for I would say nothing. "You will never see me here again," said she, "nor have me again, and may do with Louise what you like, I shan't be here, you will throw her on the town." Then she veiled closely, and made me go out first. I waited at the top of the street ten minutes, out she came, veil down, and shot off in the direction of G°°d°n Sq°°°e like an arrow.

I now with perversity longed for Camille, instead of Louise, but never had her afterwards, never sent my tallow up her, although I tried once or twice.

I began going about elsewhere, sleeping with Louise at times; but she was always pestering me about being in the family way, which annoyed me; and wanted such a lot of ballocking, that that annoyed me also. My cousin Fred wanted me to go to Paris with him, Louise said I was going to forsake her. One night after dining with her, coming out we met my cousin Fred, nothing put him off, and he would walk with us. The next day he said in his old unchaste way, which some years in India had not improved, "So that is the woman your mother says she fears has got hold of you." It was the first time I had heard that my mother had any such suspicion, for although she had spoken to me about my wildness, she had never referred to a woman; but she had told my aunt, who told my cousin my mother was awfully astonished. For that six years I had shagged all our servants under her very nose, yet she had not the faintest suspicion of it, my pranks now coming to her ears, shocked her extremely. I told Fred, that I had had Louise's firsts, to which he replied, that he should like to rattle his stones against her arse. "Is she a good fuck? Where does she live?" I did not mean his stones to knock against her arse as long as mine did, I replied. "Oh! You are fond of her then?" "No," but I preferred her to myself. "Lord, what does it matter?" said he, "white women are scarce in India, there was one that all in my regiment were fond of, there was not an officer who did not stroke her, none of us minded; we say, 'the more a cunt's buttered, the better it grinds.'" I did not see it in that light, so with the remark from him, that she was a damned fine piece, we parted.

Two or three days afterwards he spoke of her again, said he knew where she lived, so I thought he was hunting after her which annoyed me; not seeing that if he had got into her, I could have left her with good excuse.

I had tried to learn from Louise if she knew where Camille went all day, but could learn nothing, one night in bed with her however, whilst handling each other's privates, and under the sympathy generated by the rub of my fingers on her clitoris, she on my solemn promise of secrecy told me that an old friend of Camille's had opened a glove and lace shop in O°f°°d Street with Camille's money, and that he was going to marry her. In O°f°°d Street I saw a small shop, there was a Frenchman in it whose face I seemed to know. I waited near it one night, and saw Camille leave the shop closely veiled, and take the best way towards G°°d°n Sq°°°e. Madame Boileau was like an oyster. I could get nothing out of her, although she took my money. I was sure that Camille went to the shop daily, or nearly so, and as no man came to the house, suppose she got her cunt plugged in the shop parlour.

Afterwards Fred talked so much about Louise, that I said I kept her. "There are two there, do you keep both?" "Yes." "Then you are a fool, you can't be sure of one woman's cunt if you are not with her always, but two together are sure to make a couple of whores, — no wonder your tin goes so fast."

Meanwhile I went out with him of a night, and we had different women. One night three of us went to a cigar-shop kept by two women just by °°°, it was not an unusual thing then for two to have a cigar-shop, with a big sofa in a back parlour, one keeping shop whilst the other fucked. From talking we got to business without intending it. Fred began joking the girls, we went into the back parlour, and had wine, one asked my cousin if he did not want to lie down and rest himself. He said "Yes," but wanted warmth to his belly when he rested. "You may have my belly to warm you," said she. "What, here?" "Oh! They can wait," said the girl, "and your quiet friend can find his tongue with my sister. (The other girl.) I had not spoken, being at times timid at first with a woman, and especially a gay one.

We said jokingly, that we had no money. "I will take you all for a sovereign," said she, "and the one who I say is the best poke shall give me another half-sovereign." It was agreed, we tossed up for the order of the fucking, two went outside while the other had his pleasure. My turn came last, the excitement in thinking of what was going on made me in such a state, that I was no sooner up her than I spent; when I went out the other girl said, "You have been in a hurry." My cousin was pronounced the best fucker. Whilst the strumming was going on in the parlour, people bought cigars, and tobacco — for it was really sold there, — little did they guess the fun going on behind that red curtain of the shop-parlour.

A night or so after, I slept with Louise, felt uneasy in the tip of my prick, and saw unmistakably that it was the clap. It was not Louise's gift, for great was her surprise when I saw her twice afterwards, and never attempted to have her. She was annoyed, and said she supposed I had another friend, and put herself in such luscious attitudes, that I got a cock-stand, and could scarcely resist putting it up her, but saying I was ill went away. Fred said he should go to Paris without me, I was to join him in a fortnight. What with being indifferent to Louise, annoyed with her randiness, her vulgarity, and temper, being in fact tired of her and the expense, and now having the clap, I determined to break off; so wrote to Camille to meet me.

I told her I had the clap. "I thought there was something wrong," said she, "but Louise, I can swear, has never had any other man than you, take her to any doctor you like." Then she told me that in three weeks she meant to leave England, and Louise must do the best she could, she had taken means to bring on the girl's courses, would I send her back to France, or must she go gay in London.

I could not bear the idea of the girl being gay, so agreed to give her money to take her abroad with her, and she accepted. By her advice I wrote to Louise, said I had the clap, and feared I had given it to her, that she would not forgive me I was sure, and so never meant to see her again.

I sent a cheque to Louise, it passed through my bankers, and suppose the girl had it. Then went to Paris, my illness kept to me, so returned to London, got a little better, longed for Louise, stood opposite the house one night, nearly crossed over to have her, but resisted, and seeing a nice woman in Regent Street went home with her. I was so impatient, that I pushed her to the side of the bed directly I was in the room, felt for her cunt, and spent in her in a minute, she had not taken her bonnet off. My spending hurt me, my doctor had told me I could go with a woman without fear of injuring her, but that for my own sake I had better abstain. She got up, and took off her bonnet, to see if lying down had hurt it. "I'll have you again," said I. "Let me wash, you've spent such a lot, it's all running down my thighs." Again I fucked her; and next morning my ailment came back. My doctor said it served me right.

Shortly after, "lodgings to let" was posted up in Camille's windows. On calling, Madame Boileau came to the door. The two women had left, the shop in Oxford Street was shut up, and I never heard of the women afterwards.

I am astonished now, that I was wheedled out of so much money for a French virgin. How I could have done much that I did makes me now laugh, I must have been very green, and Camille very cunning; but I was also rich, and generous, which accounts for much. I see now how largely I was humbugged, but cannot explain or reason about it. I am telling facts as they occurred, as far as I recollect them, it is all I can do. Certainly I had a splendid full-grown virgin for my money, the toughest virginity I yet have taken, a regular cock-bender, and had an uninterrupted honey-moon. Camille was a most superior harlot, genteel, clever, and voluptuous, such as are not usually found; with her and her findings I had a year's enjoyment, leaving me lax, blasé, and a half-cured clap. What with women, horses, carriages, cards, dinners, and other items, I was a few thousands poorer than at the beginning of my acquaintance with Camille.

It's my fate to have sisters, — how curious! — and thrice to have had the clap, and yet not three-and-twenty, — how hard!

I was very much used up, and needed rest for body and mind; never had I been so much so before. Up to the time of getting my fortune, want of money curbed my lascivious tastes, and although I had servant after servant in my mother's house, the difficulties of getting them gave me frequent rests, and prevented me generally from exhausting myself; perhaps I got just enough fucking to keep me in health. The year's rioting with Camille and her troupe would have tired a strong man; I never counted them, but think that in that year I must have poked something like sixty or seventy different women; I poked every one of Camille's acquaintances, I am sure, — so it was time I had a rest.

CHAPTER IV

Enforced chastity. — A stricture. — Health restored. — Mrs. Pender.
— A peep from a hay-stack. — In a cow-house. — Stable and barn.
— Mother's satisfaction.

My clap brought on a stricture, obliging me to have a bougie passed every other day to stretch the pipe open, and causing me to piss clots of gruelly blood about an hour afterwards. I dared not fuck, but once frigged, and it brought on the inflammatory stage again. At length I got better, but with a gleet which wetted the tail of my shirt through daily; doctors advised me to get a change of air, I went to my aunt's place in H**°tf***d-shire where I took cold baths, and did all I could to get myself well, — I was forbidden to touch a woman until permitted by the doctor.

Touch women I did not, think of them I did eternally, and deplored the time that I was wasting. I used to look at my female cousins, and long for them; my aunt whose flabby, brown-haired, thick-lipped furrow glanced at in my boyhood I used to think about, and should not have hesitated in getting a pleasure up it, had no other cunt been ready for me. I eyed the farm-women (coarse, strong, healthy bitches) with lust that made them look beauties in my longing eyes, I was boiling over with spunk, at the closet one day my turds were hard, and hurt me; the irritation affected my ballocks, my prick stiffened rigidly, I could not piss for it, the tip looked dry, as if gleet had ceased, I merely touched the top (not frigged), and out shot my sperm as I sat on the privy seat. What a relief! But what a loss of pleasure not to have injected some dear little cunt nicked in some smooth white bum! My prick seemed quite well, and I went into the fields to get hold of some girl doing field-work, or any woman, old or young, who had a cunt available,

when with a throbbing my gleet returned; so I went to town to see
my medical man about it. He pointed out to me how needful it was
to restrain myself, I followed his advice, in two weeks was much
better, and had determined to go to town to see him again about
it, when I got well without him.

Some years before I had seen a farm-girl whose name was
Pender, a fine lass with a merry face, and lightish brown hair; she
must then I suppose have been about seventeen years old. From
ogling and laughing, I got to kissing, with that she was pleased
enough, and often I think put herself in my way to get it; a pinch
on the bum she did not resent. Thinking all safe, I one day poked
her near to her notch, and she only saying, "Adun now sir, do," my
hand went up her petticoats, I struggled with her, and we both fell
on the grass near a barn, when my fingers touched her cunt. She set
up a yell, my fingers were stained with her monthlies (not the only
time that has occurred in my life), she sat for a minute crying, then
walked away, leaving me in fear lest she should tell my aunt. She
never did, but avoided me, and would not look me in the face.
When older, I only thought of her when there, or when my memory
ran back on the quims I had touched in my then short career.

Having now nothing to do, but to read, and idle about, I was
wandering in the farm, fields, stable, cow-houses, everywhere, and
soon knew all the faces on the estate. Among them was Pender, still
so named, she having then been married about a year to a man
bearing her own maiden name, and was then about twenty-three
years old; a tall, strapping woman, with a bum as big as a washing-
tub; brown she was from working in the sun, but fucking regularly
as I supposed had cleared her complexion, she was a good, comely
country-woman. Our eyes met, both at the instant thought of the
day when I got my fingers red up her petticoats; she curtsied, and
blushed, I laughed with a baudy look I expect, and said, "Well, you
still keep here."

I spoke to her again on other days, her husband worked on the
farm, and she was dairy-woman. Whenever I saw her my prick
stood, and I avoided her, for fear of an erection increasing my gleet.

There was hay-making, — lolling about with a book I went to
look on, it was at one or two fields off from a large rick-yard which
was near to the farm buildings. There was a half-made hay-stack
with a ladder against it, up which without any object I went idly,

and laying down went on reading. It became cloudy, the head-man calling out said, "We'll have rain, cut off all on yer, and get the hay up into cocks, yes you, — you, — yes you too." (I did not know who he was talking to.) Men and women crossed the rick-yard, and went off in the distance, Pender was one, and was well ahead, when he called out, "You had better get the dairy-work done though." She turned, and coming slowly back stood still a moment, then comfortably squatted, and pissed.

I, laying half-buried in the hay, was not visible to her, but seeing her piddling, raised myself and looked. As she finished she gave her clothes that usual hitch against her cunt, looked up and saw me, turned round quickly, went away from the yard, and then as if she had forgotten, turned round with her head hanging down, and came through the rick-yard. I slipped from the stack, and met her at the foot of it, — we were surrounded with stacks.

Her face was red. "A comfortable piddle you had," said I, stopping her. "Adun sir," said she. "A kiss, for old acquaintance'," snatching one. "I am married," said she. "Don't care, so much the merrier, it's not so wet as it was, when I felt it some years ago?" "Oh! Lawk don't, I'm married."

We had moved a little, were by the hay-stack then making, a heap of hay had fallen as they had lifted it from the cart to the stack. I closed with her, kissing and hugging, gave her a push, and we both tumbled into a sitting position together on the heap, she half laughing, half resisting; then kissing her, suggesting pleasure, pulling out my prick, seeing a thick pair of legs in dark stockings, big thighs, a belly, some brown hair at the bottom of it, I felt cool flesh, a wet warm split, and was on her, up her, and spent in her.

I came to myself with a tingling aching sensation inside my prick, the stiffness and spending had hurt the urethra which had been split by the bougie. I had a notion that blood must be coming, and still stiff pulled it out of her; the little lingering sperm on the tip looked all right, she had not spent, for I don't think I could have shoved more than once before I had emitted my semen. I threw myself on her to put it into her again, but she balked me. "Oh! Now for God's sake, if my husband caught us there would be murder," but I was burning with want, it was more than two months since I had clutched a woman's backside, and spent up a cunt. Furiously I pulled her back, rolled over her, and fingered her; she rose spite of me, and went off. "Pray don't come with me, we may be seen,

I wouldn't for the world we were seen coming oot the rick-yard together."

A minute's reflection made me wiser. I got upon the hay-rick again, saw men and women in the hay-field a long distance off, I called out names of one or two I knew — no one answered, went into the farm-yard, hallooed there, no one answered, thence went into the cow-house, — there was she milking.

I stood by the cows, pulled my prick out, begged her to let me do it again, talked all the baudiness I could, reminded her of when first I wetted my fingers in her red-stained cunt, lifted up the cow's tail, swore if she did not let me I would put my prick up the cow. It was funny to see a woman whose cunt was full of sperm pulling vigorously at a cow's teats, whilst a man with his prick exposed was holding up a cow's tail, showing its cacked arse, and not too clean cunt. What absurdity will not a lewed man do?

"I must get this done, I am frightened, we shall be seen, we shall be caught," said she. I dropped on my knees, and as she went on milking, put my fingers up her petticoats, the slit was wet with my leavings. I pulled her face towards me to kiss, whilst she kept tugging at the cow's teats.

When the cow was dry she took the pail across the yard to the dairy, emptied it, and came back, looked in all directions, called out some name, but all were at the hay-making, heavy drops of rain were falling. "Come to the stable," said I, and laying hold of her pulled her in that direction.

I partly coaxed, partly pulled her, she looked uneasily round the farm-yard, and we entered the cow-shed. At one end of it was a cart-horse stable, close to that a large barn. With arm round her I led her towards the barn, there was straw and hay there; but in the stable in the first empty stall was a heap of fresh straw. I pushed her down on to it, the next instant I was fucking her, and what a fuck! I shall recollect it to the last day of my life, it was delicious. It was two months since I had had a woman; here was a stout, fat-arsed, hard-fleshed, healthy country woman; rough, dirty with work, but whose thighs were white, and whose cunt was a clipper, who was randy, had every capability of giving a man delight. No highly fed woman clad in silks and satins could have ministered to me as she did, as replying to my thrusts her cunt sucked my prick up her, and we spent together.

I raised myself up without uncunting; the straw rustling and crushing under us, too excited to lay still, after I had spent. She lay in quiet enjoyment, till putting down one hand to feel round our bellies, I roused her, then she wriggled, and out slipped my cock. "I must get up, for God's sake let me."

We got up. I don't suppose that more than twenty minutes had passed between my first and my second poke, still my prick remained stiff. She went quickly to the cow-shed, put down the milking-stool, sat down and began again tugging at a cow's teats, I again standing by her side with my privates hanging outside my trowsers.

I wanted to see her limbs, to feel her breasts. The idea of her cunt squeezing out its moisture on to her chemise as she sat on the stool, the desire to see every part of her, that irresistible want to see all, feel all, and satisfy every sense which springs up in the mind of a man when a woman has satisfied his voluptuousness for the first time overcame me. She tugged at the teats. "Oh! Go, pray do, — I won't, — you shan't, — ye've done me over, — oh! if you are seen here what will be said? — don't now get a poor woman into trouble, the milking must be done, if it's not what shall I say?" And tug, tug, went both hands milking.

Said I, No one would come back until they had raked up the hay out of harm from the rain. She knew better. "Yes, they will if they are kept late, some one will go to the Hall for beer, and they come back through the rick-yard for cans; go away for God's sake." I went back to the rick-yard, and saw a man coming as she had said, did not know which way to make off, but the hay-stacks helped me, and I dodged up to the Hall; it was about three minutes only from the farm-yard, and led to it by a lovely shady walk.

Female servants only were in the house, even my aunt and cousins had gone to the hay-meadow; soon a man emerged from the Hall with two huge cans in his hands: it was Pender's husband. He went off with them filled I suppose. I walked across the lawn and pleasure-gardens which the fields surrounded, saw him in the distance, then made my way to the cow-house again. "He's gone." "I have been so frightened," said she, — but did not say it was her husband. She was still at the cow's teats.

I would not be repulsed, nearly upset a pail of milk, and swore I would have her again. She refused, prayed me, then promised she would, if I would let her take the milk into the dairy. Permitting it, she stayed a few minutes, then out she came, looked all round, again called out a name before entering the stable. The next minute we were on the straw, my hand between her thighs. "You have washed your cunt," said I. "I did it in the dairy," said she.

I had a grope, tickled her clitoris, got my mouth on to her belly, my lips outside her cunt, we fucked, and again she went to her cow's teats. All this was in broad day-light, although evening was coming on.

She finished milking. "I ought to go to the hay," said she; but I would not let her, held her back, and swore if she went I would follow her. "What have I done?" said she. "I must be mad." Then she took as was her custom milk up to the Hall, I awaited her return, looking at my cock from which, to my delight, all signs of gleet had gone.

For some time I had had mostly gay women, this was a return to old times. It was pleasant to have a fuck on the sly, with a woman who showed real pleasure, who shivered with delight, and grasped me like a vice. Besides there was the stinging element of adultery. I laughed to myself at the idea of her husband's prick going up where I had been three times; my prick began to stiffen, and then droop, then rise again. I felt sure that at the feel of her quim I should be all right. "If I can once get it up her, once feel her cunt-lips closing round it, get a good clip round her buttocks, I am sure I can fuck her again before they come back from the hay-field," thought I, gently frigging my cock, and looking through a crack in the door.

She came back. I went at her in the cow-house; the only immediate fear now was that a servant might come from the Hall. To make the story short, I got her into the barn, where the light was less; and she let me do more as I liked. I had a look at a thick brown-haired motte, a belly, and a pair of white round thighs a duchess might have been proud of, I kissed her cunt, and fumbling about from her navel to her arse-hole, fucked her with a long lingering fuck which left us both silent, and enervated. My cock lingered up her as I lay quiet, squeezing my belly up to hers, my lips still against her rosy mouth, and said, "You will have a boy this day nine months."

And she did have a boy that day nine months. A second time that prophecy had come true, alas!

With a kiss we parted; men were returning from the fields. I got to the Hall. At dinner my aunt said, "Walter, you should have given us a help, all should help hay-making, when rain comes on; but you are too lazy; what have you been doing?" "Dear aunt, I have been reading steadily ever since." Said she, "How fond of reading you are for a young man of your age; how you can like to be so much alone, as you have been lately, I cannot imagine, it would be better if you took more exercise." She did not know the condition my cock had been in. And my mother was delighted at my being in the country, thinking I was getting steadier, and away from bad company.

CHAPTER V

Aunt at the dairy. — Morning amusements with Pender. — Female hay-makers. — Mrs. Whiteteeth. — An exhibition of cock. — Against a field-gate. — A night on the grass. — A sight from the barn-loft. — Robert the page. — Molly.

I could scarcely sleep that night. Pender seemed to me the most delicious woman I had ever poked. What if excitement had brought back the clap! What if I had clapped her! I had never after the clap had a woman until the doctor said I might. When I awakened, to my joy my prick was as dry as a bone, a woman was what I had wanted to complete my cure. The next minute my prick was stiff as I thought of Pender's charms.

It was a lovely morning, every available hand in house and farm was sent off to scatter the hay which on the previous night had been heaped up, Mrs. Pender excepted, whose dairy duty kept her at the farm. I caught her in the cow-house to her astonishment, for it could not have been more than six a.m. To rush up to her and kiss her was instantaneous. She repulsed my wandering hands. "Oh! Sir, don't now, — no never, — never again (married women always say that), Missus will be coming, — no never, — I'm a married woman, — now pray, — you shan't." I got her back up against a wall, my hand on her fringe, my mouth pressed to hers; how was it possible to resist? At ten paces was the stable, and the friendly hay. What a ballocking I gave her, with the summer sun shining through a window on to us, as we lay together in the early morning.

She sat down to milking with her cunt full of me. "They be all up at the hay," said she, "but Missus comes every fine morning to the dairy (that was true), she won't be here for an hour; but if she were, what would I do? My husband will be back, he'll take break-

257

fast to the fields, to save time, in chance of wet again coming on. Oh! Do go." There was certainly all those chances. Off I went across the rick-yard, round the belt of trees which skirted the house and gardens, so that I seemed to enter from the opposite side to that where Pender sat milking.

"Is my aunt up?" "No sir, she won't be down till seven o'clock when she goes to the dairy." I took a book, sat down till the servant disappeared, then running by the path soon to be described, was in two minutes in the farm-yard. Pender was in the dairy, resistance was vain, and with her back up against the dairy wall we fucked. I cut back to the house, and sat outside reading. Soon after, aunt appeared.

Said she, "What is the matter, that you are up so early?" (I usually was asleep at that hour.) "I could not sleep, dear aunt." "It would do you good if you always got up early, come with me to the dairy." In five minutes aunt and I were there. Lord, how Pender looked when she saw us together!

Aunt took pleasure in her farm. Every morning, if well, she walked down to it, saw how many eggs had been laid, and if butter-making, etc., went on rightly. Pender attended, whilst aunt with spectacles on was looking at the cream-pans, and asking questions, I looking as if deeply interested in the matter, was pinching Pender's bum as she stood beside my aunt. "How hot you are, Pender," said my aunt, looking at the woman. "It is hot, ma'am," she replied, perspiration streaming down her face. How very uncomfortable she looked.

At breakfast aunt said, "What do you think? Walter has been to the dairy with me." "Lor!" said my lady cousins, "that is wonderful; he to get up so early!" "Have you had that dairy-maid long, aunt?" "Why, don't you recollect she was housemaid here once?" "No." Then aunt told the history, which till then I did not know.

At the time of my unsuccessful attempt at a feel, she was engaged to a young man; they quarrelled, he left the village to go for a soldier, came back; again a quarrel, and again off he went. After a time he wrote to say he meant to marry another girl. Pender was in great grief. Just then a head-man on the estate, about fifty-five years old, offered her marriage, and in a reckless state of mind, she accepted him. Directly afterwards her sweetheart came back, his statement was a falsehood, told to try her. It was too late, and he went to America. "She is a very nice, steady woman," said aunt. "They lead a quiet life, but I don't think she is very happy, twenty-three and fifty-five are not a good match."

Food was sent to some of the farm-laborers at a meadow half-a-mile off. I had the pleasure of seeing my cousins, aunt, and two of the female servants, in big straw hats, go off to the field. They thought hay-making good fun. I promised to join them, and directly they were out of sight cut off to Pender, dodged all round the rick-yard to see if I was alone, and found her tranquilly churning butter. The stable still appeared the best place. Thither we went, and for the first time quietly, so to speak, I saw the article, and all its surroundings, which had given me several pleasures; and after fucking her I went to join my aunt, as I had promised her.

I had soon enough of hay-making myself, so laid down in the shade watching the hay-makers (nearly all women). As they moved along in rows, lewed thoughts occupied my mind. One biggish woman attracted my notice by her magnificent white teeth; looking at her short petticoats, and thick legs, lewedness increased to a cock-stand. I stared so as she approached me, that she could not fail to notice it. "It's hot," said I. "It be sir." She stooped with her bum towards me, and lying down as I was, I saw nearly to her knees. "What would I give," I thought, "to be close up to your bum-cheeks." Dirty linen, dirty clothes, sweaty flesh, none of those objections occurred to me. Then I moved farther up the field to get nearer, for working along the ridges, they had got away from my resting-place, and again laid down reading a newspaper. I covered my lap with it, feeling my prick beneath it, then I pulled my prick out (what risk!), and just as she, heading the file of women, came towards me, and began turning round; I again spoke to her. She stopped, the others went on; I lifted the newspaper; there stood my prick, red-tipped as a berry. She looked at it, at me, and putting one hand up to her mouth as if to stop her laughter, turned and followed on the others with her work. Soon returning she was again facing me, I saw her white teeth as she smiled, and her eyes fixed on me; the other women turned round, she stopped for a moment, off went the newspaper, and she gazed at my doodle for a second or two again. She was further off then, and I saw her speaking to the woman just in front of her, who looked round; I thought she had told, and in a funk left the hay-field.

In the afternoon in the farm-yard, there were people about, and no chance of having Pender. My desire to have her was intense. After dinner I went to the farm, Pender had gone home, so I strolled into the lane which the farm-buildings abutted on.

Between the Hall and farm-yard was a shrubbery path; laurels, hollies and evergreens nearly met overhead. It joined a belt of walk and plantation which skirted the lawns, gardens and a small paddock, and hid the farm-yard from the house. It took two or three minutes to walk from the farm to the house. The farm-yard on the other side opened on to a lovely village lane running between fields for a mile or so; on one side the land belonged to my aunt, the other to another proprietor. No one scarcely went along it but farm people. At one end were the two cottages in which I had fucked the two sisters years before; lower down past the farm-gates, were one or two other cottages in which lived farm-labourers, and in one of them the Penders. The lane then joined the high-road, which led by half-a-mile to the front of my aunt's house, and to the village. The farm-gates were always closed at dark. A great bell which when pulled set a dog barking was the way of getting in, after dark.

Leaving the wicket-gate ajar, I went down the lane, it was darkish, a fine summer night, but no moon. I knew where Pender lived, and by cunt attraction strolled in front of the cottage, though fearing to be seen.

As I left the farm-gate, female hay-makers who had worked till dark passed, curtseying as they recognized me. I thought of Whiteteeth but saw her not. Turning back from Pender's after I had strolled past the cottage, I went up the lane languishing with lust, and leaned against a field-gate. I heard a step, — it was the woman with white teeth.

"Good night." "Good night sir." "Come here." She stopped, came close, I laid hold of her arm, and drew her close to the gate. "Come into the field with me, I will give you five shillings."

A slight chuckle, the white teeth show. "I dare not." But as she spoke I had got her back up against the gate, and my hand on her grummit.

"My old man will be waiting me, — I can't." Lifting her clothes I tried to impale her as she stood. "No, no, — some one will pass," said she in a whisper. I put my hand on the latch, the gate opened, and we were in the field; the gate closed with a snap. I led her along by a ditch to a turn in the hedge; she made no resistance, in a minute we were buried in deep grass, my doodle buried in her cunt, we had spoken in whispers, all was silent excepting the insects which chirped in the hot summer's night.

How delightful these chance pokes are; there was my prick which had not been washed since it had left Pender's cunt, now wetting to its roots in the cunt of an unknown woman, — and I'd only just recovered from a clap. Not a word had we spoken from the moment we entered the field. We copulated in quietness. My prick did not uncunt, but I moved my arse outwards, when with tightening grasp, a heave up, and a tightening of her cunt, she whispered, "Go on doing it."

I could see the white teeth, but indistinctly, there was just sufficient light to see outlines, and anything white, but no colour. "I don't think I can, I have been doing it all day," I said.

"You've had one of the other women," said she in a whisper. "If I'd knowed it, you should not have had me," and with a jerk she uncunted me.

"No," said I, "it's a joke." She raised herself slightly to look me in the face, but it was too dark. "I thought not," said she; then she caught hold of my prick, fell on her back again, I saw indistinctly a broad expanse of thigh and belly. "Let's feel, — let's look." Wide open were her legs in a minute, I felt a great, cool belly, strong, thick, crisp hair, my fingers moved easily up the buttered love-trap, I could not see the opening.

"Hush!" said she, "there is a footstep." Quiet on the grass we lay; tramp, tramp it came past, and died away. "I wonder who it be," said she.

She had kept hold of my prick, and soon our bellies met. When done she hurried me not out of her, seemed to like my indulgence, till she whispered, "I must go, keep here till you can't hear my footsteps before you come out, we be near the yard, and if I be seen I don't know what they will say. My old man's at the 'Lion,' but I'll go straight home." "Perhaps he'll have gone home." "Not he, — they allus sticks at the Public late, when they works late." And with her cunt reeking, off she went.

I followed, intending to walk round to the front of the Hall. Passing Pender's house, to my astonishment she was standing at the door. I went up to her. "Oh!" said she, "Pender will be home, I expect him every minute." She could hear his footsteps a mile off, but she would not let me into the house.

Opposite to Pender's was also a field-gate, I persuaded her to come out and stand there with me; the hedge hid anyone coming along the lane. "At the first sound of a footstep," said I, "I will go into the field, and you can cross to your house." I was longing for the woman, but scarcely thought I could do it after my day's fucking. The idea of putting my prick still wet with Whiteteeth's juices, into Pender's quim, stimulated me; my cock stood (in those days if it stood it was sure of doing duty). I closed up to her whispering love and frigging her, she gradually getting beside herself with pleasure. At length up went my prick into her, and after a quarter of an hour's ramming, finished.

Meeting her husband in the lane might have caused suspicion, so into the field I went, intending to wait till he passed, laid down, fell asleep, awaking when it was broad day-light. I then waited two hours, walked around to the Hall, waited in the front till the door was opened, then went up to my room, and to bed. The servant saw me go in, and I imagine thought I had been out in the grounds without her knowing it. — certainly it never was known that I had been out all night.

I went to bed to rumple it, then down to breakfast, all the time thinking of some lie as an excuse for being out all night. "You were tired, and went to bed early I expect," said aunt. "Yes," said I. My limbs were aching from exposure to night-air, as I spoke.

Three days had made a great change in me. My prolonged abstinence from women, and now my recovery, my taking more to animal food, wine, and my usual mode of living, the quiet life I was leading, all put my physical forces at their highest. My cock stood from morning till night, not a woman passed me, young or old, without my desiring them. I thought of nothing else, and to this perhaps is due the variety of poking I got. Luck usually falls to those who look out for it.

I have said there was a shrubbery round the grounds connecting with that from the Hall to the farm; quite on the other side of the Hall were the stables, and the gardener's house. None of the stablemen or gardeners were on the farm-side. The servants of the Hall slipped down to the farm to gossip, but it was not allowed.

The only person who regularly traversed the shrubbery was Mrs. Pender, who twice a day took milk and dairy produce to the Hall.

Half-way down this shrubbery-path was a path connecting with that which went quite round the grounds. Cunningly contrived, and leading out of it was one to a large privy, usual in such grounds as my aunt's. A large octagonal house covered with ivy, with a door and two glass windows, a house devoted to shitting, but large enough to hold a dozen people.

One or two days after I had had Whiteteeth and Pender, I dodged about after the latter, but there were people about. I went off to the hay-making, but there were only men carting hay; so I went sniffing about the servants in the house, but nothing came of that. In the afternoon I went to the farm-yard, and prowled about to find some chance and place to get Pender, and went up into the big loft in the barn over the cart-shed. Why I went up there I don't know, and had not been there a minute before I heard a scuffle, and a kiss. "I shan't, now, — you saucy boy," said a female voice. Another kiss, and a scuffle. "I must go to the house," said the female. I peeped: it was a nursemaid, and my aunt's page. The girl ran off, leaving the page. They did not see me.

My aunt's male in-door servants consisted but of a middle-aged butler, who had been in her service many years, a slow, solemn man, a widower, and a page taken on when small, who had recently grown rapidly, and was a heavy, stupid, gawky lad, between fifteen and sixteen years old, too big for his place. My aunt, although always intending to dismiss him, kept him on out of kindness, but at length had said, "Page must go, I shall not give him a new suit, it will be waste of money." He looked stupid as an owl, and as if an idea about cunt would never have entered his mind.

This boy stood still, reflecting, then unbuttoned his trowsers, pulled out a stiff, big prick, and after pulling the prepuce down once or twice, buttoned it up again; stood still, again unbuttoned, sat down on some straw, reflected, and then frigged himself. After wiping his fingers on the straw he went off, leaving me wondering at his lust, the size of his doodle, and the quantity of spunk he shot. "That lumpish boy to do that!" forgetting what I did, when only a little older than him.

"Hullo! What are you doing here?" said a voice, — it was Pender's. He made no reply. "You'd better be off to the Hall, you've no business here." "I was fetching the nursemaid." "Well she's no business here; you cut, they will be ringing for you." When the voices ceased I descended, and went to the Hall.

The head farm-man had recently died, he, his wife and daughter, had lived in the cottage in the farm-yard. Pender's husband had taken his place, but still lived in his cottage in the lane. The woman whose husband had died attended to things in general, the daughter assisted in the dairy, and worked very often up at the Hall. A pretty girl of a common, rustic style of beauty, and about sixteen years old; she used to curtsey to me when she met me, but I had never cast my eyes at her. As I skulked out through the rickyard into the shrubbery-walk leading to the Hall I met her, stopped, and had a chat, a joke, and finished by a kiss, which she took in very bad part, and wiped away with her hand, as if I was quite disgusting. She was an only child, her name Molly.

CHAPTER VI

Joey and nursemaid. — The privy in the laurel-walk. — Scared.—
Whiteteeth in the ditch. — The nursemaid's bed-room. — Robert
amusing her. — A lost virginity. — Aunt and Joey. — Nearly caught.
— Amatory instructions to nursemaid.

Lusting worse after the kiss, I went to the house. My cousins
were out, my aunt taking her afternoon's nap. I rang my bed-room
bell for something, simply to get a woman near me, in the shape of
a housemaid who was as ugly as sin. I pulled out my cock when she
left, and thought of imitating the page, but did not; from my window saw the nursemaid was out with the child, and strolled out to
meet her. I must mention that the child (about four years old), was
a married cousin's child who had gone to India with her husband;
leaving the infant in charge of her mother, my aunt.

Nursemaid was a dry, plainish little woman whom I had
scarcely noticed until the previous three days. I talked to the infant,
and played with him, asked her if she would like a child, if she
would let me be the father, and got a chaffing reply. Suddenly it
struck me from the scuffle I had heard in the barn, that she and the
page were very intimate, and said as a random shot, "You would
not mind Robert cuddling you, would you now?" She coloured up,
looked confused, then said, as if she did not recollect, "Robert? —
who is Robert?" "Fat Robert the page." "Pough!" said she, "that big
boy!" She took up the child, and walked off, — not to the house,
but a long way away from it. After a time I followed her; she entered a grotto, or very large summer-house which formed part of
an artificial ruin in the grounds, and which was the scene of an
amusing adventure with this very child some years later on in my
life. There she sat down.

I saw what a good blind the child was, so went into the grotto to talk to him. He was sitting in her lap. In a minute said he, "I want to pee-wee." "Hush!" said she, "I will take you for a walk." "I will pee-wee," said he, scuffling down from her lap, running outside the summer-house; turning round, lifting his petticoats, and pissing in front of us.

"You naughty boy," said she. "What a little cock he has," said I. She snatched up the child, went towards the house, and there was an end for the time of my talk with her.

I dodged from hay-field to farm-yard, thence to the house, saw Pender, saw the young wench (Molly) I have named, looked out for Whiteteeth; it was all no go. I had dinner, then strolled down to the village, saw Whiteteeth outside the public with her husband. Back to the house, saw nursemaid, said in a whisper, "I shall come and sleep with you to-night." "That you won't," said she, "Master Joe always sleeps in my room." Randy and weary I went to bed, after nearly spending in my trowsers as I looked at my cousins' white necks in the drawing-room, and thought to myself, "I will go to ° ° ° (the market-town a few miles off to which I have before alluded), and have a woman tomorrow. During the hot night thought of cunt, cunt, cunt, would not frig myself, slept, awakened again with a stiff one, frigged, and then got repose.

The next morning I increased my acquaintance with the young wench Molly, chaffed the nursemaid, and besought her to let me sleep with her. Again went to the hay-field, but hay-making was finished, the weather dull, and further hay-making postponed till finer weather.

Keeping a sharp eye on page Robert, I soon saw he was spooning nursemaid; detected him kissing her, and putting his hand on her belly outside her clothes. She, seeing me, gave him a violent slap on the head; when I chaffed her, turned up her nose again and said, "A boy like that indeed; I beg you won't talk like that to me sir."

She slept in a room which was properly entered from the servants' corridor, which connected with the best part of the house through folding doors. But a door had been made in the room from the best part of the house, so that my aunt, who had had a large family, could more easily see how the children, when there, were being looked after. This door was just by a lobby which led to the

W. C.; any one going there might seem to be either going towards
the W. C., or towards the servants' staircase, the nursemaid's room
therefore could be entered from either door, and on two sides.

By the door on the servants' side was a housemaids' W.C. and
the servants' staircase which led also to the attics, where some slept,
and to a lobby with rooms mostly used for lumber, and where the
page had been put to sleep, away from females, or anyone else.
The butler slept in a little room adjoining the pantry and plate-
room, on the ground-floor.

Several days passed, I did not get a gay woman, but hunted
incessantly in hopes of getting Pender, or Whiteteeth, or the nursemaid. Young Molly I did not much think of; she seemed so young,
so chaste, so looked after, that I had no expectation, but do not
recollect what my views about her exactly were. Then I did not
care about young ones. A full-grown woman, large-arsed, with a
full-sized and fully-haired cunt was my greatest delight; above all
I liked room inside it for my cock to swell out, a tight cunt had no
delights to me.

After a few days my luck came as it mostly has. I went again
with my aunt to the dairy. Whilst she was talking to Pender a notion occurred to me. I did not go into breakfast, but waited in the
turning leading out of the shrubbery between the Hall and farm-
yard; and hiding, saw Pender take up the milk; a few minutes later
heard her returning, and stepped out. I had made up my mind to
have her in the privy; I have had women in similar places before
and since, and dare say that other men have.

She gave a start. "Come here." "No." But I clutched her. "Oh!
Now pray, — if anyone comes?" "But there won't, you know that,
— come this way," and I pulled her out of the main-walk. "Oh!
don't, there's a dear gentleman, — hush! Perhaps someone is near."
"Why they are all at breakfast." "I don't know where my husband is."

I had edged her down the path, and pushed her into the large
privy. Pender was randy, that I see now. A woman in fear yields
reluctantly, but she yields when she wants a man.

I locked the door and pressed her up against the wall. "Oh! I
am so frightened," said she, "later on I'll let you, — Oh! If we
should be found." She was in a funk, but what can any woman do,
who feels a man's warm prick outside her belly, and his hands

fumbling at her clitoris? the sensuous touch goes through her like lightning. Soon we were both spending.

My head was on her shoulder, my prick oozing its last drop of sperm, when she clutched me violently with a stare of terror in her face. It scared me. "It is he, it's he!" she said in a screaming whisper. "Oh! My God!" Tramp, — tramp, went a heavy male step in the shrubbery. "Oh! My God, I know his step!"

My prick flopped down, her petticoats dropped, but we stood close against the wall breathless. Tramp, — tramp, nearer, nearer it came, it passed the door, and died away in the distance. As he passed I peeped through the little red curtains over the window, and saw it was her husband's cap.

She sat down on the privy-seat, and buried her face in her hands. "My God," said she, "what would have happened, if he had found me here? But what does he do up this path? He has no business here," she added.

After a few seconds I went off in one direction, she as she told me, to her cottage, where she found her husband, and they had breakfast together; the good man not suspecting that his wife's cunt was full of sperm. Such are the chances of men.

I went into breakfast. My aunt was annoyed at my being so late. A female cousin, — a pretty girl, — whom it was wished I should marry, poured out my tea. I thought, "Ah! My dear girl, if you knew where my prick had been a few minutes ago, it would astonish you."

I went through the farm-yard a little before mid-day into the lane, and passed Pender without speaking. I met Whiteteeth carrying a mug and other things in a basket in the lane. She smiled, I followed to the memorable gate, then stopped. "Come into the field," said I. "I can't. I'm taking my good man his dinner, some of the women may come this way." "I owe you five shillings, I'll make it ten shillings, — come." "I don't want your money." "Come for love then."

"We must be quick," said she, following me, and cautiously she looked round. We passed through the gates to the place where we had laid down before; now in broad day it seemed dangerously near the lane. There was a sinking in the surface a little further on where cows had trodden the ground down to get to a ditch; there she put down her dinner-basket. Throwing up her petticoats, I saw her cunt was dark-haired. We fucked rapidly, no fumbling, stink-fingering, or frigging. I gave her ten shillings. "Give it me in silver," said she, "if I change it in the village it will be known." I took it back, gave her all the silver I had, owing her some. She said she would meet me again in the evening, unless her husband was working in the same field with her; he was mowing then.

I had luncheon, and a cock-stand again, walked round the grounds, and saw the nursemaid with the child. A cunning little bitch she was, — I did not see that plainly then, — she was rolling on the lawn playing with the child, her clothes went up to her knees; it was carelessness, she believing herself alone with the boy. She had a thin pair of limbs in nice boots. I peeped out from the shrubs, expecting to see higher, but did not. The little boy again wanted to piddle, she pulled out his cock, and held it. Whilst so interestingly engaged I advanced, she put his clothes down. I walked by her side. "You like holding that?" said I. She turned away. "Let me sleep with you." "This is my bed-fellow," said she, laughing, and went towards the house, I in the opposite direction of course.

I waited in the lane in the evening. Whiteteeth came along with others, eyeing me with a smile, and there was no opportunity. It was lightish. I thought to get Pender in the privy again next morning. It was not probable that her husband would pass that way again at that time. I went to bed. In the middle of the night was obliged to go to the water-closet, and sitting there thought of the housemaid, recollected that my aunt had said she would have Joey, who was not well, sleep with her that night. "Why, she will be alone, that nursemaid, she is randy one," I thought; but was by no means sure I should succeed, having known others who would go a long way, but stop short at fucking. If she resisted and there was a row, I should be obliged to leave my aunt's. All this ran through my mind whilst sitting on the water-closet. Water-closets had not long been known, they were quite proud of having them in my aunt's house.

My cock rose up, as the girl's neat thin legs came before my eyes. Cock stiffer, I went towards my bed-room, passed her door, heard her moving inside, and that settled me. Going to my room

I put in the candle, and in my dressing-gown went softly back, turned the handle, and pushed her door. It opened, and a sight met my astonished eyes.

She was lying on the bed, leaning on her elbow, in her chemise which was just above her knees, her legs partly up and open, her back turned partially from me as I entered. By the bed-side stood page Robert with his breeches opened, she was frigging, or feeling his great cock as she lay; the page's hand was between her knees, either on her cunt, or trying to get at it. They were in the enjoyment of mutual investigation. Whether it was going further I can't say. I believe she was frigging him, although she always denied that afterwards.

I had fairly entered the room before they (so engrossed were they with their pleasures) saw me; when with a shriek of, "Oh! My God, I am ruined! — Go (turning to the page), go out sir, or I will scream (to me). What's he here for? — What do you do here sir?" Without a word the page turned and bolted, pulling up his trowsers which fell down to his arse as he shuffled out of the room. She turned on one side without attempting to hide her legs or breast, and hid her face crying, "Oh! What shall I do? — What shall I do? — Go sir, go, — I don't know what he did here," and other excited, incoherent phrases.

I do not recollect saying a word, but bolted the door by which the page had gone out, then that by which I had entered; the bolts of that had been shot, only they had not quite closed the door before locking. "Be quiet, don't be a fool, I'll fuck you, — let's be comfortable," said I.

She refused. "Robert has fucked you." "No he ain't." "You were frigging him." "No I wasn't, — Oh! I don't know what you mean, or what you are saying." In her fear and agitation she had been betrayed into answering my assertions. "Oh! Dear, — Oh dear! — but you won't tell, will you sir? — It will be worse for you if you do," said she with a sort of threat, and altering her tone.

"I won't tell if you let me, — don't be a fool, — I will have you. If there is a row I will say I found you with Robert, and you and he will go out neck and crop. If they think badly of me I don't care; I shall leave, and in a few months they will overlook it; but you will have no character: you have been seen in the cart-shed with Robert." She started at that. "It's a story," said she, "who saw me?" and then she began to cry.

I pulled up my night-shirt, threw myself beside her, and pulled up her night-gown. My hand in an instant was on her cunt, her thin thighs closed to prevent me, but she was silent. "I will have you," said I, laying on her, and forcing open her knees with mine. Her resistance grew less. "I can't help myself," said she. "You are a blackguard, all the women say you are, — don't, — oh! Don't hurt me." "Nonsense, you have had a prick up it before." "No man has ever touched me." "Let me feel then." Her thighs slightly opened, I put a finger on it. "You have a very little cunt." "Don't be rough," said she. At length my belly met hers, my hand was round her slender bum, my prick on the slit. I pushed, it did not enter as I expected, then I felt her cunt roughly, and made her cry out. "What a small cunt you have," I said, and with a violent lunge pushed up it. She gave a suppressed gasp, "Oh! You hurt, oho." I pushed home, fucked and finished triumphantly, for I had had her spite of herself. We had spoken in whispers till she split, and then her cry was sharp, and loud.

I drew my prick out and myself upon my knees, to see how the cunt looked. She did not close her legs. By the light of the small candle I could see she had not much more hair on her cunt than a girl of sixteen years old. I laid by her side talking to her, then noticing my night-shirt said, "You are poorly." "Nothing of the sort." To put my fingers up to verify that, and look at them was the work of a moment. "Then I have made you bleed." "You have hurt me very much, you brute."

I did not like the girl nor her manner, didn't feel kind as I always do towards a woman I have had. "You little devil, to hear you talk one would think you had never had a man before." "Think what you like, but I never have, — go away now."

Her tight cunt, her freedom in permitting me to feel it, her sulky submission to all I wanted, astonished me. I fucked her again, and found her cunt very tight still.

She was taciturn, and when I said, "I had better go." "Go," she replied, "I suppose we shall be kicked out, — what will Robert say?" We agreed that she was to tell to Robert, that unless he held his tongue he would be kicked out without a character; that I was to tell him, that hearing conversation I had opened the door; that out of consideration for the poor girl I would not tell my aunt; but that I should notice him, and if I found him misbehaving himself, would tell my aunt that he was not a proper person to be in the house. Then I went to my bed-room.

I slept but a short time, awakened with a cock-stand, and slipping on my dressing-gown sneaked without slippers to her room again; knocked gently, heard a sleepy voice say, "Yes ma'am," and the door was opened. Spite of her opposition I got into bed with her, another fuck, she spent, and we both fell asleep.

A violent push awakened me. A knock at the door. "My God, it's Missus." We were in the dark. Pulling my dressing-gown off the chair I slipped with it under the bed, forgetting the door thro which I might have escaped. "Let her in," I whispered. Trembling she opened it. It was my aunt. "Here," said she, "take Master Joey, he has kept me awake all night." The nursemaid put him into the bed, my aunt standing by the side, her feet actually against my slippers. "What did you lock this door for?" said she. "Have I not told you always to keep this door unlocked?" "I felt frightened," said the girl. Away my aunt went, the girl sunk on the chair. There was now a light. In a whisper from under the bed I said, "Play with the child." She got into bed, took the boy in her arms, cuddled and talked to him, whilst I slipped out and regained my room. It was not day-light.

I had had three women the same day, had washed after neither, their lubrications had mixed with mine on my prick-stem and balls. A day or two following I had a stock of crabs; were they Pender's, or Whiteteeth's, or nursemaid's, or did I breed them? I had all three women afterwards, and never got the crabs again whilst at my aunt's. At the market-town I got a remedy, and was soon cured, but had to leave off fucking for a little while.

I had had the three women at a cost of five shillings; such luck never occurred to me before, or since.

I don't know when I have had such a jolly month's amusement as then followed, in getting first one, and then another of the women. All three met my wishes, but there were many difficulties, dodges, manœuvres to get either of them. Nursemaid moving about with the child in all sorts of places, came in for the most cock. She was small-boned, skinny, and her face had the expression that people have when they have just taken medicine. Under other circumstances I should never have noticed her, but the extreme smallness of her cunt was a novelty. I thought at first she was a regular intriguer, but came to the conclusion that I had had the first of her; and that until then she had been a masturbatrix, and frigged her flesh off her bones. Rub her clitoris for a second, her eyes would open wide and roll with such intense voluptuousness that for a moment her face looked beautiful. I used to tell her that she frigged herself thin.

I took, you may be sure, a great fancy to my little cousin Joey, for that gave me an opportunity of getting near the nurse. She was always out in the grounds with him in fine weather. I would throw the ball for the child to run after in the direction of the grotto, then walked round to see if any gardener was near, and tip her the wink. In we would go, and either against the seat, or up against the wall, or more frequently laying her with back on the big rustic table, and her legs round my hips, I poked her. Once she laid the little child on the table, and played with him there, whilst I threw her clothes up behind, and fucked her dog-fashion. "Lay hold of his cock," said I, as bum-wagging indications told me she was coming, and she kissed his little cock rapturously till she spent. The little beggar! — I wonder if in later years he recollected anything he saw. Years afterwards it was my fortune to see him fucking a servant in that very summer-house.

Whether the child was old enough or not to notice what he saw was a subject of talk with us. We came to the conclusion that we were safe. After luncheon, when my aunt took a nap and my cousins went out driving (if I could avoid driving out with them, and what lies I told to do that), was my most fortunate time; for the servants were lazy after their dinner, and the garden excepting from gardeners, quite free.

The summer-house, called the grotto, was a big one, there were wide seats nearly all round, chairs, and a big table in the middle capable of dining a dozen people. I was once frigged in it by a young lady, and two different servants did I fuck in it. These adventures will be told in their place. There were several summer-houses about the grounds, and I had the nursemaid in most of them.

Once only I slept with her the whole night, or rather lay fucking her, we were frightened to sleep, for fear of being caught. Joey was away. She told me the page had been showing her his prick for nearly a year; and she let him come to her room that night just to see what he would do. "You were frigging him, were you not?" "I was feeling it about." Then I told her I had seen him frig himself in the barn. "The servants at the Hall wonder at your being so much at the farm," said she. "How the devil can they know that?" I thought to myself. It put me on my guard.

She swore no man had ever touched her before me. "You forced me, and made me bleed; I would not have let you, only I feared you would tell what you had seen, and I should lose my character." She, however, took now to fucking, and was insatiable in getting me up her; her thin little form clung to me in a wonderful way and she loved my penis to push to the utmost up her tight little cunt.

"So my fanny's small?" she asked several times. "Tell me about other women's; are they much larger than mine? I know I have very little hair on mine." What nice talk we had.

She had been always nursemaid, had frigged herself as long as she could recollect, had nursed a girl eight years old who frigged herself incessantly, she had to slap her, and tie her hands to prevent it. "Now tell me truly, did you ever frig any boy?" "Never," but she had made their cocks stiff. She had frigged a girl, and been frigged in return. So much for nursemaids. She said she was 27.

The morning after I first had her, I told Robert to come to the garden directly the breakfast was cleared away. He came. "I heard a noise last night as I was passing, opened the door, and caught you; I have a good mind to tell your mistress, but the nursemaid has begged, and prayed me not; but if I hear you have ever mentioned this, or see you near her again, I will have you kicked out the next five minutes, and she too. — Be off." Away he went, without a word.

CHAPTER VII

Molly and Giles. — A country ale-house. — Pender's history. — How her virginity was taken. — Whiteteeth's ailment. — Molly in the loft. — Interrupted. — Molly tailed.

I fucked Whiteteeth in the meadow one night again. We selected a field further off, which led to another bit of luck. She had left me, and I was stopping quietly, so that if met, no one might suppose we had been together; when I heard on the other side of a hedge movements, and the voices of a male and female. They sat down within a few feet of where I was. I only heard imperfectly, and tell as well as I could gather what was said.

"I can't stay," said she. "Mother will be after me, — she don't know I am out of the yard." A kiss, — many kisses, — a scuffle, — "be quiet," — then all was a mumble. Then "I won't, — I won't, — never again, — you shan't." "Hush!" said he. "Suppose some one is near." "Do let's feel it, let's do it," said the male, "do it once, do it twice, it's all the same once done." I kept as quiet as death.

"No" (here something I could not catch), — "no, — it warn't no pleasure to me, — I've been crying ever since, — you won't marry me after all I dare say, though I let you do it." "So help me God I will, I'll marry you." He swore quite loudly. "Hish!" "Mother won't let us, she hates you." The female wimpered, then was mumbling, kissing, soothing, quietness, then all of a sudden, "Oh! You're a hurting me with your fingers." "Hish! — Hish! — Be quiet!" Then I could hear nothing; — then, "No, I'll be getting in a mess like Bess." Said the man half angrily, "She were a fool, she needn't a had a child; I knows a mother who can stop any gal having a child." "Now don't, — oh! It hurts, — no, — oh! — hoe!" The voices sank; kisses came quick, a slight rustling, and all was quiet.

Then I heard broken words from both, but in a subdued voice. "I'll never let you no more," said the female. "You go that way." Kiss, kiss, and they cut off, the female towards the gate I had entered the field by, he across the fields. She piddled, and waited till he had gone. Dodging her I moved after her, and saw her enter the farm-yard, but could not identify her. It must be Molly, I was sure, no other female at that time was likely to enter there. Why, Molly has been fucked!

Next day I asked nursemaid about Molly. "Oh! That's why you go to the farm so often," said she, laughing jealously. "She's a good girl, her mother looks after her sharp."

I had most difficulty in getting Pender. She would not go into the privy again. I fucked her once or so in the barn, but at railroad pace; both anxious, the fuck barely worth having. "I'll go to mother's next Sunday," said she. "If P. goes to the Red Lion on Saturday night, I'll be outside in the lane." We met in the lane, but I could only get a feel, and arrange about Sunday. "I'll go to mother's at °°° (the market-town), if the day be fine; P. won't come, he don't like mother, or he'll only come in the evening."

On Sunday I rode to the town, passing Pender on the road in her Sunday finery, went to a lane where was an ale-house and bakery below, a baudy house above, and took a room (Fred told me of the place years before). Pender went to her mother's, and so soon as people were in church came to the appointed corner. I kept well ahead of her, entered the house, and after hesitating at the door in she came after me.

"How could you be such a fool as to walk about outside like that?" said I angrily, for I had feared she would not enter. "I was frightened," she replied, "and oh! I must get back to mother's by dinner-time at one, when the Publics and the bake-houses open."

It was a delicious day, and beats in my recollection many others of fevered enjoyment. Little by little I stripped a tall, fine, stout, healthy, country woman, a regular spanker; with white flesh, firm, soft, satiny, and smelling like new milk. She was bashful without affectation, ashamed to expose her charms, yet proud to do so to me. She was clad in snow-white coarse linen, neat and clean from her boots to her head. What enjoyment we had! How we spent! I fucked her three times before the dinner-hour, my prick or my finger was in her cunt for an hour and a half.

At half-past twelve, off she went; in less than two hours back she came. She had said that a friend of hers was ill, and she had promised to sit with her (a woman cocking is never at loss for a lie). It was raining. The umbrella helped to hide her, but she was nervous about being seen. I had dinner at the house, the woman cooked well; the keepers were really small traders who did not mind their rooms being used for love-making, and had none of the dirty tricks of a London baudy-house keeper. They fetched me a bottle of good sherry.

I got as lewed as could be, and to her astonishment turned her face against the bed, threw up her clothes and had her with my belly against her rump. I shall never forget the comicality of that fuck, her protesting against it, and her wonderment at such an attitude. The novelty upset her.

I don't recollect much more what I did, but it was an afternoon of baudy teaching on my part, of confidences on hers; it was the first time we had a chat together on general matters. Speaking of her husband she said, "Why you have done it as much almost as he has done since we have been married." "What, in a year?" "Yes, we were married several weeks afore he did it at all, so I told mother, and that's why he don't like her."

She was warmed with wine, we were on the bed cuddling, my fingers at work on her clitoris, we were enjoying each other's nakedness. I pressed her to tell me more, and now narrate briefly what I heard of her first fuck, her grievances and troubles.

"After I spoke to mother, mother said to him, 'You don't want a wife much Mr. Pender, I think.' 'Why of course I do, I should not have married had I not.' 'Well it don't seem like it,' said mother. Then Pender said, 'You mind your own business, mother, or you'll make it hot for your daughter,' and with that he went out, and slammed the door. Mother did not like to say any more, for fear he would ill-treat me. Soon after he said, 'What have you been saying to your mother?' 'Nothing,' I answered. He looked queer, and still he did not do anything to me for some time."

"When I was in bed I used to lay and cry, he'd say, 'What are you crying about, woman?' but I never told. After that, one night he took my hand, put it on his thing and said, 'Feel that, lass.' Then he felt all around me you know," said Mrs. P., laughing, "and he had never done that before, — and with no more ado he got atop and said, 'Now don't be a fool,' and then he did it, — and that's all," said Mrs. Pender, describing her first marital poke, — the real beginning of her married life, — as she laid side by side by me, with my prick in her hand.

I was curious, — a man always is in such matters. "Did it hurt you? — Did he get up you quick?" "I'm sure it was pretty quick, I cried out, and it hurt. I was all in a tremble; then he said, 'Well you were all right and tight five minutes ago.' I bled a lot."

"Perhaps your old sweetheart had done it before?" "He never laid hand on me, but to kiss me." "Nor any one?" "Oh! Yes, they have tried all round I think," said she laughing. "You have, — so has the squire, and lots of 'em, you can't help that, — if a girl's taken unawares, a man can get his hand on her thighs, but he won't get more; and I always slapped their heads, and there was an end of it." I recollect certainly her slapping at mine hard enough.

Then she relieved her mind. "He's not a bad man, he don't get drunk, and we don't quarrel; but I don't care for him, and never did." "Ah! You lost your young man, and thought you would be fucked by someone." "I did not think at all about it, but in a sort of spiteful fit, when he asked me to marry him, I said yes. I didn't think about his not doing it to me much, till a woman asked me how I liked it, and how often he did it; but I told her he did it a lot. Then I talked, and found men did it often to their wives, and he does not do it to me once in three weeks. So I fretted." "What do you do?" said I. She laughed, I gave her clitoris a rub. "That's what you do?" "Yes," said she. "Do you often want fucking?" "Every day," said Mrs. Pender frankly and openly. "Did you want it the day I had you by the hay-stack?" "I just did." Then she added that her husband knew she frigged herself, and usually said to her when she intimated that she should like him up her, "Oh! Do it yourself, if your cunt's so hot, I'm tired."

She had married a man much more than double her own age, who poked her once in three weeks; this healthy, well-fed woman of twenty-three who wanted a nightly roger, and could have spent half-a-dozen times daily with ease. She now had got me, liked me, was ready to do anything with me or for me as I found out, and was sorry for it.

At six o'clock she was obliged to leave. We were both fucked out, and parted, regretting that a month must pass before she could venture to go to her mother's again. I had left her enough to think about, for I fucked her in several attitudes. It gave me pleasure to teach her.

Next day Molly ran in my head, so I fished about to hook her. She had seemed to me so young, that I had taken but little notice of her; liking the fat-cunted, biggish-arsed females best. Now I noticed her being so plump and fresh, and wondered I had never noticed her previously. When I met her, I looked in her face thinking, "Innocent as you look, your cunt's been wetted by a man." I longed for her, but she was nearly always in the farm-yard, either with her mother or Pender, when not assisting up at the Hall; but when a man hunts a woman he is sure to get a chance, as will be seen I did.

Just after I had Pender on the Sunday, an annoying thing occurred to me. Whiteteeth worked in all parts of the parish, and she just now came to do something on my aunt's grounds, — weeding I think. Catching her one day alone I took some liberty. She resisted sullenly, looked up, and nodding her head said, "You gave me a bad illness." "What!" said I. "Did you not?" said she. I swore I had not; did she think me such a blackguard? Would she see my prick? "Then my damned old man's given it me, and he swears I gave it him," said she. She had a clap. I never had her afterwards, and was told that lots of men had had her. Fred told me soon afterwards, that he had, but that she had been quite steady since her marriage, he believed. I didn't undeceive him.

When the farm-work was over Molly stood sometimes at the lane-gate. Loitering about I saw a man named Giles there, who when he saw me moved off. I laid hold of her once or twice, kissed and made the usual approaches, at last got a hot fit of lust for her, and felt I would do anything to get her once. After two women with well-haired cunts I did nothing but picture to myself that she had a small cunt, and but little hair on it, like nursemaid's, — and the idea excited me.

I have already described the barn, step-ladder, and loft; the chickens sometimes flew up the ladder into the loft. I had seen Pender go up, and whisk them down. Looking about one afternoon (hay-making was again going on), no one seemed about, though

Pender was in the dairy. I entered the barn from the rick-yard side, just as Molly was going up the ladder, showing her legs innocently enough.

"What pretty legs," I cried. The girl scuffled up as hard as she could to get out of sight, I after her. She was chasing some chickens, and was as red as a turkey-cock in the face. I caught hold of her, prick standing, heart beating, and kissed her. She resisted, I put my hand up her clothes, and in the struggle we both rolled on to a heap of loose hay; I had felt the flesh of her thighs. "Leave off," said she, "or I'll call mother." Her mother was then ill in the farm-house.

"Don't be a fool," said I, attempting it again. "Don't you do such things sir, — I'll call mother, — it's wrong of you." "If you do," said I brutally, "I'll tell your mother Giles fucked you in the field last week."

Never shall I forget the look of the poor girl's face. "Oh! — oh!" said she breathless, "you didn't, — it's a story, — oh! Now pray, — Oh! it's a shocking story, — I warn't in the field." "Don't. — Oh! It hurts," said I, repeating other words which had been wandering through my brain ever since I heard them. "I heard you and the man say that."

She began to cry, putting her head in her hands. "Let me do it, and I won't tell, — no one will know, and you won't tell Giles, that's certain." She ceased crying, and fixed her eyes on me wildly, I got my hand up her clothes, her thighs were closed, she kept pushing me away, "No, — no, — no." Forgetting where I was, or that anyone might come up the ladder, I had my prick out, and with a struggle got my hand on her cunt. "You won't tell, really now?" "Not if you let me." A little more scuffling, and I had her down. She was quiet, and I was fucking with all the delight and energy which a fresh woman gives a man, when I heard "Molly, Molly" shouted out. With a violent start she uncunted me, and I spent over her motte. "Where are you such a long time, Molly?" "There is a hen up here," said Molly, who had started up, "and I think she has laid, but can't find the egg." And Molly disappeared down the ladder. "You're wanted up in the Hall," said the voice, — it was Pender's; — their voices died away. How pleased Pender would have been had she known the condition of Molly's motte!

Nothing is so irritating as spending outside a long-coveted cunt, when another thrust or two would have left the sperm up it, — it is maddening. I could think of nothing but the girl; although I had barely felt, and had seen nothing of her charms, she seemed to me perfection. For a day or two I got no chance, so I wrote on a bit of paper, "You will get into a mess, unless you meet me to-night; I'll be in the barn at eight o'clock; come in through the wicket," — or something to that effect. It was intended to frighten her, for she avoided me. I pushed the note into her hands at the Hall.

I walked through the farm-yard afterwards and saw her, she shook her head as I passed. I said rapidly, — Pender was in sight, — "You had better." In the evening I hid myself in the loft, allowed the barn-doors to be closed, and should have had to stay all night there if some one had not undone one of the wickets; they fastened them outside.

I had been there a long time, it was dark. "I am in here till tomorrow morning," I thought, and walked up and down barely restraining myself from frigging, such was my state of lust. It was possible that circumstances might prevent her from coming, and I had given up hope, when the wicket opened. It was she; she came up into the loft; I caught her in my arms.

"What do you want? — You ain't agoing to tell? — You ain't heard anybody say anything?" said she. I could not see, but felt her tears, reassured her, told her I loved her; who would know but us two? "What harm have I done you?" said the poor girl, "Giles is going to marry me, that's different, — oh! don't now." I had pushed her on to some hay, threatening her one minute, coaxing her the next.

I was feeling her. My hand was roving over a plump little bum and belly, my finger entered a tight little split on which was a little crisp hair, my prick followed my finger, and on the new sweet hay, belly to belly, but not mouth to mouth (she would not kiss), my prick revelled in a cunt which seemed divine, and was soon drowned in a pond of its own making.

"Mother's better, and has gone down the lane to Pender's," said she, "if she comes back she will wonder where I am, — let me go." I would not, until I had again enjoyed her; and then the lass enjoyed me. She unclosed the wicket in the rick-yard which let me out. I got across a field into the lane, went past the farm-gates, and there stood Molly with her mother. "Good night," said I to the mother, then passing Pender's cottage, I went round, and up to the Hall.

I thought that having fucked Molly I should be contented; but the little cunt, the little hair, the small bum, made me want Molly again. I could not get her, she evidently did not wish for me; I had had her against her will, and so had her again afterwards. Perhaps only seemingly against her will, for though she resisted, and accused me of breaking my word, she had spent with me, and was to spend again, perhaps in spite of herself.

I cannot recollect the name of Molly's swain, though I have tried hard, so call him Giles, — it is a bumpkin's name.

CHAPTER VIII

Field-women. — Fred at home. — Smith, the field-foreman. — A rape of a juvenile. — Funking consequences. — Nelly consents. — Fred looks on.

Strolling into the fields one day, idly smoking my cigar, later on in the year, groups of girls and women were at work. I talked to the field-foreman and looked at the girls, especially the younger ones, and wondered if they had smaller cunts than Molly; of one whether she had any hair on her cunt at all. Some were apparently not more than twelve years of age. I longed to see their cunts, and joked with one or two of the larger girls; but a decided longing for young cunts had set in on me. "Pender," said I one day, "what a lot of fast-looking chits there are in the fields." "They are a bad lot," said she, "there is one gal there only just fourteen in the family way." I was just going to fuck Pender, and daresay finished quickly enough, for at at that age if I was fucking, and thought of anything very baudy, with a sudden spasm I spent right off, even if I had only just got my cock up. Indeed women used to say to me, "How quick you are; why did you not wait for me?"

What with Molly, Pender, and nursemaid I was so well kept in cunt, that I only occasionally went back to London. I had dissipated a large part of my fortune; fucking here had not then cost me five pounds, so that besides the novelty and delight of the intrigues and the risks I ran, it was economical; and things might have gone on so, when back came my cousin Fred.

A wide-awake fellow was Fred. When my aunt said how delighted they all were to see me so steady, and had never seen me enjoy myself so much at the Hall before, he stared. "He goes often," said aunt, "with me to the dairy." "Yes, and pats the cows," said a cousin. Fred winked at me, and when we were alone said, "What's your little game Walter, where are you cunting now old fellow?" "Cunt," said I, "is of no use, my clap's not gone; but thank God I think it's getting all right again." He was quite taken in. "You have done the best thing you could," said he, "there is nothing here much to excite you, no woman worth having, is there?"

We wandered daily over the farm and grounds, smoking and talking; he had been so much away, that faces were unfamiliar to him. "What a skinny bitch that is with Joey," said he (that was nursemaid). "That's a fine woman," said I, indicating Pender. "Yes," said he, "I recollect before she was married trying to grope her, and she nearly knocked me over." "I would not mind having her." "No chance for you my boy. Ah! has not that little Molly grown," said he with a laugh, "I have often seen the little devil's arse, and her cunt too when a child, playing about the place, — she is nice; I think I'll have a try on her." "Aunt's partial to her," said I. "Don't care." "She is very young." "Tighter cunt, and more to teach," replied he, — and I noticed he began to be very sweet to Molly afterwards.

One morning we walked into the fields, the foreman came up and saluted us. He had been on the farm before Fred and I were born. "Well, Smith," said Fred, "still at the old games, — any bastards lately?" "Oi am tow ould for that now, Master." "Perhaps the girls don't like poking now?" "Oi they do, but they doon't like me as they did." Smith (my cousin told me), had had the credit all his life of poking all the agricultural laborers, and had been threatened with dismissal on account of it. "He might have had a worse berth," said I, "there are half-a-dozen girls in the field I would not mind sleeping with." "Why don't you have them?" said Fred. "I don't want to lose my character here." "That be damned, you can always have a field-girl, nobody cares, — I have had a dozen or two."

I turned this over in my mind. We were again in the fields, on the way there he gave me a long account of how old Smith used to wink at his having the field-girls; and indeed I had often heard him tell it. "You tell him you would like any one, and see what will come of it." There was a pretty sun-burnt girl about fifteen years of age that had given me a cock-stand. "That's a pretty girl Smith, I'd give a sovereign to have her, — is she loose?" "Don't think so yet squire, she be skittish; her sister's not fourteen, and they say she be in the family way, when one sister takes to it squire, the others generally do." "Where do you pay their wages?" I asked. The old fellow leered at me. "Why you be a taken a leaf out of young squire's book sir (it was Fred's advice); I pays them next at the root-stores," a shed about a quarter of a mile from the farm-yard, and in which he had a desk. The women waited outside the shed, each being called in and paid in succession. They were paid every night, excepting in hay-making times.

At pay-time I strolled into the shed. One by one he paid. The girl I wanted came last. He told her he wanted her to take a parcel to the village. "Yes sir," said she. Off old Smith went to fetch the parcel, — it was the dodge, Fred told me afterwards, the old goat always adopted to get a girl left alone with him.

Very randy but nervous I went out with Smith, then strolled back into the shed. The girl had seated herself on some loose straw, she got up and curtsied. "Sit down my dear," said I, "you may have some time to wait," and talked to her. "You are very pretty, — you will keep your sweetheart waiting." Smiling, she said, "I ain't got no sweetheart sir." Another look or two, and my randiness getting the better of me, I began chaffing suggestively, she sat down besides me, then I talked for a quarter of an hour warmer and warmer, then kissing, tickling, and pinching her legs. This did not seem to affect her, she enjoyed it; then out I pulled my prick, and all changed at once. "Oh!" said she, rising up scared to go. I pulled her back.

"Let's do it to you." "I won't." "You've been fucked." "I ain't, — I am only fifteen years old (she did not affect ignorance of my meaning), — leave me alone." I threw her down, and got my hand up her clothes. She loudly screamed, and that is all I recollect clearly: I know that I struggled with her, offered her money, told her I knew her sister had been fucked, and a lot more. I was so much stronger that she had no chance, I rolled her over, she screamed, and screamed again (there was no one nearer than the Hall), I exposed her bum, her thighs, her cunt, and all she had. I was furious with lust, determined to have her; at last she was under me, panting, breathless, crying, and saying, "Now don't, — oh! pray don't," but I lunged fast, furiously, brutally, and all I heard was, "Oh! Pray, — pray now, — oh! — oh! — oh! Pray," as I was spending in her holding her tight, kissing her after I had forced her. Her tears ran down. If I had not committed a rape it looked uncommonly like one, and began to think so as I lay with my prick up her.

I got off her, saw for an instant her legs wide open, cunt and thighs wet and bloody, she crying, sobbing, rubbing her eyes. I was now in a complete funk, I had heard field-women so lightly spoken of, that they were so accessible, that I expected only to go up a road that had often been travelled. This resistance and crying upset me, the more so when at length rising, she said, "I'll tell my sister, and go to the magistrate, and tell how you have served me out."

I really had violated her, saw that it would bear that complexion before a magistrate, so would not let her go, but retained her, coaxed, begged, and promised her money. I would love her, longed for her again, would take her from the fields, and every other sort of nonsense a man would utter under the circumstances. She ceased crying, and stood in sullen mood as I held her, asking me to let her go. I took out my purse, and offered her money which she would not take, but eyed wishfully as I kept chinking the gold in my hand. What a temptation bright sovereigns must have been to a girl who earned ninepence a day, and often was without work at all.

In an hour and a half I suppose, old Smith came back, he had really got a parcel for her to take. She began again to cry, and blurted out that the gentleman had insulted her. "What, has he kissed you?" "More than that, — boo hoo." "What has he done?" "Been dirty with me, — and I'll tell my sister, and go to the justice."

"Pough, child," said Smith, he arn't done you any harm, — a gent like him, — don't make a fuss, — make it up, — it's all fair yer know twixt a young man, and a maid, — daresay yer wanted him to be dirty with you, — a gent like him, you ought to be proud of sich a one making love to you, — here, take this parcel, and be off."

"Take the sovereign (she had refused it before), I'll give you more another day; it will help to keep you a while, — hold your tongue, and no one will know," said I. She hesitated, pouted, wriggled her shoulders, but at last took the sovereign, and took up the parcel, saying she would tell her sister. Then said the foreman, "None o' that, gal, an I hears more on that, you won't work here any more, nor anywheres else in this parish, — I knows the whole lot on you, I knows who got yer sister's belly up, — she at her age, she ought to be ashamed on herself, and I knows summut about you too, — now take care gal." "I've done nothing to be ashamed on," said the girl, "you're a hard man to the women, they all say so, — ohe! — ohe!" "Well there," said he, dropping his bullying tone, "the square won't harm you; I think you be in luck if he loikes you, — say you nought; — that be my advice." The girl, muttering, went her way.

I followed her (it was getting dark), was so kind and coaxing, promised her so many fine things (I'm not sure I didn't say I'd marry her), that as we neared the village, the little lass let me pull her into a convenient grassy corner, and fuck her again. She promised she'd say nothing to anyone about it.

Next morning I had a fear, and was annoyed with myself. If the girl said anything it would be all over the parish in the afternoon, and in my aunt's ears the next day; all that for a dirty little farm-laborer. I had had none of that sensuous delight which both mentally and physically is found in getting into a virgin, had never thought of having her as one, nor did I recollect much cunt resistance to my penetration: but she certainly was a virgin. In my furious lust, and with my unbendable stiff prick I must have hit the mark, and burst through it at one or two cunt-rending shoves. She had given a loud cry in the midst of it, "Oh! Pray now, — oh! Pray," — but I had heeded it not. What excited me was her youth, her size, and the idea of having a little cunt with but little hair on it, something smaller than Molly's. In bed, thinking of, and funking consequences, I longed for a girl still smaller, for one with no hair on her cunt at all. On further reflection I calmed. She had taken the money, and let me do it a second time; it was all right, and I rose, and went to the scene of my exploit.

The girl was not at work in the fields, and my funk returned. "Smith," said I, "is Nelly (let's call her Nelly) here?" "No, nor her sisters." "Sisters?" "Yes, there are two: one a woman called ***, very much older, the other younger than Nelly, and the young un they says be with kid."

I went to the farm-yard, there saw Fred talking to Molly. "Ulloh, you have taken a letch there." "I'll have her," said he. Pender went across the yard. "I would sooner have her," said I. "Aye, a damned fine woman, but coarse, smells strong I should say when she sweats, or is randy, and I like them younger." I was jealous about Molly, and walked away. Fred joined me, and after dinner, I like a fool told him all about the girl ravished in the root-shed in the Twelve-Acre field.

"Was she a virgin? — she is a plump little bitch, — you were in luck, — oh! never fear there will be no row; the saying down here is, 'They all take it by the time they have half-an-inch of hair on their cunts.' She will be rather proud you have fucked her than otherwise. Has she much hair there? — has she any bubbies?" I told him all I knew, which was but little, not recollecting even if she had any cunt-wig at all.

Next day the two sisters were at work again. I told Smith that after his dinner I wished to speak to the girl. The old cock-bawd told me to wait at the root-shed; and the girl came there to fetch his handkerchief which he left purposely. When she saw me, how she started. No, she had told no one, but was not going to let me do what I liked. A kiss. "I don't like your hand on my legs, — oh! Now you said you would not, — take your hand away."

My finger was on her cunt, I was feeling what little hair she had, my finger went up it, oh! How tight it was! "Now darling, let me, I won't let you go till you do, — there, what a dear little belly, — let me kiss it." "They will wonder why I am gone so long, — my sister will be asking me questions, — do let me go." "No." "Oh!" I had her on the straw. "Be quiet, dear, — my prick's up you, — be quiet — ah! — ah!"

With her cunt well buttered, off she ran. I buttoned up. Just then at the door appeared Fred holding his sides and laughing. "What's up Fred?" "Oh! — Oh! — Oh!" "What's the fun?" "Oh! — Oh! — I've been looking at you fuck the little bitch. I saw her go in, and you go to the shed an hour ago, but did not know you were there then, so thought I would like the young one; it's five days since I've had a woman, and as I was going in heard your two voices, listened and looked till you had done the job."

"It's a damned unhandsome thing," said I in a rage. "You would have looked at me if you had caught me," said Fred. "You leave the girl alone, it's my manor." "All right, but I'll have little Molly, I have given her a kiss." Off he went, leaving me jealous about that one as well. He was treading on my heels a little too much to please me.

Four women I had poked now, being like a cock among hens, cared about neither, but could not bear the idea of Fred going up them, though I knew it was useless to try to prevent the young squire, the future master, a fine officer. Pender said to me one day, "The squire means harm to Molly; it's a shame for an officer like him to harm a poor girl; I caught him kissing her, and putting his hands up her petticoats. I'll tell Missus if I see any more of it." "Do," said I, "you tell my aunt."

So she did, and aunt requested Fred not to go to the farm-yard, and Molly was all but locked up. In a few days Fred said it was damned slow, and went to London. I, for a change, went with him.

My departure put Pender in tears, she did all she could to get me up her, and before I left I got Molly into the loft on promising never to ask her again, and there had my first good look at her belly and cunt, and fucked her. Nursemaid I advised to avoid the page, or I would never have anything to do with her more. She grinned and said, "What a loss." Nelly I caught in the lane, fucked her and she promised to be chaste and never let any other man put his finger on her. Then I departed with Fred to virtuous London.

Before leaving, Mrs. Pender said, "I'm afeard I'm in trouble, my poorliness ain't come on for two months now."

CHAPTER IX

Laura and Fred. — Vauxhall amusements. — A juvenile harlot. — A linen stopper. — The hairless and the hairy. — Ten and forty. — A snub. — At my aunt's. — Nursemaid and page missing. — Pender with child. — Molly and Giles caught. — Mr. Pender's letch.

Theatre every night, heavy lunches, heavy dinners, much wine, and cigars never out of my mouth, that was the first few days' proceedings. Fred was keeping a woman named Laura of whom I shall say more; she was always with us. I don't recollect having a woman for a few days, but it may have been otherwise. On the fifth or sixth night we went to Vauxhall Gardens to a masquerade. It was a rare lark in those days. A great fun of mine was getting into a shady walk, tipping the watchman to let me hide in the shrubs, and crouching down to hear the women piss. I have heard a couple of hundred do so on one evening, and much of what they said. Such a mixture of dull and crisp baudiness I never heard in short sentences elsewhere. Although I had heard a few similar remarks when I waited in the cellars of the gun-factory, it was nothing like those at Vauxhall, and it amused me very much. There were one or two darkish walks where numbers of women on masquerade nights went to piss, and many on other nights.

At supper Laura said, "Where have you been the last hour?" I laughed. "Tell us." "Hiding in the shrubs where ladies go by ones, twos, and threes without men." Laura understood. "Serves them right, they should go to the women's closets; but you are dirty." "Well, it was such a lark hearing them piddle and talk." Fred, always coarse, said he never knew a woman piss off so quickly as Laura. Laura slapped his head. She had not been gay, and was very modest

290

in manner and expressions; but loved a baudy joke not told in coarse language.

The signal sounded for fireworks. Off we ran to get good places. I cared more about women than fireworks, and lagged behind, seeing the masquers and half-dressed women running and yelling (fun was fast and loose then). I passed a woman leading a little girl dressed like a ballet-girl, and looked at the girl who seemed about ten years old, then at the woman who winked. I stopped, she came up and said, "Is she not a nice little girl?" I don't recollect having had any distinct intention at the time I stopped; but at her words ideas came into my head. She — what a small cunt, — no hair on that. "Yes, a nice little girl," I replied. "Would you like to see her undressed?" "Can I fuck her?" I whispered. The little girl kept tugging the woman's hand and saying, "Oh! Do come to the fireworks." "Yes, if you like, — what will you give?" I agreed to give I think three sovereigns, a good round sum for a common-place poke then.

She told me to go out of the gardens first, get a cab, and stop at a little way from the entrance. In three minutes the woman and child joined me. At about five minutes drive from Vauxhall we stopped, walked a little way, turned down a street, and after telling me to wait one or two minutes, she opened the door of a respectable little house with a latch-key, went in and closed it. A minute afterwards she opened the door, and treading lightly as she told me, I found myself in a parlour out of which led a bed-room, both well furnished. Enjoining me to speak in a low tone I sat down, and contemplated the couple.

The woman was stout, full-sized, good-looking, dark, certainly forty, and dressed like a well-to-do tradeswoman. The girl's head was but a few inches above my waist, and she certainly was not more than ten years, but for such age as nice and fleshy as could be expected. She had an anxious look as she stared at me, and I stared at her. The last month's constant desire to have a cunt absolutely without any hair on it was to be realized, I was impatient but noticed and remarked, "Why, you have gas!" — a rare thing then in houses. "Beautiful, is it not?" said the woman, and in a voluptuous and enticing manner began undressing, until she stood in a fine chemise, a pair of beautiful boots, and silk stockings. Engrossed with the girl whom I was caressing, I scarcely had noticed the woman;

but as she pulled up her chemise to tighten her garter, and showed much of a very white thigh, I said, "I've made a mistake, I did not mean you." "No," said she, "but it's all the same." She came to me, pinched my cock outside saying "oho" as she found it stiff, and then undressed the child to her chemise. I had white trowsers and waistcoat on, and was anxious about rumpling them. At my request she drew my white trowsers off over my boots with great care; then divesting myself of coat and waistcoat I stood up with prick spouting. "Look there, — feel it Mary." The girl not obeying she took her little hand, and made her feel it. Sitting down I lifted the girl on to my knees, and put my hand between her little thighs.

"Give me the three pounds," said the woman. All my life I have willingly paid women before my pleasure; but thought I was going to be done, so demurred, and asked if she supposed I was not a gentleman, took out my purse, showed I had plenty of money, gave her one sovereign, and promised the others directly I had the child, — and then pulled off my boots.

We went into the bed-room, she lighted candles, the gas streamed in through the open door. "Lay down Mary," said she. "Oh! He ain't going to do it like the other man, — you said no one should again," said the girl whimpering. "Be quiet you little fool, he won't hurt you, — open your legs." Pushing her back, or rather lifting her up, there I saw a little light-pink slit between a pair of thighs somewhat bigger than a full-sized man's calves; the little cunt had not a sign of hair on it. To pull open the lips, to push up my finger, to frig it, smell it, then lick it was the work of a minute. I was wild, it was the realization of the baudy, dreamy longings of the last few weeks. I was scarcely conscious that the old one had laid hold of my prick, and was fast bringing me to a crisis.

Pushing her hand away I placed my prick against the little cunt which seemed scarcely big enough for my thumb, and with one hand was placing it under the little bum, when the girl slipped off the bed crying, "Oh! Don't let him, — the other did hurt so, — he shan't put it in."

"Don't do it to her, she is so young," said the woman in a coaxing tone. "Why, that is what I came for." "Never mind, it hurts *her*, have *me*, I am a fine woman, look," and she flung herself on the bed, and pulled up her chemise, disclosing a fine form, and to a randy man much that was enticing. "Look at my hair, how black it is, — do you like tassels?" said she, and throwing up her arms out of her chemise, she showed such a mass of black hair on her arm-pits as I have rarely seen in other women, and rarely in an English woman at all.

"What the devil did you bring me here for? — it was for her, not you, I have hair, — I like a cunt without hair."

"Have me, and look at her cunt whilst you do it, — here Mary," and she pulled the young one on to the bed, cunt upwards. But dis-appointed, lewed, and savage, I swore till she begged me not to make a noise, and saying, "Well, — well, — well, — so you shall, — hold your tongue (to the girl), he won't hurt you, — look, his cock is not big." She pulled the girl on to the edge of the bed again, and brought her cunt up to the proper level with the bolster and pillows. Then said the woman, "Let me hold your cock, you must not put it far in, she is so young." I promised I would only sheath the tip; but she declared I should not unless she held it. "Wrap your handkerchief round it," said she. I did so, and that left only half its length uncovered. Impetuously I tore the white handkerchief into pieces, wrapped round about an inch of the stem of my prick with it, which then looked as if it was wounded, and bound up; then hitting the little pink opening I drove up it. I doubted whether I should enter, so small was it. It held my prick like a vice, but up her cunt I was, the woman promising the child money, to take her to Vauxhall again, and so on, and then put her hand over her mouth to prevent her hollowing, — she did not hollow at all really.

I spent almost instantly, and coming to my senses held her close up to my prick by her thighs, — there was no difficulty so light a weight was she. There I stood for a minute or two. "My prick is small now," said I, "unroll the handkerchief." "No," said the woman. "I will give you ten shillings extra if you do, my prick can't hurt now." The oddity of a woman attempting to unroll from a prick a slip of white rag, whilst the prick was up a cunt! But out came my prick from the little hole before she could accomplish it.

Desire had not left me, holding her thighs open I dropped on my knees, my prick flopping, and saw the little cunt covered with thick sperm. There lay the girl, there stood the woman, neither speaking nor moving, till my eyes had had their voluptuous enjoy-ment. "I will give you another sovereign now, and then fuck her again." "All right," said the woman. "But she must not wash." "All right." I gave it, then took the girl up like a baby, one hand just under the bum, so that the spunk might fall on my hand if it dropped out, and laid her on the sofa in the parlour, where the gas flared brightly, opened her thighs wide, gloated, and talked baudily till my prick stood again.

Then I lifted her back on to the bed, and rolled the strip of handkerchief round the stem again; but I longed to hurt her, to make her cry with the pain my tool caused her, I would have made her bleed if I could; so wrapped it round in such a manner, that with a tug I could unroll it. The woman did not seem so anxious now about my hurting her.

Sperm is a splendid cunt-lubricator, my prick went in easier, but still she cried out. Now I measured my pleasure. With gentle lingering pushes I moved up and down in her. Under pretence of feeling my prick, I had loosened the handkerchief, then tore the rag quite away, and afterwards lifted her up, and then with her cunt stuck tight and full with my pego, and both hands round her bum tightly, I walked holding her so into the sitting-room to a large glass. There seeing my balls hanging down under her little arse, I shoved and wriggled, holding her like a baby on me, her hands round my neck, she whining that I was hurting her, the woman hushing, and praying me to be gentle, till I spent again. I held her tight to me in front of the glass, her thighs wide apart, my balls showing under her little buttocks, till my prick again shrunk, and my sperm ran from her cunt down my balls. Then I uncunted, and sat down on a chair. We were both start naked.

The girl sat down on a foot-stool, the woman sat in her chemise. I gave her the remaining money, and to the little one some silver. Although I had had her twice, I scarcely had looked at her; both fucks must have been done in ten minutes. Now I longed to see the little cunt tranquilly. "Let me wash her cunt," said I. "You can," said the old one. I took the girl into the bed-room, she left a large gobbet of sperm on the stool, which the old one wiped off. I washed her cunt, threw her on the bed, looked at the little quim. It seemed impossible I could have been up it; but from that day I knew a cunt to be the most elastic article in the world, and believed the old woman's saying, that a prick can always go up where a finger can.

Then after cuddling her, straddling between her legs and feeling my balls hanging between her thighs by passing my hand round her arse, I laid her on the bed, took a glance at the little cunt from a slight distance, and saw the old one in an exciting posture. She had thrown herself on the bed, and resting her head on one hand was watching me. Her chemise had slipped from her shoulders showing big white breasts, and the black thicket of hair in one armpit. Her chemise was up to her waist, one leg was bent up, the fat calf pressed against a fat thigh, the other extended along the bed, the thighs wide open, the middle finger of her left hand on her cunt, whose mass of black hair creeping up her belly and along the line of junction with the thighs could not be hidden by her hand. She was frigging her clitoris with her middle finger, and she smiled invitingly. "Come and do it to me, I do want it so, — I have not had a poke for a fortnight."

My love of a fat arse and a big hairy cunt returned suddenly. I stood turning my eyes, first to the little hairless orifice, then to the full-lipped split, then to the little pink cunt, and then back again to the matured cunt. "Come, do me." "I must go." "Why?" "I came to have her." "So you have, — now have me, — you can have her again if you like after." "Can I?" "Yes, — oh! Come, I am so randy." "It's late." "Stop all night." I said I would. Off the bed she got, put a night-gown on the child, laid her on the sofa, told her to go to sleep, and throwing off her boots and stockings, got on to the bed again.

I threw off my socks. "Shall I be naked?" said she. "Yes, it is very hot." Off went her chemise, and the next instant cuddling up to me, she was tugging at my prick, kissing me, and using every salacious stimulant.

Though a hot night, naked as we both were, we felt a chill, so covered ourselves with a sheet.

"How old are you?" said I. "Guess." "More than forty." "I am not thirty-eight, although I am so stout, — feel how firm my flesh is, — how my breasts keep up." I threw down the sheet to see her fully. She was delighted, turned round and round, opened her thighs, pulled open her cunt, exposed herself with the freedom of a French whore, and by the time I had seen all my prick was at fever heat, and I fucked her. Our nakedness was delightful.

We talked afterwards. She was not the mother, nor the aunt, though the child called her so; the child was parentless, she had taken charge of her and prevented her going to the work-house. She was in difficulties, she must live, the child would be sure to have it done to her some day, why not make a little money by her? Some one else would, if she did not. So spoke the fat middle-aged woman.

I was sleepless. After an hour or two I longed to see them side by side, that strange contrast in age and size, and to try the difference with my finger as I had with my prick. She brought in the child, sleepy and peevish, I plunged my prick in the little one, took it out, and put it into the woman. It was a delight to feel the difference, — the room in one, the confinement in the other's cunt.

The aunt annoyed me by putting her hand between our bellies to prevent my penetrating too far. It was not the stretching, nor the plugging, it was the boring too deeply which hurt the little one, she said.

I laid on my back and put the little one's belly upon me; stretching her little thighs I felt round them, and guided my prick up her, then the aunt put her fingers round my prick and squeezed my balls. How funny to have that little creature on the top of me; how funny to be able to feel at the same time a big hairy cunt at my side. Such thoughts and emotions finished me, and after spending in the little one, she again went to the sofa, then with my arse to the aunt's arse we went to sleep.

She was the youngest I ever yet have had, or have wished to have. We laid abed till about mid-day. I fucked as much as I ever did in my life, and found that a tiny cunt although it might satisfy a letch, could not give the pleasure that a fully developed woman could. Tight as it was, it had not that peculiar suction, embrace. and grind, that a full-grown woman's or girl's has. When I was getting drier and drier, the old one stiffened my prick, and I put it into the child; but oscillate my arse as I might, I could not get a spend out of me; then in the aunt's clipping though well stretched cunt, I got my pleasure in no time. A fuck is barely a fuck if a man's prick is but half up a girl, it wants engulfing. A very young girl never has the true jerk of her arse, nor the muscular clip in her cunt; so if languid prick be put up it, it will slip out, unless the letch be strong; whereas a flabby, done-for prick, once in the cunt of a grown woman may be resuscitated, and made to give pleasure to both, if she uses the muscular power which nature has given her between bum-hole, buttocks, and navel.

We eat and drank, I paid liberally, and with empty ballocks

and a flabby tool went away. White trowsers and a black tail-coat were then full evening dress at Vauxhall; but ludicrous in the day. I recollect feeling ashamed as I walked out in that dress in the sun-shine. She would not fetch a cab as she was most anxious about noise. She gave me full instructions where to write and have the girl again. About a fortnight afterwards I made an appointment, but she did not keep it. I went to the house and asked for her; a woman opened the door. "Do you know her?" said she. "Yes." "She is not here, and I don't know where she has gone, — perhaps you're as bad as she is," and she slammed the door in my face. A few years passed away before I took a letch for a hairless cunt again, — and then I was a poor man.

We went to Vauxhall on an ordinary night, and I showed Fred where I had heard and seen the girls make water. Laura I got to like, and she to like me which led to something at a later date. In about three weeks or more I went back to my aunt's, through an in-definable longing to poke, in a quiet intriguing way, the women I had had there. In London I had changed my women twice a day, and fucked every nice French woman who walked in Regent Street.

My mother was again going to see my aunt, and was delighted that I would go with her. Fred had gone to Paris with Laura, and wanted me to go, but money was getting short with me, for I had been heavily robbed, and as ten pounds a day (a large sum then) was the usual cost of Paris to me, I declined, and to the old Hall went with mother.

I did not see nursemaid or page. "You have a new nursemaid for Joey," said I to my aunt. "We dismissed the other, we found her to be an improper character, — and Robert has gone, — he was too big," said she. For two or three days I could not get Pender, who looked miserable when I met her, shook her head, and looked up to the skies. I went with my mother and aunt to the farm one day, Pender for a second stopped behind, and said to me in a hurried whisper, "I *am* in the family way," and then ran after my aunt.

Next day I saw her for a second. "Meet me next Sunday at *** ." "I must," said she. We had no opportunity of speaking before, for her husband or someone was always in the way. To make sure, I next day slipped an envelope into her hand, in which was one addressed to myself, and a scribble asking her to say where I was to meet her. It came back by post containing in execrable writing the words, "My dear, same time and place, if he be out, on Saturday night." I did not comprehend, but waited outside her cottage that night. She did not show. On Sunday I went to * * *, and long after eleven she appeared. Soon we were in the room over the beer-shop.

"I am in the family way, whatever shall I do?" I had thought over this, and replied, "Well, you have a husband, so it does not matter." "I don't think he will believe it's his." "He can't say it is not, and will be proud of it." "That may be true, I did not think of that," said she, and until I had fucked her I learnt no more.

I referred to the change in the servants at the Hall. "Oh!" said Pender eagerly, "There has been a row; do you recollect the nurse-maid? — well they saw her feeling — hoh! hoh!" — she burst out laughing, — "feeling the page's thing, — hoh! ho! ho!" "Feeling his prick?" "Yes, — ho! ho! ho! — and Missus turned her and page out the same night, — ho! ho! ho!" laughed Pender. "She was a dirty hussy." "Why?" "Why a woman like that to be a taking liberties with a boy like that, a hobble-de-hoy; poor Molly told me that one day when he came here he pulled out his thing before her." "What, Molly?" said I, thinking the young girl had had manifold tempta-tions. "Yes, poor thing." "Why poor thing?" "Well, I am sorry for her; I told Missus about the young squire as you told me, and Missus told her mother to look sharp after her, — and so she did, and found that she used to get out of a night and meet Giles, — you know Giles?" "No I don't," said I, lying. "He works here sometimes, you must have seen him," said Pender. "No." "Well, he works here, is a likely young chap, but Molly's mother hates him, — well she watched and watched, till one night she caught them, and him on top of her in the large barn, — he had got through the rick-yard, and she had gone through the wicket on the farm-yard side, and let him in through the rick-yard wicket." "How could she do that?" Pender explained to me what I knew perfectly well.

"On the top of her?" "Yes, they were adoing it, — and she hit him hard on the head with a stick, and nearly stunned him before they knew she were there." "Who hit?" "Why her mother, he were nearly insensible.

"Then Mrs. Brown asked me what to do, and I said he had better marry her, and she said he should not. So she went to Missus, asked her advice, and on account of Molly's character to say nothing about finding Giles taking liberties with her daughter. Missus said

Giles at the end of the week was to be sent off, — and he's gone. Mrs. Brown scarcely lets Molly out of the house, and when I sees her I laughs to myself, that a young thing like that has had it done to her. Her mother told me you know, — I have sworn to tell nobody, but I don't mind telling you." "She has seen two pricks," said I, "page Robert's and Giles'." "Yes, she has."

I wondered whether he had spent when he felt the stick on his head. "I think he had," said she, "for Mrs. Brown said she found his stuff on her child's chemise. Every day there is a row between them, Molly says she will go to service, her mother says she shan't, and that she will turn out a bunter, and bring her in her age with sorrow to the grave. Poor thing."

"Pough," said I, "why make such a fuss about such a natural action?" "Well, it be natural," said Pender, "but she might have waited, she is very young."

In the family way Pender was, and by me, — of that I had no doubt. Pender thought it was done the first time I had her in the rick-yard. "Did he not do it about that time?" I asked. Pender hesitated, and on being pressed to reply at length said, "It's funny, I am always thinking about it, but it is a fact that he did it that very night; and when you have done it, he generally do it also that night. I can't account for it, — can't abear him to do it when you have, — can't abear his doing it at all now, and he does it more than he used." "You spend with him?" "I don't, — I hate him then, I hate him altogether since I have known you."

Now for a bit of experience which I write now, and years after I wrote this chapter of my narrative. I had a married woman who was fond of me. She assured me that whenever I had her, it was perfectly certain that her husband would do it to her that night. She thought that my fucking acted as a charm to fetch the other man. He neglected her for other women, and used, although a young vigorous man, to do it but rarely to her; but whenever my sperm had suffused itself in her cunt, his went there the same night. "You spend too then?" said I. "I do," said she. "I think so much of you, so much of the coincidence and go home so wondering whether he will do it or not, that directly he pulls me about I think of you, and then fancy it is you doing it to me, not him, and I spend. I am angry with myself afterwards, but can't help it."

Pender had said her mother was unwell as an excuse to get

to ***, so must be back quickly. She was lying speechless, with eyes closed and my prick up her, I silently reposing on her, when the clock struck. Up she jumped, uncunting me, saying, "I must go, I am to fetch the dinner from the bake-house, then I must get back home, unless P. comes," and rapidly off she went scarcely dressed, and without washing her cunt.

CHAPTER X

Nelly and Sophy. — The beer-house again. — Sophy's belly. — On the road. — Against a tree. — At the baudy house with Sophy. — Her narrative. — Tom and the three sisters. — Fred on the scent. — Pender's troubles.

I had some food at an hotel, then returning on foot saw at the end of the lane two peasant girls in their Sunday finery. I looked at first without recognizing them, but as I got close saw one was Nelly, the girl I had raped. She stopped, I smiled. "You here, why?" "Taking a walk sir." "Come with me." She hesitated, looked at the other girl. "Never mind," said I, "bring your friend with you." Two minutes brought us to the beer-house again. "Stay here," said I. I went to the side entrance which was up a yard, told the woman who stared when she opened the door to me to show the girls up the other way. They came through the shop, and stood curtseying when they came into the little sitting room.

I wanted Nelly when I saw her, and hence what I did; but was embarrassed now, for with the other in the room I did not know how to proceed without compromising her; so sent for some spirits. They sat sheepishly. I said to Nelly with the view of getting rid of the other, "Perhaps your friend would like to call for you presently." "She is my sister," said Nelly. Impulsively I cried, "Your sister? — why she is the girl who was in the family way before she was fourteen."

"Oo — h!" said Nelly's sister. "What a lie, — what a shame to say such things of a girl, — who said so?" I was disconcerted. "I heard it, but can't recollect who." Nelly never spoke, but sat looking at me with her tongue out on one side, and a funny expression in her eye. "I'll go," said her sister. "Don't go," said Nelly, "the gent's asked us in, and will be offended, — won't you sir?" "Yes," I replied.

The liquor came, I dosed them with it, and a letch for the sister came over me. "She in family way, that young thing, — is it so? — how I should like to see her belly." My conversation got warm, then baudy, the girls got warm, and laughed at my smut. From kissing one, I got to kiss the other, then to pinch, poke and feel their legs. I spoke about women being in the family way, made light of it, wished I was so myself, and so on, and they let out as the liquor worked, and I questioned.

The younger was a little over fourteen years old, Nelly only eleven months older. Said I, "A girl can't be in the family way before she is fourteen." "Oh! Yes she can," said Nelly. "How do you know?" She laughed. I plied the liquor, got the young one on to knee, and my hand up her clothes. A yell, a threat to go, "Nonsense," from Nelly. Then I shoved my hand up Nelly's petticoats, — which she permitted quietly. Then I had a strange whim.

"Stand close together with your backs to me, and put your hands behind you, and I will give you something before you go; then each shall ask the other to guess what I have put in her hand." They did, and expected money. I pulled out my prick and balls, one girl's hand I guided under my balls, the other's round my prick. They touched at the same time and knew what it was, and turning round, "It's his thing," said the youngest.

"You knew it was a man's prick," said I, "you have felt one, and one has been into you, — let's feel your cunt, do, — you are in the family way, I know you are."

Then I sat between them, talking outrageous baudiness with my prick out. "Come into the other room," said I, "and let me see if you are in the family way, and I will give you this (producing a sovereign); if you are, or are not, you shall have it." She refused, but eyed the sovereign. Said Nelly, "Well, I wish he would ask me." "So I do, but she shall come first, you afterwards." The girl asked, "How will you tell?" "My dear I shall lay you on the bed, throw up your clothes, look at your belly, and feel your cunt." "I shan't then." "Then you won't get a sovereign," and I put it by. "I'll go with you," said Nelly, but I would not accept her offer. There was a pause, the sister sat reflecting, her gaiety was gone.

Soon afterwards I renewed the request. "Let him," said Nelly, "he won't talk, he don't know people in the village." The girl shook her head sullenly, Nelly looked at me, nodded her head, and put her tongue out. I did not know what it meant, at last guessed. "Is she?" I asked. Nelly kept on nodding. "Well, Nelly says you are in the family way." The girl began to cry. "What's the good of crying?" said Nelly, "you can't hide it long." The girl kept silently crying. I persuaded, Nelly persuaded, and at last she came into the bedroom. I could feel the poor little girl's hard belly, lifting her clothes I opened her thighs and looked; then she rested, but a little only. I frigged her, kissed her a little, coaxed her, and then fucked her. She spent freely. It's my luck to get sisters.

"Tell me Sophy, all about it, — how long since you were got in the family way? — your sister will wait."

She counted on her fingers and said, "Four months and about a week." "Are you sure?" "Yes." "How can you tell?" "I have never been done but on one day." "Nonsense." "It's true." "Do you mean that once putting it up you got you in the family way?" "I didn't mean that," said she, "he were only once with me, but he did it all night, and nearly all the next day." "A dozen times?" "Don't know, I was so ill, so sleepy." "Who is the father?" She shook her head. "I can't say, — dare not, — it would be worse for me if I did." "What are you going to do?" "Go to the workhouse if they won't keep me," said the poor girl, crying again. She was rather watery headed.

It was an exciting termination to the day. After frigging her till she was in the seventh heaven, I fucked her again. It was the same bed I had fucked Pender on.

"You've been an hour," said Nelly, when we went in "what have you been doing?" "Nothing but examining." The girl stuck to that also. "Oh! Gammon," said Nelly.

"You come now," said I. She would not, was sulky, and another hour went away. It was getting late, I pulled Nelly into an open-legged posture over mine as I sat on the chair, and lifted her clothes. Her back was to her sister. I got my cock between her legs, it rubbed her thighs, but she slipped away, turned sulky, and would not let me fuck her, though I felt her. They left, and I directly after.

When clear of the town, and on the road it got dark, I joined them and learnt where Sophy lived, and could be met. Because Nelly would not let me I felt a want for her and made baudy requests. She got randy, and told Sophy to go ahead. Then I got her up against a large tree, and straddling my legs wide to get into her, found it difficult as she was short, but was poking with vigor when we heard footsteps and voices. "Oh!" said she. "Let me go, it's so and so." Although I held her on my peg, grasping her bum, and hoping to spend before they came up, I being empty was long about it, so she uncunted me, and slipped away just in time. It was two or three men she knew, who seeing girls ahead ran after them, I dodging round the tree as they ran past. They overtook the girls, I followed at a distance sufficiently near to hear their low chaff, their attempts to kiss the girls, and the yells of the sluts when they attempted more.

When I saw Pender again I heard that her husband had for some reason gone to °°° on the Sunday she was there with me. He stayed, and took his wife home. "Did he do you?" said I. She colored up. "It be a fact he did, — it be most curious. I were hot with running, and fetched the meat from the bake-house. After dinner he said, 'Well you do look comely, you do today, where as you been?,' and he pulled me on his knees, and put his hands up my clothes, — and in all my life he never had done such a thing afore in day-time. Says he, 'Lass we'll have a game at mother and father.' Said I, 'Why P., you must have been drinking.' He pulls me down on to sister's bed which were in the corner of the room, and I would not let him. He says, 'Don't make a row, for I means it,' and so I let him do it."

Such games went on until full Autumn, I was always after one or the other as fancy led, or opportunity offered; but was obliged to be more and more cunning, for fear I should be found out. Although I had heavy fucking at times, yet had good rests between. It was a jolly time, but mainly with three of the four women now. Nelly got the most of my cock at first, Sophy very soon after.

The little one in the family way had taken my fancy. I fucked her in the lane and fields, but mainly upright, the grass being now damp. One evening we went to the baudy house. I had pleasure in fucking her, but she was always crying. "Why do you meet me?" said I. "To get money to help me if they turn me out." "When?" "When they find I am in the family way." At last but with difficulty, I got out of her much about her seducer and give the narrative as near as I can in its order.

"Yes, it is a big man, a fine, tall man, and quite a man, not old, not young, — Oh! I dare not say who, it would be worse for me (a cry), — you won't tell Nelly, — how came you to know my sister? — do you do anything to her? — now do tell me." "Well, tell me your history, and perhaps I will tell you about Nelly."

"Well, he got into bed with me saying, 'It's cold, — and it were, — let's lay here, it will be no harm, no one will know.' I said I would hollow, but there was no one in the house — Now I am letting out, and I won't." She stopped, and would not tell more.

Persuasion, kisses, promises, and she answered my questions again. "He cuddled me, he was big and strong, and I could not help it; and then he pulled up my shimmy, and his shirt was up, and he put his belly close to mine." "Then his prick was up against your belly?" "I shan't say," said she with a modest fit, no sham. "Was it? — was it just as my prick now is?" Her story was exciting me, I pulled her belly up to mine, and my prick, a right good stiff one, was between us. "I suppose it were," said she, "I don't recollect, all seems in a muddle, he hurt me dreadful, I screamed, he put something over my mouth, and I don't know no more; but he was doing it right up, and I were hollowing, — and then I cried."

"Are you sure you cried out?" "I hollowed I know, but I knowed there was no one to hear." "Then you were in the house alone?" "Yes." "What house?" "I shan't say, — Nelly is always asking, and I *won't* say, — you won't tell her, will you now sir, what I have told you?"

"I don't recollect more," she went on, "but he lay on me, oh! A long, long time." "Not up you?" "Yes, oh! A long time." "Did he keep on fucking?" "He kept on adoing it and stopping, — no he never pulled it out, at last I fainted or slept I suppose, for when I recollect more he was out of bed. Then he got into bed, and he did the same I can't say how many times. When it were day I said, 'Ain't you going to work?' and he said, 'No. If any one comes they will think I am gone, and if you say a word if anyone knocks, I will murder you.' Then he got up, and showed me his razor, and said, 'Do you see that? — I bloody well meant it, mind.' Then he got into bed again, and he did it again."

"Did you like it?" "I don't know, I was all pain, but I think I must at last; I was so muddled like and ill I could not move. Then he dressed and says, says he, 'If ever you tell I'll cut your bloody throat; now you say you were ill, and stopped at home from work,' and he went away to his work." I guessed she had been raped.

Another day I had Nelly, and questioned her. She said she wanted to know, but did not; she guessed, but dared not say. Sophy had said there would be murder if she told who the father was, but she guessed. She was only eleven months older than Sophy, who must have been in the family way just before she was fourteen, had had her courses when thirteen years old, and was "hankering after the chaps" quite early. "Mother used to slap her for it." Nelly's courses had only recently come on, she said.

Sophy, although younger and slighter built, had more hair on her cunt than Nelly, and gave me the idea of being older. Neither were tall, both were larger in their thighs, haunches, and bubbies, than town girls of the same age, as far as I can recollect.

I can't recollect the order, but only the broader features of this part of my amorous history. I think that after the Sunday when I had Pender and Sophy I could not get to Pender, for the farm-yard from morning to night was full of laborers; so busied myself with Sophy, who two or three times the same week met me at °°°, and what I have narrated was told me there. It delighted me to hear about her virgin offering, it made my cock stand. Then I would fuck the little wench, and make her arse wag like the tail of a duck that had a thwack with a stone, then would question her again. If she said she should say no more, I used to remind her of what she had let out on the previous night. What delighted my sensuous imagination, was the evident fact that the man was big, and with a big prick, and must have kept it up with her without uncunting till he had fucked her three times. Her praying him to go, trying to get from under him, his grasping her to him so that she could not move, his laying quiet on her, then commencing his shoves, — all proved it. He seems to have begun his assault on her about nine o'clock one night, and never went out of the bed till two o'clock the next afternoon.

"Has he ever done it since?" "Never, he has never had a chance; he has tried to catch me coming home, but I always come with someone else; he has asked me, but I never would." "I dare say you egged him on; had he never made a baudy sign? Never shown you his prick?" "Both Nelly and I had seen that," said she. "We looked through the key-hole if we heard —." Here she stopped short, and nothing would make her go on, she saw she was on the point of giving the key to the riddle.

I advized her to get as much money as she could, and then if unkind she might snap her fingers at them. She had kept all I had given her. I had a feast with her of rump-steak and onions one night; she eat till she could eat no longer. I tippled her up with hot spirits and water, and then tumbled on to the bed with her. She was very communicative, I frigged her about till with a sigh she said, "Oh! Let's do it."

"Tell me who did it to you then, and I'll give you another sovereign to keep you through your confinement; feel my prick, and tell me." She reflected, she was so lewed, I knelt on the bed, my prick standing stiff in front of her face. "You won't ever tell anybody," said she, "will you?" I swore I would not.

Rubbing her eyes she hesitated, then said, "Tom." "Who is Tom?" "Hester's husband." "Who is Hester?" "My sister, — oh! Don't tell, or he will murder me." I saw the whole story at once. In another minute we were fucking. Afterwards she told me all.

There were three sisters. Hester married Tom, a laborer; Sophy lived with them, Nelly lived with their mother. Tom and Hester had a two-roomed cottage, in one they slept, in the other, which was sitting-room and kitchen, was a bed in the corner, where slept Sophy. The mother was dangerously ill, Hester went to assist Nelly attending her; so Sophy was alone in the house with big Tom, who took the opportunity to put his big prick into Sophy's little cunt, get her in the family way, threaten to murder her if she ever told, to turn Hester into the streets, and do any other amount of devilry. Sophy was frightened of Tom and at first of her sisters knowing about her swelling belly, till it was found out. All was quite probable. I believed it implicitly. The size of Tom's prick, and the number of times he had done her were all described with modesty. I pitied the girl, and resolved to help her. Tom bore I found a bad character, and Hester no better, had been confined soon after she was married. The child was dead. All three sisters now lived with Tom since the mother's death.

"You knew all about fucking long before he did it to you." "Of course we did. Nelly and I often talked about it, Hester told us what pleasure it was; we could hear Tom and Hester doing it. Nelly, if sleeping with me, used to listen. They used to hang a cloth before the door, — there were cracks in it, — if they did not, we could see through if there were light, and sometimes they forgot. Nelly and I have both seen Tom's cock that way. Once he showed it to me as it were by accident; he was in the privy, and he called out to me to bring him a leaf. When I took it him his cock was out and stiff; he grinned, I looked, he took the leaf, and ran a hole in it with his finger, and put his cock through the hole, then he said, 'If you tell Hester that, she will turn you out.' So I never told, but I told Nelly. He did the same to Nelly one day, but we held our tongues."

That is all I have to say about Sophy here. I had her from time to time until within three months of her confinement, for simple curiosity. I had no pleasure in it when her belly got big, but I kept her in money.

Nelly I also had. She became a saucy, lewed, low-tongued little bitch; but I liked her fuck. I found her larking with men, and stroked her more than once in the lanes. One night I caught her by surprize, and saw some male going off in the dark as I thought. "That was a fellow with you," said I. "No, it was not." But her cunt had a most unusual wetness. I hesitated, and said that some one, I thought, had just wetted her. She was confused, denied it, and whimpered at my suspicion. I again felt her, and putting my fingers and thumb together was sure it was spunk, and turned away; but felt so randy, that I turned back after her, wiped her cunt with my handkerchief, made her piss, and then fucked her up against a fence.

As I relinquished my hold of her bum I heard something fall with a chink. "Oh!" said she, "I have lost some money." It was very dark, I picked up the money, could not see what it was, but was sure from the feel it was gold, and said so. She had got it back before I made the remark, and would not let me feel it again. "You told me you hid the money I gave you." "I've been carrying it about for fear of its being found." I told her she was lying.

I had been out that day with my gun. On returning found Fred had come down from town, and been there all day; he had had a quarrel with Laura. I don't know how it struck me, but I asked, and found he had only just come in, and said to myself, "He has fucked Nelly, it was his money she dropped, it was his sperm." I did not tell him so then.

The farm-yard now was never empty, they were thrashing in

the barn. Molly was scarcely visible, and if in the yard, her mother was at her back. When I did see her I winked at her and she laughed. She was growing wonderfully, and my desires turned to her. I had Pender one night or so; but a few hurried words, a smooth of the buttocks, a hurried grope with the finger, a silent kiss or two, shove, shove, shove like a steam-engine, and a pull out of my prick almost before the spunk was well out, was all I could get.

I was out shooting most days, and would walk across the farm-yard just to see if the coast was clear. After several Sundays had passed I got Pender again at the baudy house. P. took her being in the family way rather grumpily, and she hated him since she had been with child. She loved me, begged me to take her away, where, how, she cared not, so long as she knew that I alone could have her; she would live alone if I only came to see her once a month, she said.

I was sorry for this. What had been pastime to me was going to be misery to her. I had to show her the impossibility of my keep-ing her; then she said she would drown herself. Altogether it was not a very comfortable meeting apart from the fucking, which was as good as usual I dare say, though I don't recollect much about that.

Fred went backwards and forwards to London, I did occa-sionally, but not on his days, for he was in my way. I did not tell him now much about my little games, and got most of my women when he was absent. My mother and sister also went home, and I was glad of that, but it made it more needful for me to walk and drive out with aunt and cousins. I was constantly scheming and dodging how to get one or the other of the women, and that seemed to give zest to the affair; but I think now that the pleasure I gave the girls when I had them had much to do with it. Sophy and Nelly now came after me, as much as I went after them. Each now knew that I fucked the other. "When did you do it to my sister?" was a frequent question put by both of them to me.

CHAPTER XI

Out shooting. — A female carter. — A feel in the train. — Molly in London. — Giles in town. — Fred on the scene. — Molly at the Hall. — Copulation in uniform. — A sham illness. — An afternoon with Molly. — She turns harlot. — Gets clapped. — Her baby.

I was in wonderful condition. Early to bed, out-of-door exercise, good plain living, everything to make me so. I felt as if I could fuck all day. If one day I had neither of the women, the next day my prick stood from morning till I got to sleep at night. When standing quietly in the woods waiting for the driving of the game, I used if alone to pull out my prick and look at it, and thinking of cunt forgot to fire at the rabbits. Once I recollect shooting at a rabbit with my prick out of my trowsers.

Among the laborers I had seen was a strapping woman with big legs, withered face, and parchment skin, middle-aged, yet not actually bad-looking. The old foreman had said to me, "She ha bean the biggest whore in the parish, I bet that there beant a man but what have had she when she were young. The first chap as had she, were the banker; she say it herself. I be sworn she likes a bit yet when she can get it." She was as strong as a horse, if no one were handy, she would groom a horse, was often driving a farmcart, and had the reputation of having whored since she was fifteen years of age.

Waiting with my gun by a ride one day, my prick throbbing in my trowsers, I pulled it out, and felt it, laid down my gun, and in the trembling state of erection I was in had determined to frig myself, when I heard the wheels of a cart which soon came in sight. I saw it was driven by this woman who sat on a shaft with her legs dangling, and showing her big calves. Lust made me indifferent to

310

consequences, had it been my grandmother I think I should have done the same. There was a cunt between those legs, that was enough. I forgot her age, position, the risk I ran of beaters coming, and everything else; I only thought of how to ease myself.

I nodded, "Good morning mother, come and help us a bit," and out stood my cock in front of her. She laughed, and jumped off the cart which stopped. "Come here." "No," said she, standing still and grinning. I winked and turned to the left out of the ride, she did the same. Without preliminary, almost without a word, I laid her on some grass drier than the rest, and had as good a pleasure out of her as I ever had in my life, or thought so. She went off with her cunt full, I tipped her. In a few minutes I was banging at the rabbits again. I don't think I was three minutes about it, and never had her again nor spoke to her, though I occasionally saw her and winked.

"I hain't heard much of your gun, squire," said one of the game-keepers, "there ought to have been lots o' rabbits pass you in this beat." I said I had scarcely seen any, — how could I?

Rainy weather set in, Nelly and Sophy were available but al-fresco, copulation impossible, and the long tramp or ride to ° ° °, to the bawdy house not to my taste. I had now no excuse for going to the farm, and no Pender. So one morning I set off for London. Just as the train started Molly and her mother appeared; she put the girl into a third-class carriage. At the first station the train stopped at I got into the carriage with Molly, who opened her eyes wide when she saw me. We were soon in conversation. Molly was going to an aunt's in London who was to meet her at the Terminus. You may guess which way my talk ran. I kept whispering lewed things in her ear. An elderly stern-faced woman got in at a station, fixed her eyes on us, especially on me, and at length said, "Do you know that young woman?" Her coolness nearly settled me, but I said I did, kept on talking, and was delighted when about two or three stations further on she left with the remark to Molly, "Take care of yourself my gal, and don't have anything to say to strange men or women."

There are tunnels on that line. There were no lights then in third-class carriages. In one tunnel I kissed her, and on my kiss being returned, got my fingers on her cunt, and kept them there till approaching light made me withdraw them. It was a cold, foggy day. I sat close to her wrapped in a traveling-cloak, and partially covered her with it and with my rug. I got her hand under my cloak with the pretence of warming it, gradually introduced my prick into her hand, and there I kept it a quarter of an hour, she looking in such a fright all round at the people every now and then, but enjoying the warmth of the feel. Just before entering London is another tunnel, I had another grope at her warm quim, and arranged my clothes.

I got her London address, and entered a cab, determined to follow her, and see if she was deceiving me. She waited, no one appeared to meet her, one or two men spoke to her, and as she told me later asked her to go and have a drink. Then I got out. "No one is here," said I. "Come and have some wine, you can say you waited ever so long should they come, — there is some error about meeting you."

How could she refuse? Already had her fingers been playing round my cock, mine still smelt of her cunt. Telling the cab to wait, and putting her bag inside it, in three minutes I had her in a baudy house close by the Terminus (I dare say it's there now), and Molly's little cunt was again moistened by me. If her mother had known the risks, she never would have allowed her the journey to London.

When our heat was cooled by two hours dallying, kissing, and fucking, she got uneasy about being found out. We put our heads together for an excuse. The address was Paddington, she was to say she waited an hour at the station, then made a mistake, and went to Islington, and not finding the street there came to Paddington. The excuse turned out good, Paddington and Islington looked much alike on the scrawl.

I have often wondered at the rapid success I had with country women at that time. With women whom I saw daily, and with whom I had much opportunity, such as mother's servants, I was a long time getting my aim; but at that period of my life I was often diffident; even with gay women, a slight thing would at times make me cease speaking to them. But here I no sooner attacked than the females fell to me. I attribute it to the suddenness and impetuosity with which I made at times my advances, and the boldness with which I proceeded to baudy extremities. When I was once lanced, I was so strong, so lewed, that I am sure I communicated my lewedness to them by some subtle magnetism, even before I spoke. Then I was a London swell, a relative of the lady of the Manor, there was the pride which women of the humble class have in being singled out for notice by a London gent, all these told. But my baudy, rapid assaults, lustful cunning and an innate power of stirring up voluptuous sensations in women when once I spoke, got me them more than anything else. When in the country, I was thinking of nothing else, and had nothing else to do but to hunt down cunts, and feed myself up for fucking them. When in London the case was different.

Molly's aunt was a greengrocer. Molly did not keep her promise to meet me, so I went to the place, saw her standing in the shop, and beckoned; she shook her head. I passed and repassed, on foot, then in a cab, till I thought the whole street would know me. At length she came out and said, "Aunt won't let me out alone, mother's told her not; I can only stay five minutes." She wanted a post-office, — could I find her one? I did close by. She slipped a letter into the box, and begging me not to come near the shop, went back. I asked her to write me, and arranged to send my letters to this post-office. I wrote twice, and got no reply. Angry, I wrote that I must see her, and had something to tell her; then I got a scrawl in reply. She met me, and I took her to a house near her aunt's.

Molly did not like me. When I got her into the room, she refused to let me have her, and begged me to tell her what I had heard. I invented some nonsense; and she said that was not what I had to say, she was sure. I recollect sitting and talking with my prick out, and she looking at it sulkily; but she resisted me. I said, "How is Giles' head?" "What," said she, "who told you?" "Nobody knows but me," said I. (It was one of the most blackguardly things I did in my life, and am ashamed of it.) She shed tears, but no longer refused me. I gave her a sovereign saying, "That will be useful when you marry."

I made her meet me again, and then she told me she would go to service. She went after a good many situations I know. I fucked her whenever she went out. She was getting hot-arsed, and she liked the poking. One morning I passed the shop, and saw, loitering about in the streets in a velveteen costume, Giles. She had written to him, I was sure.

I dodged them in a cab, saw her come out, and as fast as they could they went to a low coffee-shop where there were beds. I daresay my money paid for their refreshments.

Going to the street one day, there to my astonishment I saw my cousin Fred walking about. I was in a cab, and he did not see me. I asked Molly the next time if she knew if Fred was in town. She said no, seemed astonished, and I believed her; but I was sure Fred was after her, and could not imagine how he had found out her address. Laura perhaps took the starch out of him, for I never saw him in the street again. Molly now got fond of money. One day I took her to a baudy house near the Haymarket, feasted her, and fucked her till I was empty, and she full. Then I went back to the country to see my aunt, and soon again I got Pender. Said she among other gossip, "That gal Molly Brown will give her mother trouble, she has been after a situation in London, and her aunt says has been seen going into a house with a man, Giles has left the village, her mother believes he is after her, so she has sent for her back." Sure enough in two or three days there was Molly, looking as fresh as a daisy, and as modest as a whore at a christening.

The mother told no one anything except Pender, and Pender told me. Molly then went to the Hall assisting whilst a servant was ill, and then I saw her every hour or so. Then Fred came back, and I saw he was making up to her, and told him of it. He acknowledged it, remarking it was a pity such a nice young girl should not taste the sugar-stick. "Perhaps she has," said I. He thought not, there was a country lout she wanted to marry, and the mother looked after her closely. "I would give a ten-pound note to have her," he said to me one day.

Shortly, Molly appeared ill and pining; her face lost its bloom, I could not understand it. The bad weather keeping people at home had given me no chance of having her; if I saw her alone it was only for a minute, but I used to pull my prick out and show it her. I have done it in the corridor, my aunt walking in front of me. I tried to get her to come out, but she would not, besides Fred always appeared on the scene. My delight was to get in the way when I knew there was the best chance of his seeing her alone. So we baulked each other.

There was some military inspection not far from us, Fred was going in his uniform, with my aunt, cousins and self, and all but two servants were allowed to go. The carriage was at the door when I was taken short, and being in my bed-room ran to the W. C. As I came out, I saw Fred at the end of the corridor near the stairs, walking quickly but quietly, and heard his footsteps descending to the Hall. "What's up?" thought I. He has been dressed a long time, why on the first floor now? He passed his bed-room without going in. A suspicion crossed my mind, and being close to it, I put my ear to the nursemaid's door (the one with two doors in which I had had the skinny nursemaid), heard a rustling, and quickly opening the lobby-door connecting with the servants' stairs, I saw Molly looking hot, flushed, adjusting her collar and hair, and going downstairs rapidly, she didn't see me. Instinct told me she had been fucked by Fred.

I rushed downstairs, Fred and all were in the carriage, aunt angry at waiting so long for me. I told her my ailment, said I would ride after them directly I felt better, so off they drove. The butler and Molly were in the hall, they and the cook the only people in the house. I sent off the butler to the village to get me some medicine, and said to Molly in a stern way before him, as if I had never seen her. "Are you doing the housemaid's work young woman?" "Yes sir." "Arrange my room as quickly as you can, for I am not well, and shall lay down there." "Yes sir," said she, looking so hard at me. "Do the room at once," said the old butler. Off she went. I saw him go off on his errand, and ran upstairs to my bed-room. There was Molly. I bolted the door, and pulled out my prick. Never had Molly resisted me more, she struggled, fought. What would happen if someone came? She would be ruined. "No one can come my darling, all are out but cook, and if she misses you she will think you have run down to your mother's." But she struggled on, begged, implored, she would meet me; she would do anything if I would desist then; she was poorly and could not. It was useless. I had been against my will chaste for some days. The fascination of the prick overcame her, she yielded, I threw her at length on the bed, mounted, fucked, and in half-a-dozen thrusts the job was done.

I recollect keeping her under me, and with my dawning senses what I had seen a quarter of an hour before came through my mind. Prick up her, and leaning on one elbow I looked at her long; the possibility of my prick then laying in Fred's spunk mixed with my own, instead of horrifying me as it would have done, had I thought about the matter before in a cool state of mind, sent a delightful titillation through me. I grasped her firmly, drove my prick home again, and said looking her in the face, "Fred has just fucked you."

"Oh!" said she with such a start that she uncunted me, "oh! what a wicked story, — let me go." But I was flat on her, she writhed, said I was insulting her; but my prick drove on, it hit, and went up. "I am sure he has, — shove, shove, — I saw him — shove — leave the room — shove — and you came out the other door, — shove, shove, shove, — lay quiet, — shove, shove, shove." "Oh! Let me go." "I shan't, — shove, — wriggle, — shove, — oh! My love, — ah! — ah — ah! — oh — o! — ah!" Our wet lips met, and the final wriggle settled our movements, sighs and conversation. She was quiet enough now, tranquillized by her pleasure.

"Oh! If someone comes." "I will say you are not here, and no one can enter. Fred has just fucked you." "It's a lie," said she, rolling off the bed, and going off quickly with her cunt full.

The butler came back with the medicine, I threw it down the closet, and went down to the dining-room. In an hour or so, I rang for some tea (How was I to get him out of the way again?). I went to my bed-room, rang; up came Molly. "Let us do it again." " I won't, you have insulted me." "Bring me a great can of hot water." Then I rang for all sorts of odd things, making believe I had a bad attack of colic, showing her my prick each time, till again she let me do it at the edge of the bed. Her cunt had been well washed. We were quiet, afraid of being overheard, a woman knows how to avoid being compromised when she has once intrigued, — but the poor girl was in an agony of fear.

"I've been into the nursemaid's room," said I, "and there is the mark of someone having been on the bed-edge." "Well, it's not me." She stuck out that she had been in the room alone. "Why there at all?" She had only passed through the room to piddle.

In the afternoon I called the butler, and sent him to the village again, to get me another mixture. In the dining-room I rang, and Molly answered. "I am going to ring in my room again," said I, "you come." No, she would not. I went up and rang.

The cook answered my bell. What a baulk! But I was equal to it, — the cook had no business to come up, it was Molly's place. "Do you think that Mrs. Brown or Pender, or some one on the farm has got anything good for diarrhœa?" "I'll go and see," said she, good-naturedly. I knew she must be gone ten minutes, or a quarter of an hour.

I followed her downstairs, soon rushed into the kitchen, bolted the kitchen-garden entrance, laid hold of Molly, whose horror was extreme at the idea of being caught, and I fucked her in the butler's pantry, where he slept. With my cock dripping as I pulled it out, I ran up to my room. She had just had time to unbolt the door before the cook appeared, and she brought me some medicine from Mrs. Pender, which of course went down the closet.

I went to my bed-room, revelling in the intrigue of the day, and wondering how often Fred had had her, and whether that day was the first time. Whenever my cock grew stiff I rang for Molly, and showed it to her. She grew demoralized at the constant sight of the cock, but there was no time for a fuck; I promised her a new bonnet to get me another opportunity. In a couple of hours she came, I had a voluptuous caprice, turned her belly on the bed, her rump towards me, for a fuck from behind. She objected, "What are you going to do? You can't do anything like that." "Yes my love, easily." "I don't like my clothes up like that." Two or three times I had to turn her round before she was quiet, and then we consummated. Molly was astonished. She had never been tailed in that attitude before, I am sure.

It was about eleven o'clock when Fred and the others had set forth; they returned to a late dinner. I had fucked Molly five or six times. Then I went to bed, my aunt and cousins came up to me, and were so kind. So was Fred, who told me all about the inspection, and never suspected my game in the least, nor anyone else. The last words I said to Molly that day were, "Fred has fucked you." Again she swore that he never had. To keep up the deception and excuse my staying at home, I had eaten scarcely anything all day, and felt, I recollect, awfully hungry when abed.

The empty pleasure of occasionally showing my doodle to Molly was all I could get afterwards. Nelly or Sophy — I forget which — I got to the baudy house at ° ° °; whichever of the two it was, came half wet through with muddy boots and under-linen which so upset me that I did not poke. The servant who had been ill came back to the Hall, and Molly left. I had Pender (whose belly was then showing its intentions awfully) up against the gate opposite her cottage one wet night (but "cock and cunt will come together"). Said she in the slight interval between our meeting, fucking, and parting, "If that gal Molly is not in the family way, — her mother's found it out,— oh! Such a row." That accounted for Molly looking depressed.

Soon Molly went again to London, and I did the same day, but not in the third-class carriage. We spoke at the station. "For God's sake go," said she, "aunt's coming." "I'll write to the post-office," said I, and did. Then she met me, she got a situation directly, but I tempted the girl. "Tell your aunt you are wanted a week earlier than you are, and come and stop with me." The devil was with me, Molly got into a cab with her box, and was set down at a station; there I got her into another, and we drove to a small hotel where I had taken a room. She only staid with me five days. I took her to theatres and other places, but not out in the day; fed her up, and fucked her and myself out. The sheets were always slobbered with spunk, and once or twice I made the woman change them. Molly had become lecherous, and no doubt reckless, and I had the delight of teaching her baudiness (which is the main pleasure a virgin gives you over a gay woman), but she did not care about me. She was often crying, but a little friction on her clitoris usually cured that. On the last day I asked her if she was in the family way? She admitted it, and went to her situation. "I think it's you who have done it," said she to me. I told her it must be Giles.

She stopped a fortnight in her situation, then went no one knew where. Pender told me when I went back. I was sorry, went to town hoping to find her, and wrote to the post-office. By some chance — perhaps to get a letter from Giles — she went there. A week afterwards my landlady said a young woman had called on me. "A lady?" said I. "Not at all, an overdressed young woman." It was Molly, who called again. I went to her poor lodgings, she fenced my questions, said she meant to go back to her mother's. Pressing her as to how she lived, she said she had the money I had given her. "But your bonnet, your clothes, — what do you do of a night?" She could not evade it, Molly had turned whore. I never knew who had put her up to getting her living by her cunt; but a fellow servant had left with her, and had got the next room to hers.

A woman who takes to whoring takes to lying. I could not learn exactly how long she had stayed at her situation, or much about her movements. I stayed with her the night, she let me pull up her clothes, and open her thighs with a freedom she never had done before; from which I inferred she had had more than one prick in her split since I had been up her last; she was voluptuous, and her cunt was unusually juicy.

I went back to my aunt's, sorry, for I seemed to have been largely the cause of Molly going astray, and did not know then that a gay life is as happy as that of the wife of a farm-laborer. Restless, I went again to London, saw Molly who looked fearfully wretched, would neither let me fuck, nor feel her, and then broke out in an agony of tears, saying she was ill, something was the matter with her. "With your cunt?" "Yes," said she, "do look." Poor Molly opened her plump thighs, stretched open her cunt, and gave me every facility. Her quim was in a high state of inflammation, and it had a discharge. A medical student who saw her said she had the clap, and gave her medicine. "Oh! Do look again, tell me if I am very bad, — shall I be worse? — Oh! I am so sorry I did not keep at my situation," said she.

Once in my life since, another girl made me a similar confession, and those are the only two who confessed to an illness at the time they had the illness on them.

I told her she could be cured, but horrified her with the description of the diseases to which she might be subject, took her to a doctor, paid her lodgings, counselled her to go home, to hold her tongue, and refuse to tell anyone anything, excepting that she had left her situation. She promised, but was frightened of her mother.

She said she had never been into the streets since I had left her. I had a fear of the clap, and did not intend any commerce with her; but lust overcame me, and we fucked all that night to the damage of the sheets again. I wrote an anonymous letter to her mother, telling where the girl could be found. She came up to town and took her back. Molly's cunt proved to be all right.

A woman is such a fool that she must tell someone everything. Mrs. Brown told Pender about the anonymous letter, and Mrs. P. told me; but I don't think any of them knew the girl had been on the streets. Molly's belly soon afterwards showed, Mrs. Brown thought better of Giles, he married her and they went to live a few miles off. She had a child, and every one thought it was Giles' begetting. I suppose he knew nothing of the girl's pranks, for luckily a cunt cannot speak. Then Mrs. Brown left aunt, and Pender and his wife came to live in the farm-yard.

When it became known that Molly Brown was delivered of a child, my aunt remarked (Fred told me) that she was not married a bit too soon." "I had that little devil two or three times," said Fred, "and on the first day I was in uniform. Do you recollect Walter, the day you were ill?" And he told me how it came about; but I never told him that I had had her; I never spoke of having had a woman, if I thought I should injure her, whatever my desire or vanity might have been.

CHAPTER XII

Nelly and Sophy. — Nelly at the Argyle. — In town with Fred. —
On the sofa with Mabel. — The effect of black stockings. — Inter-
ference. — In bed. — Mabel's bad habits. — A ladies' school. — The
bath-room. — My cousins naked. — Maria the curate's wife. — Cunt
inspections. — Servants washing. — Flat-fucking.

I may as well finish about Nelly and Sophy, although the occurrences I now narrate happened some time afterwards. Nelly got
in the family way, told me I was the father, and told Fred he was,
for he had had her. We both cheeked her, and said that half a dozen
might claim the honor. She and Sophy left the village. Sophy I
never heard of or saw again, that I recollect. Two or three years
afterwards, I was at the Argyle Rooms. A woman looked at me
smiled, and pointed me out to another woman, then came up smiling and said, "Don't you know me?" It was Nelly, who had become
harlot by profession. I was then a poor man, but slept with her at
Brompton. She had heard I had ruined myself. I had her afterwards
once or twice, but soon gave her up. Harlotry was successful with
her, and I could not pay her price. Though she was a swell woman,
she did not want me to pay at all, but I was proud. She always
declared that I had had the first of her, but could not say I was the
father of the child.

Mrs. Pender now had a chance. At night there was often no
one in the farm-yard but her, she could therefore go into the barn
when she liked. Her husband finding the dark nights dull went
frequently to the village Public; then I used to enter the big barn
from the rick-yard, she having left the wicket open, and she had a
good bumbasting on the straw and hay. But I grew tired of her big
belly, liked a bed and nakedness, and to see and feel in comfort the

321

cunt I was to bestow my attention on. Fucking on straw was all very well with a new piece. I could generally not tell her face from her arse, excepting by feel, for of course we had no light in the barn; so I grew tired, and gave it up.

Then Fred and I went to town, he to see Laura, I to get promiscuous fucking, and other amusements. Laura who was one of the few women of her class whom I have found to be well educated, had a female friend stopping with her from her native place Plymouth. Her name was Mabel, a pretty, modest-looking girl. Laura had given out that she had married Fred, and this girl had been entrusted to keep her company. I tell the tale as it was told me. I dined with them daily, and in fact all but lived there.

One night we went to the theatre, and back to Fred's, had a jolly supper, and got as merry as sand-boys. It was a cold, foggy night, I said I would not go home as it was about three a.m., and would sleep on the sofa. Our conversation had been pretty warm. Fred remarked that I had better sleep with Mabel. Laura was surprized at Fred. Mabel laughed, and baudy insinuations passed without baudy words. Fred said he should go to bed, and off he went. Laura expected Mabel to go to bed, but she put it off laughing and joking. Laura got angry, Fred came out in his night-gown swearing if Laura did not come, he would go out, and get a woman; and off Laura went. Fred wanted a fuck before he went to sleep.

Mabel and I sat talking, both heated and randy. It got colder, she got sleepy, I would not let her go, so she laid on the sofa. I drew a chair to her side, and both drinking whisky and water time rolled on. "Oh! I wish I were Fred," said I. "Why?" "Because he is between Laura's thighs, belly to belly, how warm, how delicious, this cold night." "Oh! For shame!" "Nonsense my dear, quite natural and proper, we are made to keep each other warm, and give each other pleasure." "When we're married," said she. "Married, — pough! — then millions would never taste the pleasure." My words grew warmer, I kissed, and was kissed, edged myself on to the sofa, little by little felt my way from her ankles to her thighs, and behold me smothering her with kisses, with my hand on her cunt, her hand on my prick.

A modest woman will let you take liberties much more readily if you kiss her whilst taking them. Sit at the foot of a girl on a sofa, and try to force your hand up her clothes, she may resist you; sit close by her side, bend over her, kiss her, and at the same time your hand may find its way to her cunt, almost without hindrance.

So it was now. Mabel was scarcely modest. I recollect the conviction coming over me that she was no virgin, and if I had doubts before, the way my finger slipped from her clitoris up the love-pit and plugged it, confirmed them. She lay with her eyes fixed on me, palpitating gently with voluptuousness. Her petticoats up to her knees, I saw legs in black stockings, one in wrinkles, the other half-way bagging down the calf, and her feet in shabby slippers.

I had at that time a horror of black stockings, which affected me at times so much as to deprive me of all desire. Once with a gay woman who had black stockings I was unable to poke her, spite of her blandishment, till she put white ones on. As I now saw Mabel's legs a disgust came over me, desire left me, and my prick began to shrink; I may have been tired, or had had my sperm drawn too much the night previously; that is likely enough, I don't recollect; but know I got nervous, a fear lest she should doubt my manhood, a sense of shame overcame me. I tried to rally, but in vain, for once that nervousness on me, it vanquished me. I ceased to probe her quim with my finger, my prick shrunk out of her hand, and the titillation ceasing, Mabel turned away her eyes, repulsed my hands, and drew her clothes down, looking at me full. I sat speechless.

"Are you ill?" said she. "Yes," said I, overjoyed with the suggestion, "a faintness came over me, and a giddyness, — I shall be better directly."

She believed it, gave me cold water, and we sat for a time. I looked at her beautifully white neck, thought how white her bum must be, tried to get the black stockings out of my head, but could not. It must have been past four o'clock in the morning when I asked her to lie down again, but she refused; the spell had been broken, the weakness gone, and she said she should go to bed.

"Is your bum as white as your neck?" said I. "Laura says I am the whitest-fleshed woman she ever saw, all the girls at school used to say so."

In my mind's eye I saw the white bum and thighs, my lust came back at a rush. "Let me see it," I said, and I laid hold of her. The flood-gates of my bawdiness were loosened, and as she afterwards told me, I let fly a torrent of voluptuous words, enough to have excited the passions of all the women in London. I had forgotten the stockings. She kept refusing, denying, and evading me. "Hish! Hish! Laura will hear you." Laura did, and came in in her night-gown. "I came to see if you had gone to bed," said she. "You need not have troubled yourself," said Mabel. "As long as you're here I shall look after you; when you're at home you can do as you like." "I'm quite old enough to take care of myself." They quarrelled. Mabel resented her interference. Fred roared out from his bed-room, "What the devil are you going in there for?" and Laura not replying, came in in his night-shirt. After an altercation Fred and Laura went back to bed.

Then Mabel said she should go to bed, must go up for five minutes, but would be down again. "To piddle eh?" Taking off my boots I blew out one candle, took the other, followed her, and opened the door. She was on the piss-pot. I closed the door, and locked it. Five minutes afterwards I was on the bed fucking her with her legs in black stockings, and five minutes afterwards un-cunting, the first words I said were, "I loathe black stockings."

"I can't bear them myself," said she, "but I am in mourning." People in mourning wore black stockings then.

She was anxious for me to go, so that Laura could say nothing positive, whatever she might think. I would directly I had her again. We got into the bed together, and I had her, and then again. That is all I recollect, and that after the fuck we both fell asleep, and were awakened by a knock at the door. It was late in the morning, and broad daylight, Laura was knocking. I opened the door. Laura looked at me, and then at Mabel, and said, "Well, the sooner I send you back the better." There was a somewhat bitter row between them, short but sharp, in which Mabel gave as good as she got. Laura went away. Mabel turned round and wept; then we fucked, and went to sleep again.

This is the only point in my history with Mabel much worth noting, except that when I knew her from top to bottom, and found she got out of bed, and washed her cunt after my sperming it, I asked her, "Why did you not wash the first night?" "Because it's unlucky," said she, and I never got any more out of her; but she had known the sensation of a prick in her cunt before mine, that I found out the first night.

She was a well-arsed, well-made, plump girl about twenty-one years old, and had a wonderfully white skin. She had been fucked before, but I believed from all I learnt from her, Laura, and Fred, that for two years a prick had not entered her. A man who had paid his addresses to her had deceived her, then cleared off, I expect after tailing her.

I did not profess to keep Mabel after this, but paid for the second-floor rooms (Fred had taken the upper part of the house, three bed- and one sitting-room), and my share of the living, and slept with her almost regularly for a short time, gave her money, dressed her, and did all a man does who keeps a woman; but I never cared much about her, and was not constant. She, like Laura, was fairly educated. A few months afterwards she went back to her native town, and although she wrote to me, I never saw her again, and had some idea that Lord A*** kept her, why I shall tell further on. One reason of my being indifferent to her was that she never properly washed herself. Her beautiful white flesh never seemed to need it, but I did not like a woman who just smeared her face and neck, and never below. I told her of it, and she was offended.

About three weeks after I first had Mabel, Fred and I went to shoot with some friends at ***shire; it was towards the end of November, all the leaves were well off the trees.

As said, I had female cousins by several aunts, two of them about seventeen or eighteen years of age were at a finishing-school for young ladies. It was a large old-fashioned house kept by three ladies of whom one had been married a year, although then forty years old, to a curate about sixty-five years old. The sisters unmarried were between fifty and sixty years old, stern and stiff-rumped. Maria, the married one, fat and forty, with jet-black hair and merry hazel eyes, had been disappointed in her youth, and when this clergyman, whom she had known all her life, proposed, she accepted I suppose for companionship, and because it gave her consideration in the neighbourhood.

The house was originally a very big old mansion, large enough for two schools, and had been roughly divided by walls and partitions into two houses. The smaller was inhabited by Maria and her husband, and the kitchen-garden was attached to it. All access to the pleasure-grounds of the other, or school part of the house, was bricked up. In an establishment for young ladies, all of a fuckable age, and none without hair on their cunts, it would never have done to leave a male access, not even to a curate sixty-five years old. The gardeners were elderly men, they came round by the house to go to the kitchen-garden, which supplied both houses. Mrs. Maria used to go round to the school daily.

The air of the neighbourhood was fine, and although not professing to lodge people, if any of the female relatives of the young ladies at the school desired it, they could go and stop for a week or two at the curate's, of course paying for so doing.

Fred and I had invitations to shooting not far off, just as my aunt went to stay a week at Mrs. Maria's and to see her girl. Our friends could accommodate Fred only, and sooner than be separated, and for other reasons, we wrote to the old curate to know if he could receive us two men, — and my aunt as well, — which he did. We took up our quarters there. I had unpacked, and went into Fred's room. "Here is a jolly cupboard," said he, opening the door of one big enough for four people to stand in. "If a woman were sleeping here, she would always be thinking some one was hidden in it; it's a jolly place for boxes and clothes." He was hanging up something, when he stopped and listened. "Damned if there are not women laughing," said he. "Hish!" But he heard nothing more.

Two or three minutes afterwards he said, "Here, Walter," and both listening heard the voices of women, but very indistinctly. Fred lighted a candle. Said he, "Here is an old door screwed up, it leads into a room. What a lark to get it open, or a hole through it; nothing I so like as to hear what women say, when they think no one hears them."

I suggested it was unfair, it might be his sisters' room. "It don't matter," said he, "it's all in the family." We went to dinner, and then back to his room. He at once got to the closet, undid his gun-case, and taking out the gun-screw, tried to loosen the screws of the door, but could not. Off he went to the village, came back with a screw-driver, and with some labor opened the door. Then we found ourselves in another empty place nearly as big, and at the end of it rough boards nailed across a frame horizontally, and as we supposed covered over on the other side. It evidently had been a passage, and when they separated the house, they had screwed up the door into the room of which we did not yet know the use, leaving the door at the end next Fred's room as it was, and had fixed up some wood-work across the end of the passage, thus making the large closet at one end, and the empty space at the other. We were dusty with our job.

After breakfast next day, aunt, Fred, and I went round to see his sister and cousin. We saw their bed-rooms, accompanied by them and aunt, we were in fact shown over the house. Fred had previously looked well at the outside, to see how the windows ran. "What is that room which is shut off?" "Oh!" said his sister, "that is a bath-room; look, such a nice one." We entered it; it was the room up to which the passage at the back of the closet led. Fred winked at me, and when we got back he roared. "Oh! Lord, we shall see them naked — the boards have twisted, there are cracks next the bath-room, — we'll run a knife between one, and through the canvas and paper; then we will see through — oho! Ho! We shall see the girls bathing, — there are two or three damned fine girls."

Had it been servants, I should have been delighted at a peep; but to rip a hole to spy young ladies, and one of those his sister, revolted me. "Damn it Fred, it's not the thing, one is your own sister." "Pough! You have seen their cunts." (It was not the two I had seen.) "Ah! Those were children." "Well °° and °° are only larger, and have hair on their cunts, and you need not look." "But if we are found out, we are disgraced; if it were at an hotel or elsewhere, I would not mind." "It won't be found out." "They will see the crack in the paper." "They won't, they will think it split by the boards warping, if they do; besides there are cracks and some shelves put up, I know exactly the place."

Nothing stopped him, and after boring, prodding, and getting a chair to stand on to find the right place, he at length made some cracks a few inches long with a knife, and we saw day-light through, the bath, towels, clothes-pegs, and a large cane settee or sofa. I would not look at first, but so weak is man's nature concerning a woman, that at length I did, and a thrill of pleasure shot through me as I thought of seeing the naked girls, and strange enough, I recollect a feeling of curiosity about the figures my two cousins would cut if they were naked. I thought of the quims of his sisters some years before, and wondered what difference between these and those.

Carefully locking the closet we went out. When we returned

Fred peeped at every opportunity, but saw nothing that day. The next morning Fred awakened me. "Get up, they are going to bathe, a servant is filling the baths." It was a cold, dark morning. "I shan't." "Don't," and off he went. In a minute or two however I was by his side. We saw two young ladies enter, strip, and take their baths; the candle-light was imperfect, but we saw them rub their bodies dry, and scrub the wet off their cunts; we saw their hair above and below, and all their little secrets. They were, we afterwards knew, sisters.

"I shall burst," said Fred, "how do you feel, Walter?" I was maddened by desire like him at the sight of the fresh, modest, naked girls cleaning themselves so unsuspectingly; all this in whispers.

Another girl or two came in, they hurried through the operation as if they did not like it. "Here is Carry," said Fred. I peeped and in came my two cousins. "Lord, what a lot of hair she has got on her cunt," said my shameless cousin. "It's a damned ungentlemanly thing Fred." "Well, don't look then," said he. But I did, — I could not help it; my sense of honor was strong, my lust stronger, and I saw both naked. "Holloa! Here is Mrs. Maria," — it was. She stripped. A fine, round, plump, middle-aged woman with a mass of black hair between her thighs, that would have sufficed to stuff a sofa-squab. Fred was smitten. "I'll be damned," said he, "if I would not sooner have her than all the others." I could not get his eyes away to let me have a full look, so much was he taken with her. Indeed, when she put one leg on the chair, and rubbed the towel well round her cunt and arse, showing two big, well-set globes, and round arms and thighs, the black hair in her arm-pits, the black hair below, she looked in the feeble light not more than thirty years old, and as fine an arm-full as a man could desire. "What a pity she has never been fucked," said Fred. "I'll swear old ° ° ° can't do it to her, — he can only frig her."

Only four or five ladies took a morning bath; we saw the same on two or three mornings. We were shooting all day. Fred then went to shoot with a friend some miles off, I stopped with my aunt at the Rev. ° ° °'s house till his return, and walked out with them. Fred went away on a Saturday afternoon, I went to my bed-room, thought I would have a peep into the next house, and

went to Fred's room (he had left me the closet-key), and saw the
bath-room quite bright with a large fire. I asked for a fire to be
lighted in Fred's room which was bigger than mine, observing that
it was so much better to write in than mine; then making a great
display, I sat down to write letters, locked the bed-room door, and
stationed myself at the crack in the closet.

Oh! What an evening! It soon became evident that the whole
household would wash that night. The young ladies came in mostly
one at a time, sometimes in pairs, the mistress came in from time
to time. The ladies came in, in loose gowns, a chemise and slippers,
all but undressed. Everything was quite decorous, the mistress
mostly present. Each girl would deposit her gown and chemise on
a chair, turning her rump to the other, and get into the bath. When
they left it, they stepped out, and came straight to the spot where
I could best see them, their cunts towards me, and began to dry
themselves. Servants came in and emptied the baths. Some only
used a foot-bath. All was done so quietly and demurely that I could
scarcely hear a word they said; no girl was supposed, I think, to see
either the bum or belly of the other.

Once when the mistress left, a pair of girls were together, and
threw off reserve. One time they got into the bath together, and
smacked each other's bums. The younger girls had come in first
in the evening, the elder ones later. The mistress did not come in
with the elder ones. This pair talked about my cousin and me. They
stood in front of the fire; one tripped across the room, and bolted
the door, then each one in succession put a leg on the chair, and
they looked at each other's cunts. Able to bear it no longer, I frigged
myself, and may as well say at once that having begun so, I went
on. From half-past eight till about ten o'clock did bathing go on,
I looking, and frigging myself as often as my cock stood. I saw in
succession nearly all the ladies, and four female servants.

Most of the girls who took cold baths in the morning did not
come in at night, my cousins excepted. Every one had hair on her
cunt. I knew and recollected some for years afterwards, and when
I saw them walking out, or in the grounds from our bed-room
window, and when my cousins came in to dine with us at the
Reverend's house, bringing two of the other young ladies with them,
I recollected the look of their bums and bubbies, the quantity and

colour of the hair on their cunts as well as if it had been my own prick. I could not converse, my eyes went from one to the other of the girls as their charms rose up in my mind, my prick throbbing. Aunt noticed my silence, and joking me, asked if I was falling in love.

It was difficult to hear the conversation; what I did was for the most part chaste, and about trifles, the only exception was the two girls who looked at each other's quims, and stood near me, half facing the fire. It ran something like this: "I wonder if men look at each other's things." "I dare say they do." "Boys do, Miss Y°°° said she saw two of her brothers rubbing each other's things hard." "Law!" "Yes." "Is it not funny that the men's things should be put right up ours?" "Lor yes." "It seems nasty." "I wish you could ask °°° to let us see that book again." "I have, and she has not got it now." "It was fun." "Yes," — and they both laughed. "Make haste, they will wonder why we are so long." "Ring the bell." "Yes." "Open the bolt." "Hish! Here is some one."

The servants came in two by two, the mistress came in with the first pair, and told them to put the fire out. When she had gone, "The old skinflint," said one servant, and put coals on after saying "Yes" to her mistress. To me it was always more exciting to see a woman in stockings and boots, than quite naked. The young ladies had come in undressed from their rooms; the servants came dressed, bringing candles with them. They were full-grown women, I felt more pleasure in seeing them gradually undress and uncover. One, a middle-aged woman, said aloud, "I shall only wash my feet, it's so cold." She took water out of the big path, put it into a hip-bath, pulled off her shoes and stockings, tucked her petticoats up to her thighs, and washed her feet by the fire. She was a big-limbed woman, I could not see her cunt. I had seen a dozen that night, yet because I could not see this one's cunt I seemed to long for it. The other had stripped, and got into the bath, and I could see her naked. She was ugly and middle-aged. I would sooner have fucked any one of the young women than her, and yet I recollect feeling the most furious baudiness about her, and frigged looking at her.

Then in came two strong-looking women, but much younger. "Stir the fire, — don't make a noise, or there will be a row about coals," said one. "They are all abed," said the other. Both stripped to their chemises, one went to the bath. "I shan't wash after cook," said she, and she let off the water. "The water won't be warm, they have drawn off so much." "Then I won't wash," she replied. Then one woman stood by the fire with her back to it, and lifted up her chemise to warm her arse. I saw it sideways as she stood, boots and stockings on.

The other came to the fire. "It will take five minutes to run clean out," said she. Both drew chairs in front of the fire, sat down, and raised their chemises, one edged closer to the other, inclined her head to the other's thighs, and kissed it, then looked, and placed her hand on the cunt. I could not see the cunt, her back hid it, for she had turned her back to me; then the other one's hand crossed and the two women sat feeling each other. I don't think they said a word; if so I could not hear it; their heads were from me. They sat for three or four minutes, kissing and feeling each other.

"Is the door locked?" said one quite aloud, and getting up, went to the door, and tried it. Then one laid her clothes on the big settee, and laid down on her back, the other threw up her chemise, kissed, and perhaps licked her cunt. I only know her head covered the cunt, and then she mounted her. I thought it must be fun, for although I had once seen a woman on the top of another, and had heard of such things, I was incredulous. Now I saw them together like man and woman, sometimes between each other's thighs, sometimes with legs interlaced, and hands grasping each other's buttocks, the thighs of one raised up round the other's limbs, the mouths meeting, the backsides wriggling and twisting without ceasing. If they laid so one minute, they remained in each other's embraces nearly half-an-hour, sometimes quiet, then wriggling again. I heard not a sound, don't recollect hearing kisses, or anything; but it was difficult to hear, unless they talked loud.

The light went out, there was a glimmer from the hot fire. Said one getting off, "Is there no other candle?" "No." "You must get down to the kitchen for one, we can't go up without light." Off went one, slipping her gown on first. The other gently stirred the fire, sat down, put her hand on her cunt, and frigged it. I can't say if she had pleasure, but her head fell back, and one side of her face was then towards me. I saw it all by the flame of the fire, which she had poked. The other came back with two bits of candle, and they went away, having put on their gowns, carrying their other clothes with them, neither having bathed. Then I went off to my own bed-room, frigged out. The loudness with which the servants talked, compared with the young ladies, was very noticeable, though when on the top of each other on the settee at the end of the room, I could not hear a word.

CHAPTER XIII

Fred on flat-fucking. — In town with Laura. — Back at the school. — Pictures for young ladies. — Fred's ankle. — Mrs. Maria's weakness. — To London alone. — Laura and Mabel. — Three in a bed. — A risky poke. — Groping for the pot. — Nearly caught. — Fred joins us.

When I awakened on Sunday I thought I had been dreaming, the images of a dozen and more modest naked women passed through my brain. I could think of nothing else, waited at the gate to see the young ladies go off to church, and followed at a distance, walking with Mrs. Maria. I tried to guess from the backs of the ladies which was which, every now and then looked at Mrs. Maria, thinking of the hirsute charms of her cunt and arm-pits. At church, in an old-fashioned square pew, I could see many of the young ladies' faces, and looked at them during the whole service, thought at times that I mistook one for the other; — but no, although each had a bonnet on, and was in full dress, I recognized each face, recollected bum, bubby, and motte of each. My well-frigged cock stood from Psalms to Sermon. I went to church in the afternoon, because a few pious girls liked two services. My cousins, and two other young ladies dined at the Reverend's, it always was an early dinner, to let him get to church. In the evening I again went to church, because the servants went; and sat close to the two women who had played at flat-fucking. The astonishment of my aunt at my going to church three times was so great, that although I told her I went because I did not know what to do with myself, she wrote to my mother about it.

On Sunday night Fred returned. You may guess we saw on the Monday the morning bathings. I told him all excepting that his sister had come to bathe. "Did °°° and °°° come?" (Naming her and cousin.) "No." He was satisfied. I told him about the two servants. Why I lied about my cousins I cannot think, but was half ashamed of looking at all, and it seemed more sinful to have seen my cousins than anyone else.

Afterwards Fred told me that in India he kept three young girls all together in a bungalow; had bought them from their parents as virgins at about twenty shillings each. He was conversant with female life there, and explained how the women satisfied their letches with each other in harems, if they could not get men. His girls, he said, did it, and did it before him. I was amazed and wondered, and half thought him lying. All my knowledge of women extended to their relations with men, and although I had seen twice women on the top of each other, and seen one gamahuche another, I still regarded them as baudy tricks got up for my amusement; and had never realized the idea of women having letches for each other, as men have for frigging each other. The latter had indeed passed away from my mind as a boyish habit, no desire to feel a prick then entered my mind, I even disliked touching a man. So I heard what Fred told me, but remained incredulous, and was approaching middle-age before I realized the fact that frigging another fellow's doodle was agreeable, and that some women find similar pleasures with their own sex. The flat-cocking of the two if they were at it, which I now don't doubt, left no agreeable or voluptuous impression on me.

After breakfast, having no shooting, Fred and I went to town to see our women. Five minutes after our arrival, both were being fucked. We found, sitting with Mabel and Laura, the mistress of Lord A°°°, and will call her Lady A°°°. After we had pumped our sperm out, we all went into the sitting-room, Lady A°°° was there still. Fred asked me what I had been doing, I asked him the same, there was a general warm talk without coarse language. Lady A°°° told the girls they were lucky, for she had not seen Lord A°°° for a month, and had not had anything done to her for that length of time.

Fred then went out, and returned in an hour. Taking me aside he showed me baudy engravings, which he meant to throw into the garden of the school, where the young ladies walked daily after breakfast, if fine. I objected that his sister and cousin might find them. He did not care. "It will make them all so damned randy, that they won't know whether their arses are at their backs or fronts." This was all through my telling him what I had heard the two girls in the bath-room say to each other; and he actually that night got over the wall, into the pleasure-grounds, and laid the prints in a long building, half shed, half summer-house. From his bed-room window we could see over the wall which separated the Reverend's garden from the school-garden. I suggested sending them to a young lady by post. "No, she would keep them to herself." I must mention that each lady had a separate bed-room; they were not allowed to go to each other's bed-room, they met only at meals, or in the class-room, or drawing-room, or when out of doors. No, — the prints had better be seen by several, they would tell each other, and thus all see them. The idea of the girls seeing baudy pictures tickled us immensely. I had then wondered why the school-mistresses made it a rule that no lady should go into another's bed-room, and once asked my female cousin. She said she did not know.

Directly after breakfast we saw the ladies in the garden, pulled down our blind, and peeped. "There is Carry," said Fred, laughing as his sister showed among them. We saw a group approach the spot, the next instant all their heads were close together, looking at something. Every now and then one would stealthily look up towards the house, then another would, as if they feared being seen. On being joined by two or three others, they all moved out of sight into the shed, and we saw no more.

Fred was delighted, he did nothing but suggest how such and such a one felt at that moment. "I dare say their cunts are as hot as fire, their thighs squeeze, their arses wriggle as they walk; they will all frig themselves tonight."

Fred soon afterwards said he must go to town by the next train. I would go too. "I must go to so and so," said he, "so can't be with you much." I resolved to stay. Going into the house I saw Mrs. Maria dressed, she was going to town. "I will walk with you," said Fred, "to the station, we shall go up together." Mrs. Maria went to London to make purchases, and do all the business for the school. Neither came back till the latest train. I was sitting smoking with the Reverend when his wife returned, she looked worn out. Soon afterwards in came Fred, who looked as if he had been out all night. Said he to Mrs. Maria in a surprised manner, "Have you only just returned?" "Yes," said she, in an innocent way. "We have both come by the same train then, without knowing it," he replied.

I don't know what thoughts led to it, but the conviction came over me that he had seen Maria's thighs closer than he did through the cracks in the bath-room partition. I noticed his manner next morning, saw him look at her, and she at him at breakfast, and said to myself, "He has fucked her."

Next day we had shooting. At night Fred went to town. Next day Mrs. Maria went, and came home late, Fred not returning till the following morning. Mrs. Maria looked so tired that her husband noticed it. "She has had her belly-full again," I said to myself. As she took her bath next morning (Fred not with me), she rubbed herself dry, put on her chemise, and felt her cunt; it was a prolonged feel. I told Fred of that. His remarks were evidently intended to mislead me.

We wanted to see the Saturday night bathing, though my aunt wanted to return home; but as we had shooting on Saturday, she consented to remain over Sunday. My cousins again dined with us at the Reverend's, and two of my cousins' special friends. What pleasure I had in looking at them, knowing the looks of their backs and bellies as well as their faces, wondering what they thought of the baudy pictures, at the way in which women continue to look so modest, talk softly, look in a man's face, and keep a demure demeanour, even if lust be stinging their cunts. It is the training in hypocrisy, which is so large a part of female education.

On the Friday, Fred sprained his leg, on the Saturday was too stiff to go out shooting. I did, and returned to dinner. Mrs. Maria had attended to him, her husband was at church nearly all Saturday, so perhaps she had rubbed a little higher than his ankle. My aunt spent all the time she could at the school, or walking out with her daughter and niece.

Fred's sprain was an excuse for going to his bed-room whither I accompanied him. In the dusty closet Fred's lameness was better. In came the young ladies, the younger ones first. It was a pretty sight, a decently voluptuous one, to see the dainty white-fleshed creatures throw off their dresses, and stand naked, one by one entering the bath, rub their flesh dry, and their cunt-wigs free from moisture; to see cne with her bum towards you, rubbing her back vigorously with a towel pulled straight with both hands, whilst her bum-cheeks, loins, and thighs quivered with the motion and friction. Another put one leg on a chair whilst she rubbed her quim dry. Then came the servants. Again I recollect having my lust more stirred at seeing the fuller-grown women strip, and stand with boots and stockings on, than at seeing the virgin ladies naked. I can't account for this at all. I write exactly what I recollect.

When we saw Fred's sister, he whispered that all his family had a good deal of hair on their privates. I saw his prick soon afterwards. He spoke as if he were intimately acquainted with the cunts and pricks of the whole family. The two young ladies who looked at each other's privates did not do so again, the flat-fuckers took no pleasure in each other's arms, they soaped each other's backs, and helped to dry each other; both rubbed themselves in front of the fire — a fine couple of women. "I want to piddle so," said one just as she finished bathing. "Piddle in the bath," said the other, "there is no one else going into it." And she did so standing up, then jumped rapidly out, and they both laughed.

I have seen before and since through key-holes and peep-holes women and men wash, but it was with difficulty. Here all was fairly clear. The crevice admitted enough sight, to distinguish form, face, feature, and colour of hair and eyes. I thought of it for years, but never told a man. Oftentimes when fucking, the bathing spectacle came into my mind, and fetched my sperm out of me in a moment.

The next morning we jabbed a few more holes between other boards, so as to make it look as if the shrinking of the wood had cracked the paper in more than one place, carefully closed the door and dipped the heads of the screws in vinegar to darken them. The whole looked rusty, and as we hoped when we had done no one would ever guess the game we had been up to. We swept up dust from the carpet, and pushed it under the bottom of the door, and I think our prank never was known. The old house is pulled down now.

I went to church again for the pleasure of staring at the ladies, it was rapture to look at them, and think of their virgin cunts, think they had seen the baudy prints. My cousin Fred had gone out somewhere, Mrs. Maria, who usually went to church with her husband, was ill. In the middle of the service a thought came into my head. Feeling sure that Fred was after the middle-aged plump lady, I left the church, and went back, knocked at the door twice before it was opened, and then by Mrs. Maria. Said she, "I let both servants go out." She told me this without my asking her anything, her hair seemed a little rough, her manner excited. I sat down, told her I had felt faint, and had a colic in church, and so had come home. "Fred has been unwell too," said she. "Indeed? — I thought he was out." "He returned, and has been in bed this hour." "Oh!" said I. It was clear to me why her hair was rough. Fred was abed, but awake. Had Mrs. Maria been fucked on that bed?

My aunt and I left the next day, and went to the Manor-House; Fred to my astonishment could not get out of bed, so bad was his sprain; so we left him there. At the Hall I got so lewed that I went up to London, and rushed to Laura's lodgings the next night.

"Both abed, sir," said the servant who let me in. Finding no one in Mabel's room, I went down to the first floor. The women were in bed together. Laura opened the door to me, and got into bed again in the dark; for company's sake they slept together when we men were both away, she said.

Lewed with prolonged chastity, the two servants in the bathroom ran in my mind as I sat chatting in the dark room. After having slipped in my hand under the clothing on to Mabel's cunt, "Have you been amusing each other? — which was man, which woman?" were questions put and answered with real or assumed ignorance, but with some giggling. Laura, as I have said, never allowed a baudy word, so I ceased; and Laura, I suppose savage at Mabel having all the groping to herself, said, "You go first, and warm the bed, and Mabel will come up to you." "No, you go and warm it for me, Mabel." "I won't." "Then I won't." Mabel seemed to me thick in speech, muddled in manner, and half asleep.

I fetched my candle. The women looked so fresh and handsome. "I'll sleep with you both," said I, beginning to undress.

A slight altercation, — what would Fred say? — the servants think? — no, she would not permit it, — she knew the games we should be up to. Mabel said, "No, — no, it wouldn't do." The more they said no, the quicker I undressed, and with prick lifting up my shirt, forced myself into bed, by the side of Mabel. Laura jumped out the other side, her white legs showing half-way up her thighs as she did so.

She stood by the bed-side wrangling, and looking at me as randy as possible, spite of herself. I should not stay, — she would not go to bed. "Well, my dear Laura, go up to our bed." "I shan't." Tired of standing in the cold she said, "Well, will you promise to keep quiet?" "Perfectly." "Come on," said Mabel, "Fred won't know." So putting out the light, into bed got Laura. Perhaps she thought she would like on the quiet to hear the amatory talk of Mabel and self, — hear if she could not see or feel our tricks, — who knows?

"Turn your back to Mabel, — go to sleep Laura, — now you won't see or hear." "You know your promise, — don't you let him Mabel." "How can I help it?" said Mabel in a muddled manner. "You are a couple of dirty beasts," said Laura, turning her rump towards us. We heeded not, for we were fucking. Laura spoke not another word, she lay as if asleep. Then I fell fast asleep on the edge of the bed cuddling Mabel. It was close packing.

I awakened cold on one side, hot on the other next Mabel, who lay snoring profoundly. The regular breathing of Laura told me she was asleep. My prick was stiff, and as I thought of the two women by the side of me, it got ungovernable.

"How I should like a put into Laura," I thought, but had a high sense of honor, and checked the desire. "What, Fred's woman? — for shame, Walter. — Well (reflecting), he took my two women in the country. — Yes," replied my conscience, "but nothing made them yours, — not completely at least, one had had another man, but Laura is *his* woman, his temporary wife, he is fond of her, he keeps her." But my prick kept throbbing with desire to be up her.

I thought of Fred's description of the thick hair on her cunt, of the quickness with which she pissed, of all he had foolishly told me of her perfections, until my brain whirled. "There can't be any harm in just feeling her flesh, — no one will know." I could only guess where she was in the darkness; but carefully stretching my hand over Mabel quite slowly, it touched a bunch of night-gown, and then warm flesh. She was lying on her back, Mabel had her rump towards her. I raised myself gently up to feel further; touched the hips, the thighs, then the smooth belly, further on, and my hand laid in the thick hair of her cunt.

Up to that time I had my reason, could reflect, pause, control myself; the woman of any friend of mine was safe from attack from me, but I had had a fancy that there had been once or twice in Laura's look and manner towards me, a slight gleam of desire; yet the idea of having her never had entered my head, I should have chased it instantly. But from the moment my hand lighted on the crisp thicket, reason left me, voluptuous desire overwhelmed me: I forgot Fred, almost forgot Mabel.

Slowly, inch by inch, I moved myself half up and my arm over Mabel as she lay, fearing it would wake her, and slid my finger down between Laura's cunt-lips, and gently frigged, listening to Mabel's snoring, and Laura's breathing. At length I must have produced a voluptuous sensation, she got restless, and opened her thighs, moved, clasped my hand, and in a peevish sleepy tone said, "Don't Mabel, — what are you doing?"

"It's I," I whispered, frigging on. "Oh!" said she, pushing my hand away. "Oh! If you wake Mabel." She kept repulsing my hand saying "Don't," I replacing it, my hand frigging her clitoris.

She turned her backside towards Mabel, I then fumbled between her bum-cheeks; but she was too far off. Slowly I got out of bed, and feeling my way round the foot in the dark, I got to Laura's side. She heard me. I put my mouth to her ear, "Let me, dear," and thrusting my hand under the clothes felt her cunt from motte to bum-hole. "Oh! No, if Mabel —." Mabel's snoring reassured me. Little by little I uncovered her, lifting off the clothes, got on to her, up her, and without a word, without a whisper, without resistance or denial, we fucked gently, pausing at intervals to listen, hiding our emotions and pleasures as we spent, Laura's flanks and my hand close to Mabel's rump, my leg almost touching Mabel's leg, she still snoring like a pig.

"Go," said Laura, her mouth to my ear, and uncunting me. Quietly, without reply, I got off, and back again crept stealthily to Mabel's side, and at the very moment that I was lifting the bed-clothes Mabel awoke, and said directly, "What are you getting up for? — Where are you going?"

I was for a moment at my wits' end. "Where is the pot?" said I. "Under the bed," said Mabel. "Laura!" Laura did not answer, and breathed heavily. I pissed, and got into bed. It was a close fit. Mabel took hold of my prick. "It's wet," said she drowsily. Down went my hand, the hairs were wet and sticky. Mabel was too sleepy to notice what the wet was, yet I feared. "Turn on your back, dear," said I. She did. I got on her, and put my prick in though not stiff. "Don't, — I'm tired, — wait till morning, — get off, Laura will hear." "Here is a lark," thought I, and got off her, turning my bum towards Mabel's belly, as the best way to economize room, and I was soon asleep again. She snored off instantly.

Excitement wakened me early. The house was quiet, it was quite dark, we all three talked. Laura laid sulking, I reminded her of Fred's remark at Vauxhall about her pissing quickly; that only made her sulkier. At length upstairs I went with Mabel to our bedroom, to prevent the servants knowing anything. When we came down to breakfast, Laura and I looked at each other hard. When I got a chance of speaking to her privately, she would not hear the deed alluded to; reminded me that Fred was my cousin, and a good fellow. After that I never spoke to her on the subject for weeks, I felt ashamed of myself; but for all that my cock would often tingle, and raise its head when I looked at her. One day there, she being alone, we fell talking about that night. I had never known her so warm; we wondered Mabel had not heard. "And the hair of my prick was wet with our spending, Laura." "No, it was yours." "No, yours." "Let's try again." She rushed out of the room.

The night after poking Laura I took them to the play, at supper Mabel drinking rather freely, Laura said that she had better not take as much as she had the last night. Then I found she had lushed rather freely, which accounted for her sleeping so soundly. She had a strong liking for liquors of all sorts.

A day or two afterwards Fred arrived, looking as if his prick had never left a cunt for a month. I asked him how Mrs. Maria was, he laughed, and repeated that he should not mind having her; but said no more. Soon after we went back to the country, to spend Christmas at my aunt's. My mother, Tom, and one of my sisters also came. They were much in my way.

For brevity I compress the events of the next few months; it is a pity, but it would print to three the length otherwise. Briefly

I was obliged to get back once or twice to my aunt's to see Pender privately, though I did not want to have her. I was mostly in London. One or two funny whoring incidents I must leave out altogether, and for the same reason: brevity.

CHAPTER XIV

My cousin at home. — Pender's belly. — A lawyer's letter. — Action for crim con threatened. — Suspicions. — A compensation. — The Penders leave. — Wholesale whorings. — A frolic at Lord A°°°'s. — After dinner. — Newspaper readings. — A strange rape. — Bets on pricks. — Pricks felt. — Fred on his head. — Beds on the floor. — Free fucking. — End of the orgie.

My cousin came home from school, and when dancing or talking with her, I used to think of the look of her bum. One young lady from the school whose posteriors I also knew came to stay. Fred and I used to laugh about the adventure, and about his sister and cousin as much as about the others.

Mrs. Pender's belly was like a mountain, her husband I fancied scowled at me. Mrs. P. looked scared, and whisking past me in the farm-yard one day with a milk-pail, said in a low voice as she passed, "For God's sake keep away," — and I did, feeling uneasy. In cold weather my aunt ceased to go to the farm-yard, our own shooting was over, and I had no reason for crossing the farm-yard; but at the end of a week my cock was so much in want of amusement, that I made up my mind to have a poke up Pender if I could, and way-laid her in the shrubbery-walk. She told me that on a particular day her man would go some distance to buy cattle, and she would try to meet me in the barn. Chance favored us, we fucked, and talked at intervals for two or three hours, she having a poke, then going out for a time, coming back again, and so on.

I heard that her husband suspected her and me, he was sure it was not his child. Some one had seen me and her together in the lane, he would not say who. Said Mrs. P., "I don't know what, but I am sure he is up to something bad to you or me, and I live in

343

a fright; I can scarcely eat, drink, or sleep for thinking about what's to happen."

About a month after this, I received a letter from a lawyer in London saying he wished to see me. I went, and found that he was instructed to bring an action against me for seducing Mrs. Pender. I denied all, but it was of no use. I at once went to my solicitor, who after a time feared the case could be proved against me. The action would be brought for damages (there was no divorce possible then), and there would be the scandal, the annoyance to my aunt, and the horror of my mother. The only chance of getting a word with Mrs. P. was way-laying her in the laurel-walk. When I saw her she looked the picture of misery, her husband had refused to sleep in the same bed with her. At about five o'clock one evening, it being quite dark, she had given me a signal during the day, I went to the privy. There I fucked her, she said how utterly miserable she was, and asked me to take her away. Uprighters were never to my taste, and now her big belly made it far from pleasurable. I got worried, and at length after much legal annoyance, agreed to give five hundred pounds, on condition that I had a letter from Pender saying that he was very sorry for what he had done, that he was convinced he had made a mistake, and was then sure of his wife's fidelity, or something to that effect.

Before this was quite settled, Mr. Pender got leave of absence, and went away somewhere. My solicitor asked me whether I had any reason to suspect that Mrs. P. had told her husband. Immediately I became savagely suspicious, went to the cottage under pretence of asking for Pender himself, although I knew he was away, and insisted she should meet me at the town. I thought of nothing until we met, but how I should entrap her into a confession, and worked myself up into a belief that the couple were making a market of me.

She undressed, I caressed her, with hand on her cunt, looked at her and said, "Your husband means to make a fortune out of me." "What, he, — ho, ho, ho," she cried, "the wretch, — oh! I shall be exposed, — ho, ho," and was as white as a sheet. When she got better, I told her all, she knew nothing about what her husband had done, and begged I would pay nothing, — she would drown herself, — and I left, convinced that the poor woman was true to me.

Pender gave notice to leave, and forfeiting wages, left his place, and went to the North of England. Months afterwards I received a scrawl saying that the child was exactly like me, that P. was not unkind, but she was unhappy, would so like to see me; and if I wished it she would run away, and be as good as a wife to me. There was no name or address to it, and I never heard of her afterwards.

I thought all settled, and that no one would know about it; but for all that it leaked out. Months afterwards being at my aunt's, I got into one of her servants, and after giving her a good fucking one night, and telling her after a fuck not to wash, she said, "I don't want you to get me in the family way like Mrs. Pender." She had heard that. How the devil did it leak out?

After Christmas Fred and I went to see our women, he wanted more than I did. I had some harlotting; not being at all faithful to Mabel, I had fits of great incontinence, and as many as three different women on the same day, at times.

Exceedingly nice women were then to be met in the Quadrant from eleven to one in the morning, and three till five in the afternoon. I would have one before luncheon, get another after luncheon, dine, and have a third woman. I would at other times go under the Opera colonnade, where they used to assemble in the summer evenings with low dresses showing shoulders and breasts; to see them, even if I did not want a fuck. I had an insatiable desire to look at their nudity, would strip them, make them piss, feel them all over, leave, and in an hour perhaps have another. I had no letches for fancy postures. To see their thighs and cunts in free but graceful attitudes was sufficient pleasure. During this time the following occurred.

An intimate friend of Fred's was Lord A***, he lived with a lady who was called Lady A***. I don't think she had been gay, and in that respect resembled Laura and Mabel. The three women were much together. We often saw Lord A***, and all became friends. Lord A*** was not very true to his lady. He lived in B*t*n Street, where he had at that time the whole of a handsomely furnished house, but only could half occupy it. His in-door servants were a middle-aged woman who cooked, a maid who was her niece, and his valet, who waited at table as well. A woman who did not sleep in the house came daily. He had grooms and a coachman, but not in the house. Lord A°°° had quarrelled with his father. He had been in the Guards, and drank very freely.

He invited us one night to dinner, and gave a splendid one. By the time we had finished, we were all noisy. It was never our custom to use baudy language when in each other's company, Laura had a great aversion to it. Mabel liked me to talk baudy to her, but did not talk it herself. Fred always after dinner would let out a warm word or so, and was at once snubbed by Laura. For all that our conversation after dinner was generally warm with *double entente*.

On the night in question our conversation got to open voluptuousness. Fred and Lord A°°° went in for it, Mabel laughed, Laura hished and hished, said she would leave, but at last gave way, as did Lady A°°°; then we men got to lewedness. Whenever any sensuous allusion was made, my eyes sought Laura's, hers seeking mine; we were both thinking of the quiet and quick fuck we had, with Mabel snoring by our side. We compared our thoughts on that night, but at a future day.

Just at that time a case filled the public journals. It was a charge of rape on a married woman, against a man lodging in the same house. She was the wife of a printer on the staff of a daily paper, who came home extremely late; she always went to bed leaving her door unlocked, so that her husband might get in directly he came home. The lodger was a friend of her husband's, and knew the custom of leaving the door unlocked, — in fact he was a fellow-printer.

She awakened in the night with the man between her thighs, had opened them readily, thinking it was her husband. It appears to have been her habit, and such her husband's custom on returning home, or so she said. The lodger had actually all but finished his fuck, before she awakened sufficiently to find out that it was not the legitimate prick which was probing her. Then she alarmed the house, and gave the man in charge for committing a rape. The papers delicately hinted that the operation was complete before the woman discovered the mistake, — but of course it left much to the reader's imagination.

Fred read this aloud. I knew more, for the counsel of the prisoner was my intimate friend. He had told me that the prisoner had had her twice, that she had spent with him; that he had often said he meant to go in, and have her, that she had dared him to do it, and that she only made a row when she thought she heard her husband at the door on the landing, although it was two hours before his usual time of return. His prick was in her when she began her outcry.

With laughter and smutty allusions we discussed the case. "Absurd," said Laura, "she must have known it was not her husband." "Why?" "Why because —," and Laura stopped. "If you were asleep, and suddenly felt a man on you of about my size, and his prick up you, very likely you would not tell if it were mine or not," said Fred. Laura threw an apple at his head. Decency was banished from that moment, a spade was called a spade, and unveiled baudiness reigned.

"I should know if it were not you," said Lady A°°° looking at Lord A°°°. "How?" "Ah! I should, — should you not know another woman from Laura, if you got into bed with two women in the dark?" said she to Fred. "I am not sure for the moment if with a woman just for size, and as much hair on her cunt," said he. "I tell you what Fred, I won't have it," said Laura ill-tempered, "talk about someone else, I won't have beastly talk about me." "I'll bet," said I, "that if the ladies were to feel our pricks in the dark, they would not tell whose they each had hold of." Roars of laughter followed. "I should like to try," said Mabel. "So should I," said another. "Would you know, if you felt us?" said one woman. "If I felt all your cunts in the dark, I'll bet I should know Marie's," said Lord A°°°. "That is, if you felt all round and about," said Fred, "but not if she opened her legs, and you only felt the notch." "I think I should." "Why? — Is she different from others?" Lord A°°° was going to say something, when Marie told him to shut up.

So we went on, the men in lascivious language, the women in more disguised terms, discussing the probabilities of distinguishing cunts or pricks by a simple feel in the dark. Each remark caused roars of laughter, the women whispered to each other, and laughed at their own sayings. Lewedness had seized us all, the women's eyes were brilliant with voluptuous desire. More wine was drunk. "Call it by its proper name," said Lord A°°° when Marie remarked that a woman must know her own man's thing. "Prick then." "I will bet five pounds that Mabel would not guess my prick in the dark, if she felt all of us," said I. "And I'll bet," said another. "Shall we try?" said Fred. "Yes," said Mabel, more fuddled than the rest. Baudier and baudier, we talked, laughed, and drank, and at length set to work to make rules for trying, all talking at once.

One proposed one way, one another. "I can't tell unless I feel balls as well," said a woman. "Will they be stiff when we feel?" said another. "Mine will," said Fred, "it's stiff already." "So is mine," added I.

"How shall we know where to put our hands, if we are in the dark?" said Lady A°°°. "If a man is in front of you, you will find it fast enough," answered someone. Laura had now yielded to the baudy contagion, and made no objection, though Mabel and Lady A°°° were the most forward. Then Lord A°°° rang the bell, and told his valet he might go out for the night, and his house-keeper and maid they might go to bed, which they did at the top of the house, as we supposed. The sequel proved that to be doubtful, and that they must have had a most edifying night.

After lewed squabbles we arranged that each man was to give the woman if she guessed the prick right, ten pounds; the men were to be naked, the women to feel all the men's cocks, and give a card to him whose prick she thought she knew. The room was to be dark. No man was to speak, or give any indication by laughing, coughing, or any other way, under penalty of paying all the bets. The women were to lose if they spoke, or gave indications of who they were.

I took three cards, and wrote the name of a lady on each of them. Then each lady took her card, and they went upstairs to the bed-room pell-mell and laughing. The women were to stand of a row in a certain order against a side of the room, we to follow in an order they did not know. They were to feel all pricks twice, each giving her card to the man at the second feel, if she knew the prick. We undressed to our shirts, took off our rings, so as to leave no indications, and in that condition entered the room. The dining-room door we closed, there was no light on the first-floor lobby, nor in the bed-room, for we had put out the fire there. So holding each other by the shoulder, we entered, closed the door, and we were all in the room together in the dark.

We lifted our shirts, and closed on the women, each of whom in her turn felt our pricks. One felt mine as if she meant to pull it off. On the second feeling, we got somehow mixed, a slight tittering of women began, some one hished, and the tittering ceased. Two hands touched me at the same time, but one withdrew directly she touched the other's hand. A card was put into my hand, afterwards another card touched me, and was withdrawn. After waiting a minute I nudged the man next me. "Have you all given cards?" shouted out the man. "Yes," shouted the three women at once. Then we all burst out laughing, and the men went downstairs, leaving the women all talking at once like Bedlam broke loose.

Looking at our cards, we found that each woman had guessed rightly her man's prick; but we changed our cards, and called out to the women who came rushing down like mad. "Not one of you has guessed right," said I, "you have all lost your bets." "I'll swear I'm right," said Lady A°°°, "it's Adolphus that I gave my card to." This set us all questioning at once. "What makes you so sure?" "She says it's very long and thin," said Mabel, "and so it is." "Hold your tongue," said Marie. "I felt it," said Mabel. "They all seemed the same to me," said Laura, "and one of you pushed my hand away." "It was I," said Fred, "you wanted to feel too much, you nearly frigged me." "Oh! What a lie." Then we told the truth, and that each woman had won, which caused much noisy satisfaction, then we had more wine, we men still with naked legs.

I have told all I can recollect with exactitude, but there was lots more said and done. Fred pulled up Lord A°°°'s shirt, his cock was not stiff. "That's not as it was when I felt it," said Mabel. "You've guessed pricks, but for all that you would not know who fucked you in the dark." "We should," cried out all the women. "Let's try," said Lord A°°°. "All right," said Mabel. "We are not prostitutes," said Laura. "A little free fucking will be jolly, let's take turns about all round," said Fred. Then the room resounded with our laughter, all spoke baudily at once, every second, "prick," "cunt," "fuck," was heard from both men and women, — it was a perfect Babel of lasciviousness.

"I'll bet ten pounds a woman doesn't guess who fucks her," said Lord A°°°. We echoed him. The women laughed, but led by Laura, refused, and squabbled. All wanted the bet to come off, but did not like to admit it. We had more champagne, the men put on their trowsers, we kissed all round, and talked over the way of deciding such a bet, the women got randier, one showed her leg to another, and at length all the women agreed to take part in the orgie.

The rest I shall tell as truthfully as I can. The drink and excitement I was under makes it difficult; but I will tell nothing I am not quite sure of. We arranged a plan with such noise and talking, that God knows how it was arranged at all. Where were we to poke? — in the bed-room? Impossible, there was but one large bed in Lady A°°°'s room, and one in the back-room. How were we to fuck all together? We all rushed upstairs, took all the beds and pillows from both rooms, and from the upper rooms, and put them on the floor in the large room, making one long bed, after moving aside the furniture. The fire had been put out. All this was done with shouts and yells, a fearful lascivious riot.

The women were to lie down in an order known to us, Lady A°°° nearest to the door, and so on. There was to be absolute silence. Each man as he knelt between the woman's legs was to put a card with a number on it under her pillow. We men knew which number each had, the women were not to know which man was to have her, directly we had fucked we were to return, each woman was to produce her card, and guess who had been up her, they were to be in their chemises, we in our shirts. I never shall forget the looks of the women as they went upstairs to arrange themselves for the fucking, but think that they scarcely knew the rules of what they were to do.

The women undressed quickly enough, for we had scarcely had time to tie up our faces in napkins to prevent our whiskers being noticed (Lord A°°° had none), before a voice shouted out, "We are ready." Then with shirts on only, up we men went. I only recollect kneeling down between Lady A°°°'s legs (we had agreed among ourselves how to change our women), giving a card, feeling a cunt, and putting my prick into it, then hearing the rustling of limbs, hard breathing, sighing, and moans of pleasure of the couples fucking fast and furiously; of my brain whirling, of a maddening sensuality delighting me as I clasped the buttocks of Lady A°°°, and fucked her.

We must have spent nearly all together, none when we compared after recollected more than his own performance. All were quiet. I was feeling round my prick which was still in Lady A°°°'s cunt, when a light flashed powerfully through the room. That devil Fred had risen, and lighted several lucifers, which then was done by dipping them in a bottle, — they were expensive. What a sight was disclosed at a glance!

All three women lay with chemises up to their navels, Lady A°°° on her back, I on the top of her (rising rapidly at the light). Next to her Mabel seemingly asleep with thighs wide open. Fred kneeling between them, holding the lighted matches, Laura on her back with open thighs, eyes closed, Lord A°°° cuddling, but nearly off of her by her side, and his prick laying on her thigh. The women shrieked, and began pulling down their chemises. I swore at Fred, the women joined chorus. "Most ungentlemanly," said Laura, getting up. That got up Lord A°°°. Mabel lay still on her back as if ready to be stroked again. But all was said. In a minute the lucifers burnt out, and it was dark again. Scuffling up, we men went downstairs, leaving the women chattering. Soon after, down they came, looking screwed, lewed, and annoyed that the bets were off, and all chattering at once.

Mabel was quarrelsome. "You," said she, turning to Lady A°°°, "said that your husband's thing was long and thin, you tried to mislead me in the bet, you wanted to make me lose." They had evidently been discussing their men's pricks.

"So you have been telling how each of us fucks," said Fred. Laura denied it. "We did," said Mabel. "It's a lie, Mabel, if you say it again, I'll tell something more than you will like to hear about yourself." Mabel retorted, Lady A°°° chimed in. It was a Babel of quarrelsome lewed women, with their cunts full.

I feared a row, and that Mabel might after all know more about my having had Laura, the night we all three slept in the same bed, than I cared for; so I pacified them. Fred said we had better try again, Laura objected. "Oh! Yes, Mrs. Modest," said Mabel. "When you found it was not Fred, why didn't you cry out?" "I didn't know," said Laura. "Ah! Ah! the printer's wife," we shouted, then more baudy talk, recriminations, and squabbling. Laura said she should go home, Fred said she might go by herself. Lord A°°°, who had half fallen asleep, said it was too late, and we had better stop. Some one said we could soon again make the beds comfortable in the upper rooms. "That be damned," said Fred, "we will all sleep on the floor as they are now." "Free fucking forever," said I. Laura said I was a blackguard, Mabel said she should like it, Lady A°°°

said she didn't care, if Adolphus didn't, Adolphus said any cunt would suit him. He was reeling drunk as he spoke.

All this time we were in shirts and chemises. One woman had thrown a shawl over her, one a petticoat, but their breasts flashed out, their arms were naked, their legs showing to their knees, the men were naked to their knees in their shirts. The scene was exciting, the women hadn't washed their cunts, Fred said so. Mabel asked him if he was sure of it. No, he would feel. Laura told him he must be drunk, and was a beast. "Drunk?" said he, "look here." He turned a somersault, and stood on his hands and head, his heels against the wall, his back-side in the air, his prick and cods falling downwards over his belly, his shirt over his head. Lady A°°° took up a bunch of grapes, and dashed it on his ballocks. Then we chased the women round the room, tried to feel them, and they us. It was like hell broke loose, till we agreed to sleep on the floor together, anyhow.

No lights; lights and piss-pots were put in the back bed-room, — a woman suggested that. "You're frightened of farting," said someone. The women went up to make the beds more comfortable, took blankets, etc., from the upper rooms, whilst we men fetched candles from the kitchen, the others being well nigh burnt out. The women had washed their cunts, we had more wine, and then we all were pretty well screwed, and Lord A°°° pretty drunk when we went up to them.

Up to that time I was sufficiently sober to know all I have written, and plenty more. Surely I could tell a lot more of our conversation, but it would prolong the tale too much. After the last bottle of champagne I was groggy, recollect less clearly, was in a half-sleepy, feverish, excited, and bawdy state, my sleep was broken by others, but when awake my prick stood immediately, and I moved all night from one woman to another, fucking, and then dozing.

To satisfy Laura, and keep up a sort of appearance, we had said we would only have our own women, who were again to lay in a certain order. Directly they had left the room, we agreed to change. A°°° doggedly insisted on having Mabel, so I was to take Laura, and Fred Lady A°°°. It was such a lark. My prick was up Laura, when she cried, "It's not you, Fred." Then were simultaneous exclamations, "I'm not Mabel," — "What a lovely cunt!" — "Leave me alone," — "Feel my big prick," — "Damn, a cunt's a cunt," hiccupped Lord A***. "Oh! — ah!" — "Ha! My love fuck, — My darling, oh!" — kiss, kiss, — spending, — "aha!" — sighs of delight, — "cunt," — "fuck," — "Oh!" — "Ah! Ah!" And I fell asleep on Laura amidst this.

Awake again. By my side a wet cunt, a heavy sleeper. Turning round, my legs met naked legs. I stretched out my hand, and felt a prick, perhaps Fred's, I don't know. Getting up, I felt my way, stumbling over legs to the wall to the furthest woman, and laid myself on her. "Don't Adolphus, I'm so sleepy," said she. The next instant we were fucking. Others awakened. "Where are you?" said someone. Then all moved, one man swore, a hand felt my balls from behind. I was spending, and rolled off the lady, turning my bum to her. Then I touched Mabel, and put my hand to her cunt. A man dropped on her, and touched my hand with his prick. Ejaculations burst out on all sides, the couples were meeting again, then all was quiet, and the fucking done. Then all talked. All modesty was gone, both men and women told their sensations and wants. "You fuck me, — Feel me, — No, I want so and so," Laura as lewed as the rest.

Again awaking. A hand was feeling my prick. "Is it you, Laura?" "Yes." I felt her cunt. "Oh! Let me go and piddle." But I turned on to her, and we fucked. "How wet your cunt is." "No wonder."

Again I awakened, someone got up, and fell down. "Hulloa! Who is that?" "I want to piss, and can't get up," said Lord A*** in a drunken voice. Someone opened the door, a feeble light came across from the back-room, we helped him up and he stumbled along with us men to piss. Then he insisted on going downstairs. He could scarcely stand, so we helped him to the dining-room, we lighted more candles, he swilled more wine, tumbled on to the sofa, where we left him drunk and snoring, and found him snoring the next morning with the hearth-rug over him. We two went back to the women. "I've fucked all three," said Fred. "So have I." "Laura's a damned fine fuck, ain't she?" Someone shut the room-door opposite, as we reached the landing. We pushed it open. Two ladies were pissing; Marie and Laura. "Where is Mabel?" "Drunk," replied one. The two were past caring for anything, pissed and went back with us to the bed-room. I took a light there. Mabel was on her back nearly naked, we covered her up, for it was cold. Then I fucked Laura, and Fred, Lady A°°°. The light we left now on the wash hand-stand, so we looked at each other fucking and enjoyed it, and then we changed women. There was no cunt-washing, we fucked in each other's sperm, no one cared, all liked it, all were screwed, baudy, reckless, Mabel snoring.

I awakened after a heavy sleep, chilly, feverish, headaching, and thirsty. I drew aside the curtains; it was late, light, but foggy; a nasty winter's morning. Fred and the three ladies lay snoring, some covered, others partially so, the floor looking as if every article of bed-furniture had been thrown down with a pitch-fork. I drank water, and fucked out as I was, my lubricity was unsatiated. I could not resist gratifying it.

Moving stealthily, I uncovered the sleepers one by one. It was easy enough, as the clothes lay loose and in shapeless heaps. I saw Fred's prick touching Mabel's haunch, contemplated Laura's thick-haired quim, saw spunk on her chemise. She looked lovely. Lady A°°° on her back, her hand over her cunt, red stains about her, and on the sheet which I pulled off her, — her poorliness had come on. Mabel on her back looked ready for a man. My cock stiffened, I laid myself on Laura, and awakened her. That awakened Fred who mounted Mabel. Both couples took to the exercise in the foggy day-light, and a long time we were in consummating. "Oh! Do leave off," said Laura, "I'm so sore." My prick was excoriated, it had not been so for many a day.

Never have I been in such an orgie before, never since, and perhaps never shall be; but it was one of the most delicious nights I ever spent. So said Fred, so said Mabel; and Laura admitted to me at a future day that she thought the same, and that since, when she frigged herself, she always thought of it, and nothing else.

I thought of nothing else for a long time. Nothing has ever yet fixed itself in my mind so vividly, so enduringly, except my doings with my first woman, Charlotte. At the beginning of my writing these memoirs, this was among the first described. The narrative as then written was double its present length, and I am sorry that I have abbreviated it, for the occurrences as I correct this proof seem to come on too quickly. Whereas we dined at seven o'clock, and it was one o'clock I guess before we all went to bed together, and the stages from simple voluptuousness to riotous baudiness and free-fucking were gradual. At eight o'clock not one of us would have dared to think of, still less to suggest, what we all did freely at midnight.

CHAPTER XV

Morning headaches. — An indignant housekeeper. — A saucy valet. — Consequences. — Fred leaves England. — Lady A***'s invitation. — Laura a widow. — Farewell Laura. — Adieu Mabel. — My guardian's remonstrances. — Parental advice. — Ruined. — Reflexions. — My relations.

With headaches, heated, irritable, thirsty, worn out, we arose; the men quiet, the women quarrelsome. The women began to dress, some where they had slept, some in the other room. We went down to Lord A***, and awakened him. He went upstairs, and bawled out to the housekeeper (he had rung the bell violently several times without her appearing). "Make us some tea directly," said he. She answered, "I shan't, — make it yourself." "I'll dismiss you if you don't." "I ain't going to make tea for prostitutes," said she, "and we are not going to keep in such a house." Fred said the wine was bad, or his head would not ache so. A*** said Fred knew nothing about wine. Mabel who had heard what the housekeeper said, bawled out that she would go up, and tear her eyes out. The free-fucking tone was gone, each man seemed jealous, and spoke harshly to his woman. At a remark of Marie's, Lord A*** told her to go to another room. No, she should not till Mabel was out of the house. Mabel, not quite sober, told me I had better go home with Laura. Fred said Laura would go home with him. Laura was quiet, and tried to get Fred to leave with her, and told Mabel she would be better if she took less liquor. At length we separated. We four were going to the same house, but went in separate cabs, then to our own rooms, and had breakfast separately there, — a thing we never had done before. We always lived in Laura's apartments, and shared the expenses.

After breakfast Mabel and I went to bed, late in the day we awakened. I was refreshed, for then a long sleep restored me from any excess. Although I did not like Mabel's behaviour, and did not care about her having had the other men as I thought, yet it annoyed me; but it had the effect of giving me a strong letch for her for some time. I used to think as I fucked her, of my prick rubbing where Fred's and Lord A°°°'s had rubbed, it delighted me to say, "Should you know it was my prick if you had just awakened?" — "Did his hurt you, when he pushed like this?" — shove, shove, — "Tell me how Fred goes just before he spends." We used to fetch each other by talking over that night; but she did not recollect very clearly, and declared she was sure I had not had her, although I certainly had her once that night, and when the spunk of Lord A°°° and Fred's was in her. It used to horrify me when I thought of that, such was my masculine inconsistency then.

We all four dined together, but were a little reserved until wine was in us, then we laughed about the night; but Laura, saying we had better forget it, we agreed not to talk about it again, nor did we with the women. Fred and I used often to do so, he never seemed so happy as when he was asking me if Laura was not a damned fine fuck, but directly I said yes, he was silent.

The frolic brought about a great deal of mischief. Lord A°°°'s housekeeper and maid left that day, they would not stop. I dare say they had seen and heard enough to tell them the games we were up to, for we were not particular about shutting doors. Lord A°°° regretted the cook, because she was such a good one. She told the valet, and soon after he was insolent to Lady A°°°, so Lord A°°° kicked him out. He summoned A°°° before a magistrate for an assault, and A°°° was fool enough to compromise it. The man told a lot. The owner of the house gave Lord A°°° notice to quit, and he and Lady A°°° went to lodgings, and the publicity embroiled Lord A°°° still more with his family.

Neither was the friendship between us all quite the same. Laura and Mabel quarrelled. Lord A°°° would not let his mistress visit them unless he was with her, Laura would never leave Mabel in the room alone with Fred. Occasionally we still dined together, and went to the theatre. One night when we had had much wine, we joked about the night, and the women got quarrelling. Laura said the affair was disgraceful, and had it not been for Mabel, it never would have happened. Mabel bounced off to her own rooms. Soon after, I took separate lodgings for Mabel. There she was always in tears, if I left her long, and if away a day or two, she wanted to know if I had been with Laura. Lady A°°° visited Mabel, and was frightened to let her Lord know it. Then Lord and Lady A°°° quarrelled, he had the clap, and gave it to his mistress. Fred and I were always excellent friends, and at some annoyance through the women, suggested we should go to Paris, and leave them alone in London.

Before going, I met Lady A°°° walking out, who asked me in, saying Lord A°°° would be glad to see me. As I had not quarrelled with him, I thought a chat might heal our coolness. When in-doors, she called out to him, and professed to be surprized at his not being there. If I would wait, he would be in soon. We got nearer and nearer to each other on the sofa, began talking about the free-fucking night, of the good aim she had made with the bunch of grapes on Fred's balls as he stood on his head. We got very lewed, I kissed her, she me. Would she know it was I who was up her, if I came in in the dark to her? She could not say, but should know it was not A°°°, — a beast. "Beast, why? — have you quarrelled?" Then she told me that A°°° was often drunk, and stayed away from her for days. "He has got a disease from a beastly gay woman, and hasn't slept with me for weeks." "And not had you?" "Of course not." "Oh! don't you want it?" "No wonder if I do." At once I put my hands up her petticoats, felt her nice plump thighs, my fingers rubbed on the smooth quim. "Oh! Don't, — I can't bear it." I pulled out a stiff prick, and put it into her hand, we toyed with each other's genitals for a minute, then she sunk back on the sofa, I on her, and we copulated.

I stayed the whole evening with her, fucking at intervals. A°°° did not come back. I am sure she knew he would not, and had asked me in because she wanted me to have her. She did not tell me she had had the clap, nor I her, — it was Mabel who had told me.

She hinted she should like to meet me again, and I made some half-sort of promise, but never did. Mabel became more and more expensive, discontented, lushy, and quarrelsome, and she was not clean. She would feel my wet prick after it had left her cunt, and then cut bread and butter without washing her hands. We had rows, and I left her, giving her a handsome sum of money. Laura said she had gone back to Plymouth with Lord A°°°, who had left Lady A°°°. Then Fred, I, and Laura were just as we used to be. He seemed to have forgotten everything, and I never presumed on having poked Laura. We went to Paris, leaving Laura in London with her sister, who came up to stay with her, — a nice girl.

Though short of money now, Fred and I at Paris took no heed, but rattled away as if our purses were inexhaustible. His furlough was nearly up. We had no end of women. "Old °°° (naming a relative) will leave you all his money," said he, "he's fond of you, and has no one else to leave it to." I and all my family thought that; my mother had repeatedly warned me that he was discontented with my goings on; but I counted on his love for me, love since I was a baby; so I played at Paris a jolly game, regardless of money.

When I came back from Paris, I tried to retrench, but found it all but impossible. I got rid of Mabel, spent five shillings for my dinner, where I used to spend twenty, went to live with my mother, put down my horses and carriage, and discharged my man and grooms. But as I diminished my amusements and extravagances generally, so I seemed more and more to need women. My cock stood all day, and half the night. Women I had by dozens. I tried to reduce their fees, and did to a little extent, but for some years I had been accustomed to a liberal expenditure in that article, and though to a country girl I could give five shillings, to a Londoner I could only give gold, and never refused more if they pleased me, and were not satisfied.

Fred then went abroad to his regiment. He made arrangements for Laura to have a small income, not a tenth of what she had had, but enough to keep her in a quiet way. I at first was to pay it to her. She was to have it as long as she remained steady, and he hoped she would go home, hoped she would keep steady till his return, — his return which was not probable in less than seven years at the least.

One night when together, we laughed at the absurdity of expecting it. "Walter, is it probable that a fine woman like that will be content with frigging herself?" "No." "She will be fucked, — I would if I were she, — it's a shame to wish her to go without fucking. If I were married to her, she would go with me, but a man can't take a mistress to India, he could not live with her, and all the regiment would be smelling at her tail, — she will be fucked, and I can't help it." Tears stood in his eyes. "You give her a grind, old boy, if she must have it, I'd rather you did it than anyone, and it will keep her quiet. You have had her, — do you recollect that night? — Oh! God, what a spree! I never had such a spree before in my life, and never shall again." I said I would take care of her as if a sister, as to having her, he might dismiss such an idea from his head, and I meant what I said. He went abroad, and was killed in battle. I loved him.

Laura went into humbler lodgings, I saw her often, but never made the slightest advances. Soon she could not make her money do. Her mother came up to stay with her, and she had then partly two to keep. She dressed plainer, sold or pawned her best things, told me all, and how it was impossible to make the money do. Then I made her a present, she kissed me, and that set my blood boiling. Her mother wanted her to go back to the country, I advised it also; it was agreed she should, and her mother went back. A day or two afterwards I called on her, she got me a chop for dinner, and sent for wine. We talked about Fred, she cried about him, I kissed her to comfort her, she kissed me again as we sat on the sofa, my arm went round her, I pulled her hand on to my shoulder; and that spree at Lord A°°°'s came into my head.

"You miss a bed-fellow Laura, don't you?" "Oh! No, but I miss poor Fred, he was so kind." "Do you recollect that night?" "Don't mention it, I am ashamed of it, — oh! don't look at my boots, they are so shabby now." I had begun at the ankles, as I always did, it was on the road. "You are not so stout as you were, my dear." "There is not any difference in me." I pinched her thighs outside her clothes. "Ah! I'm no thinner there, I'm sure." "Let me feel." "Oh! Now don't, — it's a shame." "My darling, you are as smooth and plump as ever, — I know the feel of those beautiful thighs, I've laid on them." Soon my hand was between them, my finger on the clitoris. "Poor Fred," said she, still crying, her head on my shoulder. In another instant her hand was round my prick, her thighs open, my hand restless, and roving all about her cunt. "Lay down." "I won't." "It won't hurt him poor fellow, he is far away." For a few minutes we coaxed and fondled, kissed and cried, saying it was not fair, and we never would. Then cock and cunt getting hotter and more sensitive, I pushed her flat on the sofa, and we fucked ecstatically. Rising, she sat looking at me, her clothes half-way up her thighs, I looking at her with my wet prick hanging its head. Then we hugged, kissed, and did it again.

"It was to be," said she (as if poking her was fate). "Quite true dear, but let's go to the bed, the sin is no greater if we do it ever so many times." Into bed we got, and there I think we laid for six-teen hours. Laura was a lovely bed-fellow. I had a good look at the hair on her cunt, it was very long, curled round, and completely hid her cunt, even when standing with her legs slightly open; and when she pissed, she left drops of piddle on the hair. On her that bush was handsome, but very long hair is not generally handsome on a cunt, and I have disliked it on others; but it is not often found. I am describing here what I saw more coolly, and often on future occasions, rather than what I saw and recollect of her cunt, on that night of exhausting pleasure.

I had now but little money to spare, but gave her a little from time to time, and a great deal of bumbasting. One day she said, "I'm in misfortune again." She was in the family way, had been so before by Fred, but had managed a miscarriage. She now got one, but was seriously ill, and sent for her mother, and when she got better she went home. I sent Fred's money to her there for some time, then she wrote me to send it to a post-office, and afterwards to send no more, as she was going to be married. She hoped I would never tell Fred, that I would burn her letters, and if I ever saw her, would not notice her. I never saw her again. She wrote to Fred about her marriage, and he was delighted at it, as well as at saving his money. I have finished her history, so far as it was connected with me; and must now take up my narrative at a time before this.

Friends were going to Paris, I went with them, and a jolly loose time we had for a few weeks. I made acquaintance with six or eight of the best baudy houses, and had women galore. Theatres, excursions, high feasting, unlimited whoring were the characteristics of my trip. I returned empty in pocket, and knocked up with copulating, yet had had none of the excitants with women that I have had there since. I rushed at cunt directly I saw it; my physical enjoyment was so intense, that I could not dally with my prick, but let it satisfy itself as soon as it liked. The varieties that Camille had given me left no taste for them. Cunt, belly, and thighs, seen, felt, and fucked in regular fashion, was my delight. Heaps of bills met me on my return. The thought of becoming bankrupt horrified me. I disposed of my remaining property, paid all, and was left with a few hundred pounds. I pass now over a short time of which there is nothing to be said, but that I was economical in all but women.

My remaining guardian and my mother had been always at me with advice, which I entirely disregarded, and flung away money in all directions. Had I only spent it on women it would have lasted years longer. That which women had I do not regret, they have been the greatest joy of my life, and are so to every true man, from infancy to old age. Copulation is the highest pleasure, both to the body and mind, and is worth all other human pleasures put together. A woman sleeping or waking is a paradise to a man, if he be happy with her, and he cannot spend his money on anything better, or so good.

Soon after, almost dependent again on my mother, who did nothing but upbraid me, my hopes centred in my old relative, who had promised to make me his heir. He was not so gracious to me as he used to be; he murmured at my extravagance, and supposed that any money I had would go down the same sink, by which he meant women. He died suddenly, just as he was in greatest wrath with me, and left me nothing.

All hopes were dashed to the ground. Laura was my consolation till she left. For a year of my life I was needy and discontented, but not so miserable as I was fated to be. I pass over that period, there was not much in the amatory line to tell of. Fucking is a common-place thing, the prince and the beggar do it the same way, it is only the incidents connected with it that are exciting. Voluptuous, reckless, youth and beauty together, make the vulgar, shoving, arse-wagging business poetical for the time, but it is animalism.

Then I committed a more fatal error than spending a fortune in jollity; what it was will be guessed, it is only referred to here to connect my history. I was then in my twenty-sixth year.

I add a few observations which on reading this written many years ago, seems now needful to explain even to myself.

Most of my relatives lived in the provinces, and were wealthy. We visited each other periodically, but distance (there were few railways then) prevented them from entering into my daily life, still less my secret life. Fred's mother was nearest to us, and as the episodes show, she and her family were most mixed up with my affairs. An aunt in London, childless and rich, gave me the most money, and afterwards left me a good sum. I cared but little about those living at a distance. With a cousin from the North I had some rousing debauches, which were at the time known to many of my family. He is still alive, but pious, and with a large family, and would not like to know I am writing this. Jolly old Ben, I won't narrate our sprees, for you may live to read this, — who knows?

CHAPTER XVI

Married, and miserable. — Virtuous intentions. — Consequences. — Mary Davis. — A virtuous child. — Low-class fucksters. — A concupiscent landlady. — Reflexions on my career. — On the sizes of pricks. — My misconception.

My life was now utterly changed; I was quite needy, with a yearly income (and that not my own) not more than I used to spend in a month, sometimes in a fortnight. Every shilling I had to look at, walked miles where I used to ride, and to save sixpence, amusements were beyond me, my food was the simplest, wine I scarcely tasted, all habits of luxury were gone, but worse than all I was utterly wretched. I tried to make the best of my life and could when by myself be cheerful, even in the recollection of the past fun; but there was that about me now which brought sorrow over to me. The instant I saw her, she checked my smile, sneered at my past, moaned over my future, was a nightmare to me, a very spectre.

I tried to like, to love her. It was impossible. Hateful in day, she was loathsome to me in bed. Long I strove to do my duty, and be faithful, yet to such a pitch did my disgust at length go, that laying by her side, I had wet dreams nightly, sooner than relieve myself in her. I have frigged myself in the streets before entering my house, sooner than fuck her. I, loving women, and naturally kind and affectionate to them, ready to be kind and loving to her, was driven to avoid her as I would a corpse. I have followed a woman for miles with my prick stiff, yet went to my wretched home pure, because I had vowed to be chaste. My heart was burning to have an affectionate kiss, a voluptuous sigh from some woman, yet I avoided obtaining it. My health began to give way, sleepless

364

nights, weary days, made me contemplate suicide. It seemed as if I never could have happiness again, yet my physical forces, or so much of them as lay in my generative organs, seemed unimpaired. I neither drank nor debauched, and my prick stood incessantly; neither random frigs nor night-dreams stopped it.

My only relief from misery was in thinking over the pleasures I had had, yet all seemed such a long time past, that it was like a dream. Then a desire to have other women became invincible. I had no means to get those I had been accustomed to, and seemed to have no idea of going economically to work for my pleasures, but at length began to walk through streets inhabited by very poor gay women, in a neighbourhood I had known in my early youth. Then I found out other poor quarters, and one night with but a few shillings in my pocket, after thinking of throwing myself into a canal, I found myself at a spot where women of a somewhat better class lived in its centre, and on its outskirts very poor harlots.

"I will, — have I the money? — can't help it, — if one won't another will," and I slunk into a street, half ashamed of entering it. Saw girls standing at doors, never paused for selection, nor to see if one looked nicer than another, it was cunt I wanted. The moment I turned the corner of the street, I cared not who or what, as long as she had a petticoat, and what it hid from sight. I took the nearest.

"Will you let me have you for five shillings?" was all I uttered. I recollect it as well as possible, hanging my head, ashamed of my offer, and not looking at the girl, ashamed of being seen in the neighbourhood.

"All right," said she, turning round. I followed her through the little narrow passage of a four-roomed house into a little room with a bed on one side of it. I looked at her, and she at me for an instant only. "Here are the five shillings," said I. "Shall I undress?" "No." "Shall we get on the bed?" "No, at the side," — and whilst speaking I had half lifted her on to it. Laughing with a peculiar chuckle she fell back, pulling up her clothes. I saw plump thighs, dark hair, felt giddy, could not see, recollect opening the lips, and began to spend as the tip of my prick touched her cunt. Following the spunk as it shot up the passage as it opened its way with one thrust I was up her, and had finished. Fifty times in my life up to the time I pen this, has a similar rapid ejaculation occurred to me when randy.

"Didn't you want it!" said she. They were the first words I recollect being uttered as I bent over her. How divine she seemed. "Let me do it again." "Oh! You ought to give me a little more." "I'll give you a shilling, it's all I have, I fear; but more if I have it." "Very well then," said a soft voice. Oh! What a heavenly few minutes they seemed to me, — they still seem to me, — as I fucked her again. First and second fuck must have been all over in five minutes. I had not uncunted.

"Pull it out," said she, after an interval, my cock still keeping in her; but I kept close to her, and up her. "Be still dear, do, pray, — I'll see what money I have." My hat and my great-coat were on, it was cold, I had only unbuttoned my trowsers enough get out my prick. Keeping still up her, I thrust my hand into my trowsers pocket, pulled out all the money I had, and put it on the bed beside her. "See, it is all I have, every farthing, a little more than I said, — let me do it again, — there is more than seven shillings," — and pressing well on to her haunches, I began wriggling my prick.

She turned her head, looked at the money, but did not touch it. "Very well," said she, in a low voice, "but take it out, — don't make my chemise in a mess, I have not another clean, — don't make a mess on the bed if you can help it." "I shan't." "Yes you will, you have spent such a lot, it's running out now."

I withdrew. She took a towel which was close at hand, wiped her cunt, and spread another for her bum. I threw off hat and coat. Soon now we were both on the bed, I up her, and leaning on my elbow, for the first time really looked at her. Up to that moment cunt, cunt, nothing but cunt was in my mind. Now I saw that her eyes were blueish, her hair dark and wavy, I recollect our staring in each other's faces for a minute or two without speaking. A candle on a little table close to the bed showed a strong light on us sideways; then we both fucked with vigor, and Mary Davis spent with me, — she spent with me, that poor little gay woman.

"You are a nice poke," said the girl. I got off the bed, sat on a chair by the fire, and looked at the merry face of the little gay woman as she smiled at me whilst washing her quim. The pleasure I had just had, the entrancement of the carnal pleasure contrasted so strongly with my misery at home, that I burst into tears, and sobbed like a child. She rubbed her quim dry, then silently came up to me, put her hand on my shoulder, and stood without uttering a word till my passion was over. "Are you unhappy?" said she in a gentle tone. Yes I was. "Never mind, I dare say it will be over some day, — we have all got unhappinesses."

Her kind voice and manner — she a gay woman who owed me no kindness — so contrasted with the coldness elsewhere, that it made me worse, and again I sat sobbing, and taking no notice of her; she still standing with her hand on my shoulder.

"Have something to drink," said she. "Yes," — but recollecting myself, "No, I have no money, I have given you every farthing I have." "Never mind, — do you like gin? — I do." "Yes." She called out to the landlady, "Fetch me a shilling's worth of gin, and mind you don't take any, — mind a shilling's worth fills this bottle to here (giving the landlady a large medicine bottle), don't take any, and I will give you a little. I'll pay for the gin," said she, turning to me.

I sat looking at the fire. "You have not washed yourself," said she. "No, are you unwell?" "No, I think I am all right, but we can't always say you know, and it's best to wash after us," — and I washed.

I took hot gin and water, and got cheered, even began to smile when she said, "You are a gentleman, ain't you?" "Yes, I think so." "I am sure you are by your manner, but you are poor I suppose." I told her the entire truth, my heart was so full, I told this strange gay woman all my trouble, all my misery, wanted more gin and water, and having in my pocket a gold pencil-case, a gift of an aunt's. "Get some more gin," said I, "take this and pawn it, for I have no money." She would not. "I am sure, if you say you will bring me the money, that you will. I will pay for more gin."

So sitting, talking, and drinking gin and water, she sitting opposite to me listening, whilst I told my troubles, and my burst of troubles over, relieved by my confidences, I became aware that she was plump, fleshy, good-looking, and had a mild sympathetic eye. Up to that time cunt alone had fascinated me, now I thought of the woman, and a liking for her because she seemed kind stole over me; desire to have her, caress her, spend in her on that account, rather than a desire for her cunt alone, thrilled through me as I looked at her sitting half facing me by the fire; her clothes slightly raised, that the warmth might reach her limbs, one elbow on her knee, the hand supporting her face turned towards me full of interest. And so an hour or more ran away.

"I want you again so, but I have no more money." "Never mind, you may have me, — shall I undress?" "Oh! Do, — do, — how round and plump you are, — but I have no more money." "Never mind, — give me more when you see me again. Come into the bed, — see, the sheets are quite clean, — no one has slept in them, I take the clean ones off every night, and put on others before I go to bed, — stop with me all night." We both undressed, and jumped into bed together. I was frantic with pleasure as I cuddled up to her plump warm body, and felt her from her neck to her knees; rolled over her, and kissed her, till I settled down between her thighs; and then Mary Davis and I fucked, and laid still, and then fucked again, and so on, till I could do it no longer.

It was three in the morning. "Stop all night," said she, "I will give you a nice breakfast in the morning." I would not, had a strong desire to keep up appearances of propriety and happiness at home, if I had not the reality; so with a sigh rose, and dressed, borrowed a shilling of her, and went out into the street. Silent and dirty it was, and raining hard as I walked home to my miserable bed.

At dusk next day with impatience I went off to Mary Davis', gave her what I had promised, and money for that evening besides, and when I had had her, we sat down and talked again.

She was a short woman about nineteen years old, plump without fat, but as nicely covered as any woman I ever saw; had a big bum, large thighs, plenty of room between them, and dark hair on her cunt which had strongly developed lips, it was large outside in proportion to her size. She had a soft, kind face, beautiful grey eyes, nearly black hair which craped naturally, and was altogether as nice a little woman as one could have wanted. I have wondered often how she could have settled down in a neighbourhood of coster-mongers, and taken five shillings for her person, when she might as well have been a two-sovereign woman, had she tried elsewhere. I put her up to trying at a future day, but she never would.

Her room was about twelve feet square. A large bed took up one third of it, a table next the only window, two chairs (one easy), little cupboards in the recesses by the fireplace, on which stood china and glasses, a small wash-hand stand, a chest of drawers, with slop-pail, coal-scuttle, and looking-glass completed the furniture. All was scrupulously clean, the bed-linen white.

Having broken my virtuous resolution, I never regained it, and for a week fucked Mary from six in the evening till two the next morning. My week's amusement cost me about two pounds, but then that modest sum was too much for my pocket, so I left off for a while, and gave Mary a chance of keeping her other friends. They were mostly poor clerks, she told me, and married men better off, who gave her a pound, or at times paid her rent if in arrear. She paid I think but twenty-five shillings a week for her board and lodging together. My too exclusive attentions for a week had prevented her regulars from coming. There was lots of cheaper cunt in the neighbourhood so to send them away with full balls was dangerous.

The house was kept by an old man and woman, he a carpenter almost too old, yet who went to daily work. He used to fetch gin and beer for us. There was no other lodger in the house. They were a decent couple, and after a time I used to talk to the old woman, and when Mary once went away ill, she got me a beautifully shaped girl. I had offered her money to get me a girl of about fourteen years of age, a virgin. The streets about there swarmed with girls and boys who played about at night, I could hear their smutty language as they ran after each other yelling, laughing and quarrelling. She tried, but never could; she was not a woman who undertook that sort of thing, but the money tempted her. "There are lots of girls about," said she, "their mothers don't care what they do, but you want a virgin, — Lor! Where's she to be found? — when they's about thirteen or fourteen years old they won't be kept in, they is about the dark streets at night, and Lor! If you heard what I have in the streets where the costers' barrows is, of a night!" And so the old woman intimated that all the young girls of that select neighbourhood, were got into by the coster boys, and that a virginity was a rarity at fourteen years old. I afterwards groped several young girls in those dark streets, and there was certainly no obstacle to my fingers searching their cunts.

"I thinks I knows a steady little gal, whose mother's just died, her father ain't no good, and you and Mary must ask her in; I can't have nothin to do with it except gettin her here." One day afterwards she told me she had asked the girl to tea, and that she was as curious as could be to know all about it (meaning fucking). "She knows as much as we do," said the old woman with a chuckle, "as far as talking goes, and she would like to know as much as them as does it as well, but she is timid; there is three on them, she is the eldest, the father leaves her in charge, you shall see her." Mary Davis had then gone home ill. The girl was brought in, I sent out for gin, a nice little girl she was, and she drank some of it. The old woman then left with a wink. The girl took my kisses very well, never said a word, so getting on by degrees I talked to her about naked people, and getting children, felt her ankles and legs, then told her I would give her a shilling if she would feel my cock. She did not say a word, but stood still, my arm round her waist, whilst I pulled out my stiff prick. Then she bent forward curiously, whilst I put her little hand round it, and guiding it, pulled the foreskin down from the tip. Then I put my hand up her clothes, and felt her thighs and bum; but on bringing my hand to the cunt, she broke away in tears saying, "Oh! No sir, — I would rather not sir, — I'm much obliged to you sir for showing it me, and the shilling; but I would rather not sir, — oh! Let me go, let me go, — Mrs. Smith, — Mrs. Smith." The old woman was listening, and came in instantly. "Oh! What are you doing to her?" said she in a whining tone." What is the matter my dear? — don't cry, — oh! you should not sir," — and winking at me, away she went with the girl; then came back, said the girl was scared, and she feared it was no go. "But if you heared her talk, you would think she would let any man do anything with her."

Half-an-hour afterwards the girl had composed herself, and came back. I had more gin, the old woman again left us, the girl had another shilling, and again she felt me. I began talking to her about the parsley-bed out of which children come, and generally on the subject of generation and its working tools. "Now dear, don't be alarmed (she seemed as timid as a hare), you know what a cunt is?" "Yes," said she, "it's a nasty word, — poor mother told father he was a beast cause he said it when drunk." "Well, my dear, something comes out of a man if he puts this up a cunt, and that gets children, — lay hold of my prick, and you will see," — and guiding her little hand I frigged myself with it. But she cried out when I attempted to feel her cunt, and I never had her. The old woman said she was frightened to bring her again, that she and Mary Davis might manage it together, and when Davis came back I wished her to try, but she refused to have anything to do with it. The letch passed away, for it was but a whim. At that time I liked large well-haired cunts.

I am anticipating, for this took place nearly two years after I first had Mary Davis. That girl got fond of me, and I liked her. I got a little better off, and used to give her more money; but she always took what I gave her contentedly. The only thing I can remember out of the common course of lecherous events in such acquaintances, is that I took one for spending over her, used to fuck up to spending-point, then pull out my prick, and frigging it, emit my semen on to her belly, breasts, or thighs; then I began fucking again, almost directly I had discharged, and looking at my spunk lying on her flesh. When my pleasure came on again, I would put her hand on to my spunk; and directly her fingers touched it, it fetched me, and she as well, although she always said it was a dirty trick. But I only did this a few times. I began also to use French letters, for reasons she advised me to do so.

The neighbouring streets were full of poor gay women. She heard that I had been seen going into a house in the neighbourhood, and cried about it. Her health got bad, her womb began to fall, and the doctor said she was not strong enough for a gay life. She told me she was the daughter of an under game-keeper, that a young tradesman kept company with her, she liked him, and he said he meant to marry her. Bringing her home one evening when she had got out on the sly, they felt each other's privates on the road. Very soon after she and one of her sisters were allowed to go to some village dance. Her sister walked off with her sweetheart; Mary's young man took her to some cottage, did it to her twice, and then walked home with her. She did not know whose fault it was; his or hers, for from the night they had felt each other, she thought of nothing else till she had his prick up her. Her father found it out, she ran away to London, became gay, and had never lived in any other house but the one I visited her in. "Whenever I saw him after he had felt me" (her lover) she would say, "I felt in a flurry all over, and could think of nothing else, I longed to feel his hand on my thing again," — she soon did.

She went home ill, came back, her womb got worse, she went to a hospital, got thin and fretted, again went home, and I never heard more of her. I had great pleasure in her society, it was my greatest solace to tell her all my misery, for she was a complacent, kind creature. It was wonderful to see how clean everything was in that little square room, yet with the exception of the fire-place, she cleaned everything herself. At about two o'clock in the day she was dressed, and standing at the door, to catch passers by. She never spoke to them unless they spoke to her. She was to me at first a novel experience but I soon had plenty of experience of the poor class of women in adjacent streets.

I found it not wise to go into the streets well dressed, so put on old things, drew my hat over my eyes, assumed a slouching gait, and walked along slowly, talking to the women till I found one I liked. Their salutation usually was, "Come here dear — come and see what I have got to show you." "What?" "Such a nice cunt, — such a lot of hair." "Such a fat arse," would say another. "How much will you let me for?" "What you like, — come in." "I have not much money, — let me look at your cunt for a shilling." "Come in then." Another would say, "Make it two, and I'll strip." Many a cunt I have seen for a shilling. If I did not like it, I went further on, or into the next street.

The street-doors were usually open, the women when dressed lolling just inside them, with head out, but dropping back if they saw a likely man, and addressing him as he passed in loud or low tones, according to their cheek. If a woman I had had and expected to see was not visible, my way was to step inside the passage, and listen at the door; if through the keyhole I saw a light, or heard voices, there was business on. If in the evening the outside shutters of the room were closed, I knew the woman was engaged for a long time, perhaps her own man, a cab-man, a costermonger, or some man of similar class was with her, if late. The women there, though about same price, or cheaper, had quite different manners from the Waterloo Road ones. There was rarely more than one woman in a house, and always on the ground floor, the landlord or lady living in the back room, or upstairs. The rooms were mostly let to working people, who seemed quiet enough.

Lots of children were about, who played in the streets at day, but disappeared if quite young towards dusk. If a man stopped and talked to a gay woman at the door, the children of the house usually went in, always did if more than about ten years old. They drew back as if they knew that a bargain for fucking was to be struck, and I believe knew all about it. They were mostly girls who sleeping in the same room with their parents, I dare say had seen the game of mother and father played often enough. The bigger girls frisked about the streets of an evening with boys of the same age, or not much older.

If a woman could get you to enter the passage, she almost pulled you into her room. "Come in, — don't stand there, — come out of the way of the lodgers, — I'll tell you if you come in, — well, make it half-a-crown, — I've got such a nice cunt, — such a fat arse, — feel my bubbies, — look here, — come in, and let me feel your prick."

This was all said rapidly, and according to the inducements the woman had to offer. It generally ended in my going in, and the bargain was completed inside. "I'll frig you, — do anything you like, — look here (showing rapidly her breasts, and covering them up again), — here is a big pair of legs (pulling her clothes up), — yes you may fuck me how you like, — oh! Yes I want to piss bad." I have heard this hundreds of times. Once inside I never came out without paying something. The women always said or did just enough to whet my appetite for knowing or seeing a little more, so I paid, and often enough was disappointed, and left; but saw a lot.

In these streets about seven in number, during a period of two or three years, I had many women, even whilst I visited Mary Davis. I dare say fifty women I fucked, and felt as many more before I ceased going to the neighbourhood. Two or three of the adventures there are alone worth writing. At one house I was robbed of a pin whilst actually fucking the woman.

A tall broad-built woman of about thirty, was lolling at a door one night. I do not recollect having seen her before, for I knew many women by sight, even though I had not had them. She looked like a coster's wife. I should have passed on, but for the lewed way in which her eyes met mine. I stopped, she instantly looked rapidly up and down the street, went back inside the door-way saying very loudly, "You want my lodger, but she has left here," but as she said this, she stepped inside the front room, and beckoned me in both with hand and head, her eyes wide open, and looking anxious. Slowly I followed in. She was so big that I thought I should like a feel, and if I liked that, would pay more, and have more. "I'll give you a shilling to feel your cunt." "Very well," said she, standing still, and not attempting to lift her clothes slightly as most of the women used to do. I got my hand on her thighs, she pushed it away, retreated towards the bed and sat on it. I took out a shilling, and as usual put it on the mantel-piece. "There is the money, — let me now." She no longer resisted, I felt her, and she opened her legs to facilitate my groping. She put her hand on my shoulder. "Is your cock standing?" said she in a whisper. "Yes, feel it," said I, unbuttoning. She grabbed at it as if she meant to pull it off.

Her manners struck me as uncommon, and I began to feel uncomfortable; but under the squeezing of my cock, and the feeling of her cunt the usual desire to leave one's sperm up her came over me. "Let me fuck you — I'll give you two shillings more." Without reply she fell back on the bed, I began to throw up her clothes. "Oh! No, I can't let you do that." I had when with strange women just then been using French letters, and the fear of infection came over me when she would not submit herself to my inspection. "You have got something the matter with you, and I shan't," I said.

"Nothing of the sort," said she angrily, "I'm not gay, — I'm the landlady, — I am married, and have three children, — they are abed in the next room, — you may see them if you like. My lodger's gone, — you've been here afore to see her, — I've seen you afore, — but I'm not gay, and can't have anything the matter with me, — it's impossible." All this nearly in a whisper. Astonished, I laughed. "Don't make a noise," said she, "I don't want the lodgers to know I am in this room, they know it's empty, — come on," and grasping my prick again, she surrendering herself more freely to my investigations.

"Where is your husband!" "Away on a job in the country; I haven't seen him for three months, and have not been touched for that time, so help me God; you may do it without fear, — there then look, if you must," said she, letting me throw up her clothes, and look well at her cunt, which I opened. "I'm a quiet woman." Then she turned round, twisting herself so that she could get hold of my cock as I stood pulling her about. "Come on, my dear." The next minute I was spending up her.

"Go on, you were so quick, — go on," said she in spasmodic utterances, jerking her bum, clutching me to her, and using the same endearments as any other woman, — women are all the same, from the princess to the peasant. I had spent quickly, but shoved on as well as I could, and in a second or two with a sigh, her cunt relaxed.

I moved out of her quickly, for fear of the ladies' fever haunted me a little. She lay with her clothes up to her navel, till I had washed myself. "There is no towel or soap," I said. Then she moved. "I'll get you some, — but don't afear me, — hush! — don't make a noise, — wait five minutes for me, lock the door, and put out the light." I stood aghast at this request; it was in a low neighbourhood, costermongers, tramps, and even a nest of thieves I had heard was not far off. "What the devil does she mean? — what game is up?" came across my mind. "I won't put out the light," I said. "Well, hide it in the cupboard, lock the door, and if any one knocks don't answer, — perhaps my late lodger's friends may come, not knowing she has gone, — I don't want any one to know any one is in the room." This was all said in a whisper; she went out, shut the door gently, and walked to the back of the house, leaving her three shillings. I heard her footsteps, and faintly afterwards the sounds of talking in the back room, — the partitions in the poor houses were thin.

I dried my tool with my shirt and sat on the bed, looking round at the poor room, wondering what dodge was up. She did not return, and thinking over the incidents, came to the conclusion that she was not a gay woman. There was just that difference in manners, in getting on to the bed, in taking her pleasures, and in her whole behaviour about the fucking, which there always is between a woman however loose she may be, but who does not fuck professionally, and the regular trader in her charms. I saw it then, and I see it still clearer writing about it now.

Nevertheless I began to think of leaving, feeling uneasy, as she did not return for more than ten minutes. With my hat on, I was just about to run off, after hearing a man's footsteps pass along the passage, when I heard a voice cry up the stairs, "Mrs. Brown, Mrs. Brown, I'm going out to get a mouthful of fresh air, — if the children cry, will you see to them?" A shrill voice replied, a female step passed my door, into the street. A second afterwards the door slowly opened (I had unlocked it as I heard what I supposed were her footsteps going along the passage). In she came, holding up her finger for silence, then quietly closing and locking the door, she stood smiling at me. "Don't make a noise, they think I am out," she said.

I looked fully at her now, my lust satisfied. She was a big woman of say thirty years of age, coarse, common, but clean; she had a dress on which opened in front like that of a woman who suckles, and some sort of cap on her head. I did not know what to make of it, for she stood as if waiting for me to speak. I did not, and taking the candle, she put it down on the floor by the side of the drawers, or something of the sort, and remarked, "They won't see the light through the crack of the door now." Again a man's heavy footstep was heard. "That's my upstairs lodger," said she when she noticed my listening.

"You are really not gay?" said I. Then she repeated what she had said before, and sat on the side of the bed by me. "You have big breasts," I remarked. "Yes, I was a fine woman, everyone said before I married." It is impossible to be near a woman without wishing to ascertain her hidden charms. In the hurried embrace with her I had thought of nothing but cunt. At that time of my life, to see a woman, to long for her, to make my bargain, and to fuck her, was often an affair of not much more than ten minutes; it was only after the fuck that I looked well at the female I had pierced.

"Let me feel them," I said. She hesitated, but I undid the dress, and felt two breasts large and white, and pulled one out. "My nipple is spoilt with suckling," said she, "I've not yet done giving milk." "Let's have you again." "Yes," — and she got on to the bed. "Let me see your cunt." "Oh! No, — don't, — I won't." My suspicion came back; with my prick out I still hesitated. "I've not washed myself since you did me," said she. "Well, wash your cunt." She took my basin, and washed herself. Then I had a look at her cunt, and again fucked her. Lord how she enjoyed it, and so did I, that big, coarse woman; but she would not let me look long at her belly, perhaps marked through child-birth. She had thickish, lightish brown hair on her quim; it was a cock-squeezer too, and how wet it got in our copulation. I remarked it to her. She said, "I'm wet, and no mistake."

I lay on her afterwards, my prick dangling against her cunt, and talked. Her husband was an artisan away on a job, she kept the house, and let lodgings; her husband was half his time away. "You've seen the girl who was in this room, — I recollect you, — I've seen you in the street more than once, — you've been with the woman opposite. I didn't mean anything till you spoke and stopped, but I'd been dying for it, been wishing almost I were gay; the gal opposite had just gone in with a man, and I was wondering what my husband was adoing, and just then you stopped and looked, and I thought I'd let you. Do it again," said she, slipping her hand between our bellies, and grasping my ballocks. And I did it again, as soon as I could.

"I've never had another man but you and my own man, I'll swear, — ask in the street, they will all say I'm respectable, — but don't tell on me. I frig myself almost every day, if you must know, but that don't satisfy me, a woman who's had three children, — if I'm in the family way now, I'm in a mess, but I'm not so much to blame, am I? — think, three months away from your own man! — but I tell you as you spoke to me I was adying for it, — the girl who was here in this room used to say, 'Well, Mrs. °°°, you are a fool to pass your life almost without a you know what.' Well I was adying for it, and she and the lodgers would always tell me what the men did to them; and yet I never have had but you." So we lay talking for a time, she answering my questions, and sometimes volunteering remarks; but never leaving go of my prick, and every now and then saying, "Ain't you a fine man! — you just are a fine young man!"

There were noises at the street-door, men were talking, a smell of tobacco reached us. "It's the upstairs back," said she, "he will stop there till he have smoked two pipes, so for God's sake don't leave," — and she sunk her voice lower. "Oh! I must put out the light." Saying so, off the bed she got, blew it out, and got on to the bed again. There we lay quite another hour, speaking in whispers, feeling each other's privates, never washing, the spunk drying up as our hands fumbled about each other, I talking baudy, and telling her what gay women would do, she telling me she knew all about it, for her ground-floor lodgers were always gay. I asking questions about herself, heard that my cock was about the same size as her husband's. Wondering at the tightness of her cunt, as she had had three children, she said that the size was the same as before she had had a man. If she got in the family way she would be in a mess; she did not think she should, as she had not quite done suckling. She did not know how she managed to keep so firm and plump, for she had meat only twice a week. "What then?" "Potatoes and herrings," — did not know what she would do, if she did not get another lodger soon to pay the rent, — she often could not pay for a meal.

About two o'clock in the morning there were lumping boots going upstairs. The lodger had gone to bed. We lighted the candle, I washed (there was still no towel), and no sooner had I washed than she laid hold of, and kissed my prick, stooping to do so, — and then we fucked again.

We parted, she took my money. "I will keep this," she said, "it will help me." I said it was for her. She let me quietly out, begging me never to mention what had taken place between us to any gal in the street. "Though they won't believe you if you do, for I have a good character. I've seed you often go in with them." I had fancied no one ever saw me in that low street, and wondered if any other person had recognized me there.

I never had her again. Once or twice I saw her at the street-door, but so soon as she saw me she rushed in-doors, and I had too many fresh and younger women at hand to care about her. Hers was a case of a woman who could not restrain herself, owing to the long absence of her legitimate doodle, and gave way to her uncontrollable passions for that night. That was the only conclusion I could come to.

Then soon afterwards I had the clap. Mary cried, and declared she had not given it me, and I am sure she had not. Then almost for the first time I began to use condoms, or French letters, as they are called. I did not like them, but had suffered so much from gon-orrhœa, that I carried them in my purse in readiness.

My experience with this poor class of women was soon consid-erable. Satiated, sick of them, yet I continued to frequent them for the simple carnal pleasure of coition. There was no sentiment about it, no liking for the women, for though their manners sometimes amused me, they more frequently shocked me, and the poverty of some distressed me; but I had no money for choicer entertainment. My vigor was great, my pleasure in copulation almost maddening, a cunt was a cunt, and I got my pleasure and relief up it, whatever its owner might have been. A sensuous imagination aided me. When once my prick was up a woman she was for the time more or less invested with charms, and her imperfections forgotten. I used to shut my eyes, and fancy I was stroking a houri with the finest limbs and ivory flesh, and could fancy all this up to the moment of ejaculation, the woman I was enjoying was then to me some one I had had before and elsewhere, and I fancied thighs and cunt which were not those of the woman who was at that moment doing her best to please me.

There were occasions when the women when naked revolted me, my prick refused to stand, and I departed without copulating, but those occasions with this class of women are not worth noting. I have been subject to this sudden revolt and prostration, sometimes even when the woman was most beautiful. Nervousness, fear, some sudden dislike, and even most ridiculous reasons have caused it.

I should have mentioned that gradually it had taken hold of my mind that my prick was a very small one. How this notion first arose I cannot quite trace, I certainly had it in a degree when a youth, and it became stronger owing to the remarks of some French women. The men I saw fucking at Camille's had very large pricks, and no doubt they were selected on that account for exhibition; but I did not know that then, and used mentally to compare mine with theirs, and also with those of some of my former schoolfellows, and to my disadvantage.

With many harlots of both high and low class I had talked about size; each told me of men who had big pricks, rarely of those who had small ones. Experience has since taught me that harlots like talking about big pricks, for size affects their imagination agreeably. Of ridiculously small ones they make mention for a laugh, the average sizes pass without their notice. I used to ask them how mine compared with the big ones they spoke of, and got at last into my head the erroneous opinion about my own machine. At times I would produce it with an apologetic remark. "My prick's not a very big one, is it?" — and was much pleased when the woman's reply was complimentary. I know now from the inspection of many men's, that mine compares very favourably with the average, and is larger than most; but for many years I was of a very different opinion, and at times was almost ashamed of my prick, so much so that when a woman said it was as large as most, and many said that, I did not believe them, still less did I believe them when they said it was a handsome prick; then I thought they were humbugging me.

Now as I add these few words written years after the foregoing, and after having seen some dozens of pricks, both languid and erect, I know what they said was true, and I know that there is a size. a form, a curve, and a colour in pricks which makes some handsomer than others, just as undoubtedly there are ugly and handsome cunts.

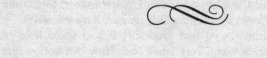

CHAPTER XVII

Irish Kate. — Drink, heat, fleas, and French letters. — The brick-layer afterwards. — I give luck. — The lost breast-pin. — The cholera's victim.

One hot night in summer I slouched along one of the streets, and stopped in front of a woman who stood lolling against the doorpost. I recollect her and my first sensations perfectly well, her white face, and dark hair hanging behind her in a net, her low dress, low in front, — showing a luscious neck and bust as white as her face. Her dress was of a very light colour, so her neck and face must have been white indeed to look so white by contrast. The street-door was close to a street-lamp, which shed a strong light on her face as it was turned upwards, and with her hands and arms folded behind her she lolled, her back against the door-post. She was a full-sized woman, but young, and exactly what pleased me then; black and white, young and full of flesh. I stopped, and gazed at her. She fixed her eyes vacantly on me, but neither moved nor spoke to me.

There were gay women standing at doors not far off, common men also at some stood smoking. They understood the habits of the neighbourhood, and never took any notice when a strange man and a woman talked together at a door. I did not like to speak to a woman if others, or men were near, and would at times walk about till the coast was clearer. But this girl struck me with strong lust suddenly. "I'll give you a shilling to feel," said I. No answer, but she kept staring at me. "Half-a-crown then," thinking my offer too small, and stepping inside the passage to get out of sight. "Come in," I said. She made no reply, never took her back quite from the wall; but turning herself round, continued looking at me, her head slightly moving about as if she did not understand.

Staggered at this behaviour I was coming out again to leave, but her lovely look fixed me. "I'll give you five shillings," said I, "to have you." "Have me," said she, "have me what?" Her voice was thick and broken. She turned into the passage. "Will you let me have you?" "Come and fuck," said the husky, thick voice. She passed me, stepped heavily into the room, staggered to the bed, and then I saw she was drunk. I had not noticed it before, being absorbed in her fleshy beauty, and the desire to see her cunt, and all of her, and join my body to hers.

There was a single candle in the room, guttering, and needing snuffing, but no snuffers. I snuffed it with my fingers. The room was in disorder, the pot full, water in the basin, the bed unmade, the whole place the picture of disorderly, drunken harlotry. A night-gown was lying on the floor, clean linen on a little table. It looked so miserable, that I thought I would go away at once, so took out five shillings, and laid it down. "There is the money," I said, "I shan't stop." "Come and fuck," said she in reply, rolling on to the bed, and pulling up her clothes. She had but a gown on, nothing else. Thighs and legs as white and fat as her neck came into sight, and a thicket of hair at the bottom of her belly as dark as the hair on her head. The sight altered my intention, I walked to the bed, and placed my hand on her cunt. "Fuck me," she blurted out in her drunken voice again. I felt wild with voluptuous delight, as my eyes gloated on the big breasts and thighs to where her garters and stockings hid the flesh from view. All was dazzling white except a nearly black crispy-haired cunt in the middle of it. The contrast was exquisite, was absolutely dazzling.

A strange train of ideas (how oddly they spring up at such times) came into my head. "You've just had a man," I said, "your cunt's wet, — you've just been fucked." "He ain't fucked me for three days, — we have been adrinking gin, we have, — he paid, — he hain't fucked me, — you fuck me," said she, making a grab at my prick which was buttoned up yet, — fuck me, — you shall fuck me." All this was said in a hoarse, drunken, incoherent manner, but the "fuck me" with a sudden violent energy, as if she suddenly felt a stinging desire to have her cunt stretched. "Fuck, — I'm bloody randy, — where's your prick?"

I took the light, pulled open her thighs, almost put the candle in her cunt. She let me do just as I liked, repeating, "Fuck me." She was beautiful, her white firm flesh, her big round thighs, the lovely globes of her arse would have excited the dead. "Pull off your gown." "I shan't." "You shall." I helped her up into a sitting posture, and pulled it off in an instant. Then she fell back naked, showing peeps of black-haired armpits. The next instant I was up her, and injected her. How beautiful she seemed as I moved my prick up and down in that cunt, spite of the drunken manner, and the miserable surroundings.

A most violent letch for her took hold of me. The women in the streets I have described had fine women among them, but for the most part they were plain in face, indifferent in form somewhere, and hideously coarse in manner; but the beauty of this woman was so great, I forgot all her coarseness. When I came to myself after my pleasures, she was fast asleep. She had perhaps spent, that and the liquor called gin overpowered her, and she forgot her business. Then the biting of fleas worried me for half-an-hour, I spent my time in hunting for them, and scratching myself, snuffing with my fingers the only tallow candle, and now and then holding it over her to look at her beautiful face, naked body, and unwashed cunt. The heat was intolerable. To be cool I gradually took off all clothing but my shirt, at last took off that, and then sat at the edge of the bed naked. I pulled open her legs, each lay just as I placed them, wide apart. I held the candle between her thighs, and opened her cunt-lips. Masses of thick sperm lay over her cunt, and hid the entrance of the prick-hole. I played with it as my baudy fancy dictated, frigged her, dipping my finger in the spunk below, and then rubbing it on to her clitoris till it was dry, twisted down her cunt-hair till it was wetted, and played every trick which a lascivious fancy dictated. Gradually I stiffened under this exciting amusement, and throwing my naked body on to hers, fucked her again. God only knows if she knew I was fucking her, or not, — I don't. She awakened after I had spent, turned on her side, and when I tried to get her on her back again, she swore.

Whether the slight dozing had relieved her brain, or whether the fumes of the liquor had evaporated, I don't know, but she soon became more conscious, and though stupid, yet more awake. Her voice had still the thick utterance, her answers still those of a person only partially understanding what was said to her. I expect I had excited her passions by my fingers, and not by what I said, for after awaking she again blurted out, "Fuck me, — I want a fuck." A grab at my prick showed that she knew where to find the means of giving herself pleasure, and I gave it her. Then I dozed.

Knocks at the door aroused me, and a shrill voice cried out, "Kate, Kate." I listened. "Are you alone?" said the voice. I shook Kate, and awakened her a little. "Some one is knocking at your door," said I. "Oh! Damn, — arseholes," said she, turning on her side, and dozing again.

"Kate, — knock, knock, — Kate, are you alone? — I'm going to bolt the door, — they are all in," said the voice.

Kate made no reply, I was dressing, so opened the door. "I'm here, and am going directly." "Is she drunk?" said the woman. "I think she is." "Do you know her?" "No." "Well, I will leave the door open." "I'm going, — wait." There lay Kate dozing. When dressed I said, "I have left five shillings on the table." "Awake her," said the woman (for I heard and saw it was one). "You had better." "Kate, Kate," sung out the woman. I shook Kate, who turned, opened her eyes, and said, "Oh! Damn, — don't." "Come in," said I to the woman. She did, and shook Kate. "Oh! Arseholes," said Kate, and again closed her eyes. "She's been lushing for three days," said the woman. "Mind there are five shillings," said I, and disgusted I left, resolving never to go near the drunken beast again.

But the woman had made a great impression on me. I was always, even quite early in life, taken with a crummy woman, quite as much as with a pretty face; and although so low a woman, I longed for her again, and before many days sought her. It was on a blazing hot afternoon of a summer's day, the sun shone brightly on the front of the houses on one side of the street, the other was in shade. A street with perhaps a dozen carts and wheelbarrows through it in a day, where children played in the roadway, and women sat on the footways. I went along slouching on the shady side, slowly looking, and not quite recollecting the number of the house, and saw Kate sitting on a chair on the footway by her door.

She looked up vacantly as I got close to the house, with that look which a low-class woman has who thinks the man above her, and not likely to take her. "Come in," I said, turning into the open door, and she followed me, bringing her chair. "I'll give you five shillings," said I. "All right." "Take off your dress." "All right, but give me the five shillings first." I gave it her. She began undressing, her gown off left but her chemise. "You don't want my chemise off?" "No, — lay at the side of the bed." She laid herself down, threw up her chemise, and the loveliest pair of thighs, belly, and cunt that ever man saw were disclosed. To look, to open its lips, and thrust my prick up her were the work of a minute. I roared as I touched her. I am told by women that at that time of my life, when thoroughly randy, and I saw the cunt I liked that I gave a low roar as I closed on it with my pego. Kate told me that I did so this time, when my prick first neared her thighs. I did not then talk when in a woman's embraces; but fucked in silence.

I pulled out my prick. "Lay still, — keep your thighs open, — let's see your cunt," said I, trying to keep her in her position. "Oh! Arseholes," said she, closing her thighs, and getting up, and looking at me.

"Did you get your five shillings the other night?" said I, "you were drunk." "Lor! Are you the gent?" said she, breaking out in a laugh, "I didn't know you, — now I see you are like him, — yes I was lushy, — so you've come agin, — Lor!" and she laughed. "How often did you fuck me?" I told her. "Sit down, and talk," said she, and we both sat down on her little cane-bottomed chairs.

"So you fucked me four or five times, — I don't know if I spent or not, damned if I do, — think of your lying there, and being bitten by the fleas, — the room was washed out yesterday, there ain't no fleas now. So you pulled me about, — what a beast, rubbing your spunk about on my cunt, — but Lor! a cunt's the proper place for it." After a few minutes' similar conversation she suddenly said, "Let's fuck agin." "Well, let's strip." Off went her chemise without reply. Gloating over her I stripped naked, and was soon on her, and up her. She had not washed. She enjoyed it. How we hugged each other's nakedness! The first words she uttered afterwards were, "You are a bloody fine fucker, — where did you learn to fuck so well?" giving me a vigorous kiss, and squeezing her cunt up to me as she said it.

I washed, and wanting soap (she had none), she went to the door, and called out for some. The woman brought it. Then there was no towel, and again standing naked at the half-opened door, she called out to the landlady to lend her one. "I shan't," said a voice, "you have now got two of mine." "Oh! Arseholes," bawled out Kate, slamming the door. "The bugger won't let me have one, — here, dry your prick with my chemise, it's quite clean."

Kate stood naked looking at me as I rubbed myself dry with her chemise, bending slightly forward, holding her fingers under her cunt. "What a lot you've spent," said she, putting down the basin with my water in it, and beginning to wash. "That's not clean," I remarked. "Oh! It's all the same spunk," she replied, and afterwards, "You may look at my cunt if you like," and she threw herself on the side of the bed, thighs wide open. She was faultless. I pulled a chair to the side of the bed, and contemplated her cunt at my leisure. The dirty white blind down in the window only just mellowed the light, it was as light as day, I could have hunted crabs, had there been any in her motte-thatch.

She asked me to give her gin. Some was sent for, then we sat drinking, she taking it neat, I mixed with water. "Let's fuck," said she again, and we fucked. More gin, more fucking, she was quicker to want fucking than I was. It was getting dusk, then she said "You're going, ain't you? I want to make a few shillings tonight,—my rent's due tomorrow." I gave her another five shillings, made her piss in the basin, and we fucked again. I was fucked out, and at last she spent twice to my once, our bodies were sticking together with sweat as we fucked. Then for a few minutes we went to sleep. "You are a gent," said she, "I likes you, — I hopes you'll come agin, and see me, — I likes a real gent."

As I went out I saw a man standing on the other side of the road looking like a bricklayer. Turning back after I had gone a hundred feet or so, I saw him cross the road, and go into the house. I went back, the street-door was as it always was, open. Stepping inside I heard a male voice through Kate's door, a woman came out from the back. "Who do you want?" said she. "Kate." "Oh! She has got a friend with her, — shall I knock?" "No," I replied, and went my way. I didn't like the idea of her having a working-man after me, or before me. I was not then a philosopher. "But what does it matter?" said I. "A man's a man."

I saw Kate next day, and told her she had had a man after me. "Yes, directly, — a chap I knows had been awaitin an hour, and he come in in a hurry. 'I'm done,' says I, but he would, — he's a rough un, and he'd fucked me before you was at the end of the street." "Why, you had not washed your cunt." "No," she laughed, "the bugger went right into your spendings, — he never knowed, and I had a good un of a cove after him, — you brought me luck. I've got two new chemises, and four towels, — let's fuck, — let's fuck," said she, laying hold of me, and unbuttoning my trowsers. My balls hung over her bum in no time.

I visited her at intervals for about a year. She had the whitest flesh I ever saw, and was very beautiful in face; hair grew exceedingly low on her forehead, yet it did not disfigure her, from her neck to her calves her form was perfectly voluptuous, but she had big feet, and her hands were large. I could not bear to see her feet in great boots, and when looking at her lovely form used to keep my eyes from them. Her cunt was perfectly beautiful and small; black, white, and carmine were never more exquisitely blended.

She was revoltingly coarse in her talk, and even when sober her voice was rough. That I did not like, but her language disgusted me. To anything she did not like she said "arseholes," said it more frequently than any other word until I stopped her. "Give me some gin," she would say. "No, you have had enough." "Oh! Arseholes." Everybody also was a bloody bugger, or a bloody shit. She was lewed on me for a time, and made me fuck her more than I wanted, but as I checked her foul language she became indifferent to me. "Oh! I'm obliged to hold my tongue I suppose," then she would sulk, and then, "Well let's have another fuck," and all would be right till I stopped her foul tongue again.

Half her time she was drunk. I would go there, not see her at the door, then call out to the woman, "Is Kate in?" "Yes, she's drunk, I ain't seen her since the morning." Sometimes her door was locked, nothing then roused her, and away I went. At other times she was in the bed, or on it, and all but insensible. Several times I fucked her, put five shillings in her pocket, and left without her knowing I had had her until afterwards.

I had now fits of timidity, and used French letters at times, even when she was quite sure she was all right. One day when she was very drunk, I had her with a letter on, and as my cock dwindled out I eased the letter off it, and with my finger pushed it well up her cunt, and went away without paying her. I should like to have known what she thought when she found the French letter up her. I never alluded to it, and she never did. Why I behaved so I don't know, it is a wonder to myself. That night I had entered her room, and left unobserved by any one.

When she was a little drunk only, she got spoony, and I could not get away from her, she would lay hold of my prick, and keep to it. "I can't do it again Kate." "Get on me, and I'll make you," — and she usually did. Then as liquor overtook her she ceased to wash her cunt after fucking, would turn on her side, and go to sleep. I left her often snoring with her cunt full, the money on the table.

It always was a wonder that she kept such a beautiful skin and look, but she did; and always was cool, fresh, and healthy-looking, even if she had been drunk for twenty-four hours previously. Her breath and body were as sweet as milk, yet she never had a bath as far as I know, but performed all her ablutions in a little basin, throwing the water into the street when she had done with it. I have seen her wash from head to foot that way in a quart of water, and a wet rag, and when done she looked like ivory.

She was called Irish Kate, why? — I never knew, nor did she. She was not Irish.

I had words with her one day, having lost a diamond pin. She had been pulling me about that night, but the same night I had been into a house with two women, and had felt their quims. I offered more than the value of the pin, but never got it back. After that I did not go near her again for a long time, but at length so longed for her that I did. She cried with joy, and kept me fucking till my back was well nigh broken.

Then I was for some time out of England. On my return, burning with desire, I went one night to her house. She had died of cholera, which was then raging.

CHAPTER XVIII

Costermongers' children. — A small girl, mother, and mangle. — A French letter fetched. — Young Gallows' exploits. — The customers' linen. — A hard-fleshed bum. — Invitation to anus. — A strange letch. — One big with child. —Fucked for a sovereign and pleasure. — A creole. — My misery. — Reflexions.

Close by Kate's was a street with a carriage way, at one end narrowing to a footway only. On one side a row of small houses, on the other a very high blank wall. Costermongers' barrows and carts stood in the carriage way at night; clothes-lines with ragged garments hung across the street in the day. One dark night, prowling about, cunt-feeling young girls and baudying generally, I went up this street. I had been up it before, and loved to hear the boys and girls chivying each other among the carts, hinting baudiness as they caught the girls, and kissed them, the girls squealing when liberties were taken with them. Occasionally standing in the shadow of the carts, I listened whilst a man would stealthily go up against the blank wall, a woman follow him. I would stand feeling my prick till I saw them come away (in two or three minutes usually), and rush into Mary Davis' or to Kate's to get a relief for my excited ballocks. There was but a feeblish light in the street, and in one part of it none.

As I passed I saw a small girl standing inside the door of a house, and thought I would like the little one. Sometimes I wanted the biggest woman I could get, sometimes the smallest. She took no notice of me, I repassed, and there she still stood. "Is she gay?" I wondered, "she does not look it." Lots of girls and women not gay stood in a similar manner in those streets. Again I passed, and stopped. "Will you let me come in, and give you a kiss?" "Yes sir," said she, stepping back.

I stepped in after her, one or two steps down. The room was below, and entered direct from the street. A miserable place: on one side a mangle, on another a poor dirty bed, a tile floor, dirty walls, wooden furniture, all miserable. Had I known, I should have been horrified at entering such a hole, but in my lust I thought of nothing but the young girl, of the probable hairless cunt, of her little bum, her smallness and freshness. She looked fifteen years of age, and was quite short.

She closed the door, and looked. I looked at her. "I'll give you five shillings." "All right, sir." "Let me look at your quim." "All right, sir," said she getting on the bed. I pulled up her clothes, and saw the little thighs, and the little cunt with a very small quantity of lightish brown hair on it. How tight it was to my finger! I took the guttering candle. "I'd like to fuck, but am frightened, — let me look well at your cunt." "I'm all right," said she, putting her fingers down, and stretching open the lips, "quite clean indeed sir." "When were you fucked last?" "It must be a week." "Aren't you every night?" "I don't get the chance," still laying on her back, and stretching her cunt-lips open, "I only go to the door quite late, when the neighbours have gone in, cause they ain't gay close here." The house was the last in the street where it narrowed to a footway.

I raised her up, laid her lengthways on the bed, and put my pego into her hand, but fear came over me, and it would not stand. "I must do it to you, but play with it a little." She laid hold of my prick. "It's not stiff." "No my dear, frig it." She began. "Do you like feeling a prick?" "I likes feeling men's things," she replied, "they are such funny things, first little, then big, then little again."

"How old are you?" "Over fifteen, mother says." "Where is your mother?" "In the back room, — look, it's getting bigger, I did not think it would be so big, — don't hurt me with your nail sir please," said she, frigging away clumsily, and when it was stiff leaving off, but looking earnestly at my pego. I kept probing her cunt with my fingers, wondering at its smallness.

A desire came to make her youthful mouth utter baudiness. "Say cunt, dear." "Cunt." "Say fuck." "Fuck." "You know what fucking is?" "Putting that into this," said she with a chuckle, "ain't you going to do it? — I'm quite clean." "Let me look again." Again the little hand went down, and stretched the lips. I prepared for action, again fear seized me, and down my doodle drooped. "No dear, lay still, and I'll frig myself over you, — turn on your belly, — let me see your bum, — there, that will do." I put some spittle on her bum, and rubbed my prick against it, but longed for the hole between her thighs. "Have you got a French letter?" "I'll ask mother," said she, going into the adjoining room.

In came a woman of middle age suckling a baby. "She will fetch one, give her the money, — make haste now, — never mind your bonnet, — run, — run. She won't be long," said the woman to me.

"Your daughter?" I said to the woman who stood suckling her baby, and staring at me. "Yes sir." The baby took to howling. Swinging it about to quiet it, she went on in a whining tone, "We are so poor, we are almost starved, we are, — what was I to do for a living? — I've nearly lost all since my husband's left me, and can't afford to keep a big gal like that; if she will go wrong I can't help it, I can't send her out, — I catched her with a young Gallows, and the mischief were done, it were, I knowed it, and I knowed it would be, so I did, — I could not keep her in, and the chaps were allus arter her, — she must live, and she's better at home doing that, than doing it away from me," — and much of the same sort in a whining, apologetic tone without stopping, without my asking.

"Has she been gay long?" "Bless you sir, it ain't more nor two months since I catched her with young Gallows, — he is in quod, — serve him right; but he'll be after her agin when he is out, he will." "Where is your husband?" "Oh! The vagabond's gone off with a hussy, and left me with three children, — this here's the last. Drat you," said she, shaking the infant which would not leave off howling. "Oh! Here she is." The girl entered the house with the condom, and the mother and baby disappeared.

The affair was not enticing, my cock was flabby again, but the little wench's naked belly stirred and stiffened me. I prepared the letter. "Did you ever see one before?" "Yes, a gent had one here one night, but he did not put his thing into it." "What did he do then?" "He blew it out, and popped it off," said the girl. "Oh! You wet it, — let me see how you do it, — does it not feel cold? — it's a nasty thing. Indeed I'm all right, — gals has diseases from doing it I know, but I ain't, — look," — and again the girl distended her cunt-lips without any modesty or affectation.

Fearful, but (as often was the case with me and French letters), my cock and the letter would not agree. My cock stiff without it, drooped its head directly the wet flabby sheep's-gut touched its tip. At length it was over my doodle, and shoved up the little cunt after much trouble. "It don't feel nice," said the girl. A few shoves more, and I lost all prudence, pulled it off, and drove my naked prick with such a thrust up her little quim, that she cried out. Her cry of pain gave me pleasure, and fetched me.

No one can lay so close up to you as a thin girl, two stout people can't stick together like two lean ones. As I came to myself the little girl was wriggling under me. "Oh! Dear, just as it was beginning to feel nice, — why did you do it so quick?" "Do you want it?" "Oh! I do, — do shove a little," — and the little cunt squeezed itself up to my belly, and wriggled my doodle in her. I accepted the invitation, the girl spent, and I had second pleasure up her, after I had pulled my prick out for a minute or two, to inspect it.

She brought me a basin, soap, and a napkin of beautiful quality and white. "Ulloh! Is this yours?" "It's something we had to wash and mangle," said the girl. "It's a table-napkin." "Yes sir."

"Don't you make a living by washing and mangling?" "No," said she, "we have lost our business, father ran away, took linen, and sold it, — people won't trust us, — none of those who lost their linen, — others don't know us. Thank you sir," as I gave her the five shillings, "we don't have as much sometimes in two days." "Wash your cunt my dear." She went out of the room, and came back saying she had washed it. I felt it, and she had. Then I talked for an hour with her.

I was curious. "Tell me who first did it to you." "I shan't." "It was a coster lad, your mother has told me." "She has not." "She has." "Yes it was a coster I knowed, he's been locked up for a row, and breaking windows, — he is seventeen." "When did he first do it to you?" "I shan't tell you," said the girl laughing, "mother's listening, I know she is." I had got the poor girl on my knee, was pulling her pretty tight little cunt about. "I'd like to do it again," said I. "You may, and welcome," said the girl. "Ain't you fucked every night?" "No, I wish I were — to get money." "Where is the five shillings?" "Mother's taken it, she always does." I fucked her again, gave a trifle more, left, and never had her after.

Then I had a woman of a singular build: she was shortish, and had the hardest flesh on her bum I ever felt, it was impossible to pinch it. She was a very large bummed woman, it was quite out of proportion to her size, so were her breasts. She was as near as I can recollect about twenty, but had the form of a woman of thirty, her cunt was almost hairless, and had no lips, the lapels and clitoris showed when she was standing up with thighs closed; when her thighs were open her cunt looked as if the lips had been cut off, she had lightish brown hair and almost colourless eyes. Her room was ragged, and I always found her cooking, she wore garters of ragged ribbon below her knees, and ragged slippers. For all that I went to see her I suppose a dozen times, and nearly always fucked her from behind, dog-fashion. The arse-cheeks were so firm, that I delighted to feel, and slap them as I fucked; and spite of her big bum I recollect no woman whose cunt I got further up in that position, as I did hers.

One day she said whilst I was fucking her, "I thought you were going to try the other hole." I looked, and her arsehole was as plainly visible in the rear as her split was visible in the front. I can't tell now how it came about, but know we began talking about that hole, and its pleasures. One night from talking I got to action, she said she would like her bum-hole broached. Such things were not to my taste, but egged on by her talk I tried; then she said she was afraid it would hurt, and although we talked more than once about it, and she always asked me to try, it always ended in nothing, and I avoided her soon after.

In the next street a woman after I had done her said, "You have got me in the family way." Something led to my remarking that I should like to fuck a woman in the family way, and her saying that she knew one who would be confined in a fortnight, a nice woman, a fine woman, her sister, the wife of a mechanic, but badly off just now. I can't tell what had made me take such a desire, but I said I would give a sovereign to see her cunt and big belly, and fuck her, and would give five shillings if she would get this for me, not believing she was a married woman, or her sister, although the wench said so.

Asserting that it was no gay woman, and that a sovereign would be a great help; she would go and see about it, if I would wait. Returning she said that if I would really give a sovereign her sister would let me, but that I could not stop long, for fear of her husband. We went into an adjacent street of poor houses, but evidently with a different class of tenants. She entered one, I waited close by till she beckoned me in, then I found a decent young woman with an enormous belly who asked me to show her the sovereign first, then to give it to her first, which I would not. She dallied, and put off the affair, and I thought I was humbugged. At length she got on to a clean although humble bed, the other woman pulled up her clothes, I smoothed her belly, and with much trouble got her legs open, and tried to see her cunt.

She resisted, but gave way under the persuasion of the other woman who kept saying, "Do now, — what did you say yes for, if you meant no? — a bargain is a bargain, — don't make a fool of me, — well, if you are ashamed now, you should abin afore," and so forth. At length I had had a good look at her cunt.

Then I longed for a fuck, indeed took a letch for it, pulled out my prick, and asked her to let me have her. "Not she," said the sister, "you have seen all, and must be off, her man may come home at any minute." The big-bellied one was much more quiet, laughed, and I said I was joking, but kept looking at my prick. I took out my sovereign, wetted it with my spittle, and balancing it on the top of my prick, told her to take it off, which she did in a very clever way; for instead of taking it off with one hand, she put one hand against the other enclosing my prick and the sovereign too in her hands. Both women laughed, and the gay one said, "Well Mary, you've had more than one man's in your hand now at all events, — you'll never tell Jack I'll swear, — now go sir, — her man don't like *me* here, and he won't like *you*, I'll swear."

My letch overcame me, I forgot how poor I was, and would have given my clothes off my back for a poke up the cunt beneath that hard big belly, so asked her again, and stood with my prick out, both women laughing. I prayed her to let me again feel, and she consented. She was then sitting down, I had to put my hands up her clothes, and stoop to do it, my back was to her so-called sister. She laughed, and looking at her sister whilst I felt her, caught hold of my prick, gave it a grasp, and immediately relinquished it. Her sister did not see this done.

I dallied a few minutes with her cunt, and fancied that if the other woman was out of the way the big-bellied one would be complaisant. So I asked if there was good gin to be had. It was a bait that the sister took at once. Yes there was. I gave her money to fetch gin, and to buy me a bun and a bottle of ginger-beer; a move to keep her out of the way as long as I could.

I had buttoned my trowsers up, and ceased feeling and asking; but the instant she was gone, out I pulled my stiff-stander. "Let me fuck you." "Oh! She won't be long." "I won't be a minute." I flew to the door, and locked it, the woman got up from the chair; made no resistance, raised her bum with difficulty on to the bed, opened her thighs, and we fucked in a jiffy. It seemed that I no sooner was cunted than we both spent. I unlocked the door, and by the time the other woman returned, not six minutes had passed. The two sat gin-drinking a few minutes, and then the harlot and I left together.

As I uncunted I whispered, "When your sister is gone I'll come back." "Very well." The gay woman made off at the end of the street in the direction of her house. Waiting a minute I returned to the big-bellied one, who was at the door, we went in, and I locked the door. "My man may be home at any minute," said she, "so we must be quick." I threw her on the edge of the bed again, her cunt was still covered with my sperm, and turning her arse towards me we fucked dog-fashion. She enjoyed it. The instant my prick was out I was off. I never saw her or her sister again.

Both women were tallish, and spoke with a strong Northern accent. I quite believe the one with the swollen belly was not gay.

These are the most noticeable events which occurred during the period of my narrowest means. In that time I must have seen the privates of fifty women, and copulated with nearly that number. Had it not been for their pleasures, coarse as they were, I think I should have made away with myself, so miserable was I. How I accommodated myself to the class I can't imagine; for although a few were nice, prettyish, healthy women, the majority were low coarse creatures, living in poor single rooms which were often not clean; but both rooms and women were as good as could be expected for the few shillings I gave for their pleasures.

My strong animal wants carried me through, and added to that perhaps was a certain amusement in noticing the difference in manner between them, and the highly paid Bonarobas, whose silks, satins, and laces I had helped to pay for at the rate of a sovereign an hour, and often higher. Besides as already said, my imagination helped me. When my prick was up one of the ill-favored ones, and I was clasping a flabby backside, I used to shut my eyes, and fancy some charming creature whom I had had elsewhere. I cultivated these dreams in copulating.

Up to this period I had tailed a neighbourhood of free cunts, as far as trifling sums would get them me. A shilling a feel, or a look at the nudity, and for half-a-crown to five shillings at the outside for complete enjoyment was a tariff generally accepted.

Then a remnant of my former fortune which had been in litigation was settled in my favour, and I had a little ready money. Immediately I left off frequenting the poor Doxies of whom I have told, and went to a higher class, in a better neighbourhood. My money was soon gone, for I had debts among other things to settle out of it. Whilst it lasted I had some very nice women, among whom I shall always recollect a tall, superbly shaped creole, with dazzling white teeth (a feature in women which always has had a great attraction for me), and who was one of the most voluptuous women in her embraces I ever yet have had; but she was plain almost to ugliness. In the rest of my amours there was nothing to need special notice, they were all fugitive, and the women were changed frequently.

It is difficult to narrate more without divulging my outer life. I would fain keep that hidden, but it is impossible, I shall however tell as little as may be and obscure it, but without falsifying or distorting any facts relating to my amorous pranks, some of which were not sought by me. I fain would have led a steadier life, and wished a home with a woman I could love; but I had an unquiet home, and a woman there whom I hated in bed and at board. I tried at times to overcome my antipathy, abstained from women for weeks at a time, so that sexual want might generate a sort of love, but it was useless, without reward, and a life of misery was before me. I broke out under it, wonder I did not break down, and should have done so, had it not been for whores. Cunt came to my rescue, and alone gave me forgetfulness, a relief far better than gambling or drinking, the only other alternatives I could have had recourse to.

And now I pass over a short period, in which I did much the same as I have just written of, until a lucky sympathy brought me a happier change in my amours.

CHAPTER XIX

My home life. — Heart-broken. — In the parlour. — Maid Mary's sympathy. — Don't cry master. — On the sofa .— Both in lust. — Impotent.

I was still poor, but had got into an employment, and was living in a small eight-roomed house. I kept one servant only, but was pinched to keep up appearances. None of the outside world could have known how much I was pinched. I went home regularly, sat for hours by myself reading, brooding, fretting, and even crying bitter tears, at the time I take up my narrative.

Our servant was named Mary. A tall woman about twenty-one years of age, splendidly built, stout of form, and with big breasts and haunches. Her face was lovely, her eye almost the most beautiful hazel I ever saw, its expression dove-like, her complexion as clear and bright as a rose. She looked as if she eat three meals a day, shit regularly, slept eight hours, and was fucked nightly, and was in brief a most lovely creature, and the picture of health. She had a mouth filled with lovely teeth, one of which was missing, and showed its absence when she laughed, it was the cnly defect visible about her. Another handsome woman whom I have had since, had also lost two front-teeth, which showed in a similar manner, but that lady always smiled, and rarely laughed, so as to avoid showing the defect. False teeth were a rarity in those days, and quite beyond the means of poor people.

She had been with us about three months. There was mystery about her, like a former servant of my mother's, she scarcely ever wanted to go out. At times we heard her singing, at others sobbing, and it used to be remarked that she was moping. I thought my wife knew more about her than she said, but to her I spoke as little as possible about anything. Mary was an indifferent but willing servant, was said to have come from the country, to have been living with an aunt a short time in London, and that ours was her first place. She was with us pretty well worked and scolded, but not by me.

I had been struck by her beauty and her ways, which were winning, friendly, and unlike a servant's, yet without being presuming, and I was as kind to her, both in manner and word as I dared to be; but I had been annoyed and suspected for speaking kindly to servants, and to avoid strife was cold, even harsh to them in manner. Mary was witness of the sullen domestic misery in which I lived. I had seen a pained, sympathetic glance at me at times when she heard our wrangles, and was confident that she pitied me.

Nevertheless I had no sensual intentions towards her, holding it as fitting carefully to respect my home, whatever I did out of it. I might have thought about her hidden charms and probably had had that tingling in my prick which a pretty woman often gives a man however virtuous he may be. But it went no further.

My last clap may have made me abstinent, or want of money had, or perhaps other motives which beset a man who wished a different order of things in his home affected me, for I know that for weeks I had barely had an emission, excepting by nocturnal dreams; and though dying for a genial fuck, yet avoided it, and worked at my occupation to get money and forget my troubles. This woman changed all my resolves, and launched me again into sexual pleasures. I may remark also, curious as it may seem, that instead of fattening, and getting strong by abstinence, I got just the reverse. Every time I spent involuntarily on my night-shirt, I awaked fatigued, agitated, nervous. I lost appetite, got thinner and thinner, and more and more miserable the less I had women.

One fine summer's afternoon I came home before my usual time, it was about four o'clock p.m. Mary opened the door, she was alone in the house. I went to my own room, then came down into the parlours, and for a time sat there looking into my garden and smoking. Grief overcame me as I looked round at the home in which there was no one to welcome me, so I walked into the garden, and saw the maid doing some work at the back kitchen door. "Your mistress is out?" I had never on any day asked that before, as far as I can recollect, not caring to know; and she might have been upstairs. "Yes sir." "Did she say when she would return?" "No sir, but it will be I dare say about the usual time." "When is that?" "Half-past five, or six o'clock, perhaps later." I again turned down the garden, and as that did not relieve my dullness, returned to the house. I could not read though I tried, sat down on a chair by the dining-room table, laid my head on my hands upon it, and thought of my unhappy home till I cried bitterly.

A hand laid on my shoulder, a voice said, "Don't you take on so Master, — don't you now, — she's not worth it, — cheer up, — don't you take on so." I looked up, it was Mary looking full at me, her eyes full of tears.

I started up astonished. "I beg your pardon," said she, looking uncomfortable, "I couldn't bear to see you so unhappy." Her interest in me struck me to the heart, without premeditation I threw my arms round her, pressed her mouth to mine, it unresistingly met it, and we passionately kissed for two or three minutes; kissed till I recovered my senses, my tears still running down, and then said, "Mary you *are* kind, — you are a dear, good girl, — a good, affec-tionate, loving creature, — I am unhappy, miserable, but how do you know that?" "How could I be off of knowing? — how could you be anything else with her? — but don't take on so Master, — she beant worth it, — and you so good, and so kind, — I hate her when I look at her, and then look at you. Oh! I beg your pardon sir — don't say anything," — and as if astonished at herself, she disengaged her-self, and stood looking at me. I closed with her again, folding her tightly to me, and we kissed till we could kiss no longer. My tears fell on her face, and hers ran down my cheeks, so close were they together.

The parlours divided by folding doors mostly open, ran from back to front. A sofa was close by the dining-table. "Sit down," said I. She did. I put my arm round her neck, pulled her face to mine, and kissed again that divinely pink and velvety cheek. Then her arm went round my waist, and lips to lips, each instant we kissed, and sat and talked of my miseries; yet as far as I recollect not the slightest desire to have her had then come into my head, all was delight at my trouble being shared, at a kind, soft, pretty woman commiserat-ing me.

After long talking and kissing, and looking at her, a sense of her great beauty suddenly struck me, just as if I had never noticed it before. I recollect telling her so.

Then a thrill of desire shot through me and staggered me. I trembled as the want overtook me, and drew her closer to me, kissed more fervently, and sighed. She sighed. My lust had kindled hers, and yet I had not spoken of it. My hand went on to her knees, I felt the thighs gently, felt their plumpness through the summer clothing, slowly my hand dropped lower kissing her all the while, and bending her forward with me, as I bent forward, with my dropping hand.

A long pause. I scarcely knew why, and then my hand went still lower, till it touched her ankles, still kissing her, and bending her with me (oh! how well I recollect it), then my right hand went quite slowly up her clothes to her knees, and there I stopped, frightened at my advances. Opening her eyes she gently repulsed me, and murmured, "Oh! Master, — Master, — what are you doing, — pray don't." Her eyes were filled with soft passion, her resistance physically would not have moved a butterfly, but morally she affected me. I became conscious of what I was driving on to unpremeditatingly.

I desisted, removed my hand, but passion now controlled me. I kissed again. "Let me feel, oh! Let me dear, feel you," bending her forward with me, I replaced my hand. "Oh! Master, pray don't, — think what you are doing, — of who I am," said she lovingly. "Oh! I won't," said she sharply, — but too late, my fingers were on her clitoris, I had begun that gentle twiddling which always ends in fucking. "Oh! — no, — oh! — Pray." Voluptuousness had overcome her, her mouth was glued to mine, her eyes fixed on mine; gently they closed, then opened, always looking into mine Her breathing was short, she was past thought, she was mine. Gently pressing her back on the sofa, she raised her limbs, I lifted her clothes, and tearing open my trowsers threw myself on her. My fingers for an instant touched her cunt, a rapid probe, and then my prick! My God! It was not standing, not a bit of swell or stiffness was in it, it was as a sucked gooseberry, a mere bit of dwindling, flexible, skinny gristle, a piece of loose, flabby flesh, and nothing more.

I had been occasionally, but rarely, suddenly unequal to love's duty as already told, had gone home with gay women, my prick standing as I entered their houses, then suddenly it had shrunk, something about them having upset me. Occasionally it was a sudden fear of the ladies' fever, or something looked less inviting when their petticoats were off, than I had imagined when drapery hid their charms, or else the fear that my prick would be thought small. At other times I could not account for it at all. I told my doctor of it. He said that it was nervousness, but the knowledge that I had once been so affected, affected me often afterwards when I went indoors with girls. "Shall I be able to fuck?" I used to think, I who had already fucked two hundred women. But so it was, a fear of inability brought on the inability. The power often returned to me a few minutes afterwards, yet sometimes not for hours.

There was nothing to account for it now, I had more or less abstained for weeks, there lay one of the choicest female forms ever presented to man's eyes, a dark-brown crispy-haired cunt with a tiny bit of pink clitoris showing between a large pair of thighs like ivory, and a sweet face above turned on one side with eyes closed, and blushing at yielding up to me. And I liked the woman, felt mad for her, yet as my belly touched hers, and my prick rubbed against her pleasure-pit, it became useless. I got up, looked at her as she lay motionless with thighs extended, stood almost frantic, frigged my prick, probed her, and again threw myself on her as I stiffened; but no sooner had my prick touched her beautiful cunt, than as if bewitched, it shrunk from entering it, I could not even thumb it up.

I broke into a sweat. "My God, what will she think of me?" I dreaded to get off, and look her in the face, feeling so ashamed, I kissed her taking her head in my hands, again got off, kissed all round her cunt, and smelt its inciting aroma, asked her to be still, said I should be all right directly. So time wore on, she never moving excepting to push her clothes down as I rose and exposed her, nor opening her eyes, nor uttering a word. "My God, what is the matter with me, I don't know but I can't," I said at last. Then she put quite down her clothes, and sitting up on the sofa gave me a kiss, said, "I must go, and see about laying the things for dinner," and off she went.

I did not stop her, but was glad when she left the room, being so ashamed that I could not look at her. It was a relief not to have to speak, to excuse, to explain. I was reeking with sweat from exertion and nervous anxiety, sat thinking and frigging, felt sensations of pleasure without stiffness, and only stiffened after half-an-hour's rubbing. With prick out and in hand, downstairs then I went, she was boiling potatoes. "Mary come up, come, I am all right, — let me." She would not. "I can't Master, I can't — what will Missus think if she finds nothing ready?" Nor could I induce her. I incited her by talk, she kept on ejaculating "oh!" to my baudy remarks, and blushing like a rose; but I could get no more. "If Missus comes home, and sees you through the area, what will she say? — Pray go up Master." Yielding under the fear of being surprised, at length up I went to the parlour.

I knew she would be up to lay the cloth, waited in the parlour till she did, keeping my prick in hand, and trembling with anxiety. When she had laid it, "Now," said I, "look here." "No, — no, — no, — Missus may be home, — pray think of me." But a stiff prick close to a randy woman is a great persuader. "Come dear, come," and I pulled her. Again she was down on the sofa, again that divine belly was under me, again as I opened the lips of her cunt my prick dwindled to nothing. "Hush! There's Mistress' step, — there is the front-gate slamming. Get up, — get up, oh! Let me get up." Upstairs I rushed to my own sitting-room as I heard a knock at the door, and had only time to button up my disgraced doodle before I heard the woman tramping upstairs to our bed-room above. How I loathed her!

Half-an-hour after that I sat down to dinner, having composed myself. Mary brought up the dishes. The instant I saw her my cock stiffened, it kept stiff all the evening, I could not sleep for it, was tempted to fuck, or frig myself, but did neither, feeling sure I should have Mary, and would not spend a drop of my sperm till I did. "What does she think of me? — will she believe I am a man? — will she let me again? — when shall I get the chance? — what enervated me so at the critical moment? — oh! My God if she lets me, and I am seized so again, what shall I do then?" — and so on ran my thoughts. I lay planning how to get her the whole night, and awakened haggard and unrefreshed in the morning.

Then I reflected less nervously. "My finger has been up her cunt," I thought, "no pain, no recoil, — how quiet she laid, — then she has been fucked before, — then what must she think of me?" and so on ran my thoughts till I was in an agony of disgrace. My haggard look was noticed. I was worried, and should not be home to dinner. "Why?" That was my business. Well then, she would spend the afternoon with Mrs. °°°, — would I fetch her? Yes at half-past ten o'clock. She wanted to come home earlier. Then she might come by herself. Well then, she would wait for me till half-past ten.

CHAPTER XX

The next day. — On the door-mat. — On the sofa. — On her belly.
— Eight hours fucking. — At a brothel. — An afternoon's amusement.

Instead of being late I went home about two p.m., just after luncheon time. "Is Mary alone, or not?" I thought, and had arranged for that. I waited in a cab, told a boy to take a letter to No. *, but not to give it unless the lady was at home; if she were not, to bring it back to me, and he should have a shilling when he returned to me. If asked, he was to say he had been told to leave it, but not to say by whom. The letter was properly addressed, but inside was a sheet of blank paper only. Back he came with the letter, — the lady was out.

Even then I was not sure, so drove up and down two or three times in front of my house, to see if I could discover any signs of Mary not being alone, and then I dismissed the cab. My prick had been standing on and off all day, I was in a fearful state of nervous erotic excitement. When I thought of her beautiful belly my prick nearly lifted me off the seat, the next minute I had fears of being taken as I had been the day previously. Would she let me now? — would she be in the mood? — would she not laugh at me, instead of putting her arms round my neck, and her eyes fill with tears? My heart beat audibly with these tumultuous thoughts as I knocked at the door. To my horror I felt my prick shrinking as I stood on the landing feeling it through my trowsers pocket.

Mary opened the door, surprize in her eyes, and a slight look of fear. "You, sir!" "Is your Mistress in?" "No sir." To step inside, close the door, place my arms round her, and kiss her rapturously was the work of an instant. She kissed me, and I her for a minute, and glory to God my prick was like a rod of hot iron standing up against my belly, and throbbing to emit its juices up the dear girl's cunt, against which its poor little tip not twenty-four hours before had dangled and rubbed so uselessly.

A stoop, a struggle. "Adun now — Master, — you shan't, — oh! You mustn't," and again I was upright, my lips on her sweet lips, my finger on her clitoris, her face scarlet with modesty, her eyes closed. What woman can long withstand that irritating, voluptuous, restless movement, of the male finger on her cunt? Soft words now. "Oh! Don't," as I stooped down to lift her petticoats, and she pushed them over my hand. Another slight struggle, again our lips meet, again my finger rubs the smooth clitoris, now her hand grasps a hot prick, and with her lips to mine she stands with her back up against the wall of the passage close to the street-door on the door-mat. So we stand kissing and feeling, I don't know how long, for who can count time in such delights.

"Come to the parlour, come." "No, no, — oh! Pray." I edged her along, one hand still up her petticoats, she trying to push them down. "No, I won't, — there now." "Do Mary dear, — let's do it, — I'm a man, — let's do it, — look, look how my prick throbs for you, — it will spend." Removing my hand from her cunt, I seized hold of both her hands with mine, and began gently dragging her along the passage to the parlour, she leaning back gently resisting, I leaning back tugging her, my prick red-tipped, stiff, and throbbing standing out in its randy glory between us.

I got her into the parlour, a flood of sunshine struck full on us from the back window as we did so (windows both back and front in the long room). There she seemed half unconscious. Kind of heart, pitying, liking me, her splendid healthy physique, her fully-developed passions, passions of which she had tasted the full pleasure, but which had been for a long time ungratified, were roused to intensity by the feel of my prick, by my groping her cunt, by the excitement of the position; all had relaxed her nervous system, and absorbed her in voluptuousness. What did she think? Did she think at all? — did she ever know? How can I recollect what I thought in that maddening moment of fierce desire to have her? I grasped her round the waist, and pushed her to the sofa. No resistance, not a word was said. My arse knocked hard against the table, and hurt me. She is down on the sofa, her petticoats up, I see the creamy flesh, large round thighs, the dark hair on her cunt for a second, I am on her, up her, a slight sob as my prick goes up with the thrust of a giant, and we are spending in each other's embraces, mouth to mouth, belly to belly, prick to cunt, ballocks to bum-cheeks, almost the instant I had covered her, and grasped her smooth fat buttocks. I have no sense of time, all is oblivion and elysium at the same time.

Our sighs of pleasure are over, there is no uncunting, no stopping; but with rigid prick still up to its roots in her cunt, on again we go fucking in earnest. Now is the higher pleasure. The first was a maddening desire for each other, a fuck finished before it was begun. Now we are fucking with soft pleasure, and the thoughts of the greater pleasure to come, of my spunk to spurt, of her juices to ooze to meet it, in a cunt already flooded. I recollect smoothing her hair back from her forehead as I fucked, of kissing and meeting her tongue with mine, and spending with rapture, then waking from a doze, and finding her half asleep, I on the top of her, my cock still up her. My trowsers not let down had ridden up, and were cutting me tightly under my balls with a painful sensation, and all this was on a narrowish sofa, a modern cheap bit of furniture unlike the grand big one in mother's house, on which many a servant had had her cunt basted by me.

She lay with her beautiful head on one side, with eyes closed, with her long hair falling loose, and her cap tumbled off. As I lay I loosened my braces, and little by little took the strain off my testicles, and my balls fell down into their natural position. I put my hand down to feel how my prick lay, the sperm was oozing out all round it. I wanted to see her quim, and pulled out, then putting my hands against the sofa-squab, I pushed myself gently up, rose on to my knees between her thighs, and looking down saw the sperm between her cunt-lips.

She opened her eyes, pushing gently down her clothes; but the glance had been enough. With prick still stiffish down I fell on her, and was up her again in the twinkling of an eye, lodging my prick in preparation for another fuck.

Now all is clear, our lust assuaged. "I've fucked you, — I'm a man you see," I cried triumphantly. She closed her eyes, my prick came out, I pushed it back, again out, again up, and so on for a time. A long business was fucking now, long friction, no result, then a long rest, our genitals joined, their hairs glued together, yet no fear of a failure. My machine went on ramming, moans of pleasure at length came from her, her hands clasped me tightly, and with a heave and a cry of "Oh! My darling," she again spent with me, my prick aching with its labour of love.

Then I dozed an instant on her, she seemed asleep, I was squeezed uncomfortably next the wall, my prick satisfied with its duty, at the first movement left her cunt. I moved her to get off, my trowsers had dropped to my knees, entangled my legs, and I gently fell on to the floor, catching at her outer thigh, and pulling it off the sofa as I did so to break my tumble. Up she sat dazed, her petticoats above her knees, I at her feet, looking intently where her closing thighs hid the seat of our pleasures from me.

"Oh! My gracious!" said she, starting up, and letting down one front-blind quite, and half of the other (there were two windows that side of the room). The brilliant sun had lowered, and came into the room in a flood of radiance from the back-window, and the room was light and bright throughout its long and narrow length. Although in a very wide street, the neighbours from the houses opposite could easily have seen right into our room, could have seen us on the sofa. Usually when sitting in the room at that hour of the day, we kept down the blind of the back-window to prevent this. Worse than that, the steps to the street-door were so close to one front-window, that by stretching forward (very much it is true, but I had done it), any one could see into the room, even on to half of the sofa on which Mary and I had been amusing ourselves. What an awful risk we had run.

We looked at each other anxiously. "Oh!" said she, "if any one saw us!" I looked through our blind. Every blind in the houses opposite was drawn down to shut out the sun. Then I sat by her side, did nothing but look at her for a time, so delighted and satisfied was I at having vindicated my manhood, until she rose to go. That aroused me, and I stopped her.

"Let me go." "No." "I want to do up my hair." "No." "If Mistress comes home —" "She won't." "She may." "No, — I've fucked you, — you thought I was not a man, did you not?" "Do let me go." "Come up again then." "Well, presently." "You are going to wash your cunt." "Hush Master." "You shan't go." "Now let me." "Kiss me then." We kissed and kissed. Could I do it again? The idea of her moistened cunt inflamed me, I pulled her back, thrust my fingers on to her cunt spite of her resistance, and never shall I forget the feel of that and her thighs. "It's dirty of you," said Mary, and disengaging herself she rushed downstairs. I followed her into the back-kitchen, where she washed her quim in a wooden bowl, but did not dry it. I chaffed her, then we went into the front-kitchen, sat down, and looked at each other without speaking, like two amorous cats, she blushing, and turning down her eyes as if she guessed what was in my mind. At length I blurted out what was there, I always did it till much later in life, and I had grown wiser. "You've had it done to you before today." "Oh!" said she starting up, then sitting down again, and bursting into tears, "Of course I have, — poor fellow, — poor fellow, — why did he leave me!"

Embarrassed and sorry at such a consequence of my speech, I tried a few words of comfort. She dried up her tears, and began her household work. I followed her about, talking, kissing, and putting my hand up her clothes, until in due time we adjourned to the parlour, and then again I fucked her, this time on the hearth-rug, the sofa-squab under her head, the sofa was too small for comfort.

Time was before us, all seemed delicious, the domesticity of the amorous amusements, the passion with which she returned my embraces, her modesty and enjoyment were all so like the days when I fucked my mother's servants. The difference between her sensuous embraces and the matter of fact fucking at five shillings a head I had been so long accustomed to, overwhelmed me with gratification. We had tea. Then as I had had no dinner, and there was none for me, I eat bread and cheese, and opened a bottle of port wine, and in an hour we fucked again, and again. At nine o'clock she had supper, and we fucked after it. She sat on my lap, I played with her cunt, she with my prick, and we kissed till our lips were sore. But nothing would induce her to let me see her limbs, nor do more than feel her cunt, and take my pleasure in it.

From two in the afternoon till ten at night was I feeling her quim, kissing, and fucking. We were both exhausted. I got into bed intending to say I had come home ill, took a pill to open my bowels, and bogged in a pot that night to keep up the sham (there was no closet in the house). As the street-door bell rang I was in my nightshirt, standing by her side, trying to frig my prick up to stand-point. In bed I jumped, downstairs bolted she. In ten minutes it was "Don't make that noise, I have a bilious headache." I never closed my eyes that night, could scarcely believe what had occurred, and tossed and tumbled, thinking of the pleasure I had had. Though we had been nearly eight hours doing nothing else, it seemed not an hour. How often I fucked her I don't know, it seemed as if I was at least half of the eight hours up her cunt, which is absurd; but it was one of my greatest feats in the fucking line, the longest, and most pleasurable.

Next morning, haggard, jaded, worn out, the bilious attack got the credit of it, I laid abed all the morning, and went out late. When at business I fell asleep, unable to work, came home at about the same time as on the previous day with no idea of chance favouring me, but it did. Mary was alone, and we fucked as hard as we could. She laid the cloth and dinner things, my sperm dripping from her cunt. I had just spent up her as the street-door bell rang, buttoned up my trowsers, turned on my side on the sofa, and shammed sleep. "Is your Master home?" "Yes, Mam, he seems quite ill." "Where is he?" "On the sofa, fast asleep I think Mam." Again the bilious attack had all the credit of it. I had pulled down the blinds which covered the window through which the room could be partly seen from the landing outside. Five minutes after I was sitting at dinner with the smell of Mary's cunt on my fingers, my prick sticking to my shirt, for I had never washed it, nor piddled since it had left Mary's body.

Luck helped me for a day or two. The illness of a relative took the other person interested in this out of the house at unusual times, and Mary and I did all we could in an hour or two. It was more exciting now than ever to see a woman bolt downstairs directly she had been fucked, to cook potatoes, or to eject me from her cunt, and leave the fuck undone, because there was a ring at the bell. It was old times come again, but with greater risk, more serious consequences if found out, yet with greater zest and enjoyment.

Then luck ceased, the house was never left, and all I could get was a stray kiss, and a slight feel of her quim. But oh! The delight of that rapid feel round the warm, smooth bum and thighs, and the push up between the warm, moist cunt-lips when I got it.

Then came her holiday. We went to a baudy house in E**t*r Street. She had a large paper parcel in her hand when I met her. "What's that?" "Cherries, — I know you are fond of them, so bought some."

What a jolly afternoon we spent. Although I had had her many times, she had not willingly let me see her person, I had had

glimpses, and no more now. In a trice she had stripped to her chemise, I to my shirt. What lovely breasts, what splendid limbs, what
thighs and arse-globes. In an instant I was on the bed with her.
After a fuck we fell fast asleep, she had done so similarly at my
house on the sofa, and on the floor. She always did after a spend.
I never met such a woman in that respect. As regularly as she copulated she went to sleep after, and said she could not help it. When
awakened she asked for cherries, and we lay and dallied, and eat
cherries at intervals. There was now no reticence, all her charms
were open to my sight and touch. "Why did you not let me at home
Mary?" "My linen warn't clean," I remember that well. "How many
times did we fuck that first day." "Don't you know? I've been trying
to recollect, and can't," she replied, laughing.

She was a lovely woman, had firm, smooth, creamy flesh, was as
plump as a sucking pig, a fat cunt of my favorite style then, and the
loveliest coloured hair on it I ever saw; but it was ample, both inside
and outside, I had experience enough to know that even then,
though its grip of the prick was heavenly. Her form and figure was
if anything, what may be called thick, the ankles and wrists were
thick, but neither feet or hands were large, her breasts and bum
were faultless. Take her all in all she was a superb creature, and had
such a complexion!

I sent for wine and biscuits, for we got thirsty and hungry, and
then amidst amorous dalliance we chatted. She astonished me not
a little about her career. I was always curious with a woman whom I
had poked, and till I had heard something about her was not satisfied. Whether lies or truth I always got a history of some sort out of
a woman of Mary's class, and usually got the main facts truly. I
have tested them. But not so with gay women, they mostly lie
heavily.

"Master (she always addressed me so in country fashion and
dialect), you know." "I?" "Yes." "No." "You do." "What nonsense."
"Ain't she told you?" "No." "Why she knows all about me, she caught
me crying one day, spoke kindly, it made me open my heart, and I
told her all! — yet she has never told you?" "Never, and if you have
told her anything about yourself that you had better have kept to
yourself, you will regret it." "I fear I shall." Then little by little,
amidst tears and caresses, she told me her history, and again did

on future days, and I saw her letters, rings, jewellery, silks, and other proofs, I knew the town she lived in, knew some of the people in it whom she mentioned, and was satisfied with the truth of every part of her story. One gentleman she named was to have married one of my sisters, — how strange!

CHAPTER XXI

The daughter of a small inn-keeper at the town of B°°t°n, she was at a public ball. A young gentleman danced with her, afterwards paid attentions to her, and induced her to run off with him. "Oh! I was just as bad as him, poor fellow! When he got me into the room I felt sure what he was after, knew it was wrong, knew he would want me, and that I should let him. I wanted to let him do it, to be all to him, I did not want it done to me for myself, not that I recollect, I dare say I might, but don't recollect *that*; but I wanted him to do with me what he liked, anything he liked, anything he wanted to do me, I would have let him do anything that would make him happy, and seem as if I belonged to him entirely, and he to me for ever."

"And he did it?" "Yes. I stopped out all night and all next day, and then went home frightened. I was father's favorite, he had been hunting for me like mad all over the town, and letting people know I was not at home. He hit me, — there was such a row! — my sister spat at me, and called me a whore. I never slept all night, and hadn't slept the night before, what with his apulling me about and doing it, and my fear of being found out. I was ill, and father kept me locked up in my room a week, because I would not tell him where I had been, and with who. I said I had been to an aunt's, he went to her, and found I had fibbed. At length he let me out, because he

wanted me to attend to his business, and the first man I saw in the
bar was my dear boy, — I nearly fainted." — These were as nearly
as possible her own words describing her seduction, they are so unlike the confessions I have had from other women, that the very
words sank deeply into my mind.

After that he used to go and drink at the bar, her father talked
with him, not knowing he was the man who had broached his
daughter. She was watched till life was unbearable, her sister worried her (she had no mother), neighbours who had thought well of
her began to sneer, a country swain who liked her was saucy to her,
one or two swells in the neighbourhood who had been accustomed
to see her about, and admired her beauty, were now free in their
behaviour. One took liberties with her, and in the public-house began asking her smutty questions. Weary with all this, liking the man
whose sperm had wetted her virgin cunt, perhaps longing to have
more (although she always declared to me that she had no recollection of that desire affecting her), one night she ran away to London
with him.

They lived in London nine months. Then came grief. He was
the son of a West India planter who had sent him to London to pass
as barrister. His father's agents found out the connection with Mary,
and wrote to the father that he was spending his money, but not
advancing his career. His father objected, then threatened, and then
his allowance was stopped. They lived on what they had, until penniless. He wrote that he was going to marry Mary, and his father
replied that if he did he need never return, and might starve. He was
a gentleman, and could not get his living, he tried but failed. Then
the father wrote, requesting him to return, and saying he would
provide for Mary. Misery stared them in the face, and he consented
to go home.

His father remitted money. The first thing he did was to take
all Mary's jewellery and clothes out of pawn, and then to arrange
for her to live. He promised to come back, and marry her, and some
sort of such promise was made by his father's agents. He begged her
to go home, but she would not. Then he put her to lodge with a
small middle-class woman whom he bribed to give Mary a character
as a servant, for he declared he would remain, and ruin himself for
ever, if she neither would go home, nor go to service. Mary remained
there a couple of months, dressing plainly, and only going to see him

in his lodgings at night, or to meet him at places where it would not be known. Then he went to India. Repeated threats of his father, and his want of money would let him stay no longer.

The father arranged that Mary should be paid fifteen shillings a week, and they paid it for some time. She wanted to write to her lover, but had mislaid his address, the agents said that their instructions were to stop the weekly payment if she corresponded with him; but *he* wrote to her, *she* replied, and then the payment ceased. Her lover then sent her money; but his father found that out, and kept him penniless. She was in London now alone, knowing not a person, again he sent her trifling sums, but begged her to go out to service, or she would become a gay woman (I have seen his letters). She used to go out, sit down on a green close by, and cry all day. One day a middle-aged woman accosted her, she told a little of her grief to her, it was something to tell her grief, even to a stranger. The woman told some plausible story, and she went to see her (I had the address). There the woman asked to see her partly undressed, and told her that with such legs and breasts she might have silk dresses and jewellery galore, in fact incited her to be a gay woman. True to her lover, she did as he advised. The female with whom she lived gave her a character as a servant, and with that she came into our house.

The way in which the old bawd got to see her legs was amusing, I often thought of it; not knowing a bawd's dodges then. She asked her if she wanted to piddle, took her to a bed-room, and as in sitting down she showed a little leg, the woman broke out into ecstasies, and asked her to show more. Much flattered she did, and then came the old woman's suggestions.

"From the time he left you till the other day, had you never been poked?" "Never, by all that is good, — I would not have injured him, — I was shocked when the old woman told me about getting money by my legs, I hoped he would come back, and always thought he would. But he never answers my letters now, although some money came for me the other day, and I know it must be from him, although the writing is not his; even when you threw me on the sofa that day, I thought I was wronging him for a moment till I forgot everything but you.

"But oh! I have had a weary life since he left, father I hear has failed, what sister's doing I don't know, — sister I heard tells everybody it was all my fault, and that the old man never held up his head after I ran away, — perhaps it's true," said she, with a flood of tears, "but I was a good gal to him, till my poor Alfred took me away."

I have never before or since heard anything more simple or touching than that girl's tale, as told me in the baudy house. I could almost swear that every word was true. We stopped at the house till time for Mary to leave. I had paid for the rooms two or three times over, being still inexperienced. When we came out we were famished, having eaten nothing but cherries and biscuits nearly all day. I bought buns, and we eat in the cab, I feeling her cunt at intervals, and once making a fruitless attempt at a fuck. The smell of her cunt on my fingers at that time I dare say gave a relish to the buns, for I liked her. She went in first, ten minutes afterwards I did. What a look we gave each other as she opened the door! Old times again, and this time as charming as those in every particular.

For some time afterwards it was impossible to have her, for we never were alone, our only chance of exchanging whispers or a kiss was on the stairs, or when the other woman went to the privy. In those few minutes we used to stand whispering, kissing and feeling each other. Then at table I used to feel her legs with my toes, putting my feet out of my slippers as she put things on the breakfast or dinner-table, and looking the other woman in the face all the time. This was so pleasant to me, that I came down in the morning without socks, saying the weather was so hot, and when I could get the naked toe up just to touch her thigh, my prick would stand at the instant. But this was poor pleasure, and I resolved on a course which I had actually to write to tell her of, so little opportunity had I of conversing with her for the time.

Our old-fashioned house was one of a row with a narrow frontage, and four stories high, had a long narrow garden, and a privy about thirty feet from the back-door, hidden by some evergreens, the common mode of building in London at that time. On the first floor was my own little sitting-room and a drawing-room, and above two bed-rooms, the back one serving as a dressing-room for me, above those a servant's attic. With one servant only we helped ourselves a good deal as may be supposed. One bath sufficed, one of us took it first, the other using the same water, it was a not very big flat tub. I usually took it first, then went downstairs, and read till breakfast-time, and so got my five or ten minutes' opportunity. But she began to take her bath irregularly, or not at all, and came down at times so quickly after me, that I was cautious, and so the opportunities with Mary were lost. She was probably suspicious, but I never knew.

The scullery, or back kitchen-door led up to the garden by a little flight of steps, and in the summer it was always wide open. Anything let fall out of back-window would fall just in the doorway. This gave me the means of signalling. It was arranged that if Mary heard a penny drop on to the stones by the door, she was at once to go up quietly to the parlour, the ground-floor room as said, was divided by folding doors, in the front was the dining-table and the auspicious sofa, in the back a small table where we breakfasted.

One morning, dressed, I waited till the woman stepped into the bath, and then looking out of the window, dropped a penny. It fell just where Mary stood cleaning my boots. Then downstairs I cut, and there was Mary in the parlour waiting. She resisted me, but she wanted it as badly as I did, and sticking her back against the partition close to the door, so that we could catch the first sound of any one coming downstairs, we fucked. My God what a rapid fuck it was, but what enjoyment! It was the old trick again of but a very few years before in mother's house. Mother still lived there.

This we did several mornings, then I lost even that opportunity, after being nearly caught in the act, and with prick throbbing to let out its sperm, I had barely time to subside into a chair, and take up a newspaper. That so scared Mary that she would not come up again when I dropped a penny out of the window.

Then she asked to go out to buy some things, which being granted, again we spent a jolly hour or so at the baudy house in E°°t°r Street. That night I sat her on my prick, and did her in the cab, I never did so to her but once. I put her up to asking to go to the post-office with a letter, it was at about five minutes walk from our house. Close by was a lane leading to large vegetable market-gardens, and there we took our pleasure, and were nearly caught at it by a man passing by. I went home first, and when the door was opened was answered, "The girl has gone to the post-office, she must have gone somewhere else, for she has been a long time." Then in came Mary. "Why have you been such a long time? Your Mistress says you have been half an hour." She got a scolding, and the Mistress went up to bed. I told Mary to come into the garden, it was a dark night and cloudy, and half-way down the garden I put into her, up against the wall, then she went in, and upstairs to bed. I followed soon, and said, "What keeps that girl up so? I have been walking in the garden, and she has only just gone upstairs." "She ought to have come up directly I did," said the other. I locked all the doors of the house at night, and was the last up.

Several other risky incidents occurred in a few weeks, and then from some suspicion I imagine, I never got a chance of having her. When I came down to breakfast the girl was rung for to go upstairs, going out was refused her, she was told in the middle of the day, "If you have any letter to post, go out now, you can't go out this evening." The Mistress seemed to stay a shorter time even in the privy than usual, and often on some pretext sent the girl upstairs or somewhere just before she went to the poopery. I was evidently suspected.

One day she did not. No sooner had she gone out of the back-door than I called up Mary. "Let's do it." "I will." "I don't care if she does catch us," said I furiously, "lean forward, look out into the garden, I will do it dog-fashion." There was a lowish-backed easy-chair which I usually sat in by the breakfast-table, up against which I pushed it. Any one stooping over it, and looking could just see through the window the head of any one coming away from the privy. My impetuosity prevailed, I threw up her clothes over her backside, and plugging her cunt, was soon in ecstasies, Mary in a funk, submitting, and with me looking whilst we fucked, out of the window for her Mistress' head, which as I have said, we could not fail to see. But our pleasure came on, and in our joint delight we only thought of the lubricity of our position. "Look out, darling." "Yes — I am." "Oh! — ah! — are." "You're loo — k — look — ing?" "Yes — oh! — ah! — be — qu — quick, — ah! — ah!" I had spent, my belly was still squeezed up against her bum, my prick still up her, my hands rubbing her flesh, when I heard a footstep at the backdoor. To pull out my prick, drop my dressing-gown over it, let fall the clothes over Mary's posteriors was the work of an instant. Rushing towards the door I met her Mistress just as she entered it. Passing her I rushed out towards the privy saying, as if ready to shit myself, "What a time you have been there, I thought you were going to stay there all day." It had been raining, the ground was wet, and just inside the back-door she had paused to wipe her feet on the mat. Had she not done so she would have caught us in the posture, for we had both spent, and lost all consciousness for the minute, I was dreamily leaning over Mary when I heard the feet rubbing on the door-mat.

I stopped a sufficient time at the privy to show that I really wanted to go there. When I went back to the house I found Mary had fainted right off in the parlour, and dropped a tray. The shock of fear at being caught had been too much for her nerves, and she rolled on the floor showing her legs. My wife jealously told me to leave. I did, but in a funk for I saw on one of her stockings unmistakable stains of spunk mixed with poorliness.

We talked over it afterwards, wondering if it had been noticed; but I never knew. Mary recovered and got up just as I went out of the room. Her Mistress afterwards remarked that she was a fine-made, but coarse, strong woman; she called all stout, well-filled women coarse.

Her Mistress asked her what she had bought the day she had gone out shopping, and she showed her some things which most unfortunately she had shown before, then her Mistress said it had been merely a pretext to get out. She told me of it, and when Mary's regular holiday came she refused to let her go. Mary insisted, there were words, I was consulted, and said she ought to be allowed to go. "You always take a servant's part." "It's a lie," said I, "and I won't come home till time to go to bed." "I shall be alone in the house then." "Serve you right,"— and off I went. Mary met me an hour or two after the proper time whilst I kept anxiously waiting and fuming, either under the portico of the Lyceum, or about there. Then we spent the rest of the afternoon and evening in voluptuous delight.

"I'm in the family way," said Mary with a sigh. "My God, are you? — how unfortunate! — are you sure?" "Yes, I knew I should be." "What is to be done?" "What I have done before." "You have been in the family way then?" "Yes, twice, he wanted me to have the child, but I would not unless I were married."

I kept out for an hour after Mary's return that night, and had a row, for the Mistress was sitting up. Next day I had a latch-key put on the door, and told her she need not sit up, then went home at three in the morning, and found her sitting up. Then I told her if she did so again I would stop out all night, but again she sat up awaiting me, so I went off and did not go home till the next night. That settled it.

Mary took medicine and was ill, another monthly holiday came, and was spent at the house. A few days afterwards Mary was looking blank. Her Mistress told me she had dismissed her. "Why?" I asked. "She was no good, and not a good servant." Mary was sacked at the end of the week, I could not of course interfere without injuring the poor woman, and implicating myself, — no good to either of us.

So soon as she had left our house I was told all that Mary had told me of herself, the Mistress evidently feared that Mary might seduce me, or go astray somehow. That is what the poor girl got for telling her true history to her. Said she also, "She has been taking strong medicine, and I believe it was to bring on her courses." She knew they had stopped. Her sister had advised her not to keep a female in the house who had diamond rings, a gold watch and chain, and silk dresses. It was evident to me that the poor girl's history had been told to more than one person.

Mary, broken-hearted took lodgings in a cottage close by, and did needle-work. "Nothing," said she, "shall make me go to service again, I only did it to please him, hoping he would come back to me, but I hate service, and don't care what becomes of me." She was always at home, I visited her regularly for two or three months, giving her what little money I could, but she was reckless, and would spend money in comfort, though not in show. She came out with me not in her silk dresses, but her plainest ones, and little by little pawned her dresses, rings, and all her finery. Then she worked harder and harder, besought me to give her just enough to keep her, however humbly, for go to service she would not again. Again she got with child.

All this time of course our fucking was regular, but although I liked her, and more than liked her, I never had a strong affection for her. When her money was gone, and she was poor in clothes, she was still cheerful. I gave what I could, but could with difficulty keep out of debt, and insisted on her going to service. "Then we shall never see each other," said she, and she begged me to go on, allow-ing a trifle; I did so, being content with her, never finding her out, never having a suspicion of her having another man, and feeling much anxiety about her.

But none of my money was my own, and what use as a beggar could I be to her? — so yielding to my solicitations at last she again went to service at a short distance from my house. Then I found out a convenient house close by, she got out as often as she could, and we had stealthy meetings and pokings in a hurry. The old lady and her middle-aged son with whom she lived liked her, and indulged her; so we often got two or three hours together, yet the difficulty of meeting became irksome, she got restless, would go as a bar-maid (she understood the business), go to America, go anywhere so as to get away from service. Then circumstances prevented my meeting her for two or three weeks; when I did again she reproached me, and hoped I had not got any one else.

Soon after she told me her sister was in the family way, having been seduced by the young man who was to have married her; I saw the letter describing this. "I am glad of it," said Mary, "for she was so hard on me." The sister came to town, I wanted to see her, but Mary would never arrange it, though I saw her letters frequently. Then I made one or two appointments with Mary which were not kept, went to the house one evening, and whilst Mary was whispering to me at the street-door, her Master appeared, and asked who I was. Mary said I was her cousin. Then he ordered her indoors, saying they did not allow their servants callers.

Then her Mistress began to treat her harshly; and we thought some of my letters had been intercepted. I was obliged to go abroad for a time, and wrote to tell her. On my return I found letter after letter from her at the post-office. She was about to leave, wanted my advice, would I allow her ten shillings a week, she would make it do, be faithful to me, and live close by me; go to service again she would not, she would sooner go on to the streets, her sister had done so. Again an upbraiding letter, — she never thought I would have neglected her so, I who was so kind and affectionate, I whom she loved so much, — if I did not reply it was the last I would hear of her.

I dressed myself up shabbily, and at dusk went to the place she had lived at. The Master opened the door, but did not know me again. She had left, had gone he knew not where. "Why?" did I ask. Then I tried all possible places, but I never heard of her for years, and greatly feared she had gone gay; but although I haunted gay places to find her, I never saw her there.

Some seven years afterwards I met her. She had gone to service again, and had written to tell me where. I never had that letter. There was again a bachelor son in the house, who made advances to her, and finally kept her. Meanwhile I had moved my residence, and oddly enough opposite to the house in which her protector had lived for many years with his mother. Mary actually knew everything about my domestic affairs almost as well as if she had lived opposite to me herself, for my neighbours knew a good deal about me. He kept her at a nice little house some miles off.

It was opposite the National Gallery that we met in the dusk of the evening. I went to J***'s Street with her, and to bed, and fucked her with rapture till I brought on her poorliness in floods.

Her protector had just married, parted with her, and given her money. She was going home to her native place, — what to do I don't recollect, — she was still lovely, although somewhat broken. I never saw her after that night. About five years afterwards she wrote to say she was badly off, would I send her a trifle. I sent her two pounds, she thanked me in a letter, and said in it, that she often cried when she thought of me, and past time, — and I never heard of her afterwards.

I could tell a lot more about my doings with this lovely creature, for everything connected with her is as fresh in my memory as possible; but must go back to that time when coming back to England I found she had left her last situation, and I could not find her whereabouts.

But I must add something which was omitted when I abbreviated the manuscript for printing. I revelled as said in the smell of a nice woman; with the poor cheap women I had for some time had, their smell offended me, I avoided kissing them even, why I can't say. With Mary this delight returned, her aroma overpowered me, and added to my voluptuous delight in her embraces. On every possible opportunity I used to lift her petticoats, and smell her flesh, it intoxicated me, and instantly made me wild with lewdness.

END OF VOLUME SECOND.